in the shadow of the sun

Prafulla Roy was born in 1934 in a village in Dhaka district, now in Bangladesh. He started writing at the age of nineteen. The Partition of India in 1947 provided one of the major themes in his writing, the other being rural poverty. Most of the stories in this volume emanate out of Roy's experience of life in the economically backward state of Bihar. His work has influenced filmmakers, particularly such major artists as Buddhadeb Dasgupta, Tapan Sinha, Biplab Ray Chaudhary and Sandeep Ray. Many of the films based on Roy's stories have been made in languages other than Bengali, and several of his writings have now been translated into other Indian languages. Nine stories in this collection have a screen version.

***

Dr. John. W. Hood is an Australian writer who has spent most of his life studying Indian culture, dividing his time now between Melbourne and Kolkata. His translations from the Bengali include Niharranjan Ray's classic, *History of the Bengali People*, poems of Buddhadeb Dasgupta (*Love and Other Forms of Death*), and novels and short stories by Prafulla Roy, including the volume of stories *Set at Odds: Stories of the Partiton and Beyond*, as well as Buddhadev Guha's *Fanfare for a Tiger* and *The Bounty of the Goddess*. He has also written extensively on serious Indian cinema. His books include *Chasing the Truth*: *The Films of Mrinal Sen; Images of Time and Dreams*: *The Films of Buddhadeb Dasgupta* (now rewritten and enlarged as *The Films of a Poet: The Cinema of Buddhadeb Dasgupta*); and *The Essential Mystery: Major Filmmakers of Indian Art Cinema*. He is presently writing a book on the films of Satyajit Ray.

Other Lotus Titles

E. Jaiwant Paul	*Baji Rao: The Warrior Peshwa*
E. Jaiwant Paul`	*Rani of Jhansi: Lakshmi Bai*
Frank Simoes	*Frank Unedited: The Best of Frank Simoes*
Girish Chaturvedi	*Tansen*
Indira Menon	*The Madras Quartet: Women in Karnatak Music*
Irene Frain	*Phoolan*
Jagdish Chander Wadhawan	*Manto Naama: The Life of Saadat Hasan Manto*
Jeannine Auboyer	*Buddha*
John Lall	*Begam Samru: Fading Portrait in a Gilded Frame*
Jyoti Jafa	*Nurjahan*
K.M. George	*The Best of Thakazhi Sivasankara Pillai*
Lord Meghnad Desai	*Nehru's Hero, Dilip Kumar in the Life of India*
Maj. Gen. Ian Cardozo	*Param Vir: Our Heroes in Battle*
Namita Gokhale	*Mountain Echoes: Reminiscences of Kumaoni Women*
Neelima Dalmia Adhar	*Father Dearest: The Life and Times of R.K. Dalmia*
Nina Epton	*Beloved Empress: Mumtaz Mahal*
Rachel Dwyer	*Yash Chopra: Fifty Years in Indian Cinema*
Ralph Russell	*The Famous Ghalib*
Rashna Imhasly-Gandhi	*Psychology of Love: Wisdom of Indian Mythology*
Savita Devi	*Maa . . . Siddheshwari*
Sumati Mutatkar	*Shrikrishna Narayan Ratanjankar 'Sujan'*
Sethu Ramaswamy	*Bride at Ten, Mother at Fifteen*
V.S. Naravane (ed.)	*Devdas and Other Stories* by Sarat Chandra Chatterji

Forthcoming Titles

Gautam Bhatia	*India Unplugged*
C.P. Surendran	*An Iron Harvest*

in the shadow *of the sun*

Short Stories by

Prafulla Roy

Winner of the
Sahitya Akademi Award
for Literature 2003

Translated from Bengali by

John W. Hood

LOTUS COLLECTION
ROLI BOOKS
Fiction

Lotus Collection

This edition published in 2004
The Lotus Collection
An imprint of
Roli Books Pvt Ltd
M-75, G.K. II Market
New Delhi 110 048
Phones: ++91 (011) 2921 2271, 2921 2782
2921 0886, Fax: ++91 (011) 2921 7185
E-mail: roli@vsnl.com; Website: rolibooks.com

Also at
Varanasi, Agra, Jaipur and the Netherlands

ISBN: 81-7436-333-5
Rs. 295

Typeset in AGaramond by Roli Books Pvt Ltd.
Printed at Tan Prints (India) Pvt. Ltd., Jhajjar, Haryana

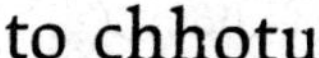

to chhotu

contents

translator's introduction

The short stories in this collection are drawn together by the common theme of poverty. While extreme poverty manifests itself in various ways and has diverse causes, in every story it is a condition that presents to a character a challenge to be overcome, a test that he or she must pass in order to survive life itself. In some cases destitution is so extreme that one might wonder whether, in fact, the test is worth the passing at all. It is in this regard that the characters are so remarkable, for most of them are people so wretchedly reduced in circumstances that all they have, effectually, is the will to live, the indomitable desire to take up the challenge, to pass the test and go on to the next day, even if, as it might seem, it is only for the sake of it. It is the way in which they do that that gives to so many of these characters a remarkable quality of humanity and lends to the lives of some of them, lowly as they may be, an element even of the heroic.

Much of India's material modernity is a feature of its cities. Metropolitan India, while perhaps appearing to be confused and disorderly, does have an advanced technological infrastructure that is very largely denied to rural India. In so many of the country's villages even telephones are rare, to say nothing of the internet. In fact, such things as electricity and made roads are not to be found in some one hundred thousand of India's villages. Educational opportunities and contact with the world at large through the mass media are minimal at best, and for an overwhelming majority nonexistent. As so many rural children are needed by their parents as labour, they cannot be spared the luxury of going to school. Modern health care, efficient transport and sufficient supply of electricity are minimal, and access to social and legal support systems is severely limited. Indeed, the picture of life in much of rural India at the start of the twenty-first century is similar in many ways to that of a century or more earlier. However, prominent in both pictures is the dominance of tradition, the centrality of a set of systems and values that owe their authority to their antiquity. In the metropolises, on the other hand, where education has led to questioning and criticism and economic diversity has given rise to social fluidity, tradition has become considerably diluted. In provincial India, however, where the economy remains predominantly agricultural, modernity and its great agent, education, have had limited effects on society; here the authority of tradition reigns largely unchallenged, supported by rigid social structures. Where education and technology are limited, traditional structures may more easily flourish. In an essentially unequal economy, poverty is taken for granted and is, to a very large extent, sustained and exacerbated by the tradition in which it has its roots. It is safe to say that in most parts of rural India there has been little significant change in social or economic structures for centuries, and whereas there have been changes in political and administrative forms, the totally subject nature of the relationship between the rural proletariat and authority remains largely unchallenged.

Much of the rigid social structure that sustains tradition, at least in Hindu India, is furnished by the caste system, which has survived from ancient times even into the twenty-first century. Hindu caste society is determined by birth, hierarchically ordered, and occupationally defined; it is by nature unequal and undemocratic and may, given the authoritarianism that is often implicit in it, be repressive. Millennia-old prescripts proclaim the purity of caste as being socially paramount and sternly condemn the mixing of castes. Such an outlook may still prevail in some of India's more remote villages, for even today the rigidity of caste values cannot be said to have relaxed greatly throughout rural society in general. Of course, as one inherits one's caste status, one also inherits the economic circumstances that attach to it. Existing poverty, then, is perpetuated through the process of inheritance. This, of course, can be the case in traditionally structured societies other than Hindu caste society, especially where education comes with privilege, technology is limited and the economy is restrictive.

Material poverty consists in the absence of property and in the relative powerlessness to acquire it. While such a condition is commonly inherited in a traditional social system, it is exacerbated by an economy that tolerates unemployment or limited employment opportunities. Day labourers – paid according to the work they do on a daily basis – are amongst the poorest of India's workforce, as work is not always available to them given the ever-increasing glut in the labour market. In the rural sector, work is often denied to contract labour by natural aberrations such as drought or flood, and day labourers often have their circumstances worsened by their own ill health. India does not enjoy the luxury of a welfare system that pays unemployment benefits to people unable to find work or to those to whom work is denied by nature or by personal illness. Needless to say, made to last over even a short period of time, the wages of most day labourers are pitifully insufficient.

Day and limited term labour are the lifelines of a number of characters in these stories. There is the pathetic irony of the two people hoping to get work in 'One Rainy Day' but missing out due to their own charitableness. Just as pathetic is the desperate need of Champiya in 'Seven Times Wed' to get casual labouring work in order to keep herself married. 'For the Sake of Survival' focuses on two people driven to scrounging in order to supplement the paucity of irregular wages and to eke out an existence when they cannot get work. The central characters in 'The Tiger' and 'The Rajput' depend on casual employment to keep body and soul together so that they may pursue what is to them a calling.

Debt is seen to be another frequent cause of impoverishment. Seeking to achieve some betterment in his condition, a man may decide to start up some small enterprise. He may, let us say, want to reclaim some unused land and develop it for agricultural use, or perhaps make a living as a cycle rickshawwallah, and so he borrows money from the ever-obliging money lender or the helpful landlord to pay off his capital expenditure. But then, as in several of these stories, the rains fail or there are floods and his efforts are all undone; when the rains fail or floods ruin the fields, the farmer has no crop and the cycle rickshawwallah cannot find customers who can afford to pay his fares, and so the loan remains unpaid. There are also the unforeseen medical expenses that are incurred by all people, including the poor – indeed, we might say *especially* the poor – and which often can be met only by taking out a loan. Perhaps the most common major expense requiring financial assistance is marriage, involving not only the cost of excessive hospitality but also the provision of a dowry or bride-price, an institution universally deplored in word yet surviving strong in deed. No matter how frugally a poor family might live, they will find it difficult to get through life without the burden of debt, and Prafulla Roy's stories are dotted with references to 'the moneylender's stomach' and its appetite for the meagre ancestral property of the poor.

No matter what the reason may be for the poor man failing to meet his commitment to repay, the lender will not lose on the deal. Usurers may take whatever the man may possess, including his home; there are even appalling instances where a wife or daughter has been enjoyed as collateral. Like moneylenders, landlords assume similar privileges when a debt is not realized. Failing sufficient satisfaction from the confiscation of property, bonded labour is the last resort of the debtor, who is then obliged to pay off his debt with work, toiling for mere rations without wages. Of course, given the exorbitant rates of compound interest imposed on the original loan, it is unlikely that a man will work off a debt in his own lifetime, and so the responsibility falls on his heirs – yet another way in which poverty is inherited. The reason why the pregnant woman in 'Human' is without her husband at such a critical time is that he is not free to leave the land to which he has become bonded.

Such arrangements are riddled with duplicity and dissembling. At the root of it all is the 'contract', notoriously a blank piece of paper on which the borrower places his thumb-print. In the utter unlikelihood of legal action ever being taken against the lender, this malleable 'contract' is his easy defence. While confiscation of property and bonded labour are the sophisticated ways of debt recovery, there are also the various violent means of extracting blood from stones. The crippling of a debtor by a thrashing, for example, will serve well to increase his dependence and maybe bring his son or daughter into the repayment cycle sooner than might have been the case.

Violence is not uncommon in rural society in situations other than the recovery of debt. Violence in its various forms, or the threat of it, is a simple and direct way for those who wield power to assert their authority, to remind the lower orders of their place and, generally, to keep the traditional order intact. Those who wield power might use strong-arm tactics for whatever purpose that may suit them. The political value of violence is well documented, and in this volume we have a reference to it in 'The Election' in Dube's threat to burn down the untouchables' village if they should renege on a promise to vote for him. In its context it may be seen as an expression of sardonic humour, but the substance of his seeming jest is grimly corroborated by the experience of the husband of Nishibala in 'For the Sake of Survival', a fine, strong young man who had had his innards ripped out with a spear in a display of upper-caste power. The violence let loose for political advantage in 'An Untimely Flood' is indirect, but carefully and callously contrived and deliberately executed nevertheless. The most blatant example of violence for political purposes seen in this volume is in 'The Dumb Show', where ruthless and utterly unscrupulous aspirants to power dispose of human life without a qualm. Violence is also used to uphold and extend the power and wealth of the rich and powerful, and we see in 'Across the Fields' a local plutocratic tyrant, sustained by his force of domestic muscle-men, torturing and even murdering his daughters-in-law for extensions of dowry.

In some of the stories we come across implied criticism of the inequality that characterizes a caste-structured society. In 'Hell', for example, we read that Sagiya, because she is a prostitute and therefore unclean, may not enter the homes of the people in Nekipur; the high-caste Jagnath, who pays her for the satisfaction of his animal needs, continues to hold his head high in the same respectable society. Nor will the respectable people of Janakpur have anything to do with the folk medico, Paonlal Sahay, because his professional responsibility extends to all members of society, including those formally regarded as 'low'. In 'The Election', the abject servility of the villagers highlights the status of Dube, while the degrading procedure of labour selection in 'Seven Times Wed' underlines the immense power that the landholders have over those who desperately need work. In 'The Feast', the abusive treatment of Dhaniya by a bullock driver contrasts meaningfully with the almost unrealistic courtesy shown to him by a gentleman on the road. As well as the violence and scant respect for human worth in 'The Dumb Show', we might also note the two performers' discomfort, born of excessive deference, regarding the propriety or otherwise of performing burlesques before 'respectable' people. Violence can be taken for granted in a society where certain classes of people simply do not matter.

So many of these stories tell of people debilitated by disease, of men who once were strong and able to work tirelessly but have now become frail and decrepit and utterly unemployable. There are very simple reasons why the poor everywhere, not only in India, get sick more frequently than the rich. Three of the most obvious causes are the nutritional deficiencies of whatever food they can afford, their obligation to endure excessive physical labour for the sake of their own survival, and their lack of the wherewithal for proper medical treatment. Most of the characters in these stories have had to grapple with illness of one kind or another – here and there a character is described as having the lingering scars of smallpox, many characters are described as having protrusive bones and sunken cheeks and eyes. There are those who once were strong and made a name for themselves for the work they could do, such as Dhaniya in 'The Feast' and Lakhindar and Bhushan in 'The Wide World'. In 'Seven Times Wed' disease ends two of Champiya's marriages and, because of labouring without respite right through her pregnancy (had she stopped work her pay would have been stopped, so how could she have survived?), ill health nearly ends her, too. The tragedy of this awful treadmill on which the poor spend and end their lives is made poignantly clear by the awful picture drawn at the end of 'Seven Times Wed' of the once hale and hearty Gaibinath, now overcome by respiratory disease and the avarice of the moneylender. Very often one has no alternative but to resort to begging, as is the case with Dhaniya in 'The Feast.' Old Natthulal, in 'The Election', like so many of the others, was once as strong as a buffalo but, like Gaibinath, also succumbed to respiratory disease and the demands of the moneylender and, like Dhaniya, had long back been reduced to the contemptible life of a beggar. Indeed, if he were able to feed his bulls more often, Bhirguram in 'Across the Fields' might make a better living, but their pathetic feebleness and his material circumstances only serve to exacerbate each other.

Vicious circles, indeed, determine the lives of the poor, for in them are caught up the causes of their deprivation, their ill health, their debts, their minimal social value and their vulnerability to inhuman treatment perpetrated by those of privileged status, and all of these causes are inextricably interconnected. There are no malingerers or wilful ne'er-do-wells in these stories; rather, the poor are seen as simple victims suffering as a matter of course the consequences of the greed and callousness of the powerful and well off, caught in the vortex of a system that consumes their labour yet does not respect their humanity.

While material means may often ensure a degree of spiritual and intellectual gratification, the absence of such means will usually deny the individual such fulfilment. A little girl with a thirst for learning may well go far in metropolitan middle-class society, but if she is part of the provincial lower class, things will not go so smoothly for her. Simply being female is a natural disadvantage in a society in which males are generally treated preferentially, so for her, as a member of a poor household, education would be seen as an extravagance. Moreover, instead of studying she could be earning, providing for herself and for whatever dependent parents she may have. In 'A Window to the Moon' Lati's mother, Rajani, cannot afford to keep her daughter as a student, and she also needs her earnings as her own earning capacity, the older she gets, is becoming more and more limited – such is the harsh reality of life for a prostitute.

While there are those who would have us believe that the life of the prostitute is caused by moral depravity, it is a lot more reasonable to regard it as a social condition brought about by material necessity, fostered by economic dependence, and, in the female line, often inherited. These three features are clearly illustrated in 'The Rajput', where the women are portrayed as being without option in their particular livelihood. In the same story, Dhaneshwar Chaube is an example of the power wielded over resourceless women by wealthy and possessive men; given his declared favour, the 'natural' inheritance of her mother's profession by the young Kunta is simply assumed. A deceptive air of light-heartedness may cloud the prominence of the same features represented in 'A Window to the Moon', but in that story Lati's determination to break free of her threatening thraldom is prompted by the same grim perception of reality as that which moves Kunta in 'The Rajput' to flee on the day of her formal initiation. When simple self-respect is compromised by the promise of a life of comfort, the young women in both stories desperately seek to preserve their dignity and personal value. Although dealing with altogether different ideas, the story 'Hell' also offers a sad portrayal of the nature of the prostitute's life.

Of course, a woman does not have to be a prostitute to be enslaved to men. The want of gender equality where tradition is dominant is well highlighted by the persistence of dowry, by definition a claim to a woman's inferiority to a man. The dowry system is frequently abused, with young wives suffering the cruelties of extortion by their in-laws and their fathers suffering the torment of knowing of their mistreatment and not having the financial wherewithal to alleviate it. Dowry deaths are by no means uncommon, even in metropolitan India, and, if they are legally recognized as 'suicides', they allow the husband to marry again and pick up in further dowry what he may have missed out on the first time. The appalling unscrupulousness of those who seek to profit from this archaic custom is chillingly brought out in 'Across the Fields', in which a young wife suffers appalling torment from her insatiable in-laws and her father is driven into penury. (In the collection, *Set at Odds*[1], the story 'The Destination' also deals tellingly with this problem.)

Spiritual poverty is widespread in the world depicted in these stories as it prevails not only in its own right but also very often as a consequence of material poverty. Yet 'Father and Son' offers an ironic twist to this rule. Bishtupada is the product of a respectable and comfortably placed family; there is no question of his inheriting the poverty he comes to know for the greater part of his adult life. While his disinheritance from his father's home as a result of his obdurate waywardness may bring him down materially, corresponding to the spiritual depth to which, it is alleged, he has sunk in marrying a prostitute, he is given the opportunity to redeem himself through his father's death by means of a spiritual wealth that had been dormant in him all these years. The pathetic end to the story is also an expression of a triumph of sorts.

For the exceptionally poor, inherent in the simple fact of being alive is the constant challenge to stay that way. A person's basic daily aim is to fill his or her stomach and the stomachs of whatever dependents he or she may have. Some people may get by, in a way, by scrounging and foraging, such as Lakhindar and Bhushan in 'The Wide World' and, from time to time, the two characters in 'For the Sake of Survival.' The exceptional lengths to which many people have to go in order merely to apply for work, often walking extreme distances and battling with intense heat or driving rain, is

---

1 Prafulla Roy, *Set at Odds. Stories of the Partition and Beyond,* translated by John W. Hood (Srishti, New Delhi, 2001).

made abundantly clear in such stories as 'Human', 'Seven Times Wed' and 'One Rainy Day.' In these stories, at least, the term 'feckless poor' carries no meaning.

While the poor have much to endure in fulfilling the simple need to survive from one day to the next, even in the extremes of deprivation they can still dream, and their simple dreams can at least temporarily carry them beyond the mundane. In 'The Feast', Dhaniya dreams of enjoying just one excellent meal before his death, and Champiya, in 'Seven Times Wed', dreams of making a marriage that will last until she dies. Lati, in 'A Window to the Moon', dreams of freedom through knowledge, and, in 'The Wide World', Lakhindar dreams of a life in profound harmony with nature. In 'The Rajput', Hiralal has visions of himself and his horse in the glamorous world of films, while Ghunuram, in 'The Tiger', lives in penury and drudgery for most of the year so that he might fulfil his dream of dancing the tiger dance in a far distant village for a few weeks each year at festival time. Especially altruistic is Bharosalal in 'Human', a man with no family at all, who is inspired by the thought of playing a part in bringing a new life into the world. Bishtupada in 'Father and Son' dreams most sadly, for his visions are of a past and can never be realized. Some dreams are fulfilled, most are not.

India's rural poor do not present any kind of a united front. As a political fact this may bring some comfort to those who enjoy privilege and power at their expense, but it highlights the essential loneliness in which the poor struggle to survive. Most of the characters in these stories are loners of one kind or another. Some choose their solitariness, others have it imposed upon them, and for some – especially the beggars in 'The Election' and 'The Feast' – it is integral to their mode of existence. Some of the characters are married but are generally depicted in detachment from their partners and families on whose behalf they conduct a lone struggle for their support. Thus, the poor are often seen here to be waging their struggle to survive individually, although some stories do represent partnerships in which support, if only in the form of company, is offered.

This generally lone struggle is often one waged against forces even greater than the powers of political economy, for the deprived and helpless are also subject to the hostility of nature. In so many of these stories the antagonist is an aspect of the natural order. In 'Human', for example, the treacherous muddy surface of the steep hill, abetted by the constant rain, is as villainous as any human character might be in frustrating the designs of the humble heroes. The ruthless, turbulent river plays a similarly antagonistic role in 'Hell', as does the simple yet awesome fact of distance in this and several other stories. The ferocity of the intense, searing heat of the dusty plains of northern Bihar is presented almost palpably in 'Across the Fields' and 'The Feast', providing an appropriate complement to the brutality of the former and the ghastly ending of the latter.

So when poverty runs its course of destruction in the life of an individual, what can be salvaged of humanity? In the actuality of life in rural India manna does not fall from heaven nor is treasure discovered under the floor of the hovel, and it is appropriate that most of the stories in this collection have no 'happy' ending, for Roy's observations of rural life are realistic throughout. Some stories end quite tragically, their grimness enhanced by ready credibility. In others, just as realistically, gain is tempered by loss. For the extremely poor, 'success' is rarely more than taking up the challenge of life itself and surviving one step at a time.

It might seem ironic that those who are so poor as to have nothing to give might, indeed, be charitable, and yet throughout the book there are to be found instances of kindness and generosity from people who have nothing to offer but themselves. The first six stories in particular have in common the notion of people putting themselves out for the good of others even more badly off or in some kind of need. Here there is a notable aspect of self-sacrifice, for what might have ended, if not happily then at least satisfactorily, is compromised by a significant element of loss. Bharosalal's gallantry in 'Human' might well have been rewarded by the young woman's becoming a mother, but it comes at the almost certain cost of his missing out on the job that he so badly needed, a job for which he had walked so many miles since before the break of day. A similar situation prevails in 'One Rainy Day', where the seriously ill are set on the road to recovery at the cost, for the two day labourers who saved them, of at least a day's wages and food for their hungry families. In 'Hell', a lone woman's tremendous endeavour in saving a man's life incurs expenditure from her meagre resources and a loss of potential earnings, as well as the fear of spiritual damnation, given the peculiar twist in inter-caste relations that evolves in the story. In 'Across the Fields', Bhirguram gets badly beaten up for his simple attempt at gallantry and loses not only his unforeseen battle but also his and his bullocks' daily bread, while Hiralal, in 'The Rajput', is successful in saving a damsel in distress – and in a very filmy way at that – but at the cost of his own dream of gracing the silver screen with his horse. In 'The Election', where Bharosaram's altruism is obviously contrived with an ulterior motive, no one gains at all except, ironically, the old beggar – at least, for a time.

Although there are notable instances of self-sacrifice, there are also instances of self-abasement, the most stark of which is to be found in 'The Feast.' Here the elderly beggar's decrepitude is highlighted against the repressive heat of the dusty road and the never decreasing distance that the old man seems to walk. His dream, brilliantly clear in his own mind, is eclipsed by reality at its cruellest. Poor to the point of bodily frailty, Champiya, in 'Seven Times Wed', values her decency above everything and the major events of her life are little more than a strategy to protect it, yet these same major events prove to be the links in a chain of humiliation and distress. The struggle with the beast in 'For the Sake of Survival' may be seen as a desperate, even heroic, endeavour to provide for oneself and one's dependents; it may also be seen as a bonding factor between the two characters in the story; but no matter how it may be regarded, a man's dignity is sorely minimized when he fights with an animal over a piece of food.

There follow four stories in which we see how, in spite of adverse material circumstances, the individual recognizes a need for spiritual freedom or self-expression. In 'A Window to the Moon', a little girl's thirst for knowledge and recognition from her peers is intensified when her mother takes her out of school, and the story is as much a quest to achieve personal empowerment through knowledge and peer recognition as it is one of escape from the degradation of the society in which she has been brought up. Ghunuram, in 'The Tiger', gains material rewards from his performances of the tiger dance in Nonpura village, but what he values more than money and from which he derives his urge to live is the respect and admiration the villagers offer him in recognition of his worth. The quest for a life in harmony with nature moves Lakhindar in 'The Wide World' to put even his wife's adultery and desertion behind him in achieving the serenity he seeks. In 'Father and Son', Bishtupada may have much to bemoan in his life, yet there emerges from his inner being a spiritual regeneration in his present moribund existence.

The last three stories focus on those who hold power – legally and illegally – over life and property. 'The Supplicant' is a study, on the one hand, in self-sacrificing idealism and the will to live merely by what is right, and, on the other, the pragmatic connivance of politicians. Political self-interest, exploitation and hypocrisy – even criminality – are taken a few steps further in 'An Untimely Flood', where they are depicted as major causes of the misery of the poorest and most helpless of people. The two central characters in 'The Dumb Show' are indeed poor, but they do at least have job security. Moreover, they are exceptionally popular mime artistes whose talent is widely recognized and valued amongst the people of their small provincial town. Nevertheless, they are still humble folk, and the story is yet another example of how little people are so often exploited by those in power – both the corrupt and the honest – for their own ends. The comprehensive and callous hold that the powerful have over the poor is starkly underlined in these last three stories.

***

Prafulla Roy, the son of a small businessman, was born in 1934 in a village in Dhaka district, now in Bangladesh. He started writing at the age of nineteen, by which time his life had been coloured by the most momentous events of modern Indian history and so many of the harsher realities of the Indian condition had made an indelible mark upon it. In his early adolescence he was caught up in the calamitous experience of the Partition of India which came as a consequence of Independence in 1947, an earth-shattering and epoch-making event for all Bengalis – for it was their land that the eastern partition divided – but especially for those Hindus living in East Bengal, which would become the predominantly Muslim state of East Pakistan. Roy's family were able to remain in Dhaka for only a short time after Partition, being forced to flee empty-handed to Calcutta in 1950. After a year in Bihar looking for work they returned to Calcutta, and Prafulla started to write. Some fifty years later a projected collection of his works is planned to fill some thirty volumes.

Naturally, the Partition provided one of the major themes in Roy's writing[2]. The other major theme is rural poverty, of which Roy became vitally aware during his extensive travel – mostly on foot – throughout India and the Andaman Islands during the 1950s. Although the language of Roy's work is his mother tongue, Bengali, one of the major languages of India, his travels have given to his work an outlook that is more national than regional. Actually, most of the stories in this volume emanate out of Roy's experience of life in the economically backward state of Bihar, although many of them might well have been set in any of a number of regions of India.

Roy's presentation of his experiences on a broad, all-India canvas has made his work popular and much sought after by filmmakers and the makers of telefilms, particularly such major artists as Buddhadeb Dasgupta, Tapan Sinha, Biplab Ray Chaudhury and Sandeep Ray. Many of their films on Prafulla Roy stories have been made in languages other than Bengali, and many of his writings have now been translated into other Indian languages, so increasing

---

2 See *ibid.*

his national appeal. (Some nine of the stories in this collection already have a screen version.)

Generally Roy's interest lies with ordinary folk, the unremarkable, unsung common people trapped in the bind of poverty and struggling to survive against all odds. He is content to simply present his characters – mostly marginalized, often unusual – as he sees them. He does not lionize them, nor does he indulge at all in sentimentalism, and the realism of his stories is enhanced by the terseness of his prose and the tightness of its construction. Indeed, among the major strengths of Prafulla Roy's writing are his candour and economy of language. In all, Prafulla Roy's fiction is immensely entertaining, profoundly moving, and often quite disturbing.

***

Perhaps an ideal in translation would be to translate every word of the text and retain no words of the original language, but this is not always possible. A lot of words belonging to Bengali and/or Hindi – such as chapati, sari, lathi, ghat – have found their way into the Oxford English Dictionary and therefore are used here without italics or explanation. There is a problem with *gamchha,* which means a cloth used for many and various purposes, though mainly for wiping moisture from the face and body; it has been left untranslated. The names of many trees, flowers, birds and fish, given their essentially regional nature, are untranslatable except, perhaps into Latin, so these generally have been left in their original form. It is possible to translate the Bengali names of months, but it is doomed to clumsiness because of the calendar difference that has the beginning of a Bengali month occurring halfway through an English month. The Bengali names have been preferred and a list of months and seasons also has been given.

October 2003

John W. Hood
Melbourne

months and seasons

Traditionally the year starts in mid-April, with each successive month starting in the middle of a Gregorian calendar month and ending in the middle of the following one.

Vaishakh	April - May
Jyaistha	May - June
Asharh	June – July
Sravan	July – August
Bhadra	August – September
Ashwin	September – October
Kartik	October – November
Agrahayan	November – December
Poush	December – January
Magh	January – February
Phalgun	February – March
Chaitra	March – April

Bearing in mind the variations that prevail throughout such a vast country, a rough guide to the seasons would indicate summer from Vaishakh to Bhadra; autumn from Bhadra to Agrahayan; winter from Agrahayan to Magh; and spring – often a very warm one – from Magh to Vaishakh.

human
manush

It was just midday when the rain started pelting down near Shermundi Hill.

The sky was hazy when Bharosalal had set off just before dawn, his colourful patchwork bag slung on a bamboo stick across his shoulder. He was coming from Hekampur, the estate of the Rajput, Thakur Raghunath Singh, and was headed for the town of Bhakilganj on the other side of Shermundi Hill.

Bharosalal could not have thought from the look of the sky at dawn that by midday rain would be bucketing down all around him. Only a few traces of very light cloud were being tossed about by the breeze then, and later in the morning the sun, like a silver plate, rose high in the sky, and the fields and the river banks and the forests and jungles shimmered in its rays that were like molten silver. But how much longer would this sunshine last? Indeed, only a little later the great lamp was suddenly puffed out and everywhere it grew dark. On his way across fields of maize and barley and through three or four ramshackle villages, Bharosalal had been unaware of the heavy masses of rain clouds covering the sky, but now he was alerted by the sudden sound of thunder and the sight of the sky being rent by lightning.

Urged by the massing of the clouds and the flashes of lightning, Bharosalal quickened his step. No matter what should happen today, he had to reach Bhakilganj on the other side of Shermundi Hill, and so, as he walked along, he kept looking up over his shoulder. Soon, far off on the horizon behind him, rain started to fall and he broke into a run, but the rain advanced relentlessly behind him and, when at last he reached the foot of Shermundi Hill, it caught up with him.

As the rain came down and the wind gusted this way and that, Bharosalal took stock of things. There was no possibility of going up the steep hill in the face of this storm. He looked all around for some shelter and saw, a little way away from him, ten or twelve rustic folk, among them a young woman, standing with their heads down under a luxuriant pipal tree, obviously sheltering from the rain. He ran towards them.

Bharosalal was about fifty. He was very strongly built, with broad shoulders and a rugged chest like a hunk of rock, and his fingertips reached down to his knees. His skin, never having been oiled in many a long year, was as dry and rough as baked brick and kept flaking off all the year round. There were tufts of stubble on his square cheeks and flat chin. Yet his eyes were enchanting, as gentle as they were innocent. He wore a knee-length thin dhoti and a red shirt cut rather like a waistcoat. A close look at his neck would reveal a number of calloused scars left by a tiger's claws.

Bharosalal was a 'beater', or what is known in this region as a 'jungle-crier'. His job was to drive a tiger or bear or any other wild beast to the barrel of a hunter's gun by shouting and beating on a tin can, and it was while he was doing this some three years ago in Raksaul that a tiger tore at his neck. As well as his work as a beater, Bharosalal had another job, which was to round up mad pariah dogs off the streets of all the small towns in the vicinity and dispose of them. No one actually retained Bharosalal as a beater or as a dog-catcher; rather, he went seeking work at the homes of hunters or at municipal offices. This was his livelihood. It was rather hard-hearted, perhaps, but simply for the sake of his stomach he had to do it.

The rain now had become heavier, and the sky offered no sign of when it might stop and let him get away from these rustic folk crowded together under the spreading pipal tree. The drops were falling through the gaps between the leaves and branches and were wetting his head and body – had he been standing in the open he would be drenched. Suddenly the man beside him spoke up. 'It's really heavy rain!'

Bharosalal looked around and saw a middle-aged man with a weather-beaten look and wearing a turban. 'Yes,' Bharosalal said.

The man immediately went on, 'I don't think it'll let up for a while.' He spoke a mixture of Hindi and Bengali, and probably came from somewhere on the Bihar-Bengal border.

'Yes,' Bharosalal said.

Now looking at his companions, the man said, 'We have to be in Bhakilganj town by midday, but how?'

So they too were going to the other side of Shermundi Hill. Bharosalal glanced indifferently at the man's companions. They were not middle-aged like him, and one of them was quite a stout young fellow, rather like a bullock. While he was looking at them, Bharosalal caught a glimpse of a young woman in their midst: the one and only woman in the group.

Bharosalal's experience of life and of people had been very limited. Since his youth he had spent his years running after wild animals and mad dogs. Nevertheless, he could tell that the young woman was pregnant and that her child must be due within three or four days.

The man beside him was a real windbag. Now he was saying that with the rain, the hill roads would be in a bad state and to go up there would be madness, for one could slip and fall and never be seen again – it would be a horrible death.

Turning his glance from the woman, Bharosalal said, 'Yes.'

Still the fellow went on, 'So if we can't get to Bhakilganj by midday, we could miss out on our work.' He looked very worried.

'What work?'

'Building a dam on the river there. Our work is digging. If we're late, the government officer might turn us away.'

'Pray God that he doesn't.' And so saying, Bharosalal turned his glance again to the woman. He had really no curiosity about the world. For the sake of keeping body and soul together he had to be occupied all the time in jungle and forest, in village and town, so he did not see much at all of anything else. And even if he did, he looked on the world and its people with very little interest. However, he had a vague idea that this woman was carrying in her belly a nine-month-old baby. Was she too going to dig, in her condition? It was not right for a woman at her time to be doing heavy work. He thought these things, but said nothing.

The man beside him spoke up again. 'But will God hear our prayer?'

Bharosalal had no answer. Seemingly distracted, he looked up at the sky, now obscured by heavy clouds, but whether he answered or not, the grumbling of the man beside him was as continuous as the rain.

Bharosalal's mind was quite blank as he stood there under the pipal tree. As the rain started to ease off, the wind became gusty, yet the clouds were still heavy and there could be another strong downpour at any moment.

The man suddenly shouted into Bharosalal's ear, 'The rain has stopped! We can now get over the hill!' Then he called loudly to his companions, 'Come on, boys, let's go! Get a move on!'

The group set out ahead, the young woman following behind. Bharosalal did not waste the opportunity either, so he started walking behind her. He too wanted to get over Shermundi Hill before the rain became a downpora again.

When he had received the news some days ago that Thakur Raghunath Singh wanted to go hunting, Bharosalal had hurried to the Hekampur estate. For roaming the jungles with Raghunath Singh and beating the tin can for four days, he had been paid ten rupees and three kilograms of grain. The money was now tucked into the waist of his dhoti and the grain was in his motley-coloured bag.

While in Hekampur he had heard that Purniya town was planning to get rid of all its mad dogs in three or four days. Therefore, no sooner had Raghunath Singh's hunt finished than Bharosalal set off. He would have to hurry over Shermundi Hill so that he could spend the night in Bhakilganj, and as soon as he got up the next morning, he would cross the river at Sagarigali ghat and set off on foot for Purniya.

Nevertheless, Shermundi Hill was frightfully steep and was covered entirely with thick forest. Here one came across mainly sal and mahua trees, but there were also many others scattered all about, including myrobalans and deodars, as well as various kinds of shrubs and bushes and jungle grass and weeds.

A winding track had been worn through the jungle, which by now had become extremely dangerous. Having been worn away by thousands of years of rainstorms, the rocky surface of the mountain was covered only by a thin layer of earth, rather like a skin, which in the rains was as slimy as rotten flesh.

They trod very carefully up the hill. Although the storm had abated in intensity and the force of the wind was much weaker, light rain still fell. Crickets had begun their continual chirping on both sides of the track and a diverse chorus of birds sang full-throated from the tops of the trees. One could also hear the sound of snakes slithering here and there.

From time to time the middle-aged man called to his companions, 'Hurry along now,' and to God, 'Oh, Lord Ram, let us be there by midday!'

Bharosalal's mind was apparently on other matters as he trudged up the hill, so he seemed not to hear him, or the natural sounds from all about. The rain had caught them all quite unawares; hence, this need for a scramble over the hill. Today, however, was Bharosalal's rest day. He would spend the remainder of it after reaching Bhakilganj relaxing and stretching his arms and legs. He would have to look for a new job next day, but for the moment tomorrow could look after itself.

He had been tramping up the hill for some time when Bharosalal heard the sound of weeping. He saw, up ahead, the pregnant woman, exhausted from the climb and panting heavily. Her mouth was open and her chest was heaving as she gasped for breath and sobbed at the same time. Her eyes were bulging like the eyes of a dead fish. She was almost staggering as she endeavoured in vain to negotiate the deep, slimy mud. Bent forward, she might have stumbled but for the steadying hand of Bharosalal from behind. He said, 'Woman, are you not well?'

Lifelessly, she replied, 'No.'

Just as he was about to speak again, Bharosalal suddenly caught sight of the middle-aged man with his young companions, all pushing like bullocks through the undergrowth some considerable distance up ahead. Anxiously, he said, 'Oh look, the others have got away from you!'

The young woman said, 'I'm not with them.'

In a flash of panic, Bharosalal said, 'What do you mean?'

'I'm travelling alone.'

'Oh, Lord Ram! In your condition!'

'What should I do?'

'Well, where's your husband?'

The woman leaned heavily on Bharosalal's huge chest and paused for a few moments. Then she straightened up and said, 'He couldn't come.'

'Why not?' Bharosalal asked.

'He's working for the moneylender. He's a bonded labourer.'

'Bonded labourer?'

'Yes.'

The woman went on to tell him that four years ago her husband had taken a loan from their local moneylender, Bishun Ahir. The debt had still not been paid. The man had heaps of money and a mountain of gold, silver and jewels, though no one knew the full extent of his wealth. Wherever one might set foot in their village, that too was the property of Bishun Ahir. Yet despite having so much land and money, he was an utterly ruthless fellow. To recover from him the paltry sum he had borrowed, Bishun had forced her husband into bonded labour on his land for two months in twelve, year after year. Taking into account the interest charged, if the woman's husband worked in this way for ten years he still would not have paid off the debt. So given all this, how could he have gone with her?

Bharosalal listened to her story, then asked, 'Is there anyone else at home, apart from your husband?'

'No.'

'Oh, Ram.' Bharosalal remained quiet for a bit, then he asked, 'Are you able to go on now?'

'All right.'

'Now be very careful where you put your feet.'

And the two of them set off again, treading carefully through the sticky mud.

The middle-aged man and his companions had disappeared amongst the sal and sisam trees and were no longer to be seen. Had he wanted to, Bharosalal could have taken longer strides and gone much further ahead up the steep hill, but now he could not abandon the young woman in her condition. Bharosalal had little interest in anything in the world other than the beasts of the jungle, mad dogs and his own stomach, but as he walked alongside this woman, a spark of curiosity ignited in him.

'Where is your village?' he asked.

'Five miles to the west. It's called Jhumritaliya.'

'And that's where you're coming from now?'

'Yes.'

'Where will you go when we get over the hill?'

'To Bhakilganj.'

'To some relatives' house?'

'No.'

'Then?'

After a pause, the young woman replied, 'I'm going to the hospital.'

'Why the hospital?' he asked, and then remembered that the woman was pregnant; obviously, she was going to the hospital to have her baby. Quickly, he added, 'Of course, I understand. May the grace of God ...'

The young woman looked down as she walked, and for a time the two of them said nothing. There was no actual road over Shermundi Hill, so one reached the top by way of the open spaces one spotted through the thickets and jungle.

Suddenly, the young woman called out in a loud voice, 'Hey, man!'

Bharosalal looked over his shoulder. 'What is it?'

'Just one thing …'

'Go on.'

But she said nothing for a few moments. Then, in considerable stress, she began, 'I'm a woman travelling on my own, and I'm in a bad way. I'm frightened of crossing the hill through the jungle. Don't go off and leave me all alone.'

Bharosalal observed the woman very carefully. Her frail, sallow body, her intensely dark eyes in their shadowy sockets, her scrawny neck, her long, emaciated face, the protuberant veins on the backs of her hands, her nine-month swollen belly and the full breast with its blackened nipple protruding from the buttonless blouse – all evoked a kind of affection in him. He said, 'Oh no, no. I won't go off and leave you alone. I'm also going to Bhakilganj. You can go there with me.'

Her face expressed her relief at being able to depend on a strong and capable man.

The two of them trudged on through the mud. A bit further on, Bharosalal noticed that the young woman was not so sure of foot and that she was starting to stagger again. Also, her breathing was very heavy. He stopped her and asked, 'What's the matter?'

In a weak, shaky voice, she said, 'My head is spinning.'

'Do you want to stop for a bit?'

'Yes.'

'Have a little rest.'

The young woman sat down on a stone. She rested for a short time, then, getting up, she said, 'Let's go.' But as soon as she was on her feet, she started to stumble again.

Anxiously, Bharosalal said, 'It seems you can't walk any more. As soon as you start, you stagger. Your head's still spinning. Let's try something else.'

'What?' she asked in a lifeless voice.

'I'll support you. If you try to walk on your own in your condition, you'll run the risk of falling.'

She nodded weakly; she had no objection to being supported by Bharosalal. That way she would survive.

Bharosalal put one arm around the woman's shoulder, and slowly she got up. After going a little distance, he could sense that her strength was running out. The weaker she became, the more heavily her weight fell against his arm. Almost hugging her, Bharosalal held her close to his chest. Somehow, they would have to get over the hill. And so they trudged on, Bharosalal muttering, 'Oh, Lord Ram. Oh, Lord Ram, have mercy on us. Have mercy on us.'

The rain kept up, though for some time the drops had been as light as fine grains of sugar, but then it suddenly began to pour again. The wind sprang up as unexpectedly as the rain had and swept gustily through the jungle.

The young woman could now barely remain standing, and Bharosalal was at a loss. He had told her he would get her across Shermundi Hill, but now he could not think how he could support her in this state – as well as the child she was carrying.

He thought carefully for a few moments.

The woman's condition would not allow her to walk any further. Moreover, there was no great spreading tree like the pipal under which she could take shelter. And there was no certainty of when the rain would stop or even if it would stop at all. It would be better to try to go on rather than wait about uncertainly, simply getting wet.

Bharosalal decided to lie the young woman down in a spot where there was not so much mud. Taking two dhotis from the multi-coloured bag he had hanging from a stick over his shoulder, he made them into a sling in which the woman could sit. He would carry the sling around his neck; the bag with the grain on his back.

The teeming rain looked like untold millions of glinting arrows. The trees all about would bend to the face of the storm, then spring upright again. In the frenzied, gusty wind some shrubs were abruptly uprooted. Flashes of lightning rent the sky. Moved by the calamity all around, Bharosalal kept muttering as he went along, 'Oh, Lord Ram, have mercy. Oh, Lord Ram, have mercy.' And so saying, he dug his toes like claws into the sticky, slimy mud as he continued up the hill.

The burden of the heavily pregnant woman weighed forcefully on his whole body. Even though Bharosalal was a strong and robust man, he felt as though his back would break, and he grew short of breath. Moreover, he could barely see at all with the pelting rain driving relentlessly onto his face, the rain and the wind together virtually blinding him and the full force of the storm pushing him this way and that. Nevertheless, intent on reaching his goal, he held his body up defiantly to the elements while all the time keeping up his plaintive prayer, 'Oh, Lord Ram, have mercy, have mercy ...'

He did not know how much longer it took to reach the peak of Shermundi and the start of the trek downhill. But then the rain eased off as the storm abated, and the clouds gradually thinned out across the sky. Bharosalal put the woman down, rested his head between his knees, and gasped, his energy almost exhausted. He felt as though every bone in his body was broken and that all his muscles were torn. From the nape of his neck an unbearable pain ran down his spine and flashed in spasms from his waist to his feet.

It was quite a while before Bharosalal recovered somewhat and remembered the young woman. He looked up quickly and saw that her body and all her clothing were sopping wet and her skin and fingertips were white. As he watched her, her face contorted in agony and her lips turned blue as she clenched her teeth in an endeavour to suppress the pain. Bharosalal was frightened. He quickly moved close to her and asked, 'What's the matter?'

Pointing to her stomach, she whimpered, 'Such a terrible pain here. You must get me to the hospital quickly.'

At last they got to the bottom of Shermundi Hill. Bhakilganj town was still about five miles away, and that was where the hospital was. Bharosalal asked, 'Can you walk?'

'No. My stomach is all twisted.'

Bharosalal had guessed as much. In this state it was impossible for her even to stand up and take one step. But Bharosalal had exhausted himself getting her over the hill and no longer had the strength to carry her on his back for another five miles.

There was, however, a small market at the foot of Shermundi Hill, nothing much – just a stall selling rice, dal, salt and pepper, another selling paan and bidis, and a third selling tea – but still, it was a market. A winding track led to it and on to Bhakilganj, through fields of maize and barley and various villages scattered here and there. Having reached the market, he could now hire a bullock cart to take them to the town, but the fare would be at least five rupees. He had tucked into the waist of his dhoti the ten rupees that Thakur Raghunath Singh had paid him, and this was all he had. Bharosalal had started to wonder how much he would have to spend, when he looked around and saw the woman crying plaintively as she gripped and rubbed her stomach.

He had no more time to think. Leaping to his feet as though someone had jerked him up, he ran off and got a bullock cart from the market. He laid the woman out on its straw-covered floor and told the driver, 'We have to get to town quickly, brother. Very quickly!'

Making a sound to stir the two bullocks, the bullock driver gave a twist to their tails, and straightaway they started to trot, panting, along the unmade road.

The sky ahead of them was clearing quickly, and the sun was breaking gently through the gaps in the cloud, but from the position of the sun it looked as though the day was coming to an end and that soon evening would be falling.

From the time they got into the cart, Bharosalal kept his eyes only on the young woman. She was sobbing continually as she lay on her side, her arms and legs contracted close to her chest and her jaws clamped in an endeavour to suppress the pain. Bharosalal leaned close and asked softly, 'Tell me, woman, is it really bad?'

She clenched her teeth hard and just nodded her head, saying nothing.

Bharosalal had no idea what to do or how to relieve even slightly her distress. He could only mutter under his breath, 'Oh, Lord Ram, have mercy, have mercy, God ...'

Then the woman said, 'I'm terribly frightened.'

With natural affection, Bharosalal took her hand and said, 'What are you frightened of?'

Suddenly, her pain seemed to increase fivefold. Her body arched like a bow, she was bathed in sweat from brow to throat, and the hairs on her body stood up as though with sudden cold. Gradually, her eyes became still.

Bharosalal was afraid. This woman had come fifteen miles and crossed a great hill in order to give birth, and he had had so little experience of ordinary affairs that he did not know how to deal with her plight. Anxiously, he asked, 'Hey, woman, what can I do for you at this moment?'

Gripping her waist, the woman said in a very weak voice, 'Could you get me a hot compress?'

How could he light a fire in the bullock cart? Nevertheless, he had to have hot water. Looking around frantically, he found, on one side of the cart, a hurricane lamp under the straw. Shouting over his shoulder, he asked the bullock driver, 'Hey, brother! Is there any oil in your hurricane lamp?'

The driver answered, 'There is. Why?'

'I need to light it for a bit. The woman has to have a hot compress.'

'You can light it, but you'll have to pay four annas for the oil.'

'All right.'

'Go on, then.'

'Do you have a match?'

'I do.' The driver took a box of matches from his waistband and tossed it to Bharosalal.

Bharosalal lit the lamp. Then he took a piece of his own very wet clothing, folded it into four, heated it over the lamp, and slowly applied it as a compress to the woman's stomach. After he had held it there for quite some time, the woman's sobbing slowly ceased and she fell asleep.

When the bullock cart reached the government hospital at Bhakilganj, it was well after dark, and the doctor had left for his quarters. Those who were there said, 'Not today. Bring her tomorrow.'

Bharosalal was thinking of how they had crossed the hill. Now he had to think of where he could look after the woman for the night. He implored them again and again to admit her.

The hospital staff explained that without the doctor's orders they could not admit anyone. Exhausted, Bharosalal went out to look for the doctor's quarters, ready to fall at his feet and tell the whole story of how he had brought this woman such a distance over the hill in all her suffering, and beg for his clemency.

And so the doctor came to the hospital and had her admitted.

Now Bharosalal's work was done. He settled his dues with the bullock cart driver – five rupees for the fare and four annas for the oil – and went off to find somewhere to shelter for the night.

In all the world, Bharosalal had no one, no attachments at all. He was as free as a bird. Wherever and whenever the need arose, he would cook his own simple meal and sleep on someone's veranda or in the fields under a tree. But he wanted to do nothing more that day. The usual daily bother of kneading dough, making an oven, fetching and cutting wood was beyond him. Instead, he went to a shop, had some paste of chickpea flour with salt, chilli and tamarind pickle, then went and lay down on the open veranda of a house. The next morning he would go to Sagarigali ghat and from there to Purniya.

When he got up the next morning, it suddenly occurred to Bharosalal to enquire about the young woman. Absorbed in his thoughts, he made his way back to the hospital, where he learned that she had not given birth yet, but might at any time.

It also distressed him to learn that she was in considerable pain. He had always been indifferent to everyday human affairs, but the thought of that young woman suffering – she whom he had carried on his back over the hill yesterday, to whom he had administered a hot compress and on whose account he had paid five and a quarter rupees out of his own pocket – made him unable to think of going to Purniya until she had her baby and was out of harm's way. Maybe he would get there to find that the municipal officials had employed someone else to get rid of the mad dogs. But what else could he do? 'Oh, Lord Ram, oh, God ...'

Bharosalal came out of the hospital and wandered around for a bit. Then he ate some chapatis and lay down for a while. It was afternoon when he awoke, and he went back to the hospital. But there was still no news.

After two days, when he was almost suffocating with anxiety, the doctor finally said to him, 'I've got some very good news.'

Bharosalal said, 'Has she delivered?'

'Yes, she has.'

'Thanks be to Lord Ram. Thanks be to God,' said Bharosalal, wiping the tears from his eyes.

'Your wife has had a little girl. A very fair little girl.'

Bharosalal was stunned. The doctor obviously thought the young woman was his wife. He quickly corrected the misunderstanding. 'She is not my wife, doctor sahib.'

'Then?' The doctor looked at him with raised eyebrows.

Bharosalal said, 'We met each other on the road. Now I must go, doctor sahib. May God bless you.'

And so Bharosalal was able to cross from Sagarigali ghat to Purniya town, utterly free of worry.

one rainy day
barshay ekdin

A long, unmade road ran through vast fields in northern Bihar straight to the highway three miles away. The fields could hardly be described as unbroken grassland, as they were, for the most part, rough, uneven and stony. Twisted sisam and pipal trees were to be seen everywhere, and in between some of the distant hills lay three or four villages, appearing as though in some rough pencil sketch.

There had been torrential rains over the previous three days, but today not a drop had fallen since early morning. Nevertheless, although the rain had stopped, there were still a few odd clouds hanging here and there in the sky, like buffalo heavy with young. The strong, damp wind blowing over the fields seemed to have stopped all of a sudden and not a leaf stirred on the trees. Wherever one looked, as far as one could see, everything seemed in a state of heavy expectancy, for at any moment the tumultuous deluge might once again fall from the sky and drench the whole of creation.

It was not yet midday. The sunbeams that timidly peered between the edges of the clouds, lending a glow to the Sravan morning had no intensity. Indeed, the dull and tepid sunshine served only to make the monsoon day all the more humid. The rain had made the earth as soft as tender meat, so that to walk on it could mean sinking up to the ankles.

Towards the end of the morning, Nathuni came trudging through the fields. She was coming from Barhouli village two and a half miles back and was going another three miles across the fields to the highway that led into Nankipura town. She had eaten nothing in two days. There was no work in her village, therefore no wages. If she went to the town, she might be able to earn some rice, dal and flour, and return just ahead of evening.

Nathuni was in her early thirties, a large-framed, big-boned woman without the slightest hint of loveliness in her longish, weather-beaten face, her rough skin, the protuberant veins in her hands, her dry, tangled hair, or the thick calves of her legs. From the harshness of the look in her eyes one might sense that she trusted no one in all the world. She herself probably had no idea when the last vestige of womanly elegance had left her. Indeed, her whole being bore a manly intractability inflected by her own personality. She was wearing a patched red blouse over a short and dirty sari that hung down just below her knees. Apart from an unattractive copper bracelet on each wrist and an artificial stone set in silver on her nose, her body was devoid of ornamentation.

Walking as fast as she could through the deep mud under that cloudy sky, Nathuni glanced all around her. No, apart from her, there was no one in this vast field. The whole place was extraordinarily still, the silence shattered only by the harsh call of a foreign parrot from somewhere towards the horizon.

There were times when Nathuni's body was remarkably strong, like the body of a wild buffalo, despite her having had very little to eat or even having gone without food altogether. Her strength was matched by an irrepressible courage that enabled her to walk through this vast and desolate field on her own without any fear at all. And as she walked, Nathuni had nothing on her mind. But suddenly there came an indistinct cry, as though someone were calling her. 'Hey! Hey, woman!' At first she paid no attention to it, but the calling continued and she had to stop. She looked all around, then saw a man a long way behind, coming towards her.

So she was not entirely alone in the field, as she had earlier thought. This put her out. No matter what, she had to get to

Nankipura to get something to put in her stomach, but what was this man doing trudging through miles of mud on a monsoon day when not even the crows had come out? At first, Nathuni was apprehensive. She might have no charm, but she was still a woman. Whether the man was good or vile, she was not to know. Who would come running and crying out for help in this desolate field? Nathuni waited, with all the suspicion of a woman's sixth sense tugging at her every nerve and sinew.

In a few moments, the man caught up with her. He was about forty or more, lanky as a palmyra tree and with long arms reaching down to his knees. He had a square face with scraggy eyebrows and whiskers on his cheeks like clumps of weeds. He was as dark as though he had been dipped from head to toe in soot, and his skin was cracked and flaky. Yet despite his unsightliness, the man's eyes seemed infused with magic; indeed, such gentle, innocent eyes are rarely to be seen. He was wearing trousers of cheap cloth and an ill-fitting shirt from which the sleeves had been cut. On his back was slung a very large cloth bundle which held, most probably, all his worldly possessions.

He bared his rotten, yellow teeth, saying, 'My name's Lakhpati, but everyone calls me Lakhua. What's yours?'

Nathuni found it quite amusing that his name indicated untold wealth, for a glance was enough to see that the fellow was poorer than poor. Nevertheless, she flared up immediately, asking, 'What's my name to you? What are you after?'

Lakhua was embarrassed by this. Hesitantly, he said, 'I'm not after anything. I was just making conversation.'

Nathuni frowned and with a sharp eye looked Lakhua over from head to toe. From his timorousness it would have seemed that the man had no kind of ulterior motive, but in all her thirty-odd years Nathuni had had a vast experience of life and had come to know the world very well. She knew that deceit was often belied by a tender-looking face, for on the surface someone might seem to be a saint or a mahatma, but a little scratching could well reveal some nefarious intent.

So she remained cautious, but in a slightly gentler tone, she told him her name and asked, 'Tell me, then, what d'you want with me?'

'I'm going to Nankipura,' Lakhua said, pointing in that direction. 'One of the villagers told me that the town is on the other side of this field. Is that right?'

Nathuni's mind filled with misgivings again. She too was going to Nankipura. Had this fellow learnt of this as he came after her? But then she told herself that Lakhua might be telling the truth and have no ulterior motive at all.

'That's right,' she said. Then, a little inquisitively, she asked, 'Do you have some business in Nankipura?'

'Yes. I heard that the big landowners are taking on agricultural labourers there. I'm going to see if I can get some work. I've been starving for a whole day, and I don't have a penny to my name.'

What a coincidence that Nathuni was going to Nankipura for exactly the same reason! Nathuni's suspicions returned. But he looked like a good man, and there was nothing suspicious in the way he talked. Nathuni said, 'I'm going there too. You can go along with me if you like. But just one thing ...'

'What?'

From a hidden fold in the waist of her sari, Nathuni flashed the blade of a short-handled knife, saying, 'Just watch it. Put a foot wrong and this'll go straight into your guts. There've been three bastards I've used it on before.'

The knife was indeed her constant companion. When looking for work in this part of northern Bihar, one has to move about quite a bit, and there are tigers and jackals and hyenas lurking everywhere in the guise of men. Who can say when one might need a weapon?

'Oh, Lord Ram!' Lakhua was startled, and fell a few steps behind. Putting one hand on his stomach he said, fearfully, 'All I'm concerned about is this.'

'Honestly?'

'Honestly, yes, honestly. In the name of Lord Ram. Believe me, I don't tell lies.'

'All right, then.' Nathuni tucked the knife back into her sari and said, 'You walk seven steps ahead of me and don't say a word.' Her idea was that if Lakhua stayed in front of her, she could keep her eye on him and be alert to any sudden move she might not be able to avert if he were walking beside or behind her.

'Just as you like.' And Lakhua carefully counted seven paces in front of Nathuni and started to move on.

Now Nathuni felt more relaxed. If the man should suddenly drop the facade of decency and reveal some hidden purpose, it would not be easy for him to do anything, and she would be prepared even before he could turn around. Whether or not Lakhua had a weapon, she did not know. But it would be extremely difficult for just one man, even if he were armed, to overpower Nathuni.

Nathuni noticed that Lakhua had still not looked around. As he trudged through the clayey mud, he muttered to himself, 'It'll be after midday by the time we reach Nankipura. I wonder if there'll still be any work available then.'

Despite the fact that Lakhua had spoken very quietly, Nathuni overheard him. She shared his concern, for she too was going to the landowners at Nankipura, and if she should miss them, all this trouble in getting there would have been an utter waste. Who could tell if she would have to go without food for yet another day?

There was just a man walking ahead of her, his feet squelching in the mud, and from his body came the bad smell of sweat and dirt, like the odour of a goat. And how much longer would he keep his mouth shut? There was still quite a way to go, and some conversation would help to pass the time.

Nathuni called, 'Hey, man!'

Keeping his eyes in front of him, Lakhua answered, 'What is it?'

'From what you say, it seems that you don't live around here. Where is your home?'

'I don't have one.'

Nathuni was surprised. 'What do you mean?' she asked.

Lakhua did not look around. Walking on, his feet sinking into the sticky mud, he said, 'This doesn't make sense.'

'What?'

'You said not to say a word. I've done as you said, but now you want to talk to me. So if I talk, you can't blame me.'

His response bothered Nathuni somewhat. It seemed from his plain words that Lakhua was not as simple as he looked. Indeed, he might be quite wily and make a surreptitious move towards her. 'All right, then,' she said, 'I take that back.'

Lakhua went on, 'What I said was quite true. I don't have any home.'

'Then where do you live?'

'Nowhere in particular. I go about looking for work the whole day. At night I sleep wherever I can – in a hut in the market, on the veranda of someone's house, under a tree.'

Nathuni wondered if ever in all her life she had met such an odd character, one who had no house and slept wherever he found himself. Whatever suspicions she may have had about Lakhua were being unconsciously dispelled. Nathuni had no interests whatever outside of her own home and family, yet she was filled with curiosity about this unknown companion.

It was not easy to carry on a conversation walking seven paces apart; moreover, Lakhua, obeying her instructions to the letter, did not even look over his shoulder at her. Now Nathuni felt that her feminine pride had been hurt. Whatever imperious, masculine front she put up, she was after all a woman of flesh and blood. And she wondered whether this strong, tall fellow thought himself to be one of the princes of the earth; he was not good-looking, yet he had such pride as not to even look back at his travelling companion.

The two went on, maintaining the same distance between them, but then Nathuni quickened her pace and came alongside Lakhua. Lakhua looked at his companion disinterestedly, then as before he kept his gaze in front as he trudged on through the mud.

'You said you have no home,' said Nathuni. 'But no one just

comes up out of the earth. Everyone has parents, brothers and sisters ...'

As he squelched through the mud, Lakhua asked indifferently, 'Do you want to know the story of my life?'

'Yes. How much longer can we remain quiet. Tell it to me.'

'You may not like it.'

'Never mind. Go ahead and tell it.'

Maybe Lakhua did not like to talk too much, but he would have had great difficulty in avoiding the wishes of this determined woman. So in a dull, monotonous voice, he told his story. He was born in a wretched village in north Bihar, close to the border between India and Nepal. He had no brothers or sisters, and he lost his parents at an early age. The little agricultural land they had was snatched from him by his uncles, who drove him away from the village and so set him on his itinerant life. From the village, Lakhua went straight to Saharasa town, where he worked for a timber yard proprietor for three or four years. The boss was not such a bad fellow, but he took to the bottle first thing in the morning and, once the booze had gone to his head, the animal in him came out; he would smash anything that came to hand, and used to beat Lakhua excessively. Unable to put up with this any longer, Lakhua left. After that he spent a few years ploughing the land of six or seven landowners, then harvesting the paddy or the wheat. But when the land was baked in drought or awash with flood, there was no work at all, and with no work Lakhua got no pay. Under such circumstances, how could he survive? So he joined up with a folk theatre company, and soon he developed a reputation as a musician, having learnt to play the tabla and the flute. But such was his luck that the company was unable to survive and had to fold up. He then got employment with a big contractor, breaking rocks and making roads. But within three years of this excessively strenuous, back-breaking work, he started to cough up blood. He went to the hospital and was told by the doctor that if he wanted to stay alive he would have to give up this kind of work for a while. So Lakhua gave it up, but he found no alternative employment and was forced to glean whatever he could, however he could. Like all the world's restless drifters, he somehow survived on various kinds of work as he wandered over northern Bihar. And so the forty or so years of his life passed by. Then, two days ago, Lakhua had come to a small town to the east of this vast field. He did not get any work there, but learned from the townsfolk that he might make some money if he went to Nankipura. No sooner had dawn broken than he set off.

After listening to all of this, Nathuni said nothing for a while. Then, slowly shaking her head, she said, 'You've come through a great deal. But my life hasn't been much better than yours.'

Lakhua did not answer, but Nathuni did not forego the opportunity to tell him about her family. They lived in a village to the south of that field. For three whole years, her husband had been bedridden, weakened by one disease or another. They had two little children. They were poorer than anyone, with no money, no valuables, no land – and there were four stomachs to feed. So every morning she went out looking for work. They got by if she could bring in some earnings, otherwise they simply had to go without.

Lakhua made no response at all to her miserable story, but seemed to express a kind of stern indifference. With his own survival perpetually at stake, he could not indulge himself in others' tales of woe.

Nathuni was about to speak again when all of a sudden the sound of a voice came from somewhere or other on the sharp, damp breeze. Someone was shouting, but they could not make out the words. Nathuni and Lakhua stopped and looked around, but they could see no one in that vast and desolate tract of land. It was as though they were the only representatives of the human race.

Again the unintelligible voice was heard, and this time Nathuni and Lakhua could catch some of the words. 'Hey, brother – sister – come!' Someone was calling them.

Nathuni looked all around the field and saw, diagonally to her right and far away, something that looked like a motor car. A man was standing beside it, waving his hands furiously and shouting out, 'Here! Here! Come over here!'

Nathuni kept her eyes on the man as she asked Lakhua, 'Tell me, what's the matter with him?'

'How would I know? It's the first time I ever saw him,' said Lakhua.

Nathuni looked worried. She said, 'He must be in some sort of trouble.'

Lakhua said nothing.

The man in the distance did not stop for a moment, but kept on waving his arms and calling out.

'What are you going to do?' asked Nathuni.

Lakhua looked up and glanced quickly at the sky. The stray clouds that had been floating about were now starting to mass together and were obscuring the sun. What glow there was in the light of the day gradually dimmed and a gloom began to spread.

Lakhua said, 'Look at the state of the sky. It's pretty bad.'

Nathuni looked up. She shook her head slowly and said, 'Yes.'

'If we go to that man now, we'll be late. And on top of that, if it rains, we'll be in trouble. We'll tell him "no" and go on straight across the field.'

'No.'

Lakhua was somewhat surprised. He asked, 'What do you want to do?'

Nathuni explained that the man must surely be in some serious trouble to be calling so urgently. It was not right that he should be left alone in such a deserted tract of land.

Lakhua raised no objection. 'All right, then,' he said.

In a few minutes they reached the man. He looked somewhat emaciated. He had a snub nose and round eyes, hair that came down to his shoulders, sunken cheeks, and a sparse beard. Thick veins protruded through the rough skin of the back of his hands, and under his broken nails was the dirt of all the world. He was wearing a khaki shirt with short sleeves and two breast pockets, and loose, ill-fitting trousers, the legs of which were completely smeared with mud. Despite this covering, it was clear that the man was very frail and that his chest was as thin as a bird's.

There was a decrepit motor vehicle standing a little way behind the man. The front of the ancient contraption was that of a rundown old car, but the back part resembled more a bullock cart, with its wooden flooring and its tin covering. The difference was that, instead of a bullock, the vehicle was drawn by an engine. Such a combined truck and dray was used to carry merchandise around this part of Bihar.

Taking in the scene in a quick glance, Nathuni said, 'Why all this screeching like a jackal? What's the matter with you?'

The man's words poured out in a stream. 'Oh, sister, I've really fallen into a terrible scrape. Having broken down in the middle of this field, what could I do? I was at a complete loss to think of what to do, when by the grace of Lord Ram I caught sight of you two. Please help me.'

There was something in the man's voice that alarmed Nathuni and Lakhua. Nathuni asked, 'What sort of scrape are you in? Be frank with us.'

The man hastened to tell them that his name was Chaupatlal and that he lived in Nankipura with Vindhyachali Singh, the proprietor of the town's main motor repair works and garage. As well as motor repairs, Vindhyachali ran a huge transport business and had many lorries and small Matador trucks. He also had a dozen or so strange hybrids of motor car and bullock cart. Vindhyachali hired out all these lorries and the like for the transportation of goods. The bullock cart brand of vehicle would be sent to all those places that were inaccessible to heavy lorries. Such a vehicle was the small truck there at the moment, which Chaupatlal had been driving for six or seven years.

One morning a couple of days ago, he was taking some merchandise through drizzling rain to Bhogbani, a big bustling market beside the Barakha river some eight miles to the south of this field. Having delivered his goods, Chaupatlal came down with a severe fever. He spent one and a half days there, then set out at dawn in his vehicle. But after he had left Bhogbani, the people of a village on the way to this field stopped him and persuaded him to take two people, a man and a woman, on board his little truck. Both were very old and were suffering from serious illness. The villagers told him to take them to the big hospital in Nankipura. At first Chaupatlal was unwilling, but relented after seeing their condition. However, having reached this field and gone some way across it, all his troubles started: the engine suddenly broke down and the truck stopped.

Having listened to all of this, Nathuni said impatiently, 'I see. But what do you want with us?'

He did not answer immediately, but unexpectedly took hold of Nathuni's and Lakhua's hands. Then he said, 'Come with me.'

'Where?'

'Just come, please.'

Chaupatlal drew Nathuni and Lakhua towards the back of the truck. Releasing their hands and pointing, he said, 'Look.'

Two people were lying side by side on the wooden flooring under the tin canopy. The man seemed as though the life had been sapped out of him. Dull, wrinkled skin hugged his bones, his neck was extraordinarily thin, and his head was like a dried up coconut. The little hair that he still had was like jute fibre. He was wearing a dirty, grimy loincloth and a very tattered cotton waistcoat. The woman was in a similarly wizened condition. A torn rag made a vain attempt to cover her body.

Neither was conscious. The woman's eyes were closed, but her mouth was open and feeble sounds of distress came intermittently from her throat. The old man's body was so dense with smallpox marks that the point of a needle would hardly fit between them. His face was deeply flushed, indicating a severe fever. His eyes were open, unlike the woman's, revealing cataracts. He made no sound of acknowledgement at all.

Nathuni was shocked to see them both. She said, 'Oh, God! Who have you brought here? How can they still be alive?' She paused for a moment, then said, 'The old man has smallpox. What's wrong with the old woman?'

Chaupatlal told them that he had heard from the villagers that she had been suffering from cholera for some days.

'Why are such ill people with you?' Nathuni asked. 'Don't they have any children, any relatives?'

'No.'

'Are they married?'

'No. They're not related.'

Chaupatlal told them whatever he knew about his two passengers. They were landless and had no house. They had survived as long as this only on the charity of the other villagers. No one to whom they held out their hands would turn them away. They could be said to be like beggars.

Nathuni then asked, 'But could none of the villagers take them to the hospital at Nankipura? Why have they put the task on your shoulders?'

Chaupatlal said, 'How could they take them so far in such rain? They have no motor vehicle. Since mine was empty, they put them in it.'

No one spoke for a few moments. Then Chaupatlal spoke up again. 'Now both of you can show some kindness to these two old people.'

'How?' asked Nathuni.

His hands clasped, Chaupatlal said, 'They have to be taken to the Nankipura hospital right away. I can't push this broken down vehicle on my own, but if you could lend a hand …' Chaupatlal paused.

Nathuni was staggered. She pointed out that they would have to embark on a journey of at least three miles pushing the little truck through the mud and slush. They could not be at all certain of when they might arrive – maybe at the end of the afternoon – but she and Lakhua had to be in the town before the middle of the day on quite urgent business.

'I'm sorry,' she said, 'we're going.' Then she prompted Lakhua, 'What are you waiting for?'

Lakhua fell in with her immediately. 'Yes, yes, of course,' he said.

Just as they were moving off, Chaupatlal took hold of Nathuni's hand and pleaded with her once more. 'Have pity, sister. Can we leave these two people to die? Shouldn't we do whatever we can to save them?'

Nathuni and Lakhua were moved by the profound anxiety in Chaupatlal's voice. They had been all the while absorbed in their own troubles, unable to think of anything other than when they might reach Nankipura and whether they would get any work and wages from the landowners. But it struck them now that there was, indeed, more to life than finding something to put in one's own stomach. Two utterly helpless people would die in the middle of this vast and desolate field unless something were done for them.

Chaupatlal could gauge Nathuni and Lakhua's feelings by looking at their faces. Still holding Nathuni by the hand, he drew her to him, saying, 'Please, come.'

Nathuni looked at Lakhua. She said, 'What can we do? If the two are to survive ...'

'All right, then,' said Lakhua.

And so the three of them started to push the little truck. Chaupatlal pushed at the front with one hand pressed against the window frame and the other on the steering wheel. Nathuni and Lakhua pushed from behind. But the vehicle's wheels were so stuck in the mud that at first they could not budge it at all.

Lakhua said, 'Our arms are not strong enough. We'll have to put our shoulders to it. See if that does anything.'

'Right,' said Nathuni.

Summoning all their strength into their shoulders, they both started to push the truck, one on each side. Chaupatlal, of course, pushed from the front, holding the steering wheel and the window frame as before. He had so little strength left, but all that he had, he used, and as he pushed, the veins in his neck stuck out like twisted cords and his eyes bulged like chickpeas. But after quite some pushing, the vehicle started to move forward, cutting slowly through the thick mud.

However, it was just then that the great mass of cloud started to do its work. At first the rain fell in small drops, and then with great force, as though the entire sky were dissolving into a storm. At the same time the gusty wind blew wildly over the field, thunder rumbled in the distance, and the sky was split diagonally with flashes of lightning. It seemed as though creation was returning to primeval chaos.

Muffled by the pervasive noise, there broke through from time to time, the sound of the sobbing of the two people under the awning of the truck. Obviously, they were suffering fearfully. It then occurred to Nathuni that the strong rain was getting in through the opening at the back of the vehicle and wetting them. The old man was covered in pockmarks and was suffering from fever; if he were to get any wetter, he might indeed die before reaching the hospital.

Nathuni cried out to Chaupatlal, 'Hey, driver!'

At first, Chaupatlal could not hear her. She got an answer only after she had called a few more times. 'What is it, sister?'

'Come here a moment.'

'Why?'

'Just come, please.'

They stopped pushing, and Chaupatlal came to Nathuni and Lakhua.

Pointing at the two old people, Nathuni said, 'If we cannot keep them dry, they'll die. Have you got a big piece of cloth or hessian in the cabin?'

'What for?'

'To cover the back of the truck.'

There was no cloth or hessian, but there was a big piece of tarpaulin under the front seat. The three of them quickly set it up as a cover over the opening at the back to keep out the rain.

Then they set to pushing the little truck once again, their drenched clothes clinging to their bodies. They could see no more than a few feet in front of them, and it seemed that in all the world there was nothing but the three of them, a broken down little truck, and two old people on the verge of death.

There was no let-up in the rain and the storm raged as though it had lasted since the beginning of time. As they pushed the truck, Nathuni and Lakhua felt as though their hands and feet had detached from their bodies and that their flesh was about to be ripped from their bones.

The rain had stopped by the time they reached the highway. The sky had cleared, but the light was dimming as the day drew to an end. Soon it would be evening.

They had almost reached the Nankipura hospital. Whatever last vestige of strength remained among the three, it managed to get Chaupatlal's vehicle there, and the two old people were admitted to the hospital. The doctors pronounced that they would survive smallpox, fever, cholera, getting wet in the rain and even the discomfort of the truck.

Chaupatlal turned to Nathuni and Lakhua and said, 'Because of you the two old people will recover, it seems. God will surely bless you.'

Nathuni and Lakhua gave a slight smile. Bidding Chaupatlal good-bye, they left the hospital.

Lakhua asked, 'What will you do now?'

'Go back home. What else?' Nathuni replied.

'You won't look for any landowners?'

'There's no point.'

'Don't go yet. Maybe one or two are still here. If we could get just a little work …'

'All right,' said Nathuni, dryly.

On one side of the town of Nankipura there were many large and luxuriant karaiya trees growing close together. Each morning agricultural labourers would come from all around and gather under these trees in the hope of being hired. The landowners' men would select their labourers from among them, according to their particular needs.

When Nathuni and Lakhua got to the karaiya trees, the place was deserted; there was not a soul anywhere. The business of selecting labourers for the day had ended long before.

'What did I tell you?' Nathuni said. 'You can see with your own eyes.'

Lakhua slowly nodded.

Nathuni looked up at the sky and grew concerned. 'It's getting dark. Will you stay in Nankipura?'

'Yes.'

'I'm going. I'll come again tomorrow to look for work. If you're here, I'll see you then.'

'Yes. But …'

'What?'

'You said before that if you couldn't take back any flour your kids would have to fast.'

'We're used to fasting. So we'll have to go hungry for another day. But we did get the two old people here alive, didn't we?'

'Yes.'

Nathuni smiled fleetingly, then she walked off across the highway to the distant, vast tract of land under the darkening, gloomy sky.

hell
narak

When Sagiya set out from Nekipur at midday there were only one or two negligible wisps of cloud floating about aimlessly in the sky and every place was pervaded by the seductive rays of the sun.

It was the end of the month of Bhadra, when the sky, washed by all the waters of the monsoon, had become a wonderful blue and looked as though someone had installed some vast cosmic mirror overhead from one horizon to the other. There were, of course, a few dark clouds to be seen each day, but no sooner had they gathered than they would seem to have been swept away by the wind.

However, today was rather different, as the clouds had not been blown away but were gathering together. Moreover, the many big clouds like lumps of heavy rock, that had been sitting on the horizon, were rising quickly and gradually covering the gleaming blue sky.

Sagiya was on her way from Nekipur to Janakpur. The narrow sealed road ran due south from Nekipur, from where she had about a four-mile walk to the ferry ghat on the Nauhar river. The Nauhar flowed out of the more important Kushi river and meandered for quite a way before joining up again with the Kushi. Sagiya would take the ferry across and get down at another pucca road, by which it was about seven miles by cycle rickshaw to Janakpur.

Janakpur was a good way off, and Sagiya was hardly two miles out of Nekipur when she noticed that it was rapidly growing dark.

As she walked, she looked up once at the sky and saw that there was not a speck of blue anywhere. Indeed, she could see nothing overhead other than masses of thick, black clouds.

Sagiya still had quite a lot of road to cover, in the middle of which, moreover, was a moderate-size river to cross. There was no way she could return and spend the night in Nekipur and then set out again for Janakpur, for that morning Jagnath had paid her her wages and gone to Saharasa. It was not that she knew no one other than Jagnath in Nekipur; it was just that none of them would admit to their homes such a base woman as she. Indeed, even to look upon her was a sin, and being touched by her shadow would entail ten baths for the hapless one to become pure again.

Growing anxious, Sagiya quickened her step. It had not started to rain yet, but the sky might well burst at any moment. Who knew when this widespread bout of bad weather would end, or even if it would end at all? In the meantime, however, she still had to get to the other side of the Nauhar river to reach her home in Janakpur, in what was probably the most depraved red light district in all the world.

Sagiya was about thirty, but age had not begun to show on her yet. Even though month after month, year after year, herds of brutes had kneaded her body as though it were dough, she was by no means finished. She had a longish face, and her skin was like polished copper. There were dark stains under her eyes and her cheeks were freckled, indicating that her appearance was starting to become rough and hard. Nevertheless, even after being mauled night after night by packs of dogs, her body was still attractive thanks to her generally fine health. She had still not started to run to fat. The bones of her limbs were thick and strong; her waist was slim and her breasts full and fleshy; her hips were broad, and her neck was elegant and well-proportioned. She had a small forehead, and her thick black hair, when loose, hung down to her waist.

Sagiya was wearing a cheap, coloured silk sari with a shiny red blouse and, on her feet, a pair of tawdry slippers of unpolished leather. She had silver bangles on both hands, imitation stones set in silver in her ears, a broad silver necklace, and a nose pin. Her hair was arranged in a large bun and secured by a comb adorned by a silver leaf. She had three thick silver rings on her fingers and rings on her toes. Between her eyebrows was a tattoo of a half moon and, on her chin, one of a small snake with its hood spread. In her right hand, she carried a tin suitcase with flowers painted on it, inside which were some clothes and items of cheap make-up.

She had gone to Nekipur about four days ago, called from Janakpur by Jagnath, a man of one of the higher castes. He was over fifty, yet even at that age his body was continually burning for women. The reason for that was Parvati.

Parvati was Jagnath's wife, married according to orthodox ritual, pure and devoted. However, it could not be said that she brought any joy into Jagnath's life, for her ability to do so had been utterly dissipated. Only a few years after their marriage she suffered an accident to the lower part of her body and for almost thirty years she had been paralysed and bedridden. Once she had been beautiful, but now the life had quite gone out of her, having suffered, confined to her bed, for all those years. Her eyes were horribly sunken, her hair was as lifeless as jute fibre, and her dry skin sagged over her bones like a paper wrapping. All that indicated that she was alive was a heartbeat.

Jagnath could have taken another wife, but for fear of his father-in-law, he did not. Ramdhariji was a big and very powerful landholder, and it was due to him that Jagnath had some standing in life as a wealthy and respected member of society. With eyes ablaze, he would raise his finger and warn Jagnath that there would be no second marriage, and that he would vehemently oppose any co-wife coming into his daughter's house.

And so Jagnath did not marry a second time, but there was still the matter of his bodily needs. How was he to cope with a sickly, sexually useless wife? Maintaining celibacy until death for the sake of his lawfully married spouse was out of the question, so he was obliged to satisfy his appetite in secret, like a tomcat.

Jagnath was a big timber merchant. His main office was actually in Saharasa, and his home was there, too. However, he also had a warehouse in Nekipur; whatever good timber could be procured from thereabouts he would send to Saharasa, from where it would be dispatched to the big cities – Patna, Dhanbad, Calcutta, even to far off Bombay.

He would go to the Nekipur warehouse whenever he had the time. He had two reasons for going there: to manage the affairs of that place, and to bring Sagiya from Janakpur for a few days of pleasure. For Jagnath this was bliss, as he found this healthy and attractive woman greatly appealing. For nearly ten years, at least seven or eight times a year, Sagiya had come and gone between Janakpur and Nekipur for Jagnath's gratification.

When Sagiya reached the ferry ghat on the Nauhar river, it had not yet started to rain, although the clouds were getting heavier. Bolts of lightning were slashing at the horizon like the blades of so many knives seeming to tear at the heart of the earth, and all the while there was the continual roar of thunder as the stormy wind gusted over the now deserted river.

A few days before, when Sagiya came from the other side, the river was remarkably tranquil, and even though it had been filled with the monsoon rains, it was not at all choppy. But that river was hardly recognizable now. Its bluish waters had turned a leaden grey and were swelling up into big waves. Indeed, one might well have thought that preparation was being made to wipe this region of Bihar altogether off the map.

There was only one boat at the ferry ghat waiting to take passengers across to the other side. The boatman was about to push off when he caught sight of Sagiya. He called out to her, 'Are you going across?'

As she looked at the state of the river, Sagiya was overcome by fear. She could not help wondering for a moment whether the fragile boat could even make it to the other side.

The boatman hurried her. 'Well? Are you coming? You won't get another boat after this.'

There was no time to stand and think. Sagiya held her breath and rushed to the boat. Straightaway the boatman pushed off from the bank with the oar and the small craft drifted out into the distance.

The stream was now running very strongly from north to south and the rough and swelling waves bore the boat with its passengers as though it were a banana skin. The boatman was a cautious and dextrous battler in such turbulence, and had vast experience of this Bihari river and its currents. At that moment he clenched his teeth, maintaining a firm grip on the rudder as the boat cut through the waves.

All the while Sagiya had inadvertently had her eyes fixed on the other passengers. There were not many, about five. They were all sitting close together on the bare decking in the middle of the boat, and their faces were stricken with fear, in the uncertainty of reaching their destination across the Nauhar.

Four of the passengers were innocent-looking, simple country folk, but Sagiya was quite taken aback when her eyes fell on the fifth passenger. From just a glance it was plain that he was from a high-caste, genteel background. He was about forty or forty-five. His skin was smooth and gleaming, and he was quite attractive, with a longish, full face with striking eyes, though a little excess flesh had accumulated under his chin. He was wearing a sparkling white dhoti and punjabi, and strong sandals on his feet. He had with him only a medium-size leather suitcase. It was also clear from the look of him that he was a thoroughly pure and virtuous man.

Sagiya was frightened herself, but this man's fear seemed immense. His eyes were fixed, and his fearful, pallid face looked drained of blood. His dry lips trembled slightly as he muttered something in an unclear, shaky voice. Sagiya could make out only the words, 'Lord Ram, in you we trust …' Perhaps he thought that in this turbulent stream of the Nauhar, under a sky heavy with the weight of clouds, death may be imminent.

A thunderclap burst over the surging river and lightning rent the sky like a saw, lighting up everything around them for a second. Sagiya shot a quick look at the frightened man, who squinted momentarily. The four timid rustics were uttering in a strange, whimpering tone, 'Oh, Lord God, be merciful ...', but as soon as the sound emerged from their throats it was blown away on a gust of wind.

With amazing strength the boatman contended with the river. He was now totally preoccupied with manipulating the oar so as to propel the boat diagonally across to the other side. From the stern he kept saying encouragingly, 'Don't be frightened, brothers. I'll get you there before the rain starts.'

The Nauhar was not a very big river, nowhere more than half a mile in width, yet after a continual struggle for about an hour the boat had reached only midstream. It was then that the wind seemed suddenly to go wild. Spontaneously, the piles of clouds burst and the rain started, at first in drops, then in torrents, falling like millions of metal blades from the sky onto the earth. Just as suddenly the waves of the river swelled up like mountains, increasing the turbulence all about and endowing the current with the strength of several thousand wild elephants. The constant roar of thunder and the accompanying flashes of lightning, the gusty, tempestuous wind and the wild and wilful stream all together made that afternoon seem like a return to the primal turmoil at the beginning of the world. Wherever one looked, the landscape was grey and obscure. It seemed as though the world had never known autumn's brilliant sunshine, its velvet blue sky and its soothing, balmy breezes.

All the while the boat was being tossed up by a wave and the next instant cast into what seemed like a bottomless pit, only to be thrown up again. The passengers were holding on with all their strength to the wooden decking as though in one capricious flash of power the wind and the river might snatch their boat away, and who could tell where one might end up if he fell into that stream!

Nothing could be seen even from a foot away, but Sagiya could make out that the others had remained sitting and were hanging on to the decking, except for the saintly man, who lay completely prostrate, grasping the sides of the boat with both his hands. The rustics kept up a ceaseless refrain of: 'We're going to die, we're going to die …', even though some time before they had placed their implicit trust in God, thinking that in his mercy he would get them safely to the other side. Now that faith seemed to be resting on very shaky foundations.

Although the clouds and the unrelenting rain had obscured visibility, it was clear that the boat was nearing the bank. But for how long could one man grapple with the supernatural power of a river in tumult? Suddenly, with the violent force of the current, the boatman's oar snapped like a matchstick. Immediately a powerful force swung the boat around twice, then it straightened up again and was swept along by the impetus of the current as the last cries of the rustics were heard, 'Oh, we're finished! Help …'

With the oar broken, the boat capsized so suddenly that no one could have known what was happening.

As she was drawn along by the stream, Sagiya thought that she would not survive, yet she remembered that she knew how to swim and the will to live surged through her like an electric current. Although her clothes clung to her body making it difficult to swim, she managed to keep above water, straining for dear life to get to the shore.

After going a little way she suddenly noticed something floating about ten feet to her right. The rain had not yet abated and the light of day was still poor, but she could tell that it was a man. Fortuitously, perhaps due to some supernatural direction, Sagiya was drawn towards the drowning man, but the current was so strong that she could not reach him and he drifted further and further from her. Sagiya seemed drawn by a power beyond herself, oblivious to the danger she herself was in. Desperately she tried to swim to the man. After a few moments of struggle she reached him at last and grabbed hold of his shirt at the shoulder. She was aware that water was gushing into her nose and mouth and that she was straining the muscles of her legs, but she had no time to think. She just had to keep herself and the man afloat and get to the shore. Now and then a sudden eddy or a big wave would try to snatch the man, but Sagiya did not relax her vice-like grip even for a second on his shoulder. When at last she got him to the river bank, she was all but exhausted.

The bank of the Nauhar river was a sandy strip about twenty-five feet wide. Sagiya, gasping, dragged the man from the water and laid him down on the sand. Having been in the water so long her hands and feet were sodden and wrinkled and she was shivering from the cold. The rain had not altogether stopped, but it had eased to a drizzle and the clouds were starting to thin out. Just a little earlier visibility had been reduced to almost nothing by the clouds and the rain, but now the clouds were breaking up and a few dim rays of light were starting to peep through.

After quite some time, when Sagiya had recovered enough to slowly sit up, she took a look at the man, still lying barely a foot from her. It was none other than the one she had thought to be of a high-caste family, genteel and virtuous. Dumbstruck, Sagiya stared at him, blinking. Then suddenly, mechanically, she leaned over to him and said, 'Can you hear me?'

The man did not answer nor did he make any response.

Sagiya was unsure of what to do next. She wondered whether, in fact, the man was alive. Leaning over again, she placed a hand under his nose. After a while, she discerned a slight breath. He was alive. Relieved, she went on calling to him, 'Can you hear me?'

Still there was no response.

Sagiya's doubts returned. Taking the man by the shoulder, she shook him gently while she moved closer to his face saying, 'Listen to me ...' The man's eyes were closed and Sagiya sensed that he was unconscious. Now she began to worry. For a moment she thought that she should no longer be responsible for him. Under extraordinarily difficult circumstances, she had rescued him from the raging river and hauled him up onto the bank. What more could she do? But the next moment she felt immensely protective of him and berated herself for thinking of deserting a man in this condition. She would stay by him until he had regained consciousness.

The rain was now but a drizzle, but although the clouds had lightened, the sky still looked as though there might be some work of destruction left, and this might occur at any moment. It was doubtful if the man, covered with water, mud and sand, could survive in his condition if left under the open sky. No matter what, he would have to be taken to a safe shelter. But how?

Sagiya looked around carefully. The area was not unfamiliar to her, and she guessed that the stream had taken them about a mile to the south of the Janakpur ferry ghat. It was a terribly desolate place. Not a soul was to be seen near or far, nor was there a bird or beast, not even an insect or a spider. It seemed as though everything had fled from the vicinity of the Nauhar in this devastating aberration of the weather. If only someone else could be found, he might be persuaded to take the man to the ferry ghat. But Sagiya had no alternative but to do that on her own.

From having been so long in the water the man's fingers, toes and lips were creased, and his skin was white and looked drained of blood. Sagiya could tell that he had taken in a great deal of water and that before anything it would be necessary to get it all out of his stomach. Holding him around the back she gently sat him up, whereupon his head slumped down onto his chest while his arms spread out. While he was in that position, Sagiya started to shake him and after a few moments he brought up a little bluish water. Then she laid him face down and pressed upon his back, and this time more water came gurgling from his nose and mouth.

As she pressed her hands against his body she felt him shiver from the cold. She knew there would be no hope of saving him unless his body could become warm again. Sagiya was resolved to take him to the ferry ghat, for no matter how difficult it might be, getting him there was essential to finding help. Seeing a man unconscious like this, no one would fail to offer assistance.

There was no longer the turbulent river or sticky mud to get through, nor was there any jungle or scrub hereabouts, only mile after mile of brown sand as smooth as a grass mat. Sagiya sat the man up again and, as before, his shoulders slumped and his head hung on his chest and his arms swung free. Sagiya then took hold of him through his armpits. The sky was again starting to loosen its heavy load, and through light rain, the river still swirling beside her, this tenacious and single-minded woman hauled the unconscious man over the sand.

After going some distance, Sagiya laid the man down on the sand and panted for breath, her tongue hanging out like a dog's. Then she set about her haul once again. By the time she reached the ferry ghat at Janakpur, she was almost utterly exhausted.

Beside the ferry ghat were many pipal trees with spreading branches, underneath which were a few stalls, one selling tea, one selling paan and tobacco, another selling sweets. Near them would be a line of bullock carts and cycle rickshaws. Throughout the day and until quite late at night the place usually hummed with crowds of people. But at that moment the shops were boarded up, there was not a cycle rickshaw to be seen, nor were there any people about. The ferry ghat was quite deserted, and it seemed that everyone had fled from the terrible storm. There were just two bullock carts that had not yet left, but who could tell what they were waiting for?

Sagiya laid the man down on the sand and, gasping for breath, approached the trees. As there was no cycle rickshaw she would have to take the man by bullock cart, but she did not know where she should take him – what town or village – or even what was his name, and she had no way of knowing until he regained consciousness.

She decided to take him to the Janakpur hospital. However, without payment neither of the two bullocks would be allowed to take a step. She remembered that, when the boat capsized, her suitcase had sunk, but the eighty rupees that Jagnath had given her as four days' wages had been tucked into the waist of her sari. Her hand quickly went there and felt for the money.

She settled on a fare of ten rupees with one of the drivers. Then the two of them struggled together to lift the unconscious man into the cart. Sagiya regretted having to part with ten rupees, hard earned by having her flesh and bones pressed and squeezed by Jagnath, but there was nothing that she could do about it.

Janakpur was a dirty and insignificant town, one side of which was dirtier and more insignificant than the other. They reached the wretched-looking hospital to find that there was no doctor, as he had gone to a wedding fifty miles away and would not return that day, nor was anyone sure whether, in fact, he would return at all. And it was not possible for those who were at the hospital to admit anybody without the orders of the doctor.

It was beginning to rain heavily again, and the wind had grown stronger as well.Evening had begun to fall when Sagiya hired the bullock cart at the ferry ghat and by now it had become quite late. The dark night was even heavier on account of the clouds, and she felt as though she were surrounded by a solid black wall.

Sagiya had thought that her duty would be done once she reached the hospital, but what was she to do now? Where could she take this totally unknown man? Anxiety spun in her mind like a wheel of fire.

Ever determined, Sagiya decided that she would take the man to her own locality, but the driver would take her there only on condition that she pay a further two rupees. The urgency of the situation and the obduracy of the driver compelled her to pay him the enhanced fare and have done with him.

The red light district was at the other end of the town and was made up by about ten or twelve tumbledown, tin-roof houses which were in such disrepair that they could have come crashing down at any moment. Somehow remaining upright, the houses stood in two rows facing each other on either side of a narrow, dirty lane.

Electricity had come to the moneyed part of Janakpur, but there was none at all here. Still, from under the canopy in the middle of the bullock cart Sagiya could see the girls of the locality sitting under the decrepit, tiled roofs – Bijri, Shuga, Lachhima, Panchhi and a few others. Two or three blackened lanterns burned in front of them.

On any other day at this time there would be a crowd gathering here like flies swarming over treacle, and all those who came to this place of perdition were drunkards, ganja addicts, thieves, swindlers, thugs, consumptives and syphilitics. Other than such worms of the lowest level of humanity, no one would tread in the shadows of this whores' quarter, but today even they seemed to have kept away.

The sight of the bullock cart created a stir among the girls. Perhaps a client had come even in this dreadful weather. But their enthusiasm was soon dampened by the sound of Sagiya's voice coming from under the awning as she called, 'Hey, Shuga! Hey, Lachhima! Come here quickly!'

There was no sign of anyone getting up. Only Shuga asked stridently, 'Why?'

'This man has to be got down. He's quite unconscious.'

Their curiosity aroused, the girls started to get up. Their faces were battle-scarred and rough, and because of their wakeful nights there were dark stains permanently under their eyes. It was hard to believe that they might once have had any charm or comeliness.

Sagiya quickly paid the driver his fare and, indicating the unconscious man, said to the girls, 'Get a hold.'

'Who is it, then?' one of them asked.

'I'll tell you later,' said Sagiya.

Two of them held the lanterns while the others struggled with Sagiya to get the man inside.

Sagiya's room had earthen walls, into one of which were set two small windows with shutters of beaten tin. On another wall hung a few cheap calendars with crude pictures of the gods Ganapati, Ramchandra, Hanuman, Shiva, and the goddess Durga, alongside which were a few pictures of scantily clad, amorous-looking film-stars cut from newspapers and old calendars, but no one could really have any objection to this juxtaposition of deities and heroines.

Where the old bed in the corner was missing a leg it was supported by a brick. The bed was dirty as a lot of dust had gathered on it in the few days that Sagiya had been away. At the foot of it were some enamel kitchen utensils, a large tin trunk, various kinds of bottles, a wooden box, a few items of silverware, and a pile of all sorts of odds and ends. Nearby was a wooden clothes rack with several saris hanging on it.

Leaving the unconscious man in the hands of the other girls,

Sagiya quickly swept the bed, took out a clean sheet from a box and spread it out. 'Lay him down,' she said, as with a deft hand she took a lantern from the foot of the bed and lit it.

The girls laid the man on the bed. Shuga said, 'He's terribly wet. He'll catch his death if we don't change his clothes.'

'Yeah,' Sagiya muttered, helplessly looking this way and that. There was nothing in her room that a man could wear.

Lachhima anticipated her concern. 'Just put a sari on him. Where would we get a dhoti now?'

Sagiya quickly took two saris from the rack. Beside her Lachhima said, 'Undress him and then put the sari on him, Sagi.' She winked lasciviously and gave a toothy grin. Since the age of ten she had regularly smoked bidis and chewed tobacco, so her teeth and gums were rotting and stained black.

The other girls laughed lewdly. Sagiya did not look at them. She covered the man's lower half with a sari and carefully undid his dhoti and drew it down to his feet. Until now the girls had not taken much notice of the man, but once they had caught sight of his face, they started to whisper among themselves. 'What a handsome man!'

Indeed, such a noble-looking man had never come into this depraved colony of whores. The girls here were tremendously jealous of Sagiya, for she was still exceptionally attractive and her body was in great demand in the marketplace. Whoever should come to the locality would agree to pay anything for her. If the other girls got two rupees, she would get ten. Yet Sagiya did not take everyone to her bed, selecting carefully the men she would allow into her room. The other girls could not afford to be discriminating; there was no question of picking and choosing for them, even if the fellow were a rotten, ulcerous worm. He only had to appear and he would be received and welcomed cordially. But in every respect they were outdone by Sagiya. None of them could remember whether they had ever in all their lives seen such a handsome man as he whom Sagiya had brought just now in the bullock cart. Envy at her renewed good fortune burned in their breasts.

Panchhi said, 'The man's very wealthy, then, is he?'

As she undid the man's punjabi buttons, Sagiya said, 'I don't know.'

'Bullshit.'

'What do you mean?'

'You go to such trouble to bring the fellow here and you say you don't know! Don't give us that. Anyway, we don't want to share him. We don't want a penny from him.'

Sagiya tried to explain to them all. 'Believe me, I had never seen the man before we crossed the river.'

But no one believed a word of what she said. Aflame with envy, Lachhima said, 'But why do you want to sleep in this stinking sewer when the fellow will certainly take you away from here and set you up in a fine house and dress you in gold and silver?'

Sagiya did not answer, for no matter what she said they would not understand. She took the punjabi and singlet off the man's body.

But then, before Shuga and Bilakhi could say anything, Lachhima cried out aghast, 'Oh, my God! She's brought a Brahmin! She's brought a Brahmin into hell!' And she pointed to the gleaming white sacred thread on the man's bare body.

Sagiya was dumbstruck. Given her lifelong reverence for Brahmins, she was momentarily overwhelmed by an awful sense of sin. Unwittingly she had brought a Brahmin into a colony of whores. The other girls in the room said nothing. To carry a Brahmin here was, in everyone's eyes, an utterly reprehensible act.

After a while, a woman called Tohori said, 'If he's a Brahmin, so what? We're not going to put an unconscious man out in the rain. If he regains consciousness and the rain stops, then we call a rickshaw and put him in it.'

They all agreed with what Tohori said. Anyhow, they had no alternative.

Feeling uneasy about any further discussion of an unknown man on such a filthy night, the girls left. They shuddered to think of what the man's reaction might be when, on regaining consciousness, he discovered himself in the bed of some despicable trollop.

After everyone had gone, Sagiya went into a corner of the room and changed into some dry clothes, then she went and stood beside the bed. The air and every single thing in this room were stained by a hundred thousand sins. Yet when she brought the man here, it had been for no other reason than his recovery. She took a dry sari and wiped his head and body, then took out another sheet and covered him from neck to toe.

Outside it was raining heavily and it seemed that the worn-out tin roof would be shattered. But then the force of the storm increased and the sound of broken branches crashing from trees could be heard along with the roar and rumble of thunder.

That day Sagiya had walked four miles from Nekipur to the ferry ghat. What had happened after the boat sank in the middle of the river had driven her body to the point of total exhaustion, so that now she felt as though her limbs were about to fall away from her body. Her eyes were heavy and she was terribly hungry, but she did not have the energy left even to light the oven and make something to eat. However, there was some flattened rice in a container; she would eat it with some water and then go to sleep.

Before taking out the flattened rice, she called gently, 'Can you hear me? Hello?'

But no, the man had still not come to. His eyes were closed as before. Sagiya felt his forehead and, although it was very hot, she could not tell if he had a fever or not.

Sagiya was unable to remain standing any longer. She managed to get down some of the flattened rice and some water, then set out a bed on the damp floor. As she lay there, it struck her as odd that she had come into this room with a man and yet she was not lying in the same bed with him. In fact, a saintly Brahmin was lying unconscious on her dirty bed and, for the first time in all her experience, she was on the floor. And as she thought about it, her eyes closed.

Suddenly Sagiya was woken by a heavy knocking at the door. Sleepily she called, 'Who is it?'

The storm was raging outside and the rain on the tin roof sounded as though a thousand wild horses were running over it. Obscured by the sound of the storm, came a drunken voice, 'It's your master, you slut. Open the door …'

She knew the voice. It was Tarjulal. He drove a tonga in Janakpur and was an ill-tempered and dangerous fellow. Not a day passed without him getting involved in one quarrel or another and at a mere word he would pull a knife. He would be on the booze the whole day and later end up dead drunk. For all these reasons he had been to jail on more than one occasion.

Sagiya called out, 'Not tonight. Go away.'

The groggy voice became a little louder. 'Open up, I'm telling you, you bitch. Otherwise I'll knock the door down.'

Sagiya hesitated for a moment. She looked at the man lying on the bed and said, 'There's a man with me. Now go!'

Tarjulal delivered a long tirade of abuse, after which he said, 'Not even a cat or a dog would go out in this rain, and you, whore, turn away a passenger! You daughter of a pig!' And with renewed earnest he uttered some unspeakable revilement and left.

A little later there was again a knocking at the door. This time it was Bhaironath, the proprietor of the bhang and ganja shop. Even though a cat or a dog would not go out in such a fearsome storm, it did not stop some of the patrons of whoredom. No beast lower than man has ever been born.

Sagiya had not thought that such a wild and stormy night would throw up such difficulties. She sent Bhaironath away too, and he, like Tarjulal before him, offered some choice obscenities before leaving.

Sagiya had no idea how long she slept after that, but she awoke with a start to a sudden sound of whimpering. Before going to bed she had turned the lantern right down low, and now, when she turned the light up, she noticed that the man had become restless and was making sounds of distress.

She got up quickly and went and stood beside the bed. She leaned over very close to him and said, 'Can you hear me? Can you hear me?'

The man opened his eyes and looked at her, but did not answer. His eyes were a flaming red and he was muttering meaninglessly. Sagiya was startled when she touched his forehead; his body was burning with fever.

Something had to be done straightaway, but Sagiya could not imagine what. At last she opened her door, went out into the next room and woke Tohori to tell her of the man's new symptoms. Worried, she asked, 'Now what is to be done?'

At first Tohori was angry at being woken in the middle of the night, but after she had heard everything, she softened a little and said, 'Have you got any money?' She thought for a second and then said, 'You have. You must have come back with a packet from your timber merchant in Nekipur.'

Twelve rupees of what Jagnath had paid her had already gone in expenses. Sagiya was thinking that, if only the man would regain consciousness, she could call a rickshaw and send him off in it, but now things seemed to have gone beyond her control. Firstly, she could not tell how long it would be before the fever subsided and the man's health was restored; secondly, it was very likely that she did not have enough cash in hand for him. Moreover, she had only the one room. As long as a man was spread over her bed, she could not bring in any clients, and as long as he stayed, she could not earn anything.

Tohori could guess what was on Sagiya's mind. Sympathetically she said, 'Call the vaid to see to him. Otherwise you won't be able to send him home cured in a hurry.'

Sagiya took hold of her hand and said, 'Go on, then. Get the vaid.'

Tohori was indignant. 'In this rain?'

'Yes. His condition is very serious.'

But Tohori insisted that neither the folk practitioner nor the Western doctor would be likely to leave his house in such terrible weather and so late at night. Sagiya had better go back to her room and wait till morning.

By the morning, the weather had improved considerably. Light drizzle continued to fall, but the sky was a lot clearer, although there were still some sparse wisps of cloud about.

Sagiya had not slept for the remainder of the previous night, sitting helplessly by the sick and unconscious man, listening to his continual whimpering and not being able to decide what to do with him. From time to time she stroked his forehead and then, as soon as daylight started to peep through, she called for the vaid, Sahayji.

Although Paonlal Sahay was a high-caste man, he did answer the calls of the residents of the red light district, and for that reason he was considered too unclean to be called to the sick of the higher-caste homes of Janakpur. But Paonlal was a man of strong will and integrity. He would say that should a sick person come to a vaid, it would be a sin not to treat him. A vaid should turn away no one – prostitute, sweeper, cobbler – no one at all. Even if a crematory attendant, a scavenger, a thief or a bandit should be sick and call him, he would go to them. In this matter he was not at all concerned at whatever anyone may think or say.

For twelve months of the year, summer or winter, Paonlal's middle-aged body was adorned with a grey alpaca coat, his dhoti was so short that it reached hardly below his knees, and he wore heavy, untanned leather shoes. Attached with a silk cord to the breast pocket of his coat was an old-fashioned, round watch. His greying hair was close-cropped and there was no regularity in his shaving habits, for his cheeks had accumulated nine- or ten-day old tufts of whiskers. Whenever he went out anywhere, he carried a very large tin box. Paonlal followed no specific method of treatment – his box contained Ayurvedic pills, numerous bottles of homeopathic globules, allopathic tablets and the wherewithal for injections. He had no cause in the least to be bothered by adherence to any one particular form of treatment.

When he went into Sagiya's room and looked at the man lying on the bed, Paonlal received quite a shock. 'My goodness!' he said. 'Do you know who it is you have brought here?'

News of Paonlal's arrival had spread quickly through the little red light quarter, and many had come and crowded outside Sagiya's door.

Apprehensively, Sagiya asked, 'Who have I brought?'

'It's Shastriji,' said Paonlal. 'The chief priest of the Ram Sita temple, Shiushankar Shastri.' Then, in a rush, he went on to say that in all of India one would never find a true celibate like Shiushankar or anyone as upstanding, holy or scripturally learned as he. In Janakpur – but why just Janakpur? – within a hundred miles thereabouts, no one was more revered and honoured than he. There was righteousness in every inch of his being, so there would have to be the most dire consequences for dragging such a man as he into this outpost of hell. If the word got around, Shiushankar's good name and reputation would be utterly ruined. Nor would the people of Janakpur overlook the bringing of the revered priest of the Ram Sita temple onto the path to depravity and would, therefore, burn alive Sagiya and all her ilk.

Although Sagiya and the others had never seen Shiushankar before, they had certainly heard of him. Various intimations of his saintliness and purity, borne on the breezes of Janakpur, had reached even their hellhole. Sagiya shuddered, and the other girls outside the door also trembled in fear.

As though speaking on behalf of all of them, with palms pressed together Sagiya said plaintively, 'I haven't done anything wrong, Paonji …', and she went on to tell in a voice quaking with fear how she had saved the utterly helpless Shiushankar from the Nauhar river.

Paonlal watched her, his face wooden, but his hardness melted once he had heard it all. Slowly shaking his head he said, 'Yes, but later Shastriji will have to make expiation for having fallen into this situation.' And as he spoke he brushed his hand over Shiushankar's forehead. From his tin box he took a thermometer and stethoscope; he took the man's temperature, then examined his chest and back. 'He has a very high temperature,' he said. 'He'll have to have an injection.' He took out a syringe and an ampoule and gave Shiushankar an injection in the right arm. He gave some pills to Sagiya and told her, 'When he regains consciousness, give him two of these three times a day – morning, noon, evening.'

'Yes,' Sagiya said, leaning forward slightly.

'He'll come to before midday. Give them to him then with some warm milk. I'll give him another two when I come back in the evening.'

'But Paonji …'

'What?'

'Is it all right for me to give Shastriji anything?'

Paonlal realized that Sagiya was worried about the impurity of her own touch in giving him milk. He told her that, in exceptional circumstances, when there is no alternative, there could be no sin in it, but she was definitely not to give him anything other than milk, such as rice or bread. It was probably due to some transgression in a previous life that Shastriji had now been brought into this hellhole. Should rice touched by a prostitute enter his pure body, he would live eternally in hell after his death as there could be no expiation for such a sin.

Alarmed, Sagiya said, 'No, no. There is no way I'd ever give him rice.'

'You must send Shastriji away from here once he gets a little better, but see to it that no one sees him come out of this place.'

'Yes.'

'Right. Then that'll be ten rupees. That's my fee, rickshaw fare, and the cost of the medicine and injection.'

Paonlal was a cautious man, careful to have the bill settled before he left.

Then the residents of the red light locality had a secret conference. They knew already that the unconscious man was a Brahmin, something that conflicted with everything in their own lives. But then Paonlal had recognized the man as Shiushankar Shastri, and that served to increase their alarm and agitation many times over. In keeping with Paonlal's instructions, they decided that they would be extremely careful that Shiushankar's honour and reputation should in no way at all be besmirched by his having been brought here. And as no sooner would evening have fallen than the horde of worthless thieves and drunks and other low-life would descend upon the place, for the few days that Shastriji would be there none of them must be allowed entry. If anyone from outside were allowed to come in, word of Shastriji would be thrown to the four winds. They could not allow infamy to be cast in his face.

By midday the clouds had rolled back to set free the clear, golden sunshine and the breeze blew gently. To look at the sky today, how could anyone believe that only yesterday the district had been devastated by such an appalling storm!

There were two big bottles of Ganges water in Tohori and Lachhima's room. The girls mixed that Ganges water with water drawn in buckets from the well and set about cleaning their old whores' quarter. As well as that, Sagiya had bought a few big steel bowls. Two of them were still unused and new. She took one of them from the box and boiled in it some milk fresh from the dairy-shed. She would have to give it to Shastriji when he regained consciousness. Indeed, what Paonlal the vaid had said had to be followed to the letter.

A little after midday Shiushankar regained consciousness. He opened his reddened eyes and looked at Sagiya. In some trepidation, he asked, 'Who are you?'

Sagiya's heart started to thump. Indistinctly she said, 'You wouldn't know me.'

Shiushankar asked nothing more. Slowly his eyes closed again.

Sagiya called softly to him, 'Can you hear me? Will you have some milk?' She did not go on, for Shiushankar did not reply, having fallen into a sleep that could not have been easily disturbed.

The afternoon passed, evening soon fell, and the hordes of drunken beasts started to assemble, but Tohori, Lachhima, Shuga and a few of the other girls sent them away. Those who had come in quest of pleasure expressed their frustration in obscene language and left.

One of them said, 'What the hell? Have you bloody harlots turned into goddesses?'

Another said, 'You're turning out the lights? Has this become a temple or something?'

No one felt the need to answer their questions.

Paonlal came again at night. He asked about the patient and gave him an injection. Not long after he had left, Shiushankar's temperature dropped considerably and he woke up from his afternoon's sleep. There was no longer that dark look in his eyes, but his face was marked by fear and anxiety when he saw a few girls sitting in the space at the foot of the bed. He did not know that they had spent almost the whole day waiting on him. Now and then one or two had got up, gobbled down some rice and dal or a couple of chapatis, and come back. And several times when the drunks had come to break down the main door and force their way in, they had gone to send them away.

With lifeless eyes Shiushankar looked at each one of them, then asked, 'Who are you?'

Sagiya answered, 'We are nobody, your reverence.'

'How did I get to this house? I don't recognize this place.'

Sagiya said, 'The ferry was wrecked in the Nauhar river in a storm yesterday. Do you remember?'

Shiushankar let his head drop slowly. 'Yes. How did you know that?'

'I was in the boat.'

'I did not notice.'

Sagiya then told Shiushankar how, after the boat had been sunk in the storm, she had brought him here.

Shiushankar looked at Sagiya with gratitude. 'Then you have saved my life! God will be good to you.'

Timorously Sagiya then told him that she had called the vaid to him and he had given him a couple of injections. The vaid had also given a lot of medicine and said that, when the patient regained consciousness, he should be given milk to enable his body to recover its strength. Would he now take some milk?

Shiushankar nodded his head. He would take some milk.

Hesitantly Sagiya said, 'But ...'

'What?'

'Will you eat anything touched by us?'

Shiushankar smiled gently. 'Why shouldn't I? Give it to me. I'm hungry.'

'We … we are the low-life of hell, revered one. There is no place in the world more vile than this.' Sagiya's lips trembled as she spoke.

Now Shiushankar realized where he had been brought. At first he was shocked. His inherited predisposition caused the muscles of his face and body to contort and his heart seemed as though it would crack under these intolerable circumstances. The girls watched Shiushankar's reaction with great fear and held their breath in anticipation of some terrible outburst. However, after a few moments Shiushankar gradually relaxed. With a soft smile, he said, 'You have saved my life. Now bring the milk.'

A thrill of excitement ran through Sagiya and the other girls. Sagiya ran and fetched the bowl, and slowly poured the milk into Shiushankar's mouth. The other girls sat there, their hands pressed together.

After taking his milk and his medicine Shiushankar fell asleep again.

The next morning Shiushankar was very much better. He got down slowly from the bed and said to Sagiya, 'Will you call me a rickshaw? I'll be going now.'

Sagiya was taken aback. 'But …'

'What's the matter?'

'What will people say if they see you leaving this godforsaken place in broad daylight?'

'I am not going to bother my head over what anyone says or what anyone thinks. You all, especially you, have given me back my life. I'll always remember that.'

'Please be so good as to never remember this hell,' Sagiya replied.

A little later Shiushankar got into a cycle rickshaw in the street outside the whores' house. Sagiya and the other girls, hands pressed together reverentially, waited on him. And then the rickshaw started to move off.

The girls thought that for just one day the holiness of heaven had come down to them. From that time on, as the years would come and go, that day would never come back. They all felt this, although perhaps they were not quite able to articulate it. And Sagiya could think only of Shiushankar as he went further and further away. Time and again she had spoken of her place as hell. But at that moment it seemed as though Shiushankar had obliterated the dividing line between hell and heaven.

across the fields

pari

Kishunpura is a small place in northern Bihar, known to the people of the region as 'town'. Some town! A few dusty, rugged stone roads with tongas, cycle rickshaws, bullock and buffalo carts; some rows of miserable-looking houses with tiled or tin roofs; in the back alleys a Shiva temple and some images of Hanuman and his army; and an open sewer over which mosquitoes swarmed: such was the town of Kishunpura, hidden away in its corner of northern Bihar.

About a year and a half ago 'the electric' had come to this municipality, but the people of the town were so poor that they were struggling even to subsist and in most houses the old kerosene lanterns still burned at night. Only one or two homes were lit by electricity. When evening fell, the roads glimmered with electric light but this was turned off after nine o'clock.

However, coming to the eastern end of Kishunpura one might be surprised, for there, avoiding the touch of the rest of the town, was 'Chaturvedi', the huge three-storey house of the Chaubes, set right in the middle of a compound surrounded by a high wall. At the front gate Bhojpuri watchmen with bandoleers around their necks kept watch night and day. On the roof of the house was a Ram-Sita temple, the pinnacle of which could be seen from about two miles away. The Chaubes were not only the biggest landowners in Kishunpura, they were the biggest for fifty or sixty miles around.

The southern end of the town bordered on fields through which a canal ran off towards the horizon. On one side of it were cultivated fields, on the other side, sandy and stony lowland. All the land, both agricultural and barren, belonged to the Chaubes.

The month of Phalgun had come to an end.

Only a few days ago, the frenzy of the region's biggest festival, Holi, had finished. As a rule, it would be only a few more days before the gentle breezes of spring would begin, but the subtleties of the weather could be very deceptive. Indeed, no sooner had Phalgun come to an end than it got very hot, and as the days got longer, the hot, dry wind gusted wildly all about like an unbroken horse.

The midday sun was directly overhead, maliciously spreading its blazing heat, and to look upwards was to dazzle the eyes. A little earlier a bullock cart, its ungreased wheels creaking and grating, had come out of Kishunpura town and was heading south across the barren land along a broken down old road which ran diagonally across the fields to the distant highway. What a road it was! For nine months of the year it was ankle-deep in dust, and for the three months of the rains the dust turned cloggy and felt like soft meat.

The bullock cart was being driven by the middle-aged Bhirguram. His body bore the marks of much deprivation and fasting; he had a sickly, emaciated look, and his Adam's apple stuck out like a peg. There were clumps of greying stubble on his cheeks, and his eyes were set deep in their sockets. He was wearing a patched and grubby shirt and, around his middle, a brief and threadbare loincloth which was little more than a strip of rag. To protect his head against the sun, he wore a large turban.

Bhirguram's two bullocks were rather similar to him, with their bones protruding and their strength burnt out, but somehow they managed to pull the dray, panting as they went.

For three successive years this region had suffered from a terrible drought. There were virtually no crops. Indeed, such scarcity had not been known in fourteen generations. As people no longer had cash in hand, who would call on Bhirguram to carry goods or passengers? His income dropped by a quarter, and what he got now was not even enough to feed himself and his bullocks twice a day. On most days their stomachs were only half full, and sometimes they had to go without altogether. As a result there was hardly anything left of them.

Bhirguram had absolutely no desire to put the bullocks to such hardship by bringing them out in this fearsome heat, but he had no alternative. For the first time in four days he had been hired at Vishunganj.

Vishunganj market was a little to the south along the highway on the other side of the fields. The son of the proprietor of a timber yard there was getting married that day, and Bhirguram had to take the groom and his party of six to a village another two miles away. He would be paid a fare of twenty-five rupees and be able to eat his fill at the excellent feast, and for the bullocks there would be chickpeas, oil cake and chaff. In such bad times, an offer like this could not be turned down, and so the poor beasts had to be taken out despite the burning sun.

The blazing sky was the colour of molten bell metal and wherever one looked the sunshine shimmered like a wave of fire, as though a thousand ovens were burning all around. Not a bird was in sight and far off in the distance a few bullock carts appeared like black spots. There were hardly any people to be seen.

Sweat was streaming over Bhirguram's body and the inside of his mouth and throat was like burnt brick. The bullocks were starting to froth at the mouth and their reddening eyes looked as though they would pop out. Indeed, the pair of them might suddenly drop in their tracks at any moment.

Bhirguram knew that the energy of his animals was quickly running out, yet he tried to encourage them, saying lovingly, 'Chunnuwa and Munnuwa, today is extremely hot, so you will have to suffer a little. But when we get to Vishunganj, you will be able to eat and fill yourselves up to your necks, so don't be upset.'

Ten years earlier there had been terrible floods for four years in a row in these parts. In times of flood, just as in times of drought, there is no income, and Bhirguram had no calls to carry goods or passengers. It was during that time that his wife ran away to Dhanbad with a younger man, leaving Bhirguram with no one in all the world. After all, how long can a woman go on fasting?

Since then life had gone on unchanging for Bhirguram in his little, ramshackle, tin-roofed hut in a corner of Kishunpura. His only company were his bullocks, Chunnuwa and Munnuwa.

Bhirguram had not mixed much with people after his wife had run off. He was happy enough to share all his joys and sorrows with Chunnuwa and Munnuwa, who would respond to his words by flapping their ears. Indeed, they agreed unconditionally with everything he said or did. They even swayed their drooping ears slowly at being told of what they would have to endure in crossing the fields to Vishunganj. They were quite forbearing.

Bhirguram told them, 'They said that there'll be a feast for you too. Oh, well, it is a wedding! You can have as much as you can eat. Understand?'

Chunnuwa and Munnuwa flapped their ears in acknowledgement.

Bhirguram went on, 'I'm sure you'll never eat so well in this life or any other. You're certain to get chickpeas and chaff and oil cake. But just remember that after the wedding feast you won't want to eat anything for three or four days. Understand?'

While this conversation was going on between a man and two beasts, in the distance someone was shouting. 'Hey, stop! Stop! Stop!'

At first Bhirguram did not hear, but when the shouting got closer he turned around. Through the awning of the cart he could see a young woman running distractedly across the burning fields. Keeping his eyes on her, he said to Chunnuwa and Munnuwa, 'Stop for a moment, children.'

The pair of bullocks stood still, and a little later the young woman, panting, caught up with them. She looked terrified. 'Save me!' she implored.

From a distance he had not been able to make out who she was, but when the woman came and stood close to him Bhirguram was taken back. He recognized her only too well – she was the youngest daughter-in-law of Kishunpura's great landowner, Vindhyachali Chaube. Moreover, Bhirguram had heard her name from someone. She was Kaushalya, and at her wedding the Chaubes had feasted the whole of Kishunpura. Even insignificant bullock-drivers like Bhirguram had not been left out. He had also seen her a few times with her mother-in-law worshipping at the Shiva temple. And so he could hardly believe his eyes when, with this hot dry wind burning all about, a wife of such a great house should come running like this across the open fields. He just looked at her, dumbstruck.

Kaushalya was wearing a fine, expensive sari, but had nothing on her feet, the soles of which were cracked and bleeding after running over the sand and stones of the barren fields. Her clothes were dishevelled and she was greatly agitated; her fair face was a glowing red, her eyes were glazed and she was sweating profusely.

Terrified, she said again, 'Save me, please, bullock driver!'

All Bhirguram could say for a few moments was, 'What's the matter, mother?'

Kaushalya told him that she was running away from her father-in-law's house because she was in great danger. However, Vindhyachali Chaube had sent his household thugs after her, and at any moment they might catch her, as hunting dogs would, and drag her back to her father-in-law's house.

Bhirguram was afraid. He did not have the strength or the courage to protect Kaushalya from the hands of such an immensely powerful landowner as Vindhyachali Chaube and his strongarm men. In a trembling voice he again asked, 'What is it all about, mother?'

'I'll tell you later. But just remember, if they catch me, it will definitely be the end of me.' As she spoke, she looked around and suddenly cried out fearfully, 'Oh! They're coming!'

Bhirguram quickly looked back towards Kishunpura town and saw far off in a shimmering haze of heat a few dark spots in the form of men, and it was clear that they were hurrying in this direction.

The blood had drained from Kaushalya's face. Her words came out in a rush, 'Don't delay any more, bullock-driver. Do something quickly. Do you want me to be murdered?'

Bhirguram knew only too well that if he helped Kaushalya, he would have a heavy price to pay. Vindhyachali's musclemen would certainly bury him alive in the middle of these fields. Yet something in him rebelled like an electric shock flashing through his frail and feeble body. He said, 'Get up on the cart. Quickly.'

It was still unclear to Bhirguram why Kaushalya was running away and why the strongarm men were running after her. However, he could see that the girl really was in grave danger, and immediately a plan to save her started to form in his mind. As Kaushalya was getting up onto the cart, he said, 'Mother, there are only some smelly old rags under the awning. You'll have to sit in there and cover yourself with them. And hide your face also with your veil. I'm afraid there's no alternative.'

'That's no bother for me.' Kaushalya covered herself with the dirty pieces of cloth as Bhirguram had directed and pulled down her veil as she shrank in under the awning.

'Do you want me to take you somewhere?' asked Bhirguram.

'Yes. To my father's house in Baihari village. If you can.'

Bhirguram did not answer immediately. Once he had got up onto the highway, Vishunganj market would be a few miles to the south, but Baihari was in quite the opposite direction, about four miles to the north. Having delivered Kaushalya there, it would be evening by the time he got back to Vishunganj. Would the bridegroom and his party wait so long for him? And yet now, having taken Kaushalya onto his cart, all these questions seemed irrelevant. He turned again to the front and said, 'Let's go, then, Chunnuwa and Munnuwa. No need to stand around in the dust any longer! Mother has asked to be taken to Baihari, so that's what we must do, mustn't we?'

The two bullocks flapped their dangling ears and set off again.

Bhirguram went on talking. 'Can we get mother to Baihari and then be back at Vishunganj before dark? What do you think?'

As before, the two beasts wagged their ears.

Bhirguram continued, 'Such a lot of bother for you both today! But what can we do? Mother is in serious danger.' And, with its wheels creaking, the bullock cart headed across the rough and barren fields towards the blazing horizon.

When Bhirguram had left Kishunpura town, the sun was directly overhead, and now it was still in the same position, making it seem that in these vast plains of northern Bihar the daily movement of the earth had come to a complete stop.

After going a little way, Bhirguram, keeping his eyes ahead of him, asked apprehensively, 'Can I ask something, mother?'

Kaushalya was sitting in silence, her chin resting between her knees. 'What?' she asked.

'You are a daughter-in-law of such a great house. Why are you running away like this?'

'Dowry. Simply because of dowry.'

'Dowry?'

'Yes. They are exploiting my father.' And as she spoke, she gave a start, for from just a little way away came the sound of many feet. Almost whispering, she said in considerable alarm 'They're coming. Be careful.'

Bhirguram turned around quickly. In her fear Kaushalya had shrunk right back under the semi-circular canopy, and over the top of her head he could see five or six highly agitated, robust young men coming close to the cart. Each of them had wide sideburns and a curled moustache and carried a sturdy, brass-banded lathi.

Bhirguram knew them all. These household thugs of the Chaubes were more savage than wild animals. They would maim or kill and they would set fire to houses; indeed, there was no wicked thing they would not do at the behest of Vindhyachali Chaube. Seeing them almost made Bhirguram's heart stop beating, but the next moment he was overcome by some divinely inspired strength of resistance. Quickly turning back to the front he gave a gentle twist to the tails of his bullocks, saying, 'Chunnuwa, Munnuwa, we're in grave danger! Run like winged horses and get mother away from here!'

The two bullocks seemed to understand him. Ignoring the unbearable heat of the sun and their own bodily weakness, they held their breath and broke into a trot.

From behind came the strident cry of one of the men, 'Hey, bullock-driver! Stop there! Stop!' As he spoke, he came up alongside them, the rest of them following him.

Bhirguram was obliged to say to his bullocks, 'Hey there, Chunnuwa and Munnuwa, pull up for a little. Whoa, there!' and he made a strange clicking noise with his tongue. As the cart came to a stop, he asked cautiously, 'What is it, brother? Do you have some business with me?'

The hugs knew Bhirguram. The one who had given the order for the cart to stop asked in a harsh voice, 'Have you seen any woman going about around here?'

Bhirguram could feel a storm blowing up inside his breast, but he struggled to remain calm. He gulped, and managed to say, 'No.'

'Think hard. Very good-looking woman. Smart clothes. Gold necklace and gold bangles. Ear ornaments . . . '

'No.'

No further questions were asked as the ruffians, their voices suppressed, went into some kind of discussion among themselves. Then one of them said to Bhirguram, 'All right, then. You can go.'

'Chunnu, Munnu, let us go, children . . . '

But no sooner had Bhirguram got the words out of his mouth than the fellow's glance fell on the space under the awning. His eyes narrowed. He took a few steps forward and asked, 'Who's that?'

Bhirguram stopped breathing. If they found out that the woman under the awning was none other than Vindhyachali Chaube's youngest daughter-in-law, Bhiguram could not even imagine what hell there would be to pay. Like a non-swimmer desperately trying to save himself in deep water, Bhirguram said sternly, 'That's my wife.'

The thug set his jaw and, clenching his teeth, said, 'You bastard son of a pig, your wife pissed off on you more than four years ago!' Frowning, he held his gaze unblinking on what was Kaushalya wrapped in dirty rags.

Bhirguram felt that he had gone so far that there was now no turning back. One slight mistake now could cost him his life. He said, 'She came back again last night, brother.'

Bhirguram's face bore an innocence that made one instinctively want to believe him. Moreover, he had a reputation in Kishunpura of being a good and honest man.

The thug asked, 'Is that so?'

'Yes, brother.' Bhirguram felt the fear build up inside him as he spoke. Never before had he been so audacious as to tell such a lie.

The ruffians appeared to believe him. Making a few obscene gestures, they accused Bhirguram banteringly of putting his nose to a plate already licked by such a dirty bugger. Did he have no pride in him? What sort of animal was he?

Bhirguram disinterestedly raised his hands heavenward and said, 'It's all the will of God.'

The thugs carried on some heated, whispered discussion among themselves, then said to Bhirguram, 'Get going, then, you bastard son of a pig.' And so saying, they ran off across the fields towards the blazing horizon.

Bhirguram could never have thought that he would escape so easily. Mumbling to himself, 'Oh, thanks be to Lord Shiva,' he twisted the tails of the bullocks and said, 'Come, children.' As the cart began to move off again he looked back at the awning. With his hands folded and his face full of repentance, he said, 'Mother, please forgive my sin. I should go straight to hell for what I said regarding you. But there was no other way than to tell a lie. Are you not too displeased?'

'No, no,' said Kaushalya. 'I don't mind what you say.'

The heavy burden of guilt that had weighed on Bhirguram like a stone lifted, and he felt much easier.

Nowhere in the sky was there the slightest sign of a cloud or of a bird, yet the cart continued on in the burning, unbearable heat of the sun.

Three or four buffalo carts passed Bhirguram on the way. All the buffaloes were sturdy and exceptionally strong. Bhirguram clicked his tongue and said sadly, 'Oh, Chunnuwa, Munnuwa, they were all behind us. If only I could have filled your stomachs, they would never have got past us!'

Chunnuwa and Munnuwa flapped their dangling ears.

A few moments later Bhirguram softly called, 'Mother . . . '

Kaushalya seemed distracted as she replied, 'What is it?'

Apprehensively Bhirguram asked, 'May I ask something?'

'What is it?'

'Why are you running away like this from your father-in-law's house?' Bhirguram had asked the question before but it had not been possible to answer it properly then.

After remaining silent for a moment, Kaushalya began to speak. She told him that she had no alternative but to flee in this manner. In Vindhyachali Chaube's home there were some six safes loaded with gold and diamonds and pearls. He had a thousand acres of land in his own name as well as in aliases. Apart from the huge house in Kishunpura town he had another twelve houses in Patna, Jhariya and Dwarbhanga. But all this land and money could not satisfy his greed, and after the marriage of each of his sons he had placed constant pressure on the daughter-in-law for dowry – pressure at first, then oppression. In fact, because of dowry, two of the wives of the Chaube home had been hanged, although the Chaubes had put it out that the deaths had been suicides.

Vindhyachali constantly pressed Kaushalya for inordinate amounts of gold, silver and land from her father, and now the poor man had nothing more to give. Vindhyachali had worn him right down to his last penny, almost driving him to the streets to beg, and still his greed was not satisfied. He had been recently menacing Kaushalya for more money and more gold, sometimes even beating her. He had told her that if she could not arrange for another ten thousand rupees from her father's house within a month she would face dire consequences.

A few days after her wedding Kaushalya had heard that three Chaube wives had been burned for dowry. To this family, indeed, wife-burning was hardly more serious than killing mosquitoes. Having lived for two years now in the Chaube house, Kaushalya had come to realize that there was nothing they would stop at.

Kaushalya's father was unable to give ten let alone ten thousand rupees, so, anticipating what the upshot of this would be, she had slipped out through the back door that day and fled. If she could get to her parents, at least her life would be saved.

Having related all of this without pausing for breath, Kaushalya fell silent. Looking downcast Bhirguram muttered, 'The richer the man, the greater the greed.' Kaushalya still said nothing.

The ungreased wheels creaked as the bullocks pulled the cart further across the fields. The sky was still an inferno and the hot wind gusted towards the horizon.

A few more buffalo and bullock carts passed them on their way up to the highway. Bhirguram had counted all the carts that had passed them. He said to his pair of bullocks, 'Have you seen, Chunnuwa and Munnuwa? Fifteen drays have passed us. If only you had some strength!'

Chunnuwa and Munnuwa flapped their ears as usual.

They had almost crossed the vast, scorched and barren fields and the highway could be seen up ahead, when Kaushalya suddenly spoke from under the awning, 'I was so lucky to come across someone like you. I can't imagine what would have happened otherwise.'

Bhirguram replied, 'Oh, mother, it's all the will of God.'

What Kaushalya muttered could not be discerned.

A little further on they came to a stretch of road that was full of potholes. Trying to pull the cart out of one of these holes Chunnuwa and Munnuwa strained, their tongues hanging out, their eyes bulging, both of them looking as though they might burst a blood vessel. But the cart would not budge at all. Had the animals been fed regularly and had strong bodies, they could have dislodged the cart with just one heave. Bhirguram had to get down and lend his shoulder to help the bullocks force the cart from the pothole. Then they were on their way again.

Bhirguram got a shock as they came up onto the highway. Standing under a huge, leafy karaiya tree were the Chaubes' strong-arm men. They were stopping and searching every buffalo and bullock cart that had crossed the fields and come up onto the highway.

In a low, frightened voice Bhirguram said, 'Mother, there's more trouble. Those fellows are waiting up on the main road.'

Kaushalya asked, 'Will they look in here, do you think?'

'They've looked once. Maybe they won't look again. But you can never trust those dogs.'

Kaushalya did not reply.

Thinking quickly, Bhirguram told Kaushalya that once they had come up onto the highway they would not, for the time being, turn right towards Baihari, as that would make the thugs suspicious. They would first head towards Vishunganj, then go roundabout by way of some other road to get Kaushalya to Baihari.

'That's a good idea,' said Kaushalya.

Bhirguram's heart was thumping when they came up onto the highway and passed the thugs, heading towards Vishunganj. 'Oh, Lord Ram. Oh Lord Shiva. Please protect mother . . . ' Bhirguram muttered as he drove the bullocks forward.

Leaving the musclemen behind them they went on a little further. But all was not yet well. Suddenly, for some reason or other, one of the ruffians came running after them, shouting, 'Stop, Bhirguwa! Stop there!'

The cart came to a halt. The fellow who had made offensive remarks about Bhirguram's wife back in the middle of the fields said, 'Your wife's sitting there with her face covered. I want to see her face – it's been such a long time. I just want to see if the returned one is real or counterfeit.'

With his hands folded Bhirguram said pleadingly, 'The woman is very embarrassed. Please don't make things any worse for her, brother.'

But the thug's eyes were aflame. He shouted, 'Take the cloth away from your wife, or we'll uncover her ourselves!'

'I fall at your feet, please don't . . . '

But hardly had Bhirguram spoken than the thug leaped up onto the cart. Instantly, something snapped inside the mind of this Bhirguram, the most timid man of all time, weak and helpless and poorest of the poor, and he seemed overwhelmed by some supernatural strength. From the depths of his lungs he roared, 'I'm warning you!' Immediately he reached in under the awning and pulled out a lathi, but before he could bring it down on the thug's shoulders another of them brought down a lathi on Bhirguram's head. At that moment everything went dim around him and before his eyes the world was plunged into darkness. As he slumped from the cart onto the ground he could hear only the terrified scream of a woman.

When Bhirguram regained consciousness, evening was starting to fall. There were now very few carts and people on the road. His only two long-time companions in all the world, Chunnuwa and Munnuwa, stood sadly beside the road.

Bhirguram noticed that a lot of blood lay congealed on the ground. It was his own, for he could feel that there was a deep gash on his head. In a corner of the cart, under the awning, there was a torn dhoti and a shirt wrapped in newspaper. Bhirguram took out the dhoti and bandaged his head with it.

A little while later, when he had resumed his journey to Vishunganj, Bhirguram said to his pair of bullocks, 'I wanted to save Chaube-ji's daughter-in-law. But I couldn't. Oh, well.'

Chunnuwa and Munnuwa flapped their ears, perhaps sympathetically.

Bhirguram then said, 'When we reach Vishunganj, we'll first go to the hospital. That dog gave my head a hell of a thumping. Then we'll go to the wedding house. But will they have waited so long for us? If they have, there'll be an excellent feast for us. Otherwise we'll have to go hungry. So? Going hungry is nothing new to us, is it?'

Chunnuwa and Munnuwa flapped their ears – as usual.

the Rajput

rajput

Right at the southern end of Nazimpura town was the red light district which the local people, censoriously turning up their noses, referred to contemptuously as 'the whores' quarter'. This godforsaken colony of twenty-five of the world's most fallen women comprised twenty-six rooms with dilapidated tiled roofs around three sides of a courtyard – one for each girl and one for Champa, the proprietor of this female enterprise. It would, however, be vain to think that because she had the name of a flower, Champa's temperament was as soft and as sweet as one, for Champa was an exceptionally authoritarian woman under whose dominion none of the girls would be spared even the slightest transgression.

On the side of the courtyard with no rooms there was a low, water-stained wall with a termite-ridden main door. Beside it were a couple of small lavatories, an enclosed space for bathing and a large well. The ramshackle tin hut adjoining the colony was somehow still standing and belonged to Champa, but was inhabited by Hiralal and his horse, Motiya. Hiralal had to pay forty rupees rent each month. Like the twenty-five girls, Hiralal too was subjected to Champa's regime.

It was the middle of Phalgun. It was still very early in the day and the sun had just risen above the horizon. The soft golden glow of spring was everywhere. In the treetops all about flocks of birds were ready to go out in search of food, and their chirping and the sounds of their wings flapping were in the breeze.

Hiralal was already awake. On other days, he would lie silently in his bed for quite some time after waking up – this was the one and only luxury of his life – but today it was not possible for him to do so. By ten o'clock he and his horse, Motiya, had to be in the range of hills about three miles away. A film company had come from Bombay and would meet Hiralal and Motiya at the foot of the hills. Yesterday they had told him repeatedly that if he and Motiya were not there when shooting began, their work would be ruined.

Naturally, Hiralal got up in a hurry. He rolled up his grubby, greasy bedclothes, bunched them into a lump and tossed them into a corner of the room. Yawning, he went outside.

Attached to the hut, under a tin roof at head height, was a narrow veranda two feet above the cemented open space in front of it. Tethered to its post was Motiya. When the horse saw Hiralal, he began stamping the ground with his hoof and emitting from his throat a vibrant soft whinny to express his happiness.

Hiralal was still drowsy, and he yawned a few more times. He raised his right hand and snapped his fingers, then said indistinctly, 'Just be a little patient, I'll be right with you.' Hiralal knew only too well that if he did not offer him a little affection each morning, Motiya would get into a bad mood.

There was no arrangement for water in Hiralal's hut, so he had to depend on the well in the women's compound. His cooking, drinking, washing clothes and the bathing of himself and Motiya had to be done with well water. The previous night he had filled three plastic buckets and left them in a corner of the veranda. He went straight to them, quickly washed his face and came back to Motiya. Stroking the horse's back, neck and ears and giving him an occasional tickle, he said, 'Oh, you old owl! Oh, you billygoat! Oh, you jackass! Now that everyone's up and about, do you think I've nothing better to do than entertain you? Oh, you bastard son of a prince!' Such were the characteristic endearments that he used for Motiya.

The man and the horse had a language of their own. Motiya would express his happiness and pleasure by closing his eyes and swishing his tail, and his whinny would become deeper and longer.

Hiralal did not stop. He said, 'Today you'll have to put on a great show for the cinemawallahs, one to make their heads spin. Understand?'

Motiya whinnied to say that of course he understood.

'Everyone in the world is going to see you on film. Just remember that.'

Motiya gave another reassuring whinny.

Their unusual conversation continued for a few moments. It was obvious that both were extremely excited about today's shooting.

Let us look a little closely at the two of them. Although there is a dazzle of jewels in their names – a combination of their names, Hira-Moti, would mean diamonds and pearls – in fact, they were poorer than the very poor. Hiralal was about thirty. He had fine features, but he was thin and his body looked malnourished, though one had the feeling that, had he been able to fill his stomach twice a day the whole year through, he might have been quite an impressive man. However, whether he could feed himself or not, Hiralal made sure of feeding Motiya. He looked after the horse very well and, as a result, Motiya did not look at all emaciated. His smooth brown-and-white body gleamed with good health as though it had been rubbed with oil.

Hiralal had no worldly wealth to speak of save a few smart shirts, some tight-fitting pants, and his horse. The one dream of his life had always been to own a horse and a fine buggy, and for that he had saved and saved. A few years ago, he had bought Motiya on a whim for three hundred rupees from Fakira, the old coachman of Nazimpura. At the time the animal was in a very poor condition, always panting with his ribs poking through his hide. It seemed as though his end was near and there was no certainty at all whether he would last even five days. Ultimately, though, under Hiralal's care, Motiya not only survived, but also became his full-time companion. Hiralal had been able to afford only the horse and still had not saved enough for the buggy. His dream was as yet half realized.

During the last few months, the season of festivals and marriages, Hiralal had been hiring Motiya out. In Nazimpura and all the nearby small towns, newly married Marwari and Rajput grooms would take their brides to the houses of their fathers-in-law on Motiya's back. At festival time Motiya would be arrayed with a canopy of flowers under which images of Ram and Sita would be placed, and a procession would be taken out. And then, of course, filmwallahs would come to do their shooting at the river nestling amid the hills some three miles off. They often required horses and called on Hiralal and Motiya, as was the case today. Motiya was not an ungrateful animal and was happy to provide not only for his own stomach, but for Hiralal's as well. But how many days of the year were given to weddings, festivals and filmmaking? Hiralal and Motiya had to struggle through the rest of the year with great difficulty. Before he started hiring out Motiya, Hiralal eked out an existence in a variety of ways, sometimes working for contractors breaking stones and making roads, sometimes carrying paddy and rice to warehouses. So even if no one hired Motiya, there was still that kind of work to fall back on.

His full name was Hiralal Singh and he was a Rajput Kshatriya, though not a trace of the valour of his ancestors was left in his blood. He was weak and timid, and he lived in a hut rented from a common whore. He was a slur on the Rajput race. Out of fear and diffidence, he did not make himself known to the other Rajputs who lived in Nazimpura. Indeed, if they knew about him, they would spit three times in his face. He had no one in the world and lived all alone, keeping to himself in this corner of the town.

Motiya was stretching his snout towards Hiralal, seeking affection. The sun had well risen by now and it was getting brighter. Hiralal looked up anxiously at the sky and said, 'I can't be playing with you any more. The morning's getting on and we have to be getting on our way. But before that there's still a lot to do. We both have to eat. I have to dress you up. Then ...'

Before Hiralal could finish what he was saying, Champa's strident voice came across. 'Hey, what's keeping you all, huh? Hurry up and get out here. If we leave any later, how will we even get near the temple?'

Champa's voice was always levels higher than necessary, and when she was quarrelling its severity was intense. At such times, even the birds would take flight.

From where he was standing, Hiralal could see that the women had now gathered in the courtyard. Ranging in age from twenty to forty, their faces bore the marks of sleepless nights all the year round in the endless inferno of the red light quarter, and their battered bodies showed the scars of exploitation.

On this particular morning, they had completed their baths and were all wearing fresh, clean saris, and their still-wet hair fanned out over their backs. Altogether there was an evident sense of occasion. On any other day such a sight would be unthinkable; bathing would be far from their minds as at such an hour – no one would have woken up. But as Hiralal knew, this day was quite different.

In the midst of the women stood the vast form of Champa, her arms like posts and her legs like pillars. Her dark skin glowed as though it had been polished and her body was adorned with garish silver ornaments. Beside her was Bilakhi – lanky and bony-faced, her eyes lined with collyrium; she was in her late thirties. Beside her was Kunta, her daughter.

Kunta was eighteen or nineteen. Although she had been born and had spent all her years in this outpost of hell, she was an extremely innocent-looking girl. There was a charming simplicity in her eyes; she had an oval face with a fine chin, her teeth were like well-set pearls, her hair hung down below her waist and her skin was the colour of ripened wheat. It was difficult to shift one's gaze from her.

Kunta was wearing a new, coloured sari and carrying a brass lamp and a small dish of gleaming stainless steel on which were arranged a few flowers and some fruit, oil, red lead and sun-dried rice.

Living next door to the women's courtyard, Hiralal was privy to much of what went on there. He knew that up until now Bilakhi had kept watch over Kunta as a miser guards his wealth. But it was impossible to keep Kunta protected all the time in a place where day and night jackals sharpened their claws and teeth to devour women. A few years ago, the richest contractor in the district,

Dhaneshwar Chaube, had set eyes on her. He was not just a contractor, but also the owner of four hundred acres of land, either in his own name or in aliases. He had immense wealth and maintained a force of well-armed protectors. His might kept the whole of Nazimpura cowering.

Although Dhaneshwar Chaube – or, to be precise, Chaturvedi – was a Brahmin, he was a man of little honour. If he saw a beautiful woman, no matter if she were a prostitute or an untouchable, he would have to possess her. After he had caught a glimpse of Kunta, he sent one of his thugs to tell Bilakhi that he would take the girl after she had reached womanhood, and that she should take care that no other son of the devil should come near her. The word spread in an instant. No one would have the nerve to lay a finger on anything that Dhaneshwar Chaube had claimed as his property, and so none of the scum who came here would dare to look twice at Kunta.

Dhaneshwar had been waiting patiently for the day when Kunta would come of age, and only the day before yesterday, he had made it known that this afternoon he would send a horse and carriage to bring Kunta to him. He had furnished a new house that he had had built for her.

The women of the red light neighbourhood followed certain habits and customs of their own. Accordingly, before a girl embarked on her career, they would all gather together and offer worship at the Ram-Sita temple. Today, they were getting ready to do that for Kunta.

However, Hiralal happened to know that Kunta had no liking at all for the red light locality and that she had an intense aversion to the prospect of being kept by Dhaneshwar Chaube, a man old enough to be her father. She wanted to break free of these demeaning circumstances, but she did not know how.

Kunta had cried a great deal to her mother and had not eaten for some days. Bilakhi explained to her that this was her destiny. Indeed, she would not be devoured by packs of jackals and flocks of vultures as other girls are, but would rather live her whole life virtually as a married woman in great luxury and happiness with a wealthy and powerful man. Did any of the girls of this locality have such good fortune? Who could say whether her persuasion had any effect. But, at least Kunta's crying had stopped.

Hiralal remembered that, for as long as he had lived there, Kunta used to watch him intently from over the wall. Whenever he went into the women's courtyard to fetch water, he wanted to say something to her, but Bilakhi was so vigilant that he could never catch Kunta's eye.

As he stood watching Kunta with a heavy heart, Champa's voice was heard again, this time even louder, hurrying them along. 'How much longer are you going to stand about? Are you aware of how much the sun has risen already?'

Motiya whinnied an exclamation of his own, for his cosseting had been interrupted for a moment. And Hiralal did not have the time to be standing there, steeped in melancholy over the plight of others. He too had to hurry up and go out. Giving Motiya a couple of gentle slaps on the head, he said, 'Wait just a little while, now. We have to go a long way. I'll get you something to eat, what do you say? We can't go all that way on an empty stomach.'

Motiya leaned his shoulders forward and neighed knowingly.

Hiralal went inside and groped around in the cupboard, but found nothing either for Motiya or himself. He had had no idea that his store of food had run out. He thought for a moment. No, he could not go hungry all that way. Taking out some money from his pocket, he said to Motiya, 'I'm going to go and buy you some chickpeas. I'll be back in fifteen or twenty minutes.'

Running close by the red light quarter was a big bitumen road that led, like some giant backbone, directly to the north. On either side of the road were sawmills, brick-dust mills, flourmills, paddy mills, lead machine factories, timber warehouses and huge storehouses for rice and paddy. After this came the busy market, then the big white-marble Ram-Sita temple. After the temple came the imposing houses of all the wealthy citizens of Nazimpura. About one and a half miles from the northern end of this locality flowed a lovely river, beyond which was the long range of hills where the filmwallahs had come to do their shooting.

In this north Bihari town things were beginning to stir. Groups of bulls were starting to amble about, and people, bullock carts and cycle rickshaws were on the move. But Hiralal did not notice any of this motion as he strode towards the market. He bought some whole chickpeas for Motiya and some chickpea flour for himself, and was returning home when he saw the residents of the red light quarter making their way along the road to the Ram-Sita temple. In the midst of the procession was Kunta, and at the head of them all was Champa.

When they got closer Kunta looked sadly at Hiralal as she walked on with her companions.

Hiralal stopped for a moment. His heart ached, but he walked on as briskly as before. For a day's work, the filmwallahs were going to pay him and his horse four hundred rupees in cash. There was no time to indulge himself, standing about on the road feeling sorry for others.

Hiralal got back to his hut and after he had fed Motiya, quickly ate something himself. Despite his dejection over Kunta, he was cheered by the promise of four hundred rupees.

There was another cause for his good cheer. In today's shooting, the hero of the film would bring down the villains, but the hero who had come from Bombay could not ride a horse. Hiralal, dressed like him and on horseback with gun in hand, would stand in for him. He would not, of course, be recognized on the cinema screen, but be taken to be the hero.

The filmwallahs asked him to dress up Motiya for the role, and if they did not like the way he looked, they would make some other arrangement. Hiralal had spent a few rupees on such things as stirrups, harness and a chain of brass bells for his horse. He brought them all out from inside and, as he was dressing him, he said to Motiya, 'Today is a very great day. We're both going to be heroes. Understand?' A wave of excitement ran through his slight frame.

Having dressed the horse, Hiralal went back inside the hut. He opened up a tin trunk and took out the tailored silk shirt and tight-fitting silk trousers he had bought a long time ago. They had, of course, become frayed in many places, but he could do nothing about that, and anyway these were the most expensive clothes he had. But could he ride on the back of the finely attired Motiya wearing torn clothes?

Hiralal put the chain on the door of his shanty and led Motiya out onto the road. Although he was thin and frail, he had learned to ride a horse a long time ago. He put one foot in the stirrups and hoisted himself up onto Motiya's back. As he rode directly to the north, he looked up at the sky. The sun had risen a little more, as had the temperature, but there was no cause for concern; they would reach the foot of the hills in good time.

As he rode along, Hiralal's mind wandered, and he saw again Kunta's frightened face. But he was timid and powerless and poorer than the poor. Whatever could he do?

On the road he met someone he knew who said jokingly, 'Hey, Hira! Are you going to play the hero of the film in those fine clothes?'

Another said, 'The heroine has come from Bombay, don't let her go. If you weren't the son of a Rajput, you could race off with her on horseback.'

Almost everyone in this insignificant little town knew all about Hiralal, such as where he was going now. He responded to their banter with a mumbled 'Mm, yeah.'

Going a little further, Hiralal heard quite a commotion coming from the vicinity of the Ram-Sita temple. He saw the women of the red light quarter running towards the north and shouting at the tops of their voices, all of them looking extraordinarily heated. However, he did not see Kunta, Champa, Bilakhi or one or two others among them.

Hiralal quickened the pace of the horse and came close to them. He was bewildered, and wondered what was the reason for all this hullabaloo. The women had simply come in a procession to worship at the Ram-Sita temple. What calamity could suddenly have occurred to set them running about in such an agitated state?

Anxiously, Hiralal asked, 'What's the matter, Aunties? Why are you all rushing about like this?' He called everyone in the red light quarter 'Aunty.'

The girls answered all at once: 'Kunta's run away!' And as they spoke, they pointed their fingers saying, 'There – that way!'

Hiralal had seen Kunta when he had gone to buy chickpeas a little earlier, but he had not had the slightest idea then that the girl was capable of such an audacious thing. Infected by the excitement and concern of the women, he asked in a shaky voice, 'How did she get away?'

One of the girls, Janki, said, 'While we were waiting to get into the temple, Kunta put down her plate with the worship offerings on the road outside and started to run. We were stunned. We all started to chase after her. Aunty Champa, Bilakhi and three or four other girls led the way.'

Another girl, Chhibli, said, 'Get after her quickly on your horse! See if you can catch the bitch!'

The idea of hurrying after her on horseback had also occurred to Hiralal, but first he asked, 'Why did Kunta run off ?'

Chhibli screwed up her nose in contempt. After delivering a rapid volley of obscenities she said, 'The daughter of a whore wants to be a goddess like Sita or Savitri! Dhaneshwar is such a wealthy man, a Brahmin. She doesn't realize how well she'd be looked after, and she's gone and run away! Get going, Hira, quick. See if you can get her. If you can't catch this daughter of a pig, Dhaneshwar will think that we've plotted to get her away and then none of us will be safe.'

Hiralal felt a little easy knowing that Kunta had run away, but the idea of Dhaneshwar Chaube and his household goondas running after her sent a dull ache throbbing inside him. He could not wait any longer – not because of Kunta, but because he and Motiya had an appointment with the cinemawallahs. Gently nudging Motiya with his heels, he hurried off with renewed enthusiasm.

Having left the market, the Ram-Sita temple and the upper class locality all behind him, he caught sight of Bilakhi running and screaming and tearing at her hair, with Champa and the other three or four women behind her. Bilakhi's words were indistinct, but Hiralal had no trouble working out that they were part of a continual flow of abuse aimed at her daughter. When she saw Hiralal, she raised her voice to speak to him, but as Motiya was moving fast, he heard nothing more than his name. It could be assumed, however, that she was pleading with him to find Kunta.

Leaving the outskirts of Nazimpura behind, Hiralal came onto a stony road that gradually rose up towards the distant range of hills. On one side there were rows of deodar, karaiya and shishu trees, and on the other was the stream that came down from the hills, flowing abundantly over rocks and pebbles of various shapes and colours, gurgling like jingling anklet bells, just as it had through the ages. On the other side of the stream, a green carpet of grass stretched into the distance, with a cactus plant or some tall trees here and there to adorn the scene and please the eye. The cinemawallahs had chosen for their shooting – from the top of the hills – various spots covering a large area.

Some way along the stony road, looking like specks in the distance, a number of tents could be seen at the foothills. That was the camp of the cinemawallahs, and for as long as the shooting lasted the whole unit, including the hero, the heroine and the villain, would be staying there.

Having gone a little further, Hiralal heard a frightened voice. 'Stop the horse. Stop the horse.'

Hiralal was startled. The whole place was perfectly silent and still with nobody about anywhere. High up in the sky, a few hawks could be seen against the blue as they floated on the breeze, and there was no sound other than the rippling of the stream. Everything else was sunk in profound silence. Who could be calling?

Hiralal cast a careful eye all around. He had not anticipated at all that he would see Kunta come out from behind the screen of closely growing karaiya trees on the right-hand side of the road. Stunned, he said, 'Kunta, is it you?'

'Yes, yes, it's me.' Kunta's voice was indistinct.

Hiralal pulled up the horse. He noticed that the girl's lips were trembling, and her face was marked by intense fear and worry. He could think of nothing to say.

Kunta spoke again, 'I'm running away.'

'I know. Your mother and Aunty Champa are looking for you with some of the others.'

'Let them. I knew you would be going along this road to the cinemawallahs, so I hid here among the karaiya trees. Please save me.'

Hiralal felt an electric shock flash along his spine. Nonplussed, he said, 'Save you?'

Her voice broken and choked, Kunta said, 'Yes, yes, if you don't help – it'll be the end for me. You know it all – don't you?'

'But your mother and Chaube-ji …'

Kunta interrupted him, shaking her head decisively and saying heatedly, 'I don't want to hear anything of them. You must have pity on me, have pity on me!' She held on to the bridle of the horse as though this were her life's last hope and she would not let it go, no matter what. She also started to cry profusely, the tears flowing continually from her eyes. In all the thirty or so years of life, Hiralal had never seen anyone so vulnerable. He could think of nothing at all to say or do.

As Kunta was about to speak again, shouting was heard from the direction of the town. She looked around quickly and saw Bilakhi, Champa and three or four women coming towards her, like hunting dogs on the scent of their prey. Greatly flustered, Kunta said, 'They're coming! Help me, please – have pity on me!'

Champa and the others were screaming hard enough to burst a blood vessel as they came running. As he watched them, Hiralal realized that something had to be done urgently for Kunta. At the same moment he seemed to be reduced to nothing by some kind of a churning inside him. Without his knowing it, there arose a champion from inside this hesitant and weak young man. He reached out his hand to Kunta and with one grab hauled her up and sat her behind him. Motiya, after a prod on his shoulder, charged off like an arrow.

Some way along, they reached a fork. The way to the right led to the foot of the hills where the film people had their camp. The way to the left led to the district town some sixty miles away. He decided to take Kunta to the left. He would worry about whatever had to be done after that later.

The weak and timid Hiralal had at last become a Rajput.

the election
chunao

Mankohal is a village of outcaste and destitute agricultural labourers. No matter how much work they do, theirs is a constant struggle to make ends meet. To get even a little for their stomachs, they bend their backs in the service of the big landowners.

In independent India there is, on the one hand, great pride and progress; on the other, there are villages such as Mankohal in northern Bihar. Here there is no electric light nor any pucca road for five miles around. Goodness knows how long ago it was when the government men sank a tubewell here. Anyhow, it collapsed long ago. Except during the monsoon, the villagers are dependent on an old canal both for drinking water and as a source of irrigation.

Far to the north one can see the misty line of the mountains against the sky, while around here the earth is hard and black. Apart from the rainy season, the people have ten months of dust, mosquitoes and disease. It is freezing in winter and scorching in summer.

The month of Magh was coming to an end. In a few days it would be Phalgun, and the intensity of winter would have abated. The paddy had been harvested at the start of Magh, and all the fields were bare except for a few where the rabi crop was coming up.

It was after midday and the sun had started its downward trek into the western sky. Since morning Mankohal village had been restless and apprehensive, as though in the grip of some unknown fear. The reason was that Dube-ji had sent word that he was coming to the village that afternoon for a special reason, and that everyone should be there. No one should go anywhere, under any circumstances.

'Dube-ji' was the respectful way in which Saubhagyanath Dube was known. Dube-ji lived in a small town about twelve miles away called Dudhlipura. There he had a vast residence with three or four wings. It was said that Dube-ji also owned another five or six grand mansions in Patna and Dhanbad. He was indeed the biggest of all the landholders in the region. The villagers knew that he owned most of the land for ten or twenty miles around, and that he also had two or three hundred buffalo and bullock carts and eight or ten horse-drawn carriages. He also had a very large vintage car.

No one could imagine what business such a great man as Dube-ji could have with the destitute villagers, and as time wore on their anxiety only increased. Soon after midday everyone's gaze was fixed nervously on the high road, from where Dube-ji would come in style in his motor car or a horse-drawn carriage.

Of all the people in the village, the most nervous and tense was Bharosaram. As the head of the village Council of Five he was the leader of Mankohal. Dube-ji had expressly made it known that he should be there, but at midday Bharosaram had to go to Naiteyar village to make arrangements for the marriage of his son.

The harvest had been particularly good that year. Moreover, having worked themselves to the bone in the fields of the big landowners, the villagers had received good wages. So when the crop had been harvested at the beginning of the month of Magh, Bharosaram had decided to get his eldest son, Shiunath, married. He was already about thirty, and in this village no young man stayed single beyond that age.

Bharosaram had chosen a suitable girl for his son in the village of Naiteyar, four miles away. It was difficult to turn one's eyes from her, for she was a girl of exceptionally fine bearing and demeanour.

Indeed, such a beautiful girl would seldom be seen even in the homes of the upper castes. A girl like her was truly one in a million.

However, there was a problem with Musafirlal, the girl's father, who had set a grand sum of two hundred and fifty rupees for his daughter. Though Bharosaram had managed to put aside two hundred rupees after years of hardship, his son could well turn grey waiting for him to raise the remaining fifty. Musafir was not likely to keep his daughter sitting at home for much longer and would surely start to look elsewhere for a match.

Shiunath had set his heart on the chosen girl, so his father tried his best to get Musafir to reduce the amount. Bharosaram had clasped Musafir's feet, begging him to waive the extra fifty rupees, but the man was such a money-grubber that no amount of pleading would make him relent. He would not accept one rupee less than the two hundred and fifty he had stipulated.

Bharosaram could have borrowed the fifty rupees from the wily moneylender of Mankohal village, Ramnagina Thakur, but he did not have the nerve. All the villagers – indeed all the other illiterate outcaste people of the region – who had borrowed money against a thumb impression on a blank sheet of paper would one day see all their land end up in the stomach of Ramnagina.

Bharosaram had wanted to finish his midday meal and go to Naiteyar to plead on bended knee one last time with Musafirlal. But now hanging over him was the fact that, if he left the village, he would be disobeying the order of Dube-ji.

The sun had begun to set when the villagers suddenly caught sight of Dube-ji's car in the distance, spreading clouds of dust along the wide, unmade road. Saubhagyanath's early model car was extraordinarily powerful, travelling with ease through undulating fields or over rough and uneven dirt roads and through all those places where no other car in the world could go. In a little while it pulled up in an open space in front of Mankohal. Seeing the car, the villagers ran out onto the road, led by Bharosaram.

Dube-ji got out of the car along with three henchmen. Then the grandly liveried driver carried a huge chair like a cushioned throne out of the car and set it down just behind him. The people of every town and village for ten or twenty miles around knew that wherever Dube-ji went, his chair went with him. He would never sit on any other chair or throne.

Dube-ji was about sixty, but he did not look his age. Many big landowners became mountains of fat after consuming so much ghee, butter, almonds and pistachios along with so much time passed in idleness, but Dube-ji was not of that ilk. Regular wrestling kept his body youthful and devoid of any excess fat. His waist was as slender as a lion's, and he had a broad chest, thick neck and prominent muscles. His face was square with small, round eyes and a waxed moustache, and his hair was trimmed short, except for a thick braid tied in a knot at the back. A man of exquisite taste, he wore a finely spun dhoti and a silk punjabi, and his slippers were ornamented with brass flowers. He wore a fine necklace bearing a tiger's claw, and all his fingers were adorned with diamonds, rubies, emeralds and pearls.

Seated in his chair, he slowly ran his eyes over the assembled people. He looked exceptionally pleased to see them.

None of the villagers could remember when Dube-ji had last visited them, though they were all certain that he had not come for at least six or seven years. Overwhelmed by the occasion, they all pressed their palms together, bowed their heads and said, 'Namaste, your worship.'

Raising his right hand slightly, Saubhagyanath Dube said, 'I have an urgent matter to put to you, so I had to come in person.'

No questions were asked as they all looked at him in suspense.

Seemingly in thought for a few moments, Dube-ji said, 'Have you heard that the elections are coming around again?'

Generally, the villagers understood that every five years there was an election when one had to vote by placing a stamp against a candidate's printed symbol. When the harvest had been in full swing a short time earlier, government officers had come to Mankohal to register everyone's name, address and age. So the villagers knew what Saubhagyanath meant when he mentioned the elections.

As the representative of the village, Bharosaram asked respectfully, 'When is the election, your worship?'

Dube-ji told them that it would occur in two months' time, towards the end of Chaitra when the rabi crop had been harvested. Bharosaram and the others had not realized that the election date was so close.

'This time I will be standing in the election,' Dube-ji said. 'My election symbol will be the peacock. You understand?'

'Yes, sir.'

'What will be my symbol?'

In one voice Bharosaram and all the others said, 'The peacock, sir.'

'On voting day, look for the peacock on the paper the election officials will give you and put your stamp next to it. In that way your vote will go to me. Will you remember?'

The villagers worked for most of the year on Dube-ji's land. He paid a lot better than the other landowners. When such a great man came in person seeking votes, one could hardly say no to him. They all followed Bharosaram in saying, 'We'll remember, your worship.'

The people were all standing close to Dube-ji. Beckoning Bharosaram to him, Dube-ji said in a quiet yet firm voice, 'You are the leader of Mankohal village and the head of the panchayat.'

Bharosaram bowed his head to him and said, 'By your grace, sir ...'

'Everyone round about respects your word.'

Bharosaram was quite dumbfounded. Even in the town ten miles away, Dube-ji was apparently aware of things in Mankohal. Maybe he had twenty pairs of ears and fifty pairs of eyes. Humbly, Bharosaram said, 'All by your grace, your worship, that is so.'

Lowering his voice again, Dube-ji said, 'I would not expect to get your votes for nothing; everyone who votes for me will get ten rupees. When I go, let everyone know this. Understood?'

At the mention of money, an electric shock ran through Bharosaram's head and the blood surged through his veins. He remembered that his family had three votes – his, his wife's, and that of his eldest son, Shiunath. The other children were still too young to vote. If the three of them voted for Dube-ji, they would get thirty rupees. He already had two hundred rupees in hand for Musafirlal's daughter. If he got another thirty rupees, that would leave only twenty, and surely he could find some way of getting that. With great enthusiasm he said, 'Understood, sir!'

Dube-ji said, 'My man will come early tomorrow morning to see who will give their votes. Three or four days later he'll come again with the money.'

'By your grace, your worship.'

'But one more thing.'

'Yes, sir?'

'Having taken the money, no one may renege.'

Shocked, and with his hands to his ears, Bharosaram cried, 'No, sir! No, never!'

Dubeji said, 'You know me. I am like a flower, delicate and sweet. But let me be candid. If you betray me, I'll burn your village. Remember that.'

Bharosaram was taken aback. Shakily, he said, 'I'll remember, sir. No one will betray you.'

Dube-ji then raised his voice a little and, looking at the other villagers, he said, 'All right. I'll be going now. If I win in the election and become an MLA, it will be good for you. I'll build a sealed road here. I'll set up an English medium school, there'll be a hospital, you'll get electric light ...'

Painting a picture of a rosy future for the village, Dube-ji got into the car with his retinue. The driver packed away the throne-like chair, got in and started the engine.

The villagers followed the car as far as the high dirt road. Then, when it disappeared around the distant bend, they all made their way back to the village where Bharosaram explained the one-vote-ten-rupees deal to them.

A great wave of excitement regarding the deal spread through the entire village. However, the excitement was probably greatest in Bharosaram's family. Why not, when for three votes they would get thirty rupees and so be able to finalize the marriage of Shiunath? They talked about it that night while eating their new rice along with the water in which it had been cooked.

In their midst burned a kerosene lantern. On one side sat Bharosaram, Shiunath, and the other three children – Manachaniya, Tiunath and Sukhiya, aged fifteen, twelve and nine – who would have no vote. Sitting facing them on the other side of the lantern was Bharosaram's wife, Lakhiya, serving the meal.

Looking at his younger children, Bharosaram said, 'If you three were old enough to vote, our worries would be over and in a few days Shiunath would be married.'

Lakhiya nodded her head. 'But what about the remaining twenty rupees?' she asked.

'I'm thinking about that. We just have to get it. With twenty rupees nothing can stand in the way of Shiu's marriage.' As he spoke something suddenly seemed to occur to him. A little hesitantly, he began again. 'Well, then,' he said.

'Well what?' asked Lakhiya.

'Has anyone seen old Natthuwa today?'

Natthuwa's proper name was Natthulal, and he was one of the people of Mankohal village. No one could say if he was sixty, seventy, eighty or a hundred. Even Nathu himself could not say exactly. But then his age was not something the villagers unduly worried themselves about.

Natthulal had no one at all in the world – no wife, no children, no brothers or sisters. He lived entirely alone. He had once had a little land, but a long time ago, to pay off a debt, his land went into the stomach of Ramnagina Thakur. For as long as he had the strength, he used to work like a buffalo on the land of others. Then suddenly he developed problems with his chest and could no longer do labouring work. Consequently, he ceased to have an income, and in recent years had survived entirely by begging. Some time ago he used to go and beg in the weekly markets of distant villages, but these days even that was too much for him. Now, at the time of the midday meal and the evening meal, Natthulal would haunt the homes of the people of Mankohal village, whining slightly and pleading, 'Give me just a piece of bread', or 'Give me the water you cooked your rice in, or I'll die of hunger.'

Some, if they felt so moved, might give him half a chapati or a piece of baked bread or a handful of rice, but most of the people of Mankohal would drive him away as soon as they saw him. After all, if they could not fill their stomachs themselves twice a day, they would not be likely to give anything to a beggar. But whether he got anything or not, Natthulal would still appear at the houses of Mankohal twice a day, at meal times, and the people would usually ignore him.

'The old man came asking for rice at midday today,' said Lakhiya.

Indeed, Bharosaram had seen Natthulal at mealtime that day, but then he had been so preoccupied with the visit of Dube-ji that he had forgotten about him. He asked, 'How was he?'

'Who knows?'

'I have some news for the old man.' And Bharosaram went on eating at the speed of a storm.

Like everyone else, Bharosaram would get irritated at the sight of Natthulal with his hands outstretched. Who would want to share his food with him? So his family was amazed by his sudden concern for one of the world's diseased and debilitated rejects.

Actually, it was quite a different kind of concern for Natthulal that had just flashed like a bolt of lightning through Bharosaram's mind. Although he had been abandoned by the world, Natthulal still had value as a voter. His one vote was worth ten rupees in cash, and looking after him for so many days could buy those ten rupees. Then there would be only a further ten rupees to find on account of Shiunath's marriage. Ten rupees was not such a problem; somehow or other he could get that.

Lakhiya asked, 'What news have you got for the beggar? If he comes here he'll only want something to eat.'

Quietly, Bharosaram explained his plan regarding Natthulal, 'Now be very careful not to mention this to anyone.

There are some real scoundrels in this village who'd take care of the old man only to try to trick him out of his ten rupees. Do you follow me?'

Lakhiya and the children's admiration for Bharosaram increased tenfold. They all looked at the man who had had such a brilliant idea, shaking their heads in amazement. Of course, they would keep the matter secret.

Hurriedly finishing his dinner, Bharosaram went out with Shiunath.

Natthulal lived at the northern end of Mankohal village in a dilapidated mud hut with its thatch in tatters. When Bharosaram reached the place, he called, 'Uncle Natthu?' This was how Natthu had been known by the villagers since their childhood.

At first there was no response. After calling out three or four times, there came from inside the hut a sound like faint sobbing. 'Who's there?'

'Just us – Bharosa and Shiu.'

'Come in.'

The full moon had risen like a silver goblet in the sky and the whole world was bathed in its glimmering light. Bharosaram and Shiunath went inside the hut where, in the moonlight that poured in through the gaps in the thatch, they saw Natthulal lying wrapped in a filthy, stinking, old bedsheet. They were appalled at the sight. The old man pushed himself up with one hand and said, 'What brings you to a beggar's hut at this hour?'

Bharosaram squatted down beside him. With a look of genuine concern he said, 'I've got some news for you. You mustn't go out any more now. We've been very worried. Are you unwell, Uncle?'

'Yes.' Natthulal went on, 'I've got no strength left in my body. I can't go out. I was coughing up blood this afternoon. I'm going to die.'

Bharosaram's heart began to thump. Whatever it took, Natthulal had to be kept alive until the election. He said, 'Coughing up blood doesn't mean you're going to die, does it? Not really ...'

'But how can I survive?'

Bharosaram thought for a few moments and said, 'Put up with

a bit more trouble tonight, and first thing tomorrow we'll take you to the hospital to see the doctor.'

Natthulal said, 'But the hospital's in Dudhlipura town, a long way away. About a ten-mile walk. How can I go there? I just don't have the strength.'

'Don't you worry. You won't have to walk. We'll see to that.'

Natthulal could not imagine why Bharosaram should suddenly be so abundantly sympathetic for a beggar like him. He could only say, 'God bless you. But one thing ...'

'What, Uncle?'

'There's no point taking me to the hospital tomorrow. I'll be dead before then.'

'Why, Uncle?'

'I've eaten nothing at all since yesterday. I'm really hungry. If I don't put something in my stomach, how can I last through the night?'

'All right. I'll fix up something for you to eat.' Bharosaram told Shiunath to bring some rice and whatever else he could.

A little later, ravenously devouring his rice, Natthulal said, 'One word, Bharosa ...'

'What, Uncle?'

'I've been sick and hungry for some time. I've really suffered. But no one's ever been interested in me. So why now?'

Bharosaram wondered then whether to tell Natthulal about the election deal and explain to him that he would look after him in return for his vote money, but immediately he rejected the idea. It would not be wise to broach the subject just yet. He would wait and put it to him when the time was right. Bharosaram said, 'What? Just because I haven't come for so long, I shouldn't have come today?'

'No, no, I didn't mean that,' said Natthulal. 'What I mean to say is ...'

Bharosaram interrupted him, 'That's right, I've not been able to see you for so long. I'm a poor man. On top of that, I've got a big family, too many kids. I am always worrying about their stomachs.

But when you suffer hunger at your age, how can I not care for you? After all, we are your kinsmen.'

Natthulal was pleased with Bharosaram's words and slowly nodded his head, 'Oh, yes. Yes, that's true.'

A little later, having returned home, Bharosaram and Shiunath made a stretcher out of bamboo, on which they would carry Natthulal to the hospital next day.

Very early next morning, while it was still dark, Bharosaram and Shiunath put a little rice steeped in water in an earthen pot and set off with it and the stretcher to Natthulal's hut. They fed him the rice and water, then they spread his bedsheet on the stretcher and laid him on it. Bharosaram and Shiunath took up the stretcher, each with one end on his shoulder. Then, uttering the names of their gods, they set out for Dudhlipura.

Mankohal was still sunk in sleep. The sun had not yet risen, but was just a bare ray of light in the east. Leaving the sleeping village behind them, the men came up onto the high road that ran straight to Dudhlipura.

After some way Natthulal called from his stretcher, 'Hey, Bharosa.'

From under the stretcher Bharosaram answered, 'What is it, Uncle?'

'Last night after you'd gone, Bhaonath brought some bread and vegetables.' Natthulal then said to himself, 'Bhaonath had never been to my place before, never asked about me. It's really strange that he should suddenly come to the hut of a beggar like me.'

Bharosaram was alarmed. 'Why did Bhaonath come?'

'Like you, he wanted to look after me in my old age. He talked a hell of a lot, and he fed me the bread and vegetables with his own hands.'

'You'd already eaten!'

'Why shouldn't I have eaten it? Nice hot chapati and vegetables. Really well cooked by Bhaonath's wife.'

Bharosaram thought of how he had filled Natthulal's stomach with rice. And after that he had eaten chapatis! The old bugger had the appetite of an animal. Bharosaram asked, 'And what did Bhaonath have to say?'

'He said he'd take me to hospital at sunrise this morning. He said exactly the same things as you'd said to me.'

'What did you say to him?'

'I said, "No, I won't go to the hospital with you. I've already said I'll go with Bharosa. I'm a man of my word – once I give it, I stick by it." Was that all right, then?'

'Yes, yes,' answered Bharosaram eagerly. 'Quite right.'

And so they went on in silence for awhile. Then Natthulal said, 'I still can't understand why everyone is so keen to look after me.'

Bharosaram did not answer.

Very soon the sun came up. It was not quite the end of Magh, so there was not much heat in the sun as yet and the north wind still bore intermittent waves of cold. But if the sun were as warm as it gets in the months of Chaitra and Vaishakh, their tongues would have been hanging out, carrying a man on their shoulders for mile after mile.

On either side of them were bare paddy fields, thickets of sarban trees, the irregularly-shaped sisam and karaiya trees, silted up drains with culverts over them and, overhead, flocks of tiny foreign parrots. From time to time, they came across some wretched rustic village. As they walked, Bharosaram thought hard about confirming the matter of the election and the ten rupees.

Ahead of them there was a small weekly market. Stalls had been set up and a crowd had gathered. When they got close to it, Bharosaram and Shiunath put the stretcher down and took a little rest, then they went and bought some snacks and sweets from the market and divided them equally into three.

As they ate, Bharosaram said, 'I've got something to tell you, Uncle Natthu.'

'What?' Natthulal looked up, chewing on his food.

'Did you know there's an election coming?'

'When?'

'In a month and a half.'

Natthulal belched casually.

For a while Bharosaram said nothing. He had resolved that he would have to raise the issue of the ten rupees. So he cleared his throat, closed his eyes momentarily, and prepared to speak.

As before, Natthulal remained apathetic. He said, 'Now, explain to me ...'

'Explain what?'

'Why you're taking such good care of me. Why you're going to such trouble taking me to the hospital.'

Bharosaram did not answer. He held his breath and went on looking at Natthulal. He was frightened that the old man might not cooperate.

Natthulal spoke again. 'Of course, I can understand why Bhaonath took the trouble to come to me.'

Bharosaram still said nothing.

Natthulal went on, 'All right, well, if you want to look after me and go to all the trouble of taking me to the hospital, then you can have my vote money.'

A smile burgeoned on Bharosaram's face and his eyes sparkled.

They finished their snack, and Bharosaram and Shiunath took Natthulal up onto their shoulders and set off once again.

They reached the hospital at Dudhlipura just after midday.

Having examined Natthulal carefully, the doctor said to Bharosaram, 'You've brought the old man virtually at his end. There's nothing left inside his chest. He's completely riddled in there.'

Bharosaram's heart sank. In a shaky voice he asked, 'Will my uncle live, Doctor?'

'I will try to save him.' He gave Natthulal an injection, and then he scribbled something on a piece of paper and gave it to Bharosaram, saying, 'Here are two kinds of medicine. You can pick them up from the hospital dispensary. Give them to him three times a day. Bring the old man back again in seven days.'

Bharosaram thought to himself: 'Anything to keep him alive until the election.'

It was nearly evening when they brought the medicine and Natthulal on his stretcher back into Mankohal. Having delivered the old man to his hut, Bharosaram suddenly thought again. No, there were too many sly buggers like Bhaonath in this village who would prey on Natthulal for his vote money. But Bharosaram would deny them that opportunity. He took the old man straight to his own house and fixed up his accommodation on the covered veranda. He told Lakhiya, 'From now on, Uncle Natthu will stay here with us.'

At first, Lakhiya was dumbstruck. She beckoned her husband behind the curtain and said, 'What? Have you completely lost your head?'

'What do you mean?'

'Put someone up in this house? Where's the money going to come from?'

Bharosaram explained his plans to Lakhiya. Natthulal's stay would be temporary. He would not be staying one day after the election, and if he did not want to go, then he would have to be kicked out. As for the cost of his keep, he could survive on just a little share of what was for them – his body needed no more. Anyhow, what were a few crumbs when they had such a great need for cash? It was almost impossible for them to raise ten rupees. Whatever happened, they had to get Natthulal's vote money. If they did not hold on to the old beggar, the scoundrels of the village would soon pounce on him.

Lakhiya was persuaded by her husband's arguments and, finding nothing further to quibble about, she said, 'All right.'

From that moment, all of Bharosaram's family made Natthulal welcome, giving him his medicine punctually and feeding him rice and vegetables.

Then one day one of Dube-ji's men came and informed them that the vote money would not be paid just yet, but would be given to them two days before the election. No reason was given for this sudden change of plan.

After seven days, Bharosaram and Shiunath again took Natthulal to the hospital in Dudhlipura. The government doctor examined

Natthulal for some time, placing the stethoscope on his chest and tapping on his back with his fingers. Then, with a grave face, he spoke to Bharosaram, setting his heart thumping. The medicine had done nothing in seven days; in fact, the old man's condition had worsened. It was hard to say how long Natthulal could be kept going. The doctor prescribed more medicine and told them to bring him back in another week.

Bharosaram kept praying in his heart that the old man might last another month and a half.

Every week from then on, Bharosaram and Shiunath would take Natthulal to the hospital in Dudhlipura. However, despite so much medicine and so many pills, Natthulal got no better, but rather, day by day, he seemed to get worse. From time to time he brought up blood and, when he did, he would just lie there, lifeless, and all of Bharosaram's family would gather around him. With the worries of the world on their faces, one of them would rub Natthulal's chest, while another would rub his cold feet with warm oil. They were all anxious to do whatever was necessary for his well-being, for the future of Bharosaram's family had become implicated in the life and death of Natthulal.

On the one hand was the election, on the other was death, and in between was Natthulal. The family kept watch over him day and night to see that Yama, the god of death, with whom they had started to wage a silent, undeclared war, did not get to him before the election. But two days before the vote money was to be paid, Natthulal vomited blood for the last time and died.

In all his seventy or eighty or one hundred years of life his one consolation was that, thanks to the election, he had had for one and a half months a full stomach and had been carried on the shoulders of Bharosaram and his son to the hospital.

On leaving this world, the beggar, Natthulal, was glad to offer his endless gratitude to democracy.

the feast
bhoj

The revelries of Holi, the region's biggest festival, had come to an end and the month of Phalgun was drawing to a close.

As is usual in northern Bihar, the breeze still carried a trace of cold, but this year the days had already started to change. It would become hot before the sun had barely risen, and later, in the unbearable heat of midday, all the fields were scorched. Gusts of wind spread fiery waves of heat from east to west and from north to south.

Overhead was the vast sky, below were the endless fields which, as far as the eye could see, were lying fallow with not a grain to be found, for two months earlier the labourers had loaded up the carts with all the harvested paddy. Even the rabi season had come to an end. Only in parts of one or two distant fields could some crops of linseed or pigeon peas be seen.

Up to his knees in dust, Dhaniya came tramping along the tortuous, unmade road that winds through those fields. He was sixty or seventy – he could not tell, having little skill at arithmetic. He could count up to, maybe, thirty, but any reckoning after that presented him with difficulty. On his body there was no flesh to speak of and the loose, wrinkled skin that somehow covered his bones was flaky and slough-like. The muscles at the back of his legs were knotted, his cheeks sunken, and his collar bone protrusive.

His hair was as rough as jute fibre, and it was easy to see that it had never been treated to oil since the day of his birth. His face bore tufts of stubble, and one could sink a finger into the sockets of his dull eyes.

He was dressed in a grubby, ragged loincloth that hardly covered him from waist to thigh, and a tattered shirt held together by numerous patches of various colours. A gunny sack tied with a cord hung on his back and contained all his worldly wealth: two extra rags, two shirts with the sleeves torn off, an old enamel plate, a few chapatis, half a melon, a piece of sugarcane, some boiled maize, some wheat and a blunt knife. All of this was for when times might get hard.

Dhaniya was coming directly from the south and was on his way to the town of Meklipura to the north. A great feast had been arranged there as part of the post-funerary rituals for Chandreshwar Mishra's late mother, and Dhaniya was going to eat at that feast. Of course, Dhaniya had not been invited to the house. He would attend the feast on his own undertaking, for Dhaniya was one of north Bihar's well-known beggars, and along with others of his ilk – and crows, hawks and dogs – he would sit down beside the gutter and join in the general scramble for the scrapings of the plates of the honoured guests.

Yesterday, Dhaniya had been wandering about the market at Dharamganj, and it was there that he heard the news of the shraddha ceremony for Chandreshwar Mishra's mother, as one eminent Brahmin read out the invitation to a fellow Brahmin. Standing a little way off, Dhaniya pricked up his ears and listened.

Dhaniya's memory was weak. In fact, he was quite dull. But although he could not count beyond thirty, in matters of the stomach he could store in his mind a host of details.

The invitation read as follows:

Respected Sir,

On the thirteenth of the month of Phalgun, my beloved mother went to her heavenly abode. Her shraddha ceremony will be held on the twenty-fifth of the month of Phalgun.

You are kindly invited to be present on that occasion to pray for the repose of her soul.

In mourning,
Chandreshwar Mishra
Meklipura

Would not a truly superb feast accompany such a shraddha ceremony? The moment he heard the invitation, Dhaniya made up his mind to spend the night on the floor of a stall at the market and at daybreak to take to the road for Meklipura. He had found out that the next day would be the twenty-fifth.

So, when it was not yet daybreak and the sky was obscured in the darkness by a light fog, Dhaniya set out from Dharamganj market. He had heard the name of Meklipura, but had never been there. As for what direction it was in or the way to get there, he had only a faint idea. Yesterday, he had decided that by asking people along the way he would discover its exact location.

There were no trucks or buses on the unmade road, but countless bullock and buffalo carts went along it, with cycle rickshaws passing by them, all raising the dust. One cart went past in a cloud of dust that floated towards the sky. And there were not only carts, but also an inestimable number of country folk on foot. Although it was not yet midday, the sun had risen directly overhead and it was starting to become blazing hot. There was not a speck of cloud in the sky as the last flocks of winter birds were carried by the breeze towards the distant horizon.

Dhaniya did not take any particular note of the dazzling sky, the birds, the lines of carts and the thick clouds of dust, for he was becoming more and more anxious as the morning wore on. He knew the shraddha feast would be soon after midday and that the best of it would be over by the middle of the afternoon; the guests would have to arrive before that, or else there would be little left for them. He asked about thirty people on the road, 'Brother, how far is it to Meklipura?'

They all gave much the same answer, 'Not far. About three or four miles.'

In fact, whoever he had asked since sunrise that morning had given him the same answer, but 'about three or four miles' never got any shorter, so naturally Dhaniya felt he had cause for concern.

As he walked, the sun hovered directly overhead, and the hot dry wind gusted over the open fields. But Dhaniya seemed not to feel the fearsome heat of the sun; indeed, he was not even conscious of it. His one and only concern was getting to Meklipura. Before his eyes was the magnificent feast, the likes of which he had only ever dreamt of in all his life.

Dhaniya was growing tired and weak. If he had wanted to, he could have taken a handful or two of the boiled maize or a dried chapati and nibbled on it, but had held back in anticipation of the shraddha feast.

He could not tell how long it had been since he had had good food in his stomach – one month, two months, three months – who could say? What he usually got in begging from door to door were leftover chapatis, burnt bread, boiled maize and wild seeds, food that dulled his senses from the tip of his tongue to the pit of his stomach.

Indeed, this chance of a fine feast had come to him after many long years. Who could say whether or not this would be the last one of his life? An irrepressible ardour inspired a great strength in Dhaniya and drove him on towards Meklipura. However, no matter how keen his enthusiasm and appetite were, his body was still very weak. With the sun beating down on his head, he had great trouble walking, and he almost staggered now and then as he went along.

A bit further on he called to a middle-aged rustic, 'Hey, brother … '

The man was walking past him and, hearing the call, looked back over his shoulder. Just a glance at the state of Dhaniya's clothes and his body covered in dust from head to toe gave the man an idea of what sort of creature he was. He frowned in contempt and asked harshly, 'What?'

'How much further is it to Meklipura town?'

'One and a half, maybe, two miles.' The man pointed to the north where the heat glimmered relentlessly on the horizon, saying, 'Over there is a carrion dump. About a mile or a mile and a quarter past that is Meklipura town.'

It had taken him all this time to get a clear idea of where Meklipura was. First of all there was the dumping ground for dead animals, then there was the town. He wanted to ask the man about Chandreshwar Mishra's house and one or two other important questions, but before he could do so the fellow had left him way behind with his long strides. Dhaniya tried to catch up, but there was no possibility of his tired body walking so fast, and after just three or four steps he became fearfully out of breath. The bones from his waist to his knees seemed to go limp and he felt as though he would cramp. Forced to slacken his pace, he staggered on, feeling a steady stream of perspiration wetting his clothes. With all that sweat, he was losing so much salt that his strength must surely have been running out.

On his way, Dhaniya looked this way and that. He saw a big leafy tree beside the road and thought that he might sit down for a little while in its shade and take some rest. But then he thought that once he had sat down he would not be able to walk any further and so would miss out on what might well be the last feast of his life, given his age and the state of his health. Indeed, Dhaniya had grave doubts that such an opportunity would ever be repeated.

When he heard the sound of wheels squeaking, Dhaniya turned to see an empty buffalo cart passing him, swinging from side to side. It seemed from the look of it that the cart was not going anywhere in a hurry. A faint glimmer of hope flashed through Dhaniya's mind. Touching the cart hesitantly as it moved alongside him, Dhaniya called timidly to the driver, 'Hey, brother …'

The rustic fellow was fanning himself with a gamchha and humming a tune. He stopped his humming and answered, 'What?'

'Where are you going with the cart?'

'Meklipura. Why?'

The faint glimmer of hope in his heart suddenly grew tenfold. Timidly, he said, 'Just a word, brother … '

'Say what you want to say,' said the driver.

Gulping, Dhaniya told the man that seeing that the bullock cart was absolutely empty and that it was going to Meklipura, and that Dhaniya too was going there, and as he was a very weak and tired old man, the driver might be so kind as to take him onto the cart and deliver him to Meklipura. If he did, of course, he would be blessed by all the gods, his crops would increase, his children would eat ghee and sugar and be joyful, and the driver's pair of buffalo would remain healthy and strong. And so Dhaniya went on, taking a thousand words to say it all.

The buffalo driver frowned and looked at Dhaniya out of the corner of his eye. Then, with a scowl, he said menacingly, 'Oh, Mr Bloody Important! You beggar son-of-the-dirt – piss off! Go on, get!' And with both hands he shook the tails of the two buffalo and made a clicking noise with his tongue, a familiar signal at which the pair ran off breathlessly into the distance, kicking up clouds of dust and leaving Dhaniya far behind. At that moment, his flicker of hope went out.

Dhaniya dragged his tired and lifeless body on further. He had not always been so wretched a beggar as to scramble with dogs and hawks and crows and other beggars for the scrapings of people's plates; however, nowadays he had to survive in this world on handouts from people in towns and villages. He could no longer remember what things had been like at the start of his life, sixty or sixty-five years ago. He carried only a vague recollection of having to toil from sunrise until midnight for many years of his childhood in the fields and farmyard of a high-caste landowner of the Naibahar estate on the other side of the river Koshi. After about ten years of that he suddenly realized one day that it was only his stomach that ever got anything. As it looked bad having to go naked, the landowner gave him some clothes, but he never had so much as a rupee in his hand.

In those days he was a strong and spirited young man, and like all young men of the world Dhaniya too had the natural desire to get married. But this was not to be his good fortune. It would have required maybe a hundred and fifty or two hundred rupees, and if he could not meet the conditions of the girl's father, how could he claim her hand as his wife?

Indeed, in a short time, he left the Naibahar estate for the jungles of Palamau in search of hard cash. After a few years there clearing the jungle, he had saved only a little, while in that time the market price of brides, along with the cost of so much else, had risen steeply and he could not afford to set up a house with the little that he had. But at that stage his hopes for marriage were not entirely dashed, for the dream, at least, still lingered in his mind.

Still in need of money, he went through a recruitment agency to distant Assam to work as a cane-cutter and was there for fifteen years without a break. Towards the end of his time in Assam he contracted a bad case of smallpox, and no sooner had he recovered from that than he caught dysentery and started suffering from respiratory trouble. His health broke down and his weak body could no longer manage hard work like cane-cutting, nor was any other labour possible. The contractor sacked him. Now with a permanent chest ailment, Dhaniya returned to northern Bihar.

There was a vast difference between the hefty buffalo of a young man who had gone to Assam and the Dhaniya who had come back fifteen years later. Assam had sucked every spark of life out of him and cast him onto the scrap heap. He came to do all the contemptible work of the world that in turn made the world contemptuous of him and reject him. Even walking became a problem, for it led to shortness of breath. The dream of getting married evaporated. Soon he had spent all the money he had brought back from Assam. Then, in despair, Dhaniya embarked on the ancient profession, gradually becoming known throughout northern Bihar as a beggar.

Dhaniya had no fixed abode. He covered about fifty miles of northern Bihar year after year in continual quest for food. Wherever he went, he might get a little maize, maybe a handful or two of rice or a couple of pieces of bread. For that he drove himself almost to death. His body knew nothing other than hunger. While begging he kept his eyes and ears open, and obtained news of where within about fifty miles there would be a marriage or a shraddha or a baby's first rice ceremony or a young man's sacred thread investiture. Perhaps even the world's best spies and newspapermen could not glean so much news. For food he would go anywhere, in summer or winter, twelve months of the year.

It had probably been a whole year – not just a month or two – since he had eaten well. With his health being so poor, the food at the shraddha ceremony at Chandreshwar Mishra's house would surely be the last fine feast of his life. Come what may, he had to have one excellent meal before his death, otherwise he would die with the great regret of having eaten only boiled maize and wild seeds, and he had no desire for such a death.

The sun seemed to be fixed directly overhead and gave no sign that it would start sinking towards the west.

On his way, Dhaniya met up with another man. It transpired that he lived in a village near Meklipura town and that he had gone the previous day to a relative's house in a distant village and now was returning home. The man's demeanour and style of conversation were affable. Unlike all the others, he did not treat Dhaniya, the beggar, with disdain, nor did he ignore his questions. Dhaniya had never met such a genial, compassionate man.

As they walked side by side, Dhaniya asked, 'Brother, you live in a village near Meklipura, then?'

'Yes,' the man nodded.

'Do you know Chandreshwar Mishra of that town?'

The man said that he knew Chandreshwar, having seen him from a distance many times. He was a very rich man who owned about a thousand or even two thousand bighas of land. Having said all of this he asked in some surprise, 'Why are you interested in Mishraji?'

'I heard that today is the shraddha ceremony for Mishra-ji's late mother.'

'Oh, yes, I heard that too.'

'So then, brother, Mishra-ji will turn on a fine feast for his mother's shraddha ceremony – don't you think?' Dhaniya looked at his companion with eagerness in his eyes.

'There could be none better! So rich a man! He had but one mother, and her shraddha will be celebrated only once. It will be such a feast that no one will be able to eat for three days after it. I have heard that Mishra-ji will not let anyone go until they are filled right up to the neck!'

Dhaniya stopped himself from asking about what would be served at the feast. He was a little shy. But privately he had made a long list of excellent delicacies.

The man went on, 'Mishra-ji's daughter was married three years ago. Musicians and fireworks were brought from Patna. Rosgullas and sweet curd and ten different kinds of sandesh were brought from Calcutta, kalakunda from Mihijam, laddus from Munger, and gulab jamuns from Bhagalpur.'

The man's non-stop naming of these delights did not mean much to Dhaniya, who had not heard of most of them. But if Mishra-ji had turned on such a grand affair for his daughter's marriage, would he not do at least half as much for his mother's shraddha ceremony?

Dhaniya asked, 'Did you go to Mishra-ji's daughter's wedding?'

'Oh, no, no!' The man shook his head quite emphatically. 'Should such an insignificant poor man as I dine at the wedding of the daughter of one so great as Mishra-ji?'

'Then?'

The man realized that Dhaniya wanted to know how he knew so many details of the feast if he had not been invited to the wedding. The man explained that as regards such a rich man there was really nothing left to know. The description of that feast had been told to him, having been circulated far and wide.

Dhaniya's nerves tingled with renewed enthusiasm and his blood quickened. Gulab jamun, kalakunda, sandesh – the very names electrified him.

The sun had become even stronger, and in the unbearable heat, the sky seemed to be melting onto the boundless open fields of northern Bihar. There were no longer any birds overhead, for as the heat had intensified they had flown beyond the horizon. The fiery dry wind kept gusting wildly all about.

However, no matter how heartened he had been, no matter what list of fine foods was in his mind, Dhaniya had been walking on an empty stomach since daybreak and his body was on the verge of collapse. He was now having severe difficulty in continuing in that fiery heat.

For some time his companion had been walking slowly by his side, but now the man said that he had to hurry home on some urgent matter and would not make it at such an easy amble. He quickened his pace and moved on.

All this time the man had walked slowly, giving Dhaniya company and conversation, even to the point of exciting his hopes and dreams with the names of so many fine foods. All that had been enough for Dhaniya. It would not have been at all proper if the man had conducted a beggar like him to Chandreshwar Mishra's residence in Meklipura.

The man had got some distance away, but from behind Dhaniya called to him, 'Just one more thing. How far is it now to Meklipura?'

Without stopping the man turned his head around and said that he would reach the carrion dump in another quarter of a mile, and from there the walk to Meklipura would take hardly any time at all. The man walked on with long strides, and the distance between him and Dhaniya gradually increased.

There were no longer many people to be seen on the road, for the human traffic had lessened as the heat had become more intense. Only one or two carts went by, and the beasts drawing them, their tongues hanging out, no longer looked where they were going.

For a while now, Dhaniya had been walking as though in a trance. Now he realized that his mouth was as dry as wood and his throat was rough like coarse sand; he had terrible trouble in trying to swallow. His hands and feet were gradually growing numb, and it seemed that he could not go on any further. Soon he might fall down on his face.

Yet somehow he struggled on, and having gone a little way, gasping for breath, he saw the carrion dump on a raised stretch of land. Several trees grew there, and above them hovered countless vultures. And on the hot dry wind came the stench of the rotting bodies of the dead animals.

The carrion dump had come into sight, the town of Meklipura would not be much further ahead. Summoning up his last ounce of strength, Dhaniya nearly started to run.

But not for long. He realized that he was frothing at the corners of his mouth. His head was spinning dreadfully and before his eyes, the shimmering fields grew blurred. As he got close to the carrion dump, his knees gave way, his shoulders slumped forward and as he fell heavily to the ground, he passed out. All the while his face had become covered with froth and now dark blood was starting to ooze from his mouth. Out of the bag slung over his shoulder, his bread, boiled maize and pieces of sugarcane fell and scattered everywhere.

Dhaniya did not get up again. As afternoon wore on, the vultures of the carrion dump, their necks craned, watched him from the tree tops. Then, with unerring instinct, flocks of them spread their wings and glided slowly down.

Just before evening, a gathering of a few hundred vultures sat down to feast on Dhaniya's dead body.

seven times wed
satghoria

The main highway or pucca road to Manpatthal village was known thereabouts as 'the pakki'. Beyond it was a dried up inlet of the southern reaches of the river Koel, now quite shallow. In Jyaistha, what little water there was amid the brown sand at the bottom of the hills was hardly knee-deep.

Manpatthal was a village of untouchables. To the north there were the Dhangars, to the south the Ganjus, and to the west the Dosads.

Having bathed at daybreak in the shallow water of the Koel, Champiya, of the Dosad neighbourhood, was sitting slumped on the veranda of her hut. She remained like that for a while, then raised her chin and anxiously looked into the distance towards the pakki. Along that road, from the east, Natwar was supposed to come.

It was so early in the morning that no one in the neighbourhoods of the Ganjus, Dhangars or Dosads was awake as yet, although some of the Dhangars' pigs – animals that always have the devil of an appetite – had already gone out looking for food. Not only the pigs, but the birds too were awake. Flocks of sparrows and foreign parrots hovered above, then cut through the air as they flew over the pakki towards the vast open fields.

Flowering paras and simar trees were to be found everywhere in Manpatthal. Three months ago, red pointed buds had appeared on them, and they had now burst into bloom. There were also numerous thickets of flowering trees, all of them crowned with blossoms.

The people who lived here were at the lowest rungs of the human ladder, people who fear the world and keep their distance from it. So if anyone of them had woken at that moment and seen Champiya, they would indeed have been amazed.

Champiya was around forty and the colour of burnt brick. Her hair was receding, making her forehead look like a fallow field. Her nose was short and flat, her brow was broad, and there was a scar on her rough chin. But if one looked carefully at her face, it was easy to sense that it had once had a certain elegance about it. Even now her eyes were sincere, innocent and attractive. Twenty or twenty-five years ago when she was just a young woman, a young fellow called Fekumal of the Ganju neighbourhood used to say that her eyes were doe-like. He was a lively and merry young man who used to enchant the people with his songs, jokes and amazing stories when he performed in the local jatra troupe.

Whether or not Champiya's eyes were like those of a deer, in those days she had the strength of a wild buffalo. Unlimited energy and sustained good health would seem to have assured her of many long years of life, but three years ago she had succumbed to a bad strain of smallpox. Her neck stuck up like a peg, black pockmarks covered her face, shoulders and neck, and the veins of her hands were like cords protruding through her skin. Her body much weakened, she was often short of breath.

The other villagers were used to seeing Champiya as a sickly Dosad woman, well past her prime, but right now her appearance would have amazed them. She was wearing an exceptionally well-washed, coloured sari and a short blouse. Her eyes were highlighted by collyrium, she had placed a vermilion spot on the middle of her forehead and fixed her hair in a neat bun with a wooden comb. She wore a silver necklace, silver earrings and silver bangles. The past three years had been very hard on her – she had hardly anything at all to eat and was forced to go hungry many times. Yet there was good reason why she had not sold her silver ornaments to fill her stomach. Despite a thousand sorrows, Champiya's one hope, her one dream, was to dress up like this one more time in her life, and that day had now come.

She had attired herself like this a total of six times since she was fifteen. The last time the untouchables of Manpatthal had seen her dressed in this way had been five years ago when she was going to the house of her sixth husband. Because she had been married to six men so far, she was known in ten or even twenty villages around Manpatthal as 'Six-times-wed'.

Champiya was getting restless sitting on the veranda. Around her were the three outcaste neighbourhoods, the flocks of foreign birds, the herds of pigs, the fiery blooms on the tops of the trees, and the open fields extending into the distance, yet Champiya was quite unaware of all this. Her eyes were fixed on the highway.

The arrangement had been that well before the sun had risen high, Natwar would come from the small town of Bhakilganj, two miles to the east, and take her straight to the market at Surathpura, some five miles to the west. Natwar was of the same caste as she, a Dosad, and was about fifty. He had been working as a day labourer for a contractor in Bhakilganj, digging for the construction of the highway that now runs that way.

As she watched, it gradually became brighter around her. Far, far in the distance, where the sky arched down to the horizon, the sun had raised its glowing crimson head. Voices could now be heard from the outcaste neighbourhoods, as the village of Manpatthal woke up.

The sun had indeed risen, but Natwar was not yet to be seen. Would he not come? The idea set Champiya's weak forty-year-old heart thumping, and tears welled in her eyes. If Natwar Dosad did not come, her dressing up would have been for nothing. However, after just a few minutes, when the sun had risen clearly above the horizon, Champiya could see him coming towards her along the pakki. Her heart thumped wildly, and her face beamed with joy.

Natwar walked through the pakki between the Dhangar and Ganju localities on either side of the road and entered the Dosad neighbourhood. He walked straight up under the trees and stood in front of Champiya. Scrutinizing her fine appearance from head to foot, he asked, 'Well then, Champiya. Ridi?' 'Ridi' meant 'ready.' While working for the contractor, he had picked up a few English expressions which he would utter frequently.

'Yes.' Champiya leaned forward slightly, but did not look at him directly. Although she was no longer a fifteen-year-old girl, coyness still tempered the joy with which her breast swelled.

'I'm a bit late.'

Champiya could not think of any reply.

Natwar spoke again, 'No sense waiting about any longer. Sun's getting higher. Better get a move on or it'll be noon before we get to Surathpura.'

'Just a second,' Champiya muttered. She went inside the dilapidated hut and came out with a bundle she had packed the night before. In it were all her worldly goods: a couple of narrow, stitched saris, three torn blouses, a patchwork bedsheet, a blanket, and two or three silver plates and mugs.

Natwar pointed to the bundle and said, 'You're taking this?'

'Yes.' Champiya nodded her head.

'Okay, then. Let's go.'

They had gone just a little ahead when Champiya turned back to look at the ramshackle house that had been her father's home. Of course, he was no longer alive and was destitute when he died. Not only had she no father, but no mother or sister either. She did have a brother, but after his marriage he had gone a long way off to the town of Jhariya, where he worked in the coal mine. Champiya had not heard of him in ten or twenty years and could not say if he were alive or dead.

This was not the first time Champiya had left her father's house carrying all her worldly goods. There had been six men, six occasions, before. Each time she left she said a prayer in her mind, 'Oh, Lord Ram! Oh, God, let me not come back to my father's house,' but six times Champiya had had to come back. This man was number seven. As she looked at the house, her hands folded, she prayed to Lord Ram to let this be her last departure from it.

Natwar was in a hurry. 'Hey, what are you waiting for? We'll be late.'

'I'm coming.' She turned around and again set out after Natwar. Along the way she noticed how fine the robust, middle-aged Natwar looked. Because of his work he was covered with dirt, but that morning after bathing he had rubbed his body profusely with oil. Indeed, he had poured so much mustard oil over his head that it was trickling down over his brow. He was wearing a fresh and bleached white dhoti with a red shirt. On his feet were a pair of untanned, strong leather shoes, and his ears were adorned with brass rings. Over his shoulder was a new, unbleached gamchha.

The couple left the Dosad neighbourhood behind them and went on through the Ganju and Dhangar localities. Those who were now awake were confronted by the remarkable sight of Champiya dressed for the occasion. Some of them asked, 'Hey, Champiya, have you found a new husband?'

Champiya said nothing; she just looked down and gave a slight nod.

'This must be the seventh, then?'

Again Champiya said nothing.

The adults of Manpatthal wished them well, calling out their advice, 'Be sure to make this one last!'

Privately Champiya too prayed that this, her seventh marriage, would endure until she were taken to her funeral pyre. Oh, God, please be gracious!

Once they had left Manpatthal, they came straight up onto the pakki and made their way towards Surathpura. They had not walked as a pair while going through the village, for as they were still not married, it would have seemed brazen to the villagers had their bodies come in contact. Natwar was very likely sensitive to such embarrassment, and he took care to keep a distance between himself and Champiya. But on the highway no one knew them, so where was the problem with Champiya walking beside him there?

From time to time, Natwar would take a look at his partner and Champiya too kept stealing a glance at him; occasionally, their eyes would meet. When all was said and done, Champiya was a live, flesh-and-blood woman with great experience of humankind. She sensed from the look in Natwar's eyes that she was acceptable to him.

Champiya could remember going like this with a man to the market at Surathpura five times. She had not gone there when she first married as her father was still alive. He had found a likely lad amongst the cultivators. After the wedding, they went eight miles to the north of Manpatthal to the groom's house in Hathiyaganj.

That first man of her life, Mungilal, was a simple, decent sort, who had no one else in the world other than his old aunt. Mungilal was a bonded peasant labourer on the estate of a Rajput kshatriya. His grandfather had made a thumb impression on blank paper to contract a loan from the landowner, a loan which he had not been able to repay. Consequently, for the rest of his life, the man had to toil on the owner's land in exchange for mere subsistence. After that, his son also had to labour on that land until his death. And then it was Mungilal's turn. By then the interest had become so inflated that despite the continual labours of three generations the debt had still not been paid.

After his marriage, Mungilal brought Champiya into the landowner's service too, hoping that if they worked together, he might be released from his bond a little sooner. But hardly two years had passed when Mungilal suddenly died. Champiya had barely got over her grief for her dead husband when the landowner's clerk, the elderly and wizened hunchback, Teraram, came to her one night and whispered a proposition. For her favours he would look after her, providing her with the things she needed, as well as new saris and some silver; and he had some money.

The landowner and his men were always exploiting the young women of the untouchable peasant labourers' homes, a practice that had gone on since time immemorial. No one had ever stood up to it. But Champiya was a spirited girl of a different disposition. Moreover, her mourning for Mungilal was still recent and she was not herself. 'You old vulture, I spit in your face!' And with much abuse, she spat three times on the face of Teraram, after which she realized that she could no longer stay in Hathiyaganj, or Teraram would surely murder her. So without a moment's delay Champiya set off, running breathlessly through the night, over field after field, straight to her father's house in Manpatthal.

Her father, Ganapat Dosad, was a very poor man. He was a seasonal labourer, getting work for three months a year – one and a half months when the paddy or wheat was sown and one and a half months when it was harvested. For the remaining nine months, he wandered through the jungle along the banks of the southern Koel, looking for edible roots, sweet potatoes and mahua in order to survive. Before her marriage with Mungilal, Champiya had followed her father many times through the jungles in search of food, and after her return from Hathiyaganj that again became her daily lot.

So the days passed, and such was her luck that barely six months after the death of Mungilal, her father died penniless.

No matter how weak or how old or how wretched, he had still been her father! Now, after she had closed her eyes in the dark of night, someone or the other would scratch at the fence of the house and whisper, 'Open the door, Champiya. I have brought sweets for you – and silver earrings.' So after her father's death Champiya used to sleep with a chopper beside her head. She would sit up in bed flourishing the weapon, the veins in her throat sticking out, and scream, 'Keep away or I'll slaughter you, you bastard!'

However, the mischief and harassment actually increased. At last, Champiya angrily brought a complaint before the Manpatthal village council. The head of the Council of Five was the old man, Dhanpat, of the Ganju neighbourhood. Having heard her case he declared that it was not right for a young woman to live unprotected and that Champiya should get married again, quickly. In every man there was something of a beast, and those beasts might well devour her. How much strength of body and mind did Champiya have?

Dhanpat was a good man, a very upright man. He was not to be ignored. Champiya said to him, 'But I've already been married once. Who'd marry me, a widow?'

'It's an extraordinary thing to suggest,' said Dhanpat, 'that in our community there is no remarriage! There are those who have been married twice, four times, ten times, and set up new homes.'

This was not unknown to Champiya. She knew the social customs of the Dosad community, but she did not like the idea of being remarried like that. She quickly tried to justify herself. 'I know, Uncle. But I am just a girl, and I have no father, no one to arrange things for me. Must I go from door to door asking for a husband? What a shameful thought!'

'Just tell me if you agree. I'll make the arrangements.'

'You do what you think is best.'

Within just a few days, Dhanpat produced a middle-aged Dosad from the neighbouring Dudhliganj village. His name was Chaupatlal. After introducing them to each other, Dhanpat told Champiya that Chaupat ran a cycle rickshaw along the pakki. He had been married twice before; one wife had died of hunger, and he had divorced the other. He had no children, and was a thoroughly hard-working man. Champiya's situation was similar, he noted, so a new marriage would be good for both.

Champiya looked down as she asked Dhanpat, 'Uncle, who owns the rickshaw?'

Chaupatlal gave the answer to Dhanpat. 'Tell her, Uncle, that it belongs to the boss. I have to pay him four rupees a day for its lease. Whatever's left is my wage.' He paused for a moment, then said, 'There's something else, Uncle Dhanpat.'

'What?' asked Dhanpat.

'Tell your girl not to cast her eyes on my wages. If we marry, she'll have to provide for herself. My stomach will be my concern, hers will be her concern. If she agrees, then we can be married.'

'But if she goes to your house, to a new place, how will she look after herself?'

'I'll see to that. Just see if she agrees.'

Before Dhanpat could answer Champiya spoke up. 'I agree.' In fact, living alone had not been easy for her, and she really did need a man's protection.

Chaupatlal now looked directly at her and said, 'In that case, put on some clean clothes and be ready tomorrow at daybreak. I'll come and get you.'

'Where will you take her?' Dhanpat asked.

'To the market at Surathpura,' Chaupatlal replied.

'Why there?'

Chaupatlal explained that it was the season for planting crops, and all the landowners in the twenty or so villages around were in need of labourers. At that time, all the landless men and women of the region would gather at Surathpura market, and the landowners would look for the strongest among them and select their labourers. If selected, it was possible to have work for the whole year. For their toil they were paid in rice, wheat or millet, and a little cash. If Champiya obtained work, Chaupatlal added, he would take her to his home.

Dhanpat was doubtful. He asked, 'What's your intention? Do you want to keep Champiya as a mistress?'

Quickly, Chaupatlal tried to correct the impression. 'No, no, Uncle. I wouldn't do that. Don't you worry, I wouldn't commit that type of sin. If your girl gets work from some landowner, I'll fix up the marriage. Then I'll take her home. But one thing ...'

'What?'

'If she doesn't get work, then there'll be no marriage. The woman will have to find her way back from Surathpura.'

Dhanpat looked downcast. He turned to Champiya and asked, 'Well then, do you agree? Think carefully.'

'There's nothing to think of,' said Champiya. 'I agree.'

According to plan, at daybreak the next morning, Champiya had taken her bath in the knee-deep water of the Koel, dressed herself and put on her jewellery, and was sitting waiting on her veranda. Her father had given her a lot of silver at the time of her first marriage. She had not been able to bring it all back as she had had to flee from Mungilal's village with whatever she could wrap in a cloth, though later, indeed, the old aunt returned the rest of her belongings to her.

And so early the next morning, Chaupatlal came and took Champiya to the market at Surathpura. Once there, one of the landlords saw her and work for a year was assured. Chaupatlal was a man true to his word. At the market the marriage was celebrated by a priest of the untouchables, and Chaupatlal took his new wife home to Dudhliganj.

Champiya's married life with Chaupatlal lasted four years, during which the time passed rather well, more or less. According to their agreement, Chaupatlal and Champiya provided separately for themselves, and their life went quite smoothly. Each day after washing and eating some bread or leftover rice, Champiya would light the stove and make the midday meal. She would fill two brass pots, give one to Chaupatlal and take the other herself. Then they would go their own ways, Champiya to the farmyard or the fields and Chaupatlal to the pakki with his cycle rickshaw. At the end of the day, the two would meet again. They would eat some hot bread cakes or rice and then, as they lay close to one another watching the stars in the sky through the cracks in the roof, Chaupatlal would have so much to tell her.

Except for Champiya's giving birth to a stillborn child, the days passed in much the same way during those four years. But at the end, there was a devastating drought that put an end to all cultivation for miles and miles around. There was not a speck of a cloud, not a drop of rain. Indeed, the sky held out no promise of rain at all, and without water there could be no cultivation. The landlord told Champiya that he could no longer keep her on.

After she had left her job, Chaupatlal, with a gloomy look, said, 'I feel really bad about this, but I have to say it.'

'What?' Champiya looked at her husband, fearful.

'You'll have to go back to Manpatthal.'

'Go back?'

'Yes.' Chaupatlal nodded sadly. 'You have no work, no earnings. And with the drought people have no money so no one can go anywhere by cycle rickshaw. What I earn in a day I don't even get to keep. If you stay, we'll both die of hunger.'

There really was no other way. Champiya packed her clothes and her silver and returned to Manpatthal, tears streaming down her face.

After such a long time her father's house had fallen into disrepair, and with no one living there the place was ankle-deep in dust and rubbish. The support posts had been so ridden by woodworm that the house could have fallen down at any time. So Champiya cleared away the rubbish, collected some timber from the jungle and replaced the posts.

Then followed a very difficult year. Not only was there drought where Chaupatlal lived, but the land of some forty or fifty estates around Manpatthal was also baked dry. Once cultivation ceased for want of rain, everyone, like Champiya, was out of work. In fact, all they had to rely on were the two sides of the dried up canal of the lower Koel. For a whole year Champiya boiled the various edible roots and tubers she got from there and tried to get by on them. But there was no doubt about the strength of her will to live; otherwise no one could have survived on such a diet of mean vegetables and weeds.

A year later, the gods were kind. Hardly had Jyaistha come to an end than heavy black clouds covered the sky. Champiya looked up, then with folded hands and bowed head she prayed, 'Oh, Lord Ram. Oh, God, be gracious. With work we can eat. My mouth has not taken rice for a year.'

She decided that in a couple of days, she would go and wait under the trees at the Surathpura market where landowners came to select their labourers. But the day before she was to go, Jagan Dosad from the neighbouring village of Hatiyara turned up. He was carrying goods to the grain depot at Surathpura market. He said, 'I hear you're without a man in your house now that your marriage with Chaupatlal has finished.'

Champiya had known Jagan Dosad since their childhood. He used to come to Manpatthal when her father was alive.

She nodded her head and said, 'Yes.'

'I'm without a woman in my house,' he said. 'If you like, you can come and stay there. But ...'

Champiya was neither embarrassed by Jagan Dosad's proposition nor did hearing talk of marriage from such a virile young fellow set her heart aflame. She just looked straight at him and asked, somewhat indifferently, 'But what?'

Jagan told her simply that she could come and live with him on one condition – that she should get a job and provide her food. Of course, such a stipulation was not unknown to Champiya, for it was on this condition that her previous marriage had been arranged.

'All right,' she said. Champiya understood that, according to the customs and tradition of the country, there should be a man for every woman. While he may not feed and clothe her, she badly needed his protection. It was indeed dangerous for a woman to remain unattached.

Pleased, Jagan said, 'By the look of the sky, the landowners will certainly be coming to Surathpura to get labour this year. If you go there, you'll get work.'

'I know. I'll go to Surathpura tomorrow.'

Jagan's enthusiasm increased tenfold. He said, 'I'll come and get you here at daybreak then. We'll go together to Surathpura.'

'All right.'

'And if you get work, I'll take you to my house.'

And so the next morning, before the sun came up, the people of Manpatthal might have seen Champiya, dressed up for the occasion, once again going off to Surathpura, this time behind Jagan Dosad of Hatiyara village.

No sooner had Champiya reached the karaiya trees at Surathpura market than she was selected for work, and what had happened with Chaupatlal happened again. Jagan got a tonsured priest from somewhere, and after the fee of five rupees had been paid, the marriage was celebrated. Then he took Champiya straight to his own house.

Champiya's third marriage did not last even two years. Hardly had the first year passed when she became pregnant, but she did not stop working. If she had not worked, she could not have eaten. Indeed, for nine months she worked on the landlord's land, bearing the child inside her, until one day she fell face down on the ground. Bleeding and unconscious she was taken in a bullock cart twenty miles to a town where she was admitted to hospital. When she came out after a three-month struggle with death, she was very frail. She had lost the child, and the doctor at the hospital had told her that she could not have any more children. She had no misgivings about that, as she feared for her health. Should she again break down physically, she would be unfit for work and would die of hunger.

After leaving the hospital, Champiya became extremely weak. Work in the fields was out of the question, as she would be panting after walking ten paces at a stretch. As a result, she lost her job. She could not provide herself with food, nor was Jagan able to provide for her. Champiya's third marriage also came to an end. She packed her clothes and her other odds and ends and again went back to Manpatthal.

After this Champiya dressed up for another three men whom she followed to Surathpura market, again under the condition that before the marriage could be celebrated she should get agricultural work to provide for herself. But her fourth, fifth and sixth marriages lasted between just one and four years. Number four broke up when the southern Koel flooded all the land under cultivation – she lost her job and, consequently, her marriage. Number five ended with the death of the husband. The break-up of marriage number six was brought about by crop failure.

Then the long-suffering Champiya, her body wasted and weakened, went off with the seventh man of her life, Natwar, to Surathpura.

Suddenly, she heard Natwar's voice beside her. 'Hey, woman …'

All this time Champiya had been walking lost in thought. Immediately, she looked up and said, 'What?'

'There's a few facts we have to get settled.'

Champiya said nothing, but she listened expectantly.

The intense heat of the Jyaistha noon was falling on them as the temperature rose rapidly. The traffic – buses and trucks, cycle rickshaws, bullock and buffalo carts – was also getting heavier, raising red dust over Champiya and Natwar as they went along the highway. The number of people on the road had also greatly increased.

Natwar said, 'I'm as hungry as ten animals.'

Champiya was not surprised. Almost all the men with whom she had walked to Surathpura had said the same thing. They had all come to marry her with the hunger of ten animals in their bellies. Champiya said nothing.

Natwar was looking at her intently. 'Do you hear what I say?' he asked.

Her voice lowered, Champiya said, 'I'm listening.'

'Whatever I earn is just enough for my stomach. At Surathpura, you have to be chosen for work.' Natwar laid considerable stress on the last words.

There was nothing new for Champiya in any of this. Her face impassive, she said, 'I know.'

Then, shaking his finger and raising his voice, Natwar said, 'However …'

Champiya looked at her companion with a degree of curiosity. She asked, 'What?'

'If you get work, I'll give you a good marriage. Everyone will be impressed.'

Champiya could not imagine what could possibly be impressive about her seventh marriage at this stage of her life. But she was not put off by Natwar's ebullience. Indeed, there was even a stirring in the flagging beat of her heart.

As they went along, Natwar noticed Champiya's clothing. Although her sari and blouse were clean, they were very old. They had become threadbare in a number of places, and he also noticed two or three patches. Shaking his head emphatically, Natwar said, 'No, no, those clothes won't do. I'll buy you such clothes in Surathpura that everyone will be dazzled by the sight of you. Oh, yes!'

No one had ever promised her this before. Encouraged by Natwar, her heart beat in hope and joy and excitement. He also said, 'I'll buy you some foreign powder, vermilion and some scented oil. And do you know what else?'

'What?'

'Some silver jewellery and ornaments, like earrings, a collyrium case …'

Softly she stopped him, saying, 'I've got them all. There's no need for new ones, so …'

Natwar held up his hand to stop her. He said, 'You're coming new to my house. Shouldn't I want to give you something? Isn't that all right? Tell me!'

Lowering her eyes, Champiya said, 'Yes.'

'I will set you up as my tender golden bride, like a real fairy princess.'

Blushing, Champiya kept her eyes in front of her as Natwar, painting his dream-pictures, brought her at last into Surathpura.

On the southern side of the Surathpura market, seasonal labourers were already gathering and waiting about under the dozen or so karaiya trees. There must have been as many as two hundred and fifty people, both men and women. Most of the women were nursing babies in their laps.

Natwar and Champiya went there directly. Pointing at the gathering of labourers, Natwar said, 'Go and sit over there.'

'And you?' Champiya asked.

'I won't sit down yet,' Natwar replied. 'I'll be back after I've had tea and something to eat.' Then, reassuringly, he said, 'Don't worry, I won't eat alone. I'll bring something for you too.'

Natwar did not wait, but went straight to that part of the market where the stalls were set up and people were crowding around, and slowly Champiya went and sat among the labourers. Champiya recognized almost everyone sitting around her. They were all of various low castes, including Dosads and Ganjus. Apart from the untouchables, there were also a number of tribals, such as Mundas, Oraons and Santals.

In this part of the market, there were still a number of gaps in the crowd. The market itself was a little way off to the north, from where a noise was coming like the buzzing of flies.

Champiya took a furtive glance around at the other labourers. Her glance came to rest at the foot of the thatched awnings in front of her. Although they were part of the market, they no longer served as stalls, which had now been moved to the other side. At that moment the agricultural proprietors of the region along with their assistants were sitting under those abandoned awnings. Apparently, the selection of workers had not yet begun.

Having walked her weak body all the way from Manpatthal, Champiya felt as though her arms and legs were broken. Moreover, she still had not eaten anything, and her hunger made her feel as though a wild beast was gradually tearing at her stomach with its sharp teeth. Of course, she trusted Natwar to bring her some tea. Wait and see told herself.

The agricultural labourers were chattering all around her. Some children were running about boisterously, dirtying themselves in the red dust. But Champiya seemed not to hear anything. She had but one thought only: whatever should happen, she must get work. And so she kept on muttering to herself, 'Oh, Lord Ram. Oh, God, be gracious.'

Suddenly, someone called out from behind, 'Champiya! Is it you?'

Champiya turned to look. Sitting just a short distance from her was the middle-aged Gaibinath. Just a glimpse of him was enough to shock Champiya. What a state he was in!

Champiya had known Gaibinath since that time many years before when she had first come and sat under the karaiya trees in hope of work, and she had met him every time she had come here after that. His body had seemed to have been made of stone or iron, and he had had the strength of ten wild buffaloes. The landlords would take just one look at him and select him straightaway.

Gaibinath was a washerman by caste. As a result of their meetings over many years, Champiya was on familiar terms with him. While showing no interest in the other workers he would ask her for her news and want to know all about her latest husband. As he listened painfully to the cause of the breakdown of one marriage after the other, he would express his genuine sorrow and sympathy. In a word, he was an exceptionally big-hearted man.

For three years, Champiya had not been able to come to Surathpura. In this time, apparently, the stone that had been Gaibinath had crumbled, and the iron had corroded. His cheeks were sunken and the bones protruded. There was no flesh to speak of on his body and one could count his ribs, for his broad frame was now just skin and bone. One could fit a finger in each of his eye sockets, and his skin was slack and wrinkled. His breathing was laboured and his jaw hung as he struggled for breath. It was clear that his lungs were not amenable to the air. And yet at such an age! He was not much more than fifty, but he looked as though he had passed seventy or even eighty.

Champiya said, 'Oh, it's you!'

'Well, then!' Gaibinath came and sat beside her.

'What a state you are in!'

'Oh, well! My chest's been no good these last three or four years. I've had this cough and shortness of breath that almost finished me off.'

'Have you seen a doctor for some medicine?'

'Medicine! What I need is a morsel for my stomach. What d'you think I am? A king? A maharaja?'

Champiya said nothing.

So far Gaibinath had not taken much notice of Champiya, but now his dull, lifeless eyes focussed on her and he said, 'You don't look too good yourself.'

Champiya sighed heavily. 'I had smallpox,' she said. 'My health went downhill after that.'

'It's hunger that's weakened the both of us, you and me. Who knows if we'll get work or not?'

'If God is kind …'

Just then Natwar came back with some tea in a clay cup, hot samosas and bread. Putting it all into Champiya's hands, he said, 'Have it while it's hot. I'm going back to the market.'

'Why?' The word seemed to drop out automatically.

'Didn't I tell you when we were coming along the road? I'm going to get you some smart new clothes. I'm a man of my word – oh, yes.' And so saying, Natwar waited no longer but disappeared into the market throng.

As she brought the cup of tea to her lips, Champiya suddenly noticed Gaibinath looking longingly at her snack. It was plain to see that the man was suffering terribly from hunger. 'Will you have some tea?' Champiya asked him.

Gaibinath said nothing, but she could tell from the look on his face that he yearned for something to eat. She was not so generous as to offer him her entire cup of tea, but without letting the cup touch her lips, she drank half of it and gave the rest to Gaibinath. She also shared the samosas and the bread with him.

Munching on a large piece of bread dipped in tea, Gaibinath asked, 'Who was that man?'

'Who d'you mean?' Champiya asked.

'The one who brought you the snack.'

'His name's Natwar Dosad.'

With curiosity in his eyes, Gaibinath again looked at Champiya and inquired, 'Why's Natwar given you tea and bread?'

Champiya said nothing.

Gaibinath kept on. 'I presume that if you get work, Natwar will marry you and take you home. Right?'

Champiya looked down and slowly nodded her head.

Gaibinath continued. 'Your last marriage was your sixth.'

He knew everything about her. She said, 'Yes.'

Natwar came back in the middle of their conversation with a bright new sari. As he gave it to Champiya, he said, 'Take this. I'm just getting you a few other things.' And off he went again.

Just then the land proprietors and their men, who were sitting under the thatched awnings, got up and came to begin the selection. Just as buyers at a livestock market are careful to seek out the best specimens of calf or goat or chicken, in much the same way the landless tribals and outcastes were appraised and sorted under the karaiya trees. The bosses wanted only those with the strength for the demanding toil of agricultural work. There was no point in taking the weak and feeble.

Robust men and women were selected first, and some of the bosses went off with them, gradually making more space under the karaiya trees. Champiya was still sitting among the leftover fifty or sixty tribal and untouchable people, with Gaibinath beside her.

He was panting constantly. To Champiya, it sounded like the gurgle that comes from drawing on an empty hookah.

In other years, a boss would take just a look at Champiya and select her, but now her luck had turned bad. After the selection had begun, so many had come and stood in front of her, but had moved on after just a glance. The same applied to Gaibinath.

However, Champiya did not give up all hope. There were still a few landlords there, and this season's cultivation would require a great number of labourers. Surely someone or other would give her work. All the time she kept on muttering to herself, 'Oh, Lord Ram. Oh, God, be gracious.'

By now the sun of the month of Jyaistha was almost directly overhead and it was scorching hot.

There were still a few proprietors going about under the karaiya trees. Champiya held her breath whenever one of them came and stood in front of her. Most of them said nothing as they moved about, but then one of them asked her, 'Hey! Can you do agricultural work?'

Champiya took a deep breath. 'I can, sir,' she said.

The man scrutinized her carefully. Her entire body was covered by her sari which she had carefully wrapped around herself to conceal her puniness. 'Take away the cloth,' he said.

If she removed the sari, her real condition would be exposed and there would be no hope at all that anyone would choose her. Fearfully, she said, 'No, no, sir …'

The man thought that it was only modesty and shyness that made her not want to remove the sari. Contemptuously, he said, 'You all think you're the daughters of kings,' and he pulled part of the sari away to reveal a good view of Champiya's sick and frail body. 'No wonder you had it covered up!' he said. Squeezing Champiya's hand, he added, 'There's nothing to you. I can't give you any work.'

Clasping the landlord's feet, Champiya cried, 'Oh, please, sir, please! Give me a chance and you'll see …'

The man saw no need for words as he snorted impatiently, jerked his feet away, and went on with his business.

Gaibinath called out beside her, 'Please take us, sir!'

The boss stopped in his tracks and said, 'Your chest is like a rat's. What sort of work can be done by a corpse like you?'

The repeated entreaties and clasping of feet by the two of them could not make him change his mind. They had been coming to Surathpura market and sitting under these karaiya trees for twenty years or more, and every time they had been picked out for work in the fields – except for this time.

When the sun was starting to lean towards the western sky, the remaining landowners had selected a few more men and women from among the leftovers and gone on their way. The twenty or so tribals and untouchables who remained had also begun leaving. Only two remained under the karaiya trees – Champiya and Gaibinath.

Champiya was sitting in silence, her head resting on her knees. Beside her, sobbing through his rasping breath, was Gaibinath. 'No work for us. Now we'll die. No question of it, we'll die.' Once it would have been unthinkable that one day this man of iron and stone should be crying in this way. The sound of his sorrow spread a heavy melancholy on the hot wind of Jyaistha.

Just then Natwar came back with some things he had bought. Seeing Champiya sitting silently in the empty space under the trees, her head between her knees, he was quick to assess the situation. He had no interest at all in Gaibinath. Quietly he called, 'Champiya.'

Champiya too was crying, but without any sound. When she heard Natwar's voice, her heart missed a beat. She lifted her head and looked at him with bloodshot eyes.

Natwar came straight to the point. 'Did you get work?'

'No.' Sadly Champiya shook her head.

'But so many bosses came. No one wanted you?'

'No.'

Seeing Natwar, Gaibinath had stopped his crying, and now a profound stillness fell for a while over the space beneath the karaiya trees on that lonely afternoon.

Coldly Natwar continued, 'You didn't get work. So how can we get married?'

Champiya said nothing.

Natwar waited for a few moments. Then he said, 'Give me the sari.'

Silently and with shaking hands, Champiya picked up the sari beside her and handed it to Natwar who grabbed it and went straight off towards the market.

Gaibinath had been sitting all the while with bated breath. Now he breathed deeply and, panting somewhat, said with intense sadness, 'He's turned you down.'

Champiya said nothing. Given the circumstances, there was nothing to say.

But Gaibinath kept talking. 'What'll you do now? You didn't get any work. And now you'll burn in this sun. It's like fire.'

Champiya now started to realize the impact of not getting work and not getting married. Yet it all seemed rather natural to her. She said, 'What's the point in staying here? I'll go home.'

'To Manpatthal?'

'Yes.'

'Because you came to Surathpura and didn't get married, you're going back to your father's house, eh?'

Champiya did not answer Gaibinath's question, but instead asked one of her own. 'What will you do now?'

'I'm thinking.' He took a few rasping breaths and said, 'I don't have anywhere to go.'

'Why? What about your village house?'

'That went into the belly of the moneylender two years ago.'

'How come?'

'I was very sick. I had no work, but I still had to fill my stomach. So I took a loan. And then I couldn't pay it back, so I lost my father's and grandfather's house.'

'So where do you live?'

'Here and there. Under the awnings at the market or under the trees beside the road. My chest got bad and blood gushed up from my throat once, so no one would come near me.'

Suddenly, Champiya felt an immense pity for this rejected, frail and ailing man, for like him she too had been abandoned by the world. She said, 'Then you have nowhere to go?'

'No.' Gaibinath shrugged his shoulders.

'Then let's go together to Manpatthal.'

This startled Gaibinath. 'What're you saying! Have you gone off your head?'

'I know what I'm saying. And there's nothing wrong with my head.'

'But you live alone. Can't you imagine what the villagers will say if you take me in?'

Champiya had not thought about that. She remained quiet for some time, thinking to herself that for so long the only thing that had ever troubled her mind was her own safety, and for that she had followed six men, one after the other, to the Surathpura market. But here now was this ailing, feeble and helpless man, and in this world of millions of men, it was he who seemed to be her one and only. Champiya had made up her mind. She said, 'Before we go to Manpatthal, we must find a priest and get married. I can sell my silver things to pay him.'

Sounding as though his lungs were cracking Gaibinath said, 'No, no, this can't ...'

'Be quiet,' she said. 'In God's name ...'

That evening the untouchables of Manpatthal were astonished to see Champiya, who had gone off all dressed up at daybreak with one man, now coming back with another. There had been six men who had married Champiya and taken her away, but this was the first time she had chosen her own man.

Everyone was dumbfounded as they watched the two rejects going home to an old, derelict house at the end of the village of Manpatthal.

for the sake of survival

banchar janya

The month of Magh had come to an end but the cold still lingered on. Since morning, clouds like big lumps of rock hung in the sky, though from time to time a sudden flash of sunshine would break through.

The winter's day was getting on and the shadows cast by the branches of the trees were lengthening when Bishtupada reached the northern field. He was about forty. His squat nose was like a lump in the middle of his face, his eyes were dull, and he had no eyebrows to speak of. His dark lips were thick and droopy, his cheekbones were sunken, and he had an unusually scrawny neck. His rough, dark skin was flaky. All in all, he was like a leafless tree, a mass of heavy bones, but if even a little flesh were attached to his frame, he would look like a man-mountain, strong and powerful. What clothing he had was a dirty, tacky loincloth around his waist, a shirt with a profusion of different coloured patches, and a gamchha which served as a turban around his head. He carried an axe over his shoulder and a sharp dagger at his waist.

Bishtupada had not had work for three days, and no work had meant no wages. In the houses of day labourers like himself there were no piles of gold that enabled one to do nothing but sit and eat; what few grains of rice there once were had lasted only until the day before. If only he could scrounge something today, his wife and children could eat. Otherwise they would have to go without.

As soon as he had woken up, Bishtupada went out looking for work. But where could any be found? As he wandered about getting tired and dejected, he thought of the northern field. This field had helped Bishtupada on many occasions; sometimes he had saved his family with edible weeds and creepers from there, sometimes with birds or a field tortoise or a rabbit. And so in great hope he decided to go there again.

Bishtupada paused for a little when he got to the field. It was a desolate place. All around for as far as the eye could see was grass-covered land, though in this cold, of course, the grass was not so green and luxuriant but rather pale and sparse. A canal ran through the field and there was a thicket of trees or shrubs here and there.

He started to walk, looking carefully all around him. In the declining day, flocks of birds flew overhead. If only he had brought his slingshot, he thought, it would have been very easy to bring down one or two of them. That had been a bad oversight.

As he went about Bishtupada examined with a keen eye the bushes and trees he came across as well as the tracts of grassy land, but he saw nothing that he wanted. After walking for some time, however, he was suddenly stopped by the sight of something beside the canal. A young woman was standing there, her eyes fixed on him. She was only about ten paces from where he was standing, and being so close he could see clearly the alarm and suspicion in her eyes.

Bishtupada could not imagine from where she had come to this desolate field on a late afternoon in winter. He took a good look at her. She was snub-nosed and had a dark complexion, a robust body and rounded breasts. She wore a carelessly tied short sari, and seemed an alert, spirited girl. In her hand she held a heavy chopper.

After a few moments Bishtupada asked, 'Who are you, woman?'

In a sharp voice she said emphatically, 'Never you mind. You just clear off from here.'

'Do I have to? But I've got things to do.'

'What things?'

'Just things.' Bishtupada paused for a bit. Then he went on, 'So you're all alone here in this lonely field.'

'I've got things to do, too.'

Bishtupada unwittingly took a step forward and the girl screamed at him, 'Watch it! Don't move another step, fella, or you'll feel this chopper.'

That startled Bishtupada. He noticed that the girl was no longer apprehensive and that her eyes were ablaze. Warily he said, 'All right. If you insist, I won't move. But where've you come from? Do you mind my asking this?'

A little softly now she said, 'I live in Taldanga. It's to the north.'

'That's some way off – about five miles.'

'Yes.'

'You've come such a long way?'

'I've come out of necessity.'

'What does necessity mean? Tell me.'

The girl said, 'If you want to know so much, I'll tell you. I've come to gather creepers and wild fruit.'

Surprised, Bishtupada said, 'That's funny. So have I.'

The girl's eyes flared up again. 'You're lying,' she said.

'God's truth, I'm not lying.' He was a little nervous as he went on. 'God's truth. My kids have had nothing to eat all day and I've had no wages for three days. If I go back home with nothing from here, they'll starve.'

Listening to his voice and noting his nervousness, the girl believed Bishtupada. She said, 'Then you haven't got any dirty ideas?'

'Oh, look, I've told you in God's name. Come closer.'

'Don't you try to touch me ... Where do you live?'

'At Payarpur. It's south.' He pointed in that direction.

'You live a long way off too.'

Bishtupada bared his crooked yellow teeth as he smiled. 'Yes. Like you. If it's necessary, we have to come a long way ...'

'That's true,' the girl said.

Bishtupada said, 'We've chatted for a bit, but we don't know each other's name. Mine's Bishtupada. What's yours?'

'Nishi – Nishibala.'

There was a pause, and then Bishtupada said, 'I've got an idea, woman.'

'What?'

'You've come for what I've come for. Then why don't we both look for creepers and fruit together? It's a cold day, so let's get started. Anyhow, you're a young girl. It's not right that you should wander around the field on your own.'

Nishi hesitated for a bit, then said, 'All right. I'll go with you.' And she moved towards Bishtupada.

And as they both wandered about the field, they acknowledged an unwritten contract, that whatever they got, they would share equally.

Bishtupada and Nishibala raided every tree and bush in the field, every hole and every ditch. But they found nothing apart from four little field tortoises, and once their shells had been taken away, there would be hardly any flesh at all.

They did not walk around in silence, and as they looked about for food Nishi asked, 'Who've you got living in your house, man?' In just this short space of time she had freed her mind of fear and suspicion of Bishtupada. She felt she could trust him completely.

Bishtupada answered, 'Just the wife and kids.'

'How many kids?'

'Three. Two boys and a girl.'

'So a family of five?'

'Yes.'

'What do you do?'

'I'm a day labourer.'

'Can you get by?'

'It's very hard. Almost every day I can manage only half a meal. Otherwise we go hungry.'

Nishi thought for a bit, then said, 'Do you have any land?'

'Where would I get land?'

'So you've got only your labour to get by with?'

'Yes.'

'It must be very hard for you.'

'It could be worse, but I can't do anything about it. I just have to survive as long as I can.'

After a pause Bishtupada asked, 'Why all this talk just about me? What about you?'

Nishi said, 'Things aren't much different with me. I too have only my labour to offer.'

'Did you think I couldn't tell? I could. But I just wanted to know, woman …'

'What?'

Bishtupada turned around and caught a glimpse of his companion. He said, 'I don't see any conch bangle or vermilion in your hair. You're not married yet?'

Distracted, Nishi said, 'I was.'

'Then?'

Nishi was aware of what Bishtupada wanted to know. If she were married, then why did she not wear a conch bangle or put vermilion in the parting of her hair? Bishtupada was probably confused. Very sadly she said, 'My husband is no more.'

Bishtupada clicked his tongue in sympathy. 'Ah, you lost your husband so young?' he asked, with pity,

Nishi did not answer.

Bishtupada went on. 'What happened? Disease?'

'No,' she replied. 'He was killed in a fight with the landlord's men. They speared him in the stomach, tore open his innards. It was seen by …' Then suddenly that desolate and still vast open space was rent by wailing. 'Oh, God! They killed my strong man, my husband!'

Bishtupada held back for a moment. Then running his hand over Nishi's unkempt hair, he tried to console her. 'Don't cry, woman. Don't cry. The hurt will go in time.'

After a while, when her grief had subsided, Bishtupada asked, 'Do you have any children?'

In a bare whisper, she said, 'No.'

'Do you have any family at all?'

'I have my old mother-in-law. Day and night she just sits and gapes in hunger, and yet because of her hunger her son is dead, and now she can never be satisfied. Filling her gaping mouth will one day be the end of me.'

'Any land?'

'If there were, why would I be punishing myself roaming around the fields looking for creepers and things?'

And so both of them went on, looking and looking; however, just like some mothers, this vast field was today tight-fisted and unsympathetic. They had found nothing apart from some five wood-apples which they gathered up after they found the four field tortoises – hardly enough to divide into equal shares!

The sunshine had gone and the winter's day was coming to a close. Indeed, so quickly had the sun gone down behind the thick foliage of a big tree in the west that neither Bishtupada nor Nishi had noticed. Soon the entire place was overcast with shadow and gloom.

Then the masses of clouds that had been building up throughout the sky since morning suddenly burst into drops of rain. On top of that came a bitter wind from the north that cut through the skin and flesh and went straight to the bone. A chill rose up from the cold grassland.

Nishi said, 'It's really cold today, isn't it?'

Apparently preoccupied, Bishtupada said, 'Yes.'

'And now it's started to rain.'

'Yes.'

Although Bishtupada answered Nishi's questions, he had something else on his mind. If he took home two field tortoises and two and a half wood-apples, whose mouth would they feed? He said, 'It won't do if we can't get anything more, woman. There are five mouths in my family.'

'Sure, but it's getting dark and it's raining. Can we get anything more now?' Her face and her voice reflected her doubt.

'Let's see.' Bishtupada's eyes narrowed. Pointing in front of him and sounding a little excited, he asked, 'What's that, d'you think?'

Nishi looked in the same direction. 'Looks like a wild pig.'

'Yes.'

'What the hell is it doing there?' Bishtupada looked very carefully, then he said, 'It's digging.'

'When a pig digs the ground, he always gets something,' Nishi told him. 'If there's nothing there, he won't dig.'

'Let's get a bit closer and see,' said Bishtupada. Another thought had just burst like a flash of lightning inside his head: if they got nothing, he could always kill the pig. It would weigh more than a hundred kilograms. After giving half to Nishibala, there would be enough meat to feed the five mouths of his house for more than three or four days. And if they could survive for three or four days, he would not have to worry about the future for a little while.

He explained his idea to Nishi, who said fearfully, 'It sounds good, but ...'

'What?'

'Oh, man. It's such a big, fat, black beast. And what if the bugger's got a tusk? That'd be too much for you.'

Bishtupada replied, 'I've got my axe and my dagger.'

'Axe and dagger to kill the god of death.'

'We'll see, then,' said Bishtupada, desperately. 'But at least I have to try. A fight with a wild pig is better than dying of hunger.' And giving Nishi no time to think or say anything more, Bishtupada moved towards the pig. Nishi could do nothing but follow him.

As they got closer they saw that the pig was old and that it had no tusk. In its digging, the animal had made holes in several places, and looking into these Bishtupada's eyes lit up. There was a giant ground potato, half of it above the surface, the other half still buried. Obviously the pig was intent on digging it up. Bishtupada estimated the great tuber to weigh about ten kilograms. If he could not kill the pig, at least they would have the potato. Then suddenly he made up his mind not to engage in combat with the wild pig, but to chase it away and take the potato instead.

From behind him Nishi said enviously, 'Look at the size of that ground potato, man!'

'Yes.'

The pig was absorbed in its digging, but at the sound of human voices it looked up in surprise. It had pink beady eyes and dirt was smeared all over its body and face.

Bishtupada started making noises to chase it away. 'Ur-ra-ra, hot-hot-hoi!'

But the pig did not budge. It took one glance at Bishtupada, its eyes filled with suspicion. Bishtupada made noises again. Nishi joined in. But the pig did not move. 'The bastard's as stubborn as a mule,' said Bishtupada. 'I don't think he'll fight.'

'He's not likely to surrender the potato,' said Nishi.

'That's true, woman,' said Bishtupada. 'Nothing happens when we kick up a row. But a blow from the axe'll bring the bastard down.' And so saying, Bishtupada went over to the pig, took the axe from his shoulder and brought it down on the beast's neck. The blow did not land true, serving merely to rip a little of the hide from the pig's neck. The animal looked at Bishtupada for a few moments, with malice in its eyes, then suddenly charged at him.

Bishtupada had not reckoned on such a reaction. He and Nishi caught their breath and started to run. The pig chased them for quite a way, then went back to its ground potato. Bishtupada and Nishi were not to be deterred, however, and in a little while returned to the pig. Bishtupada delivered it another blow, which made quite a large cut on its back. Again the bleeding pig chased Bishtupada and Nishi, this time quite a long way, and again they came back, and when the moment seemed opportune, another blow was brought down on the wild pig. In fact, quite some time was spent in this way.

The winter evening was closing in, and the shadows between the trees were becoming deep and thick. The drops of rain that had been falling a little while earlier had now become quite heavy and the north wind was still blowing.

Nishi grew dejected. She said, 'Give it up, man. You're trying to take the potato from the mouth of the god of death.'

But Bishtupada was obdurate. He said emphatically, 'Never. I'm not fighting just for the potato, but we'll get that when I finish off this son of a sow. I've got an idea. This time we won't both stand in front of him. I'll stand in front, you go behind. If he charges at me, you strike him from behind. If he chases you, then I'll land one on him.'

Bishtupada and Nishi went and stood before and behind the wild pig. Who knows what the pig thought? Perhaps he sensed that he would have his work cut out for him defending his right to the great potato. So before a blow could be delivered the beast suddenly leaned forward and charged at Bishtupada, coming at him so fast that he had no time to defend himself. Bishtupada had not had a skerrick to eat since morning and his body was very weak. A shove from the hundred-kilo pig sent him flying, and then he felt sharp teeth biting into his thigh.

Bishtupada screamed out, 'He's killing me! He's killing me! Help me …' While he was shouting, his hand reached down to his waist and he pulled out his sharp dagger, which he thrust with all his might near the beast's nose, and immediately blood spurted out.

Nishi came running from behind and started stabbing at the pig. The wounded animal released Bishtupada and turned back to run at Nishi. Unable to avoid the impact she too was sent flying. The pig then set about tearing at her sari and body with its teeth while at the same time Nishi lashed out blindly with her chopper.

Bishtupada's thigh was badly gashed and foul-smelling blood flowed from it, but he did not let that deter him. Frantically, he ran and swung the axe at the pig's head. It then left Nishi and charged again at Bishtupada; Nishi got up from the ground and attacked it again from behind.

Under the blows the wild pig went first for Bishtupada, then ran at Nishi. In the gloom of the end of a winter's day this desolate, wide open space looked like a primordial battlefield, where a man and a woman fought a wild animal over something to eat.

After a protracted struggle Bishtupada delivered a mighty blow with his axe to the vicinity of the pig's mouth, causing it to shriek out a blood-curdling howl. For some time it rolled about in the dirt in unbearable pain, then like a shot it ran off to the west and disappeared into the jungle.

After the wild pig had fled, Bishtupada and Nishi lay as though lifeless for a long time. Then, still panting, they got up and dug up the rest of the giant vegetable; and just as they were gathering up the tortoises and wood-apples to divide them, the rain started pelting down.

They had no idea how long the fight had lasted. They had felt nothing in their minds or bodies other than frenzy and primitive savagery. Now they started to feel the terrible cold, and an irrepressible shivering from their bones emanated as though their jaws were locked together.

Bishtupada said, 'This rain's a real bastard.'

Shivering, Nishi said, 'We're sure to die if we stay here, man. We'll have to go somewhere else.'

'Well, tell me where?'

Somehow Nishi managed to say, 'There's a cremation ground over to the west, isn't there? There's a hut there. Let's go to it.'

Bishtupada remembered. 'Ah, yes, yes. Let's go.'

They both ran to the thatched hut in the cremation ground that had been set up for waiting funeral parties. They sat there for a little while, puffing and wiping the blood off themselves. Then Bishtupada said, 'I'm really hungry, woman.'

'So am I.'

'Let's have something to eat.'

Nishi cut up some of the giant potato while Bishtupada separated the shells from the flesh of the tortoises. Some time earlier a body had been cremated, and from the embers of the pyre they started a small fire for their meat and vegetable. After they had eaten their fill, they belched their satisfaction.

'After a whole day my stomach now has something in it,' said Bishtupada.

'Mine too,' said Nishi.

'A bidi would be good now, after that meal.'

'Yes. I'd love a paan.'

The rain then got heavier and strips of lightning flashed across the sky. Nishi said, 'I don't think this rain is going to stop tonight.'

'No.' Bishtupada shook his head.

'We'll have to spend the night here.'

'Yes.'

After a few more moments, Bishtupada said, 'Are you going to keep on sitting up? I'm going to lie down.'

'I will too,' Nishi said.

The two of them lay down on either side of the hut, with a respectable distance between them.

The night had got even darker when Nishi called, 'Man ...'

From the other side of the hut, Bishtupada answered, 'What is it?'

'Come over to me.'

'Why?'

'It's very cold. Come and hold me.'

On that wild winter's night Nishi and Bishtupada lay in mutual embrace for a little warmth.

The next morning, having divided the remains of the tortoises and the wood-apples and the giant potato won in battle, Nishi went to the north and Bishtupada went to the south.

a window to the moon

akasher chand ebang ekti janala

At one end of a small country town stood the red light quarter in all its glory: a slum with broken tin roofs housing thirty or forty of the world's most debased women, who had nowhere else to go.

It is very likely that this godforsaken colony of women was established when the town was founded a hundred years earlier. Death, of course, has removed all of the colony's residents of those times, but the practice of their profession – its tradition – has been maintained, so that every fifteen or twenty years the old are rejected and the new are welcomed. The colony is now in its fifth generation.

In front of the slum is a raised gravel road which runs as far as the silted up river. On one side of the road is a Shiva temple and, on the other, the cremation ground. Turning to the right, the road runs straight to the original town. At some distance, safe from the touch of those fallen women, live the urbane, well-off family men. Between their genteel neighbourhood and the devil's domain there is a large, stony tract. Across the road from the slum is a teashop, adjacent to which is a licensed grog shop and several stalls selling fried snacks. Behind all of this, as far as the eye can see, are scattered here and there a sawmill, a timber warehouse, a glass factory and numerous brick kilns. Dozens of chimneys reach up to the sky and gush out polluting smoke, and these, along with the silted up river and its opposite bank, make up the view from the colony of scarlet women.

The month of Ashwin had come to an end. The sun was beginning to sink towards the west, the heat had abated and a comfortable warmth pervaded everywhere. In the clean blue sky, bright white clouds like carded cotton drifted aimlessly. High up in the blue a few hawks hung on the air, as in a freeze shot in a film.

Lalita was standing with her face pressed against the window bars in a house in the slum facing the road. Every day when the afternoon was getting on she could be seen there. She was not looking at the distant river, the kiln chimneys on its other side, the sky or the hawks or anything else. With wide eyes, she kept a steadfast watch on nothing but the tea shop on the opposite side of the road.

The neighbourhood was quite still throughout the day, overcome by a profound listlessness. The only people to come there would be the odd one or two who had lost their way. Of course, from time to time a funeral party bearing a dead body would pass through; death has no sense of time or place. But no sooner had evening fallen than everyone in this devil's domain would cast off their inertia and come to life again. Many of the world's drunkards, flagrant thieves, swindlers, thugs and other rogues would start to frequent the place. There would even be three or four incognito from the genteel neighbourhood, who would sneak in, faces hidden like petty thieves.

Lalita kept her watch. In the tea shop the middle-aged and worn-looking Uncle Phatik sat quietly dozing. As he had no customers, there was nothing else for him to do. It would not be long before many from the women's quarter would come to have some tea, and his business would build up again.

Lalita was not actually related to Phatik, but as her mother called him her 'older brother' or *dada,* Lalita called him 'uncle.' Nor did she have any interest in Phatik; rather, she was becoming anxious for Shibu to return from school. Shibu, Phatik's son, studied in Class Six. Every day after school he would come to the shop to help his father for a couple of hours, though he would be sent home long before evening when hell's joys would be in full swing. His house was somewhere in between the women's colony and the genteel neighbourhood.

Lalita was thirteen. She was very healthy and looked much older, more like a mature young woman on whom the low life of the devil's domain, wherein she lived, had made no impression. Her skin was the colour of polished bell metal. Her mouth was shaped like a betel leaf and seemed to be infused with all the tenderness of the world. Her forehead was small. Her skin, soft and smooth like fresh green vegetables, stretched taut over her arms and legs, her throat and chin, and thick lashes bordered her innocent eyes. That afternoon Lalita was wearing a sari printed with a floral design. The sari was draped carelessly for although almost thirteen, Lalita was still inept at it. Her thick hair was tied back with a coloured ribbon, and she wore green glass bangles on her wrists, a silver necklace, gold earrings and, set into her nose, a red stone which sparkled like a drop of blood.

Shibu was the same age as Lalita, and they had been classmates. However, when Lalita's body suddenly started to blossom, her mother Rajani put her foot down and took her out of school. Lalita wept and wailed, but her mother was unmoved. She started to see a rosy future for her girl now that she was flowering into youth, while at the same time Lalita was not at all interested in who thought what about her nor what dreams they might have had. Those few years during which she had gone to school were her time of greatest joy, and it was still so much a part of her.

Shibu had not come back, so she called, 'Oh, Uncle Phatik!'

Phatik was woken from his snooze. With a slight start he got up, looked around, and caught sight of Lalita. After cracking his knuckles and having a good long yawn or two, he said lazily, 'Oh, it's you. What are you up to?'

'Look and see what time it is.'

In the shop there was a battered old cupboard with broken leaf doors, on top of which Phatik kept a round table clock, its glass cracked and held together with tape; it must have been a relic from ancient times and had to be wound every three or four hours.

Phatik looked at the clock and said, 'Quarter to three. Shibu won't be home for an hour yet.'

Lalita said nothing.

Phatik knew who it was she waited for every day, standing there with her face pressed up against the window. Now he said, 'Why on earth did your mother take you out of school so soon and keep you at home? With such an aptitude for learning, what harm could it have done to have allowed you three or four more years of study? But no matter how hard I tried, I couldn't convince her.'

In his younger days, Phatik had been a pimp, presenting customers to the girls of the locality at twenty-five percent commission. It was a good living while it lasted, but it was suddenly turned on its head when he married one of the girls of the neighbourhood, Jyotsna, one who had silvery ambitions and dreamed of a genteel style of home and family life. Nor did she have any desire at all that her husband spend the rest of his life as a whore's pimp, some worm in the gutter. No one in the genteel quarter would rent them a house, and she would not stay in the red light quarter, so they set up house on a piece of land that they bought in between. Having given up pimping, Phatik opened up the tea shop at the persuasion of Jyotsna. He had been married now for fifteen or sixteen years and in that time they had had two sons, Shibu, the elder, and Jaga. Jyotsna instilled her own ambition in Phatik; their sons were not spoiled and were enrolled in school. Moreover, Phatik was continually persuading the girls of the adjoining slum to send their children of unknown fathers to school, too. It was not entirely a waste, for three or four ink-inscribed letters of the alphabet could get one work. Indeed, civilization could reach even the devil's domain. And so it was that Rajani's daughter was sent to school. But hardly six years had passed when something suddenly got into Rajani's head to make her take her girl from school and keep her at home. Phatik, of course, could guess the reason, but what could he do other than utter an impressive sigh?

'You'll have to wait a little longer. Lie down for a bit. Shibu will call you when he comes,' he said to Lalita.

'I don't want to lie down in the afternoon. I'll stay standing.'

'As you like,' said Phatik, and with renewed inclination he settled down to doze off again.

Lalita spent an hour standing at her place by the window, watching the sky, the hawks, the distant river, the chimneys of the kilns on the other side, and all there was to see in the declining afternoon. Then Rajani's listless voice, heavy with sleep, came from an inner room. 'Lati. Hey, Lati.'

Lati was Lalita's pet name. Indifferently, she answered, 'Yes, Mother?'

'Your singing teacher's coming this afternoon. Get the harmonium and do a few vocal exercises.'

Lalita did not reply.

Shibu appeared exactly one hour later. He was a skinny, sickly kid, looking rather like a grasshopper. No one would have thought that he was the same age as Lalita. There were beads of sweat on his brow because of his long walk. He wore a shirt and long pants of cheap, poor quality cloth, and patched slippers on his feet. On his shoulder hung a cloth bag containing his school books and things.

Lalita's eyes lit up when she saw Shibu. 'I've been waiting such a long time for you,' she said.

Shibu came and stood beside the window. 'I can't help that. I came as soon as school finished.'

'The history class was today, wasn't it?'

'Yeah.'

'Abinash Sir took it?'

'Yes.'

'What was it about?'

'The decline of the Mughal Empire.'

Lalita's eyes shone with earnestness. 'How did it decline, tell me!'

Having spent five hours in school, Shibu was terribly hungry. He was in no mood for talking about class work now. Frowning, he said, 'It's very complicated. I'll tell you later. I've got to go now.'

Lalita reached out through the window and took hold of Shibu's shoulder. 'All right, tell me later, then,' she said. 'Oh, but

Shibu, you said the other day that Tapati had a bad fever. Is she better yet?'

'Yes.'

'Is she back at school?'

'She came back today. She'd been away four days.'

Seemingly to herself, Lalita said, 'She's my very good friend. Does she say anything about me?'

'She used to,' Shibu replied. 'She doesn't say anything now.'

Suddenly, Lalita's face went dark. She said nothing for a moment, then she asked, 'Ganesh, Adhir, Mohan, Dipti, Namita – do they all go to school every day still?'

'Yeah.'

'I suppose no one talks about me?'

'No.'

Lalita sighed. She was quiet for a while, then said, 'They've all forgotten me, haven't they?'

'Don't be silly! Why would they forget you? Nagen Sir talks about you every day.'

Once again Lalita's face lit up. She grabbed hold of Shibu's shoulder hard. Her voice full of curiosity, she asked, 'Did he say anything today?'

'Yes.'

'What did he say?'

'That you're a good girl with a really good head for maths and science, and why would Aunty Rajani take you away from school – all that stuff.'

Lalita looked incredulous. Her eyes widened and she shouted at him, 'Tell the truth!'

'Why should I lie?' protested Shibu. 'It's true, true, true!'

Lalita's eyes started to glisten, as though she were about to cry. In a serious tone, she said, 'Nagen Sir likes me very much, doesn't he?'

Shibu nodded his head in agreement and said with special emphasis, '*Oh*. Do you want to know what else Nagen Sir said?'

'What?'

'He's going to come here one day.'

Lalita gaped. How could this possibly be! She knew only too well that no gentleman would ever set foot in this neighbourhood, so it was utterly unthinkable that someone like Nagen Sir could come here. Pressing her face against the thin rusty bars of the window, she asked,' Are you sure that's what you heard?'

'Yes, of course. And he said it not once, but three or four times.'

'Why is he coming, did he say?' Lalita's voice trembled with anxiety, excitement and unbearable urgency.

'To meet Rajani Aunty and talk about getting you enrolled again in school.'

The tears that Lalita had held back now started to well up in her eyes. She was about to say something when Rajani's strident voice called from the next room, 'Lati! Hey, Lati!'

Turning around, Lalita answered, 'What is it?'

'Who are you gossiping with at the window? Shibu, I suppose?' Rajani knew, as did the whole neighbourhood, that Shibu came here after school to chat awhile with Lalita.

'Yes.'

'Tell Shibu to run along now.'

'Later. I have something to tell him.'

Raising her voice a little, Rajani said, 'Cut the gossip. Are you aware, you shameful she-devil, that the singing master is already here waiting for you? Now bring the harmonium!'

Fearfully, Shibu said, 'Go on. I'm not staying any longer or Aunty's likely to get mad.'

'Let her get mad,' Lalita said, frowning angrily at Shibu. 'How can I begin to tell you, Shibu, what filthy songs that singing teacher makes me learn! It's enough to make me vomit.'

From inside Rajani again pressed her. 'What's the matter, Lati? Are you dead or something?'

Shibu was frightened. 'I can't stay any longer. I'm off.' And in one dash he was across the road and running into the teashop.

Lalita called out after him, 'Tell Nagen Sir to come soon!'

'I will,' called back Shibu, still running.

Slowly, Lalita turned around. Unlike the other women of this colony, they had two rooms, one for Lalita and the adjoining one for her mother. On one side of Lalita's room was a freshly made bed. On the other side, against a thin partition wall, was her wooden bookcase with its glass doors in which were arranged all her texts and notebooks from Class One to Class Five. In addition there was the *Ramayana*, the *Mahabharata, The Twenty-Five Ghosts, The Jataka Tales,* a simple book about the lives of saints and holy men, and an atlas. There was also a book of stories by Sarat Chandra Chatterjee and some other modern writers. Beside the bed were a number of boxes and a clothes rack. On a large stool sat an old harmonium covered with a cloth. Pictures of gods and goddesses and holy men covered the walls. In a colony of debased women, such a room would have been quite unheard of; it was like a touch of sanctity in the middle of the devil's domain. To the right, amid a variety of pictures was a round mirror, beneath which were such things as a long comb, a powder box, some cheap perfume, some hair clips and a bottle of lac.

Lalita removed the cover from the harmonium and, holding it by its two metal handles, took it into Rajani's room.

Rajani's room was much bigger than Lalita's. Here too the bed was freshly made. There was a mirror on the wall as well as three or four wooden ornaments. On one side there was a wicker box of clothing and various items of baggage, and some folded saris hung over a clothes rack. A few cheap cane stools were set out on the floor. On one wall there was a picture of the goddess Kali, but the other three walls were not to be looked at, for here were a number of pictures of naked men and young women variously entwined in such a way as to make one swoon at but a cursory glance.

This room was Rajani's private quarters during the day, but after evening fell it became a province of the devil's domain. After admitting a customer from among the drunks and the thieves and the thugs, Rajani would bolt the door for an hour or so. All night her slight body would be rubbed and squeezed and bitten and pinched and, when the last customer had gone at dawn, almost broken. Then, like a lifeless lump of meat, she would stay on her thoroughly threshed bed until late in the afternoon.

The singing teacher, Binod Sadhu Khan, was sitting on the bed with his legs dangling over the side. Rajani sat a little way away from him on a cane stool.

Binod was forty-four or forty-five and as thin as a ritual bull-tethering stake. He had a propensity for such intoxicants as ganja, bhang, country liquor and toddy, a combination of which had made his health very poor for his age. His cheeks were sunken and there were always black shadows around his eyes. His Adam's apple stuck out like a peg, and his back was slumped, making him look like a hunchback. The veins in his hands protruded, and his knuckles were twisted. He wore stove-pipe pajamas and a finely woven, rose-coloured punjabi. Around his neck was a thin chain, and there were several thick rings on his fingers. His neck was covered by a luxuriant mass of hair.

Binod played the clarinet in the local jatra company, the Navadurga Opera, and came to the women's quarter in the mornings and afternoons to teach singing. A girl's fee could be greatly enhanced by her being able to sing.

Having placed the harmonium on Rajani's bed; Lalita just stood there, her shoulders slumped.

Binod said, 'What's the matter? Sit down.' Smoking and drinking had made his voice rough and rasping.

Lalita disliked the man intensely. She did not sit down.

Rajani narrowed her eyes and, frowning, looked at her daughter. Angrily she snapped, 'What's the matter? Why are you standing there? Sit down on the bed.'

Rajani was not yet forty, but the debased life of her society had cast its mark on her appearance, and she would never be able to wipe it away. She had a hard look in her eyes, her jaw jutted forward, and two of her teeth were capped with silver. Till about three or four years ago, she had been in excellent health, but then her compact body became slack and now bore the signs of decay. She wore a cheap, domestic style, striped sari, and she had adorned herself with a tight-fitting silver necklace, red stones in her ears and a green stone in her nose.

Defiantly, Lalita said, 'I'm not going to learn singing.'

Rajani's face darkened. 'You're not going to learn singing? You will learn what will make you a living! You wretched girl, what a mistake I made sending you to school! Now sit down!' Her voice had gradually got louder.

Lalita was quickly subdued by the menacing look on her mother's face. Slowly she sat down on one side of the bed.

Binod said, 'Now, now, Lati's mother, don't be cross with her. If she doesn't want to learn singing, then so be it.'

'So be it nothing! Don't you sweet-talk her, Master. She'll have no trade value. Mr Paladhi has told me over and over again, you must teach Lati to sing.'

Lalita knew the name of Paladhi, but she did not understand what he had to do with her learning singing. A little confused, she looked up, then lowered her eyes again.

Binod's eyes lit up. With great interest he asked, 'Which Mr Paladhi would that be, sister Rajani?'

'Natabar Paladhi.'

'The brickworks' owner?'

'Yes.'

'An oil mill, a rice mill, a warehouse in the market. Mr Paladhi has so many businesses. A real demon for money.' Binod signalled Lalita with his eyes and, dropping his voice conspiratorially, he asked, without mentioning her name, 'Has he seen her?'

Rajani shrugged her shoulders and said nothing.

'Wonderful. Excellent news, sister. It seems that God has bestowed his blessing on your wishes.'

Lalita could barely make any sense of what he was saying. She just sat there, looking down.

Rajani said, 'Will you give your blessings too?'

'I do that all the time,' said Binod. 'If it all works out, then you'll be made for life.'

'Yeah. Now time's getting on. It won't be long before we'll

be lighting the lamps of this hell. You must start before then, Master.'

Binod sat there, a little restless. 'Yes, I will,' he said. 'Now, Lati, sing along with me.' He drew the harmonium to himself, placed his fingers on the keys and started to sing:

O my love,
I have adorned the raw youth
of my body,
come close to my breast and ripen me.
O my love,
for you I let go of
youth and life,
in my heart the fire rages,
ablaze I die night and day.
O my love,
rub your limbs against mine,
let the fire go out,
give yourself willingly and ripen me,
O my love.

Tossing back his hair, he finished the song and noticed Lalita still sitting there, silently. She had not sung one line with him. Binod was not put out for he had seen her sit like that in her singing lessons many times before. He said, 'You've not opened your mouth. Sing with me.'

'No.' Slowly Lalita shook her head.

'Why not?'

'It's a very bad song.'

'A song is neither bad nor good. It must be sung as it is written.'

Lalita protested vehemently. 'The words are filthy! Just hearing them makes me sick.'

While Binod had been singing, Rajani had stuffed a paan into her mouth. She now stopped chewing for a moment to threaten, 'You sound like the daughter of a toff. You'll not stay here to pick and choose just as you like. What the master teaches, you will learn. And look happy about it. Now pick up the song.'

But Lalita was fired by a powerful determination. She said, 'No, no, no … '

'Oh!' Rajani pressed her temples, then shouted, 'I've borne a member of Satan's family! It was a disaster sending you to school, you pig's offspring!' And breaking into a stream of abuse, she flew at her daughter like a spitfire.

Raising his hands frantically, Binod said, 'Now, now, don't quarrel! She's been to school and been influenced by others. Let it be for the time being. It will turn out all right.'

Rajani heeded Binod's words though she had not satisfied her stubborn resolve. Grumbling, she went and sat down again on her cane stool. 'We'll see in a day or two. If she's still obstinate, I'll set fire to her face.'

Binod said to Lalita, 'Your mother has such high hopes for you. We've all seen the trouble she has gone to on your behalf. She will be so happy if you learn singing. You are all she has got. Now why not try to sing just a few verses? Come on, now.'

With obvious unwillingness and extreme contempt, Lalita sang some lines and then went to her own room.

Rajani called after her, 'And be sure to bolt the door against the vultures!'

Every day just before evening when Lalita went to her room, Rajani reminded her to lock the door. That door would not be opened again for the whole night. This was a very strict rule, for no sooner had darkness fallen than thieves and thugs and drunks would converge in swarms. Rajani knew them all and had warned them personally against disturbing Lalita. She showed no lack of care. Could one trust the clients of the devil's domain who assembled there like dung beetles and were full of toddy or Black Label country liquor? Was there any guarantee that, under the influence of booze, they would not want to go into Lalita's room? So Rajani had to take her clients into her own room and keep her ears alert. If anyone ever knocked on Lalita's door, she would yell, 'Not there, you dead shit, not there! Piss off! Get away!' In fact, Rajani kept watch over Lalita as though she were a treasure, and indeed she was, for her own future was involved in that of her daughter. She had no gold sovereigns in her purse, so if she did not make plans, her dreams of wealth and happiness would turn to dust and be blown away.

The next day after school, Shibu came with some really hot news.

'Did you know, Lati, a man is going to the moon?' Shibu's face gleamed with excitement.

As usual Lalita had been waiting for Shibu, her face pressed against the window of her room. Surprised, she asked, 'Which moon?'

'What do you mean "which moon"? Haven't you seen the moon in the sky?'

'That one?'

'Yes!'

Shibu's excitement had immediately infected Lalita. Although the afternoon had worn on, clear glimmering sunlight still shone all about, and she pointed her finger to the distant blue heavens, saying, 'A man is going to go there? Get away!'

'Yes! Oh, yes!' said Shibu.

'Who told you?'

'Nagen Sir.'

Whatever doubt Lalita may have had was instantly dispelled because, for her, every word of Nagen Sir carried the weight of revealed truth. Even if he were contradicted by the whole world, Nagen Sir could not be wrong. In Lalita's mind, this master of theirs was a ship of knowledge second to none in the universe.

'When will the man go to the moon?' she asked.

'Nagen Sir didn't say. But I think it'll be pretty soon.'

'You must tell me when he goes.'

'I'll tell you.'

'Do you know what country the man is from?'

Shibu hesitated for a moment, then he said, 'Do you know the names "Russia" and "America"?' In fact he could not remember exactly which country Nagen Sir had mentioned.

'Why wouldn't I know?'

'It's one of them. Oh! I've got to go now, Lati.'

Just as Shibu was about to head for the teashop, Lalita suddenly remembered something and stopped him. 'Hey! Listen, listen … '

'What?'

'Did you remember to tell Nagen Sir anything about coming here?'

'Oh, hell! I clean forgot. It slipped my mind listening to all that stuff about the man going to the moon.'

A faint shadow of disappointment came over Lalita's face. 'Tell him tomorrow, then,' she said.

Shibu nodded his head and said, 'Yes, I will,' and ran across to the other side of the road.

Almost immediately, Rajani's voice came from the next room, 'Lati, the master has come. Hurry up and get here.'

Today, Lalita did not demur. Her mind on other things, she went into Rajani's room, did a little bit of singing, and returned to her own room where she locked the door and went and stood by the window. In fact, she had been so taken by the news of the man going to the moon that she could not think of anything else. In this state of rapture, she opened her atlas and sought out the locations of Russia and America. She looked at them in fascination.

As she looked, evening fell. It was very likely the bright fortnight of the moon, which rose up full from the horizon like a silver plate, spilling its light like a stream of milk over the distant river, the treetops and throughout the sky. Even this mean, benighted neighbourhood of a small country town seemed transformed by the light of the moon to look like a wonderful enchantress.

Of course, the worms of the devil's domain were now starting to assemble on the other side of the locked door to Lalita's room. Their voices mingled with the uproar from rooms all about, and the strains of a harmonium gave out a few snatches of song. But

Lalita was not interested in any of that. In intense wonder, she stared steadfastly at the moon. She had read in her geography book that the moon was millions of miles away from the earth. She knew that an aeroplane could not fly so high, so how could a man get there in some spaceship? It made her head spin to think of such things.

She had no idea how long she had stood entranced, looking at the moon, but it was very late when Kamini knocked on the door and brought her back to reality. At this time the middle-aged Kamini, who did their cooking for them, would bring Lalita her evening meal. She entered the room, set down the rice, the dal and the vegetables, then said impatiently, 'I must go now. Be sure to lock the door behind me.'

As Lalita was locking the door, Kamini said from the other side, 'Eat up now. It's getting late.'

'All right.' Lalita went back to the window to look at the moon.

One thing struck Lalita as strange. Since early that year, after she had been taken out of school, Rajani would not let her go outside of their own neighbourhood. She was virtually imprisoned there. On the few occasions she did go out, her mother kept close to her like an escort. Simply put, Rajani maintained her watch over her daughter all the time. What little contact Lalita had with the outside world she had through the window of her room. She was confined within the narrow limits of the neighbourhood, irrespective of whether a man was leaving the territory of their vast world to go to the moon so very far away. She could not even conceive of how many millions of miles of the vast sky there were between her and the moon.

A few days passed during which nothing changed in Lalita's daily routine and, as usual, she would spend the time until the afternoon in her locked room, getting restless. In the middle of the afternoon, she would wait anxiously at the window for Shibu. She would chat with him, and then Master Binod would come. She would somehow manage to learn a little singing and then return to her own room as evening fell. Then, after the inertia of the whole day, this province of the devil's domain would throw off its torpor and come alive. And just like other days, Lalita would lock her door, look up into the sky, and watch the moon with wonder, though of course, after the full moon the dark fortnight had started and the moon had begun to wane. Her only break in moon-watching was when Kamini brought her dinner to her.

In this short time, Shibu had come and told her that the man had not yet left for the moon, as preparations were still going on. And despite repeated reminders, Nagen Sir had still not come. She insisted to Shibu that he really must come soon.

But suddenly the established routine was turned upside down. One afternoon, when the locality was pervaded by listlessness, the sounds of a commotion came from outside, the hubbub spreading everywhere and instantly agitating the local residents. They all spoke at once, greatly excited, and nothing else could be heard.

Lalita had lain on the bed after her lunch and was browsing through some old textbooks, and as she turned the pages, her schooldays came back to her. Now, hearing the commotion, she looked out through the open door at the several parts of the women's colony she could see from her bed. It seemed that someone had entered the courtyard through the opposite door and was heading straight for Rajani's room. She caught a glimpse of some of her 'Aunties' – Tiya, Tagara, Mohini – whose faces shone with expectation. Lalita watched, quite dumbfounded. On other days in this neighbourhood there was never any fluster and excitement in the middle of the day. Most of the women would sleep, some would play board games, some would do some sewing, and some would just talk. Whose sudden arrival could throw the locality into such a frenzy?

She did not have to wait long for soon Rajani came into Lalita's room. Containing her excitement, she said, 'Get up quickly and do your hair.'

Lalita's wonder increased immensely. She never did her hair in the middle of the day. 'Why, mother?' she asked.

Rajani had no time to waste. 'You'll find out in a little while,' she said. 'Now hurry and get up.'

And without giving Lalita the chance to say another word she pulled her up and dexterously arranged her hair in a bun secured with a silver comb. 'Now,' she said, 'put on your blue silk sari with the peacock pattern.'

'Why do I have to put on a silk sari now? Are we going somewhere?'

'Just do as I say.'

Lalita responded to the sternness and authority in Rajani's voice. She could not remember her mother speaking to her like this before. An unfamiliar fear ran through her, like a chill running up her spine, a fear which goaded her to a big tin trunk in a corner of the room from which she took the peacock printed silk sari and quickly put it on.

With the end of her own sari, Rajani wiped her daughter's mouth, then carefully applied some eye shadow and placed a rose-coloured spot in the middle of her forehead. Then, she said, 'Now come with me.'

Lalita never went into her mother's room after evening, but came and went as she wished at other times. However, on this afternoon she trembled terribly as she went in there with her mother.

Some of the women of the neighbourhood were pressed together, waiting on the veranda in front of Rajani's room, eager with greed and envy to see whatever they could inside the room. 'Why are you making such a fuss here?' Rajani asked them. 'Mr Paladhi will get angry. Go on, now. You can come back later.'

Rajani was well-meaning and spoke gently, but the women did not take to her words kindly. The one called Tagara had a tongue as sharp as a razor. She said, 'You're so smug that Mr Paladhi has gone into your room. And just look at your daughter! Well, we were young once, too, and had good bodies.'

What a thing to say! But if Tagara's tongue concealed a razor, Rajani's harboured a sharpened dagger. Her blood rushed to her head. No one like Natabar Paladhi had ever shed the dust of his feet in her room, so she could not fathom why Tagara and the others should be seething so with malice. Rajani could have stopped the brawl with more obscenities and ribald altercation, but inside, the richest man of the district was sitting waiting, and Rajani believed that Lalita's fortunes and hers would be transformed by his kindness; otherwise, he would not have gone to the trouble of coming to this hellhole.

Rajani could not reveal any more of her true nature with Natabar there, except to say coldly through clenched teeth and with eyes blazing, 'Listen to me, you malicious she-devil, piss off right now, and later on I'll have your guts!'

But Tagara was not a girl to back away. Raising her voice even higher, she said, 'Get to hell, you slut! We're staying right here, so let's see what you can do about it!'

Just as Rajani was about to retort, Natabar came out and threatened stridently, 'What's going on, huh? You all clear off right now. Get away with you, I say!'

Natabar's roar did the trick. His money had such power that no one could remain in conflict with him. Lowering her voice, Tagara said, 'All right, we're going. We'll get our own back later.'

In other words, although order had been brought about and mouths had been closed, the quarrel was in no way finished, but merely adjourned.

After Tagara and her friends had gone away grumbling, Rajani took Lalita inside, where Natabar Paladhi was sitting on the freshly laundered covering of the bed. He was a flabby man in his early fifties. He was a dark man, and his skin had a glazed look as though smeared with oil, and was quite smooth for his age. His long, curly hair hung down to his shoulders; his face was square and heavy; his eyes were red and sleepy; and it was clear that he had already had a little to drink.

He had big-boned arms and legs and fingers like forceps. He wore a thin, fine-woven dhoti and punjabi, beneath which his rose-coloured net-woven singlet could plainly be seen. He had an expensive watch with a gold band on his left wrist, a gold chain around his neck and gold buttons on his punjabi; two of his lower teeth were gold-capped as were three of his upper ones. There were at least seven rings on his fingers.

This was the first time Lalita had seen Natabar, but she had heard much about him from her mother and others in the neighbourhood. She could not remember his ever coming here before, yet guessed that he had, from what Tagara had had to say. On seeing him, her apprehension increased and her stomach twisted in fear.

Now, looking at Lalita, and slowly shaking his head from right to left, Natabar said in sincere admiration, 'Ah! A flower in full bloom.' His voice sounded full of tenderness, not at all like that of the same man who had just minutes before roared to get rid of Tagara and company.

Rajani too spoke tenderly. 'All through the grace of God, Mr Paladhi,' she said.

Unable to take his eyes off Lalita, Natabar said, 'Do sit down.'

As though resisting his will, Lalita just stood there, trembling. Rajani took her by the hand to one side of the bed and sat her close to Natabar.

Natabar turned to look at Lalita. Keeping his enchanted, lustful gaze on her, he said to Rajani, 'I'd heard of her face. And you've brought her up exceptionally well. She's just what I'd imagined her to be. A few years at school, so she's not illiterate. A few lessons from the text-books – that's fine. And she has all the radiance of youth.' As he spoke, Natabar's eyes shone like sharpened steel.

Rajani kept her eyes on Natabar as steadfastly as he kept his on Lalita, noting with almost bated breath his every reaction as though their lives depended on it.

There was no equivocation in what Natabar had to say, such coyness as polite formality being very far from his manner of speaking. With utter candour he said, 'I'm very pleased to meet your daughter. I have a family at home of grown-up children who've married and given me grandchildren. Otherwise I would call the priest and go through the rituals and marry her. I still could, but the old woman and the kids would raise hell. In all there are ten of them, and any little fuss could turn into a scandal.'

Rajani was gratified by Natabar's talk of marrying Lalita. Fawningly, she said, 'Ah, but of course. Only such a respectable man as you would be so gracious to Lati. You offer her life such promise.'

Natabar smiled. Lowering his voice, he said, 'And she will also fill my life with joy! Rajani, dear, the girl is worth more than gold. So let me put something to you.'

'Yes, yes,' said Rajani eagerly. 'Go ahead, Mr Paladhi.'

'Although I can't marry your daughter, I will still keep her in happiness and comfort, away from my wife.'

'You are so kind.'

'On the other side of the river,' Natabar said, pointing through the open window, 'I've had a new two-storey house built. I'll set Lalita up there. Everything is there for her – two maids, a manservant, kitchen and dining staff. There'll be electricity, so she'll have an electric fan overhead and light at the push of a button. I've provided all of this. And … '

This description of luxury and freedom in a two-storey house far from this rundown hellhole with its cracked roof, the courtyard with its rubbish and its stink, and the inside lit by a smoky blackened lantern all seemed like a dream to Rajani. 'And what?' she asked, her voice trembling in anticipation and excitement.

'My relationship with the one whose daughter I have honoured will not be at all diminished.' Natabar turned on his seat to Rajani.

Rajani felt as though a thousand drums were beating in her heart. In a very low voice, she asked, 'Do you mean me, Mr Paladhi?'

'Who else?'

Rajani did not answer, but just stared at him intently.

Natabar went on, 'Although your daughter won't be my wife, she will be more than my wife. And in that sense, you would become a sort of mother-in-law. I'd feel better knowing that the girl's mother was there to love and take care of her. So I've decided that, to make things complete, I'll take you there as well as the girl. I can't stay in that house all the time. There's business, family and the like to be managed, but after all that I'll be there. I'd feel very happy if you agreed to this.'

The inconceivable happiness that had welled up in Rajani's breast threatened to burst right through her. There were so many words that she wanted to say, but all she could manage was, 'You are so very kind, Mr Paladhi.'

'It's not a matter of kindness, my new mother-in-law. I am doing only what is right. Now I have a wish.'

'Yes, yes, tell me what it is.'

'I want to take you both as soon as possible. Say, in three or four days.'

'But … 'Suddenly, Rajani stopped what she was saying.

Natabar frowned. Suspiciously, he asked, 'But what? You sound like you have some objection.'

'No, no!' Rajani said, waving her hands. 'Why should I object? This is our great fortune. Because of your kindness, Lati can start a new life. So I dearly wish that it might begin on an auspicious day.'

'Is that all?' Natabar's frown was dispelled and, smiling, he said, 'In that case you do what you think is best. Go to the temple and find out from the priest what would be the best day. But tell him the day must be soon. He's not to wait long for it.'

The hint of a smile appeared unbidden on Rajani's mouth at the idea of their son-in-law-mother-in-law relationship, something which otherwise might have been expressed somewhat less decorously. With great difficulty, she suppressed the smile and said, simply, 'All right.'

'In that case, I must be gone.' And Natabar got off the bed.

It suddenly occurred to Rajani that mother and daughter had not fulfilled their responsibilities and shown such an eminent man the appropriate hospitality. She too got up quickly, saying, 'No, no. You mustn't go without having some sweets … '

Natabar raised his hand to stop Rajani and said, 'Not today. Later on, I will eat so much from your hands! But now I must go. In two days, I'll call to see how things are going. In the meantime, you get that auspicious day fixed.' As he walked towards the door, he turned and looked again at Lalita, saying, 'Good-bye, then.'

Lalita remained sitting like a piece of wood on one side of the bed, sweating profusely. Now it had all become clear to her: into whose hands her mother was giving her up, why she had taken her out of school, and why she had had to learn those filthy songs from Binod. She felt as though her breast would split with panic.

Natabar left the room, crossed the courtyard and walked straight out of the women's locality and onto the road, where his old model, expensive car was waiting. He got in and the driver started the engine.

When Rajani returned from seeing Natabar off, she saw the tears streaming from Lalita's eyes, which were swollen and bloodshot. She was crying as though her heart would break. Rajani watched for a moment, taken aback. Then she sat beside her daughter and said, 'What's the matter? Why are you crying?'

Lalita flung herself into her mother's lap. Pressing her face against her stomach she sobbed, 'What've you done to me, mother? You've destroyed me!'

Rajani's amazement grew. She said, 'What's the matter with you? What are you doing?'

'Don't give me into the hands of that devil! I'd rather you killed me!'

Rajani understood who 'that devil' might be. She was so flabbergasted that she could not think of anything to say. After a few moments she controlled herself and, stroking her daughter's back, said, 'What are you saying, Lati! Even our forebears have been favoured by Mr Paladhi's generosity to you! You can live like a queen for the rest of your life, or you can live like we do now, just hardship on top of hardship to get a couple of handfuls of rice a day before giving ourselves up to the vultures.'

Lalita's tears did not stop but welled up even more.

Rajani said, 'What a girl you are! You have the chance of unlimited happiness, and all you can do is howl. Any other girl would all this time have been up in the air with joy.'

Holding her mother tighter and pressing her face against her body like an inconsolable little girl, Lalita said, 'Don't destroy me, mother!'

Lalita would not hear any word of justification, and Rajani grew impatient. 'I'm destroying you? To think of how much has been done for your happiness, how long it has taken me to arrange things with Mr Paladhi, and all you can do is blubber! You disgraceful girl, you don't know what you're bringing on yourself! Oh, what sort of a daughter have I given birth to! Go on, get up! Get up and get out of here!'

Lalita saw the menacing look on her mother's face. In fear she ran straight to her room, shut the door and threw herself onto her bed, weeping. From the next room came Rajani's harsh and angry voice saying, 'You can cry for all you're worth, but what I've decided will stand.'

Lalita did not answer. After a long spell of sobbing she got up slowly and went and stood beside the window. The street was deserted as no one was about at this time of day. The sun was so strong that the wind too was very hot. As far as could be seen the neighbourhood was tranquil in the early afternoon.

Inside the house Lalita was completely at a loss. She knew her mother well. She was so stubborn and insistent that she would not waver a hair's breadth from whatever she had decided. She would indeed hand her over to Natabar Paladhi. And then it occurred to Lalita to run away. But where could she go? She was a product of her neighbourhood, it would be impossible for her to find refuge in some respectable home. Moreover, it was common knowledge that for girls of her age there was the danger of men lurking everywhere like wild beasts. If they found her alone they would devour her. An unfamiliar melancholy overwhelmed Lalita with a numbing confusion. She had no idea how long she had been standing there when she was suddenly brought to by Shibu's call.

Today Shibu looked extraordinarily excited. It was clear that he had come straight from school, his bag of books hanging over his shoulder. His words came out in a rush: 'Do you know, Lati, it's been decided. The man is going to the moon next week. Nagen Sir said that the whole world is thrilled about it.'

On another day Lalita would have been immensely enthusiastic about this news. Man's lunar voyage was so sensational to her that she would hold her breath listening to every word Shibu might say about it. But today she hardly appreciated – or even heard – a thing. To her, now, the idea of a man going to the moon seemed quite meaningless. She looked at Shibu, thought for a second or two, and said in agitation, 'Oh, yes, Shibu, and you said Nagen Sir would come, but he still hasn't!'

Taken aback at Lalita's lack of interest in the lunar voyage, Shibu said, 'But I don't know why he hasn't come.'

'Did you tell him clearly?'

Lalita still harboured the hope that Nagen Sir would come and speak to her mother so that Rajani would send her back to school. If she was catching up with her studies she would not have to worry about Natabar for a while. This was the child's thinking, and for the moment she could think of nothing else. Of course, if her mother was not agreeable, she would tell everything frankly to Nagen Sir and ask him to save her. Nagen Sir loved his students so very much, for without a family of his own, they were all he had.

'Yes, yes, I told him,' said Shibu. Then suddenly he remembered, and with some urgency in his voice he said, 'You know, Lati, we heard something really dreadful today.'

'What?'

'Nagen Sir is leaving.'

Lalita's heart almost stopped. Pressing her face up hard against the window, she said, as though in panic, 'What do you mean, leaving? Where to?'

'I heard that he's going to be the head sir in a big school in Calcutta.'

'When's he going?'

'I didn't hear, but very soon.'

The soft, enchanting afternoon light permeated everywhere. In no time it would be dark. For a while Lalita felt like one sinking in an unfathomable ocean, unable to swim, but then she recovered enough to reach out and grab Shibu by the shoulder and say, 'Shibu, my brother, if you can, you must bring Nagen Sir tomorrow.' And as she spoke her voice trembled.

Until now Shibu had not been taking much notice, but now he

looked carefully at Lalita. Her eyes were red and her cheeks were tear-stained. Her chest heaved as she caught her breath. Shibu had not seen Lalita in such an agitated state before, and this made him a little frightened. Stunned, he asked, 'What's the matter, Lati?'

Lalita did not answer him directly but said, 'You wouldn't understand. Save me, Shibu.'

It was clear that Lalita was in real distress, but she refused to tell him about it. Yet she wanted Shibu to save her. But how could he without knowing what the matter was? It was all a tangle inside his head.

He said, 'But if you don't tell me frankly … '

Not allowing him to finish, Lalita said, 'If you can bring Nagen Sir, I'll be saved.'

Agog, Shibu said, 'Okay. As soon as I get to school tomorrow, I'll go to the teachers' room and tell Nagen Sir about you before going to class.'

Indeed, the next day after school Shibu came with Nagen. He was a tall, thin man, with a trimmed moustache, tufts of stubble on his cheeks, and dishevelled hair. He was wearing a long, loose shirt tucked into a grubby dhoti. The shirt had one broken button and two other buttons missing, and its sleeves were too long for him. He had an old pair of sandals on his feet, and he wore round, nickel-framed glasses. This disorderly appearance was characteristic of him.

Once the afternoon sun had started to decline, Lalita had gone and stood at her place beside the window. When she saw Nagen, her heart truly missed a beat and she felt as though it were about to burst.

Nagen was familiar with where Lalita lived and her social condition. Affectionately he said, 'What is it? Why have you sent for me?'

Lalita said, 'Mother has said that she won't re-enrol me in school. But I'll die if she doesn't.'

Lalita's keenness to learn made Nagen very happy. 'All right, then,' he said, 'call your mother.'

Lalita ran to get Rajani, who was flabbergasted to see Nagen. But she pressed her head respectfully against the window and folded her hands. 'I cannot invite someone like you inside this dreadful place. Please, you must stay outside.'

'Yes, yes, that's all right,' Nagen said. 'Actually, I just want a word with you and that can be done standing here.'

'Why have you called me, Schoolmaster Sir?'

'Your daughter has such a head and such a strong inclination for learning, you should send her back to school. You don't want to spoil her enthusiasm.'

Everyone in the town had great respect for Nagen. They had not known anyone to love his pupils so selflessly. But he was also a little eccentric. His reputation had spread even as far as this neighbourhood. Put simply, he was a man who could not be ignored.

Rajani said, 'We've fallen on our faces in the dirt. You know all that, Sir. What is the use of education to our girls? Lati can read three or four pages, that's more than enough.'

Nagen tried to explain the importance of education to Rajani, but her mind was quite made up and she would not listen. She had not the slightest intention of sending her daughter back to school. 'You won't be teaching her any more, Schoolmaster Sir.'

'What you say makes no sense. Look, Lalita's mother, if I were staying here, I would insist that she go back to school, but I am leaving for Calcutta next week. As you know, I have no children of my own. Let me take Lalita to Calcutta. Such a desire for learning must be satisfied. I will bring her back to you with her greatest wish fulfilled.'

Rajani was alarmed. Emphatically shaking her hands and her head, she said, 'No, no, Sir, that cannot be.'

'Why? Don't you trust me?'

'Of course, Sir, to us you are like a god!'

'Then what?'

Rajani politely explained that a woman like her, getting on in years, depended on Lalita. Without her, Rajani would starve and die. Apart from that, in her society there were certain 'done things', certain customs, in accordance with which arrangements had already been put in place in order to allow Lalita to commence her career. Under these circumstances it was not at all possible to send her to Calcutta for an education with Nagen.

Nagen looked dejected. Sadly he said, 'Well, in that case, there's nothing more to say. I'll be here for only a few more days. If you change your mind, then let me know. Goodbye, then.' And he waited no longer, but set off straight down the road.

Shibu had left for the tea shop before this exchange took place. Lalita seemed as though she had stopped breathing. With the departure of Nagen Sir her last flicker of hope had spluttered and gone out. Her ashen, lifeless face followed Nagen as far as she could see. With anger in her eyes, Rajani looked once at her daughter and, her mouth twisted, went back into her own room, suspecting Lalita's deviousness behind Nagen's visit.

Another few days passed in which time two things happened. The date was fixed for the man to go to the moon, and the priest at the Shiva temple consulted his almanac and informed Rajani of the time and date on which Lalita should commence her new life with Natabar. It was amazing that the two things should have been determined on the same day. And on that same afternoon, Natabar would send his car to fetch mother and daughter.

But there was a third thing to happen on that day. Nagen was to leave town on the nine o'clock morning train for Calcutta. Shibu had let Lalita know this two days before.

At daybreak that morning, Rajani woke Lalita, bathed her herself, and gave her an expensive new silk sari, a blouse and a petticoat, saying, 'Put these on quickly and then come with me.'

Lalita knew that Natabar had sent the new clothes the previous afternoon. She asked her mother, 'Where am I going with you?'

In a loving voice, Rajani explained to Lalita that today she would be setting foot on the path of her new life, but before that Rajani would take her, dressed in her new clothes, to worship at the Shiva temple and pray to the great Lord that she may become an empress.

After Nagen had left her, Lalita had been quite distraught as it began to sink in that her life was now utterly destroyed. The mention of the Shiva temple was a lightning bolt shot through her head. Without saying a word, she obediently took the new clothes and put them on. Rajani was delighted to see that her daughter had come to her senses.

After their worship at the Shiva temple beside the silted river, Lalita touched her head to the ground in obeisance to the priest and sought his blessing. Then it was Rajani's turn and the priest too gave her, his blessing. Rajani wanted to talk with him about her daughter's future, so she told Lalita to go and wait for her under the tree outside the temple.

Lalita could not have imagined a better opportunity. For so long her mother had kept watch over her. Just in case she should do anything to upset her plan, Rajani had shut down her business and slept by her daughter for the last few nights. Who could believe that she could suddenly let her slip through her fingers?

An old clock inside the temple had told Lalita that it was a quarter past eight, and she bore that in mind as she stepped furtively outside, her eyes cautiously on Rajani all the while until the high wall around the temple concealed her from her mother and the priest. Suddenly she was filled with a sensation of foreboding. She took a deep breath and, as though in a wondrous dream, began to run.

She did not know how long she had been running when she saw that she had reached the railway station at the end of the town. The Calcutta train was standing at its regular platform, its compartments crowded. In a short time it would be leaving and taking Nagen to Calcutta.

Anxiously Lalita put her face to the window of each compartment, calling out, 'Nagen Sir – Schoolmaster Sir … '

But no familiar voice came in reply. Tired and worried, she came to the last compartment where, in answer to her call, Nagen's voice came back. 'Who is it?'

With bated breath, she said, 'It's me, Lalita.'

'Wait there. I'm coming.'

A moment later, Nagen had pushed through to the door and looked at Lalita, amazed and speechless. Then he managed to say, 'What's the matter? What are you doing here?'

'Please save me, Sir,' said Lalita. Her voice was trembling.

'What has happened?'

'That thing that I couldn't ever mention to you.' Lalita hung her head as she spoke. 'Please take me with you.'

Nagen was quite taken aback. 'But what about your mother?' he asked.

'She has made those final arrangements for my destruction. If you don't take me …'

Lalita suddenly stopped, but Nagen could guess what she had been going to say. He made up his mind and said in a strong voice, 'Come on up.' And he reached out his hand to her.

Lalita boarded the train to Calcutta before a man walked on the moon.

the tiger
bagh

Some may well wonder where on earth the region of Chanda is, or even where Ratnagiri may be.

Actually, we are concerned here not so much with Ratnagiri but with Nonpura, a poor village of cotton-growers. This community on the furthest outskirts of Ratnagiri district has kept itself a virtual geographical secret. If one should come across it, one might well think that its inhabitants had resolved to live incognito.

Ghunuram had come to Nonpura as he had in previous years. He took the light rail out of Chanda, then began his long and tireless walk, guided by the sun, across the hills until at last he arrived in Nonpura.

It was the month of Bhadra, in the middle of autumn, when, as a rule, the clouds and rain powerfully proclaim their presence and a frenzy borne on the moist wind gusts and blusters everywhere. But whatever may be the situation in other parts, in this outpost of Maharashtra the opposite prevails, for here there is neither heavy cloud nor rain nor lightning, and someone must have captured the moist wind and shut it away. Here in Bhadra there are just a few scattered wisps of cloud in the sky, though elsewhere in Ratnagiri district the sky still remembers fondly the months of Asharh and Sravan and refuses to give leave to the rains.

For five years, Ghunuram had been coming from Chanda to Nonpura in the middle of autumn. At this time the Ganapati festival is starting throughout Maharashtra, and not a home is to be found where preparations for the worship of Ganapati – or Ganesh – have not been made. It is the major festival of Maharashtra; the formal part of it runs for two days, but if there is sufficient enthusiasm, the festivities may well continue for longer. The waves of revelry will flood even the nondescript and insignificant villages of cotton-growers in the remote parts of Ratnagiri, and even Nonpura will be borne on the tide.

There was, of course, a particular reason that brought Ghunuram to Nonpura each year at the time of the festival. He would come there dressed as a tiger and, in that guise, earn a little money entertaining the people. In full tiger array, flourishing his long tail, Ghunuram would dance at the doors of the cotton-growers, creating excitement wherever he went. Housewives and children, the middle-aged and elderly, young men and women and teenagers, would all run and jostle to see the tiger show. In no time at all Ghunuram would be surrounded by them, all raising the cry together: 'The tiger is here! The tiger is here!'

Having come for these festive days, Ghunuram would be borne on a river of joy performing the tiger dance for which the villagers of Nonpura had waited so eagerly and patiently the whole year through. Ghunuram would not disappoint them, and along with his dance he would also sing, beseeching Ganesh, the granter of boons, to hurry back again next year.

His performances were actually quite profitable. The people of Nonpura might have been poor, but they were not mean-hearted. With ready smiles they would put whatever they could into Ghunuram's bag, and after his month here Ghunuram would return to Chanda with quite a collection of largesse: his bag would be filled with about one hundred and fifty or two hundred rupees, several new dhotis, maybe fifty kilograms of rice, countless bidis, some cotton, and all sorts of odds and ends.

In all the world, Ghunuram had only himself. Four dhotis would do him quite well for a whole year; he would not need to buy bidis; and the fifty or so kilograms of rice would last him a good three months. However, he then had the problem of finding a livelihood for the other nine months of the year, and during this time Ghunuram could be seen doing various things for a living: for a while he might be a landless peasant, then a coolie, then a labourer on the roads for the Public Works Department. Sometimes he would graze the buffaloes of a wealthy householder, sometimes on the blazing hot days of the month of Vaishakh, he would carry a pole over his shoulders bearing cans of water from a spring in the hills for the rich people. And sometimes he would be simply out of work, again.

He won the heart of no one in any of these labours – abuse, obscenities and even beatings were usually reckoned as reasonable wages. With nine miserable months it was little wonder that for at least three months of the year, Ghunuram would revel in the bounty of Nonpura at the time of the Ganapati festival.

No doubt, his coming there promised three months' rations and clothes for the whole year. But there was also something else that drew Ghunuram – an attraction centred around Rati. For five years he had lodged in her house for the month of the festival, and for the rest of the year this girl in some unknown corner of Ratnagiri would pull constantly at Ghunuram's heartstrings. So after somehow surviving eleven months of the year, he would come in joyful anticipation to spend the remaining month in Nonpura.

There was yet another reason for coming, and that was the status and respect that this one month would bring into Ghunuram's dull and empty life. The people of Nonpura derived great pleasure from seeing their tiger, and they placed him high on a pedestal. Even when Ghunuram was not dressed in costume and make-up, everyone – especially the girls – would point at him and whisper excitedly. No sooner had one year's festival ended than the older folk would implore him to come again next year. Ghunuram, who in Chanda no one ever sought after, was a genuine celebrity – a marvel, indeed – to the people of Nonpura.

When Ghunuram arrived in Nonpura this time, the sun was high in the sky and there were just a few wisps of light cloud here and there. On his head he carried a battered old tin trunk containing all his worldly goods: pink, yellow and black paint, collyrium, a fur hat, his tiger accessories - teeth, claws, whiskers, tail – some straw, a lot of rags, strips of bamboo, glue, wire and numerous metal clips, all of which were his performance paraphernalia. Besides this, there were his clothes and his bedding. Seeing that he would stay for a month, he had also brought rice, dal, flour and spices.

As the sun shone over his head, a fire raged in his belly. For days at a stretch he had gone up and down over the hills, not stopping anywhere. He had then followed the road directly to the south and gone straight ahead, his feet bearing his weary body forward in long strides. And right now he was in urgent need of three things: a bath, then something to eat, and finally some continuous sleep till the afternoon.

Part of the village was hilly, part of it flat, so that the houses scattered all around, built from lumps of stone cut from the hills, looked like heads sticking up out of the ground. They were roofed with beaten tin or with a thatch of wild grass. At first glance they might have looked like rows of ancient forts. On top of a hillock, on the southernmost boundary of Nonpura, was the house of Shibal Nayek, the father of Rati. Ghunuram headed straight there.

Shibal was at home. He was sitting against a post on the front veranda, puffing on a bidi. His broad body looked as though it had been made from some ancient rock. Indeed, he had survived a long time in the world, as his timeworn, weather-beaten body abundantly showed. His hair was grey and his sight was deteriorating, but in spite of such physical decay the man gave the impression of great inner strength.

As soon as he saw Ghunuram, he dropped his bidi and ran to him. He gave his customary warm welcome: 'Ah, come, come. Come, Showman!' Everyone in the village called Ghunuram 'Showman'. The term was not uttered lightly, of course, but with great respect. Shibal took the large tin trunk from Ghunuram's head and set it down on the veranda. Then the two of them sat down together.

'How are you, Showman?' asked Shibal.

'I'm well,' Ghunuram replied. 'How are you both?'

By 'both' Ghunuram meant Shibal and Rati. There was no one else apart from her in Shibal's family, no son, no other daughter, and his wife had died after three days of fever some ten or twelve years back.

Shibal said, 'We get by. But this time you've come a little late, Showman.'

The festival would not start for a few days yet, but coming through the village Ghunuram sensed that some kind of revelry had already started. Shibal, Ghunuram's genuine champion, had wanted him to come to Nonpura before the festivities formally began and collect whatever he could from the local people. As long as the celebrations went on, people would be generous and unstinting, freely giving three paisa instead of one. But there was the risk that that generosity would, in time, decline, and that the poor cotton-growers would keep their hands in their pockets, thinking twice – or more – before giving two paisa. One step forward could entail a giant leap backwards. Put simply, one has to strike while the iron is hot, so Shibal's reasoning was plain: it was necessary to exploit an opportunity as soon as it arose.

Ghunuram said, 'Yes, I am a little late.'

While Ghunuram chatted with Shibal, his mind seemed elsewhere. Unwittingly his eyes darted around restlessly, but wherever his glance took him – in the tidy courtyard in front of him, on the rise beside the well, under the pipal tree, in the single-thatched kitchen or on the veranda of the two adjoining bedrooms – he could not discover Rati. Yet in other years, no sooner had Ghunuram entered the house than the girl had come running, her face gleaming with unbounded joy. For Ghunuram she was like a dancing hill-stream dashing all around him with her spontaneous laughter, her unrestrained delight, her never-ending questions and her free and incessant chatter. And Ghunuram would happily sink in that stream.

The hint of a shadow came over Ghunuram's mind. He had returned to Nonpura after almost a year. Had Rati been married in that time? Looking into Shibal's eyes, he was about to say something when Shibal spoke up. 'Will you take a bath, then?'

'I will, indeed,' said Ghunuram. 'I've walked for four days without a break, not even sleeping at night. All of me seems to be burning. I'll die if I don't take a bath.'

Shibal said no more. He brought some oil and a gamchha from inside and laid them before Ghunuram.

Having freshened his hot and tired body in the water from the well, Ghunuram came back to the veranda to find that his trunk was no longer there. Shibal had taken it inside. There were just two rooms in Shibal's house. Every year at the time of the Ganapati festival, Shibal and Rati would share one room, the other they would give to Ghunuram.

Ghunuram dropped the wet gamchha from around his waist and put on a dry dhoti from his trunk. Then Shibal called, 'Come and have some lunch. You've walked so much, you'll need a rest after you've eaten.'

Hesitantly, Ghunuram said, 'But … '

'What?'

'I've not given you any rice and dal.'

Each year when he stayed there, Ghunuram provided his own rations. Of course, Rati did his cooking for him. 'You can give me that later,' said Shibal. 'Now come and eat.'

Ghunuram hesitated. Still thinking of Rati, he said what he had been unable to say earlier. 'Uh, I haven't seen your daughter.'

'Don't talk about her, Showman. She's hardly been at home for the past five or six days! She does her housework somehow or other and then rushes off to North Hill. She spends the whole day there. And it's not just her, the whole village goes there.'

He was now assured of two things: Rati was in Nonpura, and she was not married. Eagerly Ghunuram inquired, 'So what's to do? Why are they all rushing off to North Hill?'

'Oh, I forgot to tell you,' Shibal said. 'There's a tiger come to North Hill that ...'

Ghunuram could barely understand. Stunned, he just sat and stared at Shibal. All he could say was, 'A tiger?'

'Yes, yes, a tiger. A live leopard, actually.' He then went on, 'Some bugger called Shambha has brought it in a great cage from Satara district. He's been here five or six days. In that time the whole village has gone mad over it.'

Ghunuram could think of nothing to say as a gust of unidentifiable fear blew through his heart.

Shibal thought for a moment, then said, 'Never mind any of that. You eat up now, Showman.'

Shibal went back into the kitchen and Ghunuram sat down to eat with a sense of unease. The meal was a simple one: rice, some fried brinjal and bitter spinach, a sour, yellowish dal, and pigeon-pea bread toasted over the fire.

Ghunuram noticed that Shibal had brought out only enough rice and vegetables for one. He asked, 'Am I eating alone?'

'Yes.' He shook his head, saying, 'The girl has run off without eating. I'll eat when she comes back. I can't eat now without her, can I?'

A sudden thought occurred to Ghunuram. In some hesitation he stammered, 'But ... '

'What?'

'What has been cooked is for you two. Have I eaten ... '

Shibal knew what was bothering Ghunuram. He smiled and said, 'Don't worry. We won't go without. These days Rati does two lots of cooking each morning. If you've finished that, have some more. She can cook again later.'

Ghunuram said nothing more after that. He drew the plate towards himself and, his mind elsewhere, took a mouthful. Not long before, he had a raging hunger, but now it was no more. His whole existence seemed to have been overcast by North Hill, a leopard, and some unknown visitor from Satara district called Shambha.

He had almost come to the end of his meal when Rati, panting, came running in from North Hill. Instantly Ghunuram felt something like a bolt of lightning shoot through his bloodstream.

To Ghunuram, Rati looked exactly the same as she had last year – indeed, as she had for the past five years. She was a dark girl from whom an intense glow radiated, as though her whole body were smeared with oil and perspiration. Rati's waist was so slender that one's hands could reach around it. A yellow sari with black flowers printed on it embraced her body. She had something of the unbounded vivacity of tribal women. Her mouth and nose were fine and taut, and she had silver rings on her fingers and a silver chain around her lovely neck. The silver gleaming against her skin simply enhanced her beauty. She was like a black peacock whose dark eyes glimmered mischievously.

She came running up to the kitchen door, her face beaming with excitement and her breast heaving. Looking at Shibal, she said, 'Oh Father, the tiger is so beautiful with its golden coat and the black round marks on it. Its eyes are like glass, and its tail … '

Shibal smiled affectionately. 'I know, I know,' he said. 'More a genuine royal princess than a tiger.'

'Ah, but listen,' she went on, impatiently. 'Its great tail … '

Shibal interrupted her. 'I've heard it all, my dear, I've heard it all. You've talked about nothing else for the past five or six days. What the tiger's eyes are like, its nose, its tail. I'm quite worn out by it all. Now have done with the tiger and think about your food. Go, take your bath.' Rati turned to go, but Shibal stopped her. 'Hey, wait, Rati! Look who's come.'

Rati turned around to see Ghunuram sitting and eating in a corner of the kitchen. Her eyes widened. 'Oh, my goodness, Showman! When did you come?'

In a flat voice, Ghunuram said, 'A little while ago.'

'I had no idea you were sitting here eating.'

'That's all right. You were excited about the tiger.'

With renewed enthusiasm, Rati went on, 'Oh, I tell you, such an amazing tiger … '

But she could not finish what she was going to say, for Shibal quickly broke in. 'There you go again! Go and take your bath. Be off!'

Hurriedly, Rati said, 'I'll tell you all about the tiger later, Showman.' And she ran off.

Utterly exhausted, Ghunuram lay on his bed to surrender himself to sleep, but sleep would not come. He felt as though a thorn were piercing his breast, though he was not sure where the thorn was, whether it was right in the middle of his heart or in some adjacent artery or somewhere else, but he could feel it there amidst an intense discomfort. Restless and distracted, he drifted between dozing and waking. He noticed as he lay there that Rati, having taken her bath and eaten her meal, had run off again to North Hill. The change in her was wrenching and twisting the core of his being.

And yet every other time when he had come here Rati had never wanted to leave him, all the time keeping close behind him. How amazing that today she had not shown even a hint of interest in him.

When Ghunuram got up and went out onto the veranda, not having slept at all, the sun had sunk low in the sky. What he had wanted was to have some sleep and then put on his tiger costume and go into the village, but at that moment he did not have the slightest urge to dress up. He felt as listless and unenthusiastic as a lump of clay. Shibal was not at home, and Rati had gone to North Hill, so he just stayed sitting on the veranda, looking blankly at the sky. He had not sat there for very long when just before evening, Rati came back. Seeing him, she said, 'You were asleep when I went out. When did you get up?'

'Not long ago,' Ghunuram replied.

'On the day you arrived in other years you always went out dressed as the tiger. Why not this time?'

'I think I'll start tomorrow.'

'Why? Aren't you well?'

'No, nothing like that.'

Rati asked no more questions. Evening was starting to fall, and she went inside. She lit the kerosene lamp and came back to Ghunuram. After a few words about nothing she got back to the subject of the tiger of North Hill. With sparkling eyes, she began, 'The trainer is as handsome as the tiger.'

Ghunuram was taken aback. 'What trainer?'

'The tiger's. He's called Shambha. He has a beautiful complexion, he's tall and broad, his moustache is curled, and his hair is like a mane. When he goes into the tiger's cage for the show, he has nerves of steel. He's a real man.' As she spoke, her voice trembled with passion and her eyes shone.

Ghunuram's eyes started to burn watching Rati as she sang the praises of the looks and virtues and virility of some tiger's trainer called Shambha. His forehead seemed feverish and his temples throbbed. Suddenly, he got up.

Rati was surprised. She curbed her eloquence about the tiger and Shambha and asked, 'What's the matter, Showman? Why have you got up?'

'My head's spinning terribly. I'll go and lie down for a little longer.' Giving Rati no chance to say more, Ghunuram went to his room.

Physical and mental listlessness notwithstanding, Ghunuram had to go out the next morning. He needed his three months' security as well as his clothing for the year.

So he went out completely made up as the tiger. First, he went to the locality to the south. In all the other years there would be quite a response to his mere arrival. They would all come out of their houses and a swelling crowd would follow him, all the while buzzing like bees. However, this time there was no excitement, nor was there any sign of his being surrounded as he always had been before. Nevertheless, he still went from door to door, singing his song of welcome to Lord Ganesh, loudly, so as to announce his presence.

It was not that no one came out to him, but there was no welcome in their eyes or warmth in their presence. In other years the villagers would all come running to him, offering words of appreciation and gratitude. This time, however, Ghunuram came to them, but no one came to him. He stopped his song, his face softened and he smiled, saying, 'I've come again to your village.'

People said, 'You're welcome.' But there was no sincerity in their voices.

Having called in front of three or four houses he came to the Bhaojis' place where Bhaoji's young adult son was standing in the courtyard. He said, 'We don't have to watch a fake tiger dance any more. A real tiger has come for us to see.'

Ghunuram had been coming to Nonpura for five years. He knew everyone in this village. He knew them by name, too. He looked at Bhaoji's son and said, 'Real tiger, fake tiger, what are you talking about, Jashwant!'

'You're a fake tiger,' said Jashwant. 'A tiger of straw and rags. But on North Hill there's a real tiger.'

In other words, Shambha and his leopard. Ghunuram's blood seemed suddenly to run cold.

When the sun had reached its final welcome in the western sky and Ghunuram, exhausted, came staggering home, he had in his bag a total of five rupees and twenty paisa and about one and a half seers of rice.

The next day Ghunuram went to the eastern neighbourhood, the day after to the north, and finally to the western locality. It was the same wherever he went – no one reached out a hand to him. There was only a cool and disinterested acknowledgement, but no gathering. Everyday his hopes remained unfulfilled.

Many of the villagers made it known publicly that they had no more interest in the tiger man, gratified, as they were now, by a real, live beast straight from the forest. Others said nothing, but took very readily to going to North Hill to see the leopard.

After some days Ghunuram realized that there was nothing to gain from his endeavours. It seemed as though he were blanketed by a thick and heavy shadow of fear. He had come to Nonpura to provide for himself for three months, but this time the cotton-growers had been so tight-fisted that it was unlikely that he would have enough to last him even a few weeks. All the waves of enthusiasm were now breaking on North Hill.

Having lived like a half-starved animal for nine months, Ghunuram was not to have his three months of relative comfort, and would have to find some other way of getting by. But where was the honour he got from coming to Nonpura? It seemed to him that his deserved and established reputation had been most unjustly seized from him by Shambha and his leopard. And not only had that beast of North Hill taken away his reputation and his wherewithal for the next three months, it had also rendered him utterly powerless.

Early morning, Ghunuram made himself up as the tiger and went out. After spending the whole day dancing and singing, trying to win over Nonpura village, he returned to Shibal Nayek's house towards evening. He did not see Rati on his return as she was still out at North Hill, where she had been for most of the day. Of course, she never stayed out after evening had fallen, but came straight home.

It grew late as Ghunuram took off his tiger costume and washed his black bag. It was then that Rati called him to eat. A lot was said while he was eating, but just as all rivers run to the sea, all Rati's talk ended up on the subject of the tiger. She asked him, as she did almost daily, 'Have you seen the tiger yet, Showman?'

As he was eating, a lump of food caught in his throat. He croaked faintly, 'No.'

'That's amazing! There's no one left in the village who hasn't seen it. Everyone has been going there three or four times a day, but only you don't go!' From the look on Rati's face it seemed that not going to North Hill to see a leopard was something of an offence.

Ghunuram said nothing more. With downcast eyes he occupied himself with his plate.

Rati quickly went on. 'But tomorrow you must go, Showman. Such a magnificent tiger you have never seen in your life, and never will. And then that trainer, Shambha – oh, Showman, how can I describe such a man!'

It was a strange affair. In other years Rati would take him from house to house to show him off to everyone in Nonpura village. She would regale them with various stories about what he liked to eat, when he went to sleep, how he made himself up as the tiger, and so on. Ghunuram knew that this black peacock-like daughter of Shibal Nayek, given the nod from Shibal, might one day follow him to Chanda. But given his precarious existence, along with its daily insults, Ghunuram felt that he could hardly ask her to go. The constant struggle and indignity that he had to endure, apart from his one month a year in Nonpura, made him reluctant. He could never find the courage to ask her.

But despite Ghunuram's circumstances and his lack of confidence, Rati had for so long doted on him, always ready to magnify his importance. It was hard to understand that the same Rati was now infatuated by Shambha and his leopard on North Hill.

Rati spoke up again. 'I know, you won't go on your own. So tomorrow I'll take you myself to see the tiger.'

Ghunuram said nothing. But waves of angry helplessness kept swelling up inside him. No, he had not seen Shambha and his tiger, nor did he have the slightest desire to see them!

In no time the Ganesh festival had come, and all of Nonpura's excitement and revelry had come to a head. Disappointed and downcast, Ghunuram was to go before the public, maybe for the last time. But he also had to be audacious and desperate if this time he were to make any impression. So his tiger make-up must be as near perfect as possible, he must dance and move with all his energy, and he must pour all his heart and soul into his singing. But now the people of Nonpura sat – it would seem, deliberately – with their backs to him, keeping their distance in callous contempt.

Ghunuram started to doubt that his well-known imitation tiger would be given the respect claimed by the real one, as he was unsure whether or not the people of Nonpura appreciated the difference between the actual and the imitation. And now that a real tiger had come and his distinction from it would be realized, would he be cast into the dust from his throne of dignity and honour?

A few more days passed.

Defeated and dejected, Ghunuram saw no point in making up as a tiger and going out any more. What good could come of it? So he simply sat on Shibal Nayek's veranda, his head between his hands, staring vacantly at the sky and wondering how the tiger on North Hill had been able to take all his prestige from him. He had decided that he would never go and see the tiger. He had gone everywhere in Nonpura except, this time, North Hill. He did not have any idea when the basis of his firm resolve had started to crumble, but now Ghunuram decided that he would visit the leopard.

With a strange mixture of animosity and excitement, Ghunuram spent the whole afternoon making up as the tiger, and when the sun was starting to sink in the western sky, he stepped out to North Hill.

It was the fifth day of the Ganapati Festival, and when Ghunuram reached North Hill, he saw that quite a gathering had assembled there. Given the crowd that had gathered, there could be no one left in the village. And standing right at the front of the crowd was his black peacock, Rati.

It was quite a spectacle. The crowd reached as far as the red awnings of a large canopy, under which was a large iron cage; inside it lay a leopard.

And there, standing with his hands on the cage, was an attractive young man, obviously the trainer, Shambha, from Satara. What Rati had said was not wrong; he was indeed a handsome man. His rippling muscles, his hands and feet, his thick wrists and his broad chest all signalled his power. In his mane of hair was a curved part, and he had a splendid moustache. His eyes bore a hint of arrogance.

He wore a rose-coloured shirt and short pants, and he held a slender cane in his hand. As his eyes moved slowly over the crowd, he began, 'This very powerful tiger was caught only a few months ago in the Satpura Hills. But he obeys only me. At my command he gets up, at my command he sits down, at my command he will clasp his paws in salutation. If he wanted to, he would also sing a song!'

Shambha brought gasps from the crowd as he gave his long litany of the tiger's qualities. Then suddenly he opened a door in the cage and went inside. He went up to the tiger and gave it a prod with his cane, saying, 'Get up, boy, get up! Greet the world with a dance!'

But the tiger would not get up. He blinked his eyes a few times, then went back to sleep. Shambha set about prodding and pulling; he even opened the tiger's mouth and put his hand inside it. But the tiger did not react; it just wanted more sleep.

Those at the front of the crowd were stunned, spellbound! Rati could say nothing. In her eyes there was an immense wonder. She was completely enchanted.

Ghunuram was standing right at the back of the crowd; he did not think of pushing to the front.

Shambha came out of the cage and said, 'No. If he doesn't get a little more from each of you, the fellow won't do anything. He won't greet you, and he won't dance, either.'

And then he waited. Immediately, from all around, small coins, even a rupee note, started to rain down. There were even a few small bags of rice thrown in. Amazed, Ghunuram saw before him more than ten times the amount it would take him a month to earn going around the village – all earned in a day by Shambha and his tiger.

Suddenly it occurred to Ghunuram that all those who had deceived him, insulted him and stripped him of his honour were represented by that leopard lying in the cage. It had deprived him of his status and had cast him out of the hearts of the village of Nonpura. It had even bewitched that girl who was like a black peacock. Having reached this depth of shame, Ghunuram's sense of honour was set alight. Suddenly he called out to Shambha, 'What a heroic performance – with a dead tiger!'

Picking up the money, Shambha was stunned. In a flash he straightened up and looked at Ghunuram. As he observed the tiger showman, a frown slowly came across his brow and his eyes took on an intense, taunting look. Through clenched teeth he said contemptuously, 'My tiger is dead?'

'Undoubtedly.'

'And you, I suppose, are a live tiger!'

Shambha's manner of speech had the crowd everywhere breaking into reckless laughter, but once it had died down, Ghunuram roared, 'Indeed I am a live tiger!'

Shambha thought for a moment. Then, through clenched teeth as before, he said, 'Will you put it to the test – who's alive and who's dead? Will you fight with my tiger?'

Ghunuram noticed that nobody was laughing any more. Some wild impulse shot through his very being making him believe that if he fought with this tiger, his lost honour would be restored to him. 'Of course I will fight!' Ghunuram said.

'Come on, then.' Shambha started to open the cage, saying, 'But whatever the result, don't blame me.'

'I won't.' Seemingly distracted, Ghunuram repeated his words, looking at the crowd, looking at Rati. Every heart was thumping, every breath was held. Dumbfounded, they all watched, unblinking.

Ghunuram looked at them all, as though in some wild dream, and then entered the cage. Straightaway Shambha fastened the door.

When Shambha had gone inside, the tiger blinked a few times then fell asleep. But when Ghunuram went in, it had to try to make out the strange sight of what appeared to be a wild animal. Swinging its tail across its body, it stood up. And before Ghunuram could do anything or even know what was happening a great paw came down on his neck and the next moment so did another. Immediately he felt himself sinking into a deep and dark unconsciousness.

Maybe a scream of terror went through the crowd, but Ghunuram would not have known. In his ears there was only a faint mumbling coming from afar. Even that he did not hear for long. In a moment Ghunuram lay sprawled out beaten, bloodied and unconscious.

All through his life Ghunuram had dressed and made up as the tiger man. Only this once, he had tried to be a real tiger.

the wide world

characħar

On any other day, morning would hardly have broken when Lakhindar, in keeping with long habit, would get up from his bed. Today, however, he had woken quite late, having suffered a bad bout of fever the night before. He had lain delirious throughout the night, covered from head to foot by four heavy cotton quilts; however, this had made it difficult for him to breathe, and he had slept only fitfully.

The rays of the sun came in at all angles through the countless holes in the tin roof and fell on his face, urging him to hurry out of bed. At that moment he heard a quiet, lilting sound; it was obviously Sari singing. Her voice was very sweet. But he could hear only the lovely tune and could not make out any of its words. Enchanted by Sari's song, Lakhindar remained sitting there as though he had all the time in the world. Although the sun had come up, the marshes and all the land along the canals would still be deserted, with no birds anywhere and all the crabs and field tortoises yet to be seen. Lakhindar quickly got to his feet.

For so long his earthen-floor house had been threatening that sooner or later it would collapse. Like the roof over his head, the tin walls too were falling apart. The whole house, with its rusted and worn tin and its worm-eaten posts, was in urgent need of repair. But where could Lakhindar find the money?

On one side of the room, some extra bedsheets and pillows lay tangled up on a tattered mat. Beside them was an old tin box with a floral pattern, a few very cheap, worn-out utensils, two and a half candles, some matches, a hurricane lamp, a small oil lamp, a bottle of kerosene, a phial of mustard oil, an earthen pot for rice and dal, six or seven little boxes, and some other odds and ends. There was a picture of Lakshmi, the goddess of wealth, hanging on one wall; some pictures of film stars had been pasted with similar devotion on the opposite wall. Sari had done this, as though she actually knew them all.

In another corner of the room was a pot of glue along with a few long sticks of bamboo, on the end of each of which was a decoy in the shape of a bird, cut out of palm leaf. Also for catching birds were a few nets with long wooden handles.

Lakhindar had no worldly wealth at all apart from this tumbledown shack and the meagre belongings inside it. A long time ago he had had some agricultural land, but that had gone into the stomach of the moneylender to pay back a loan taken to keep Lakhindar's father alive.

Lakhindar picked up the glue pot, the nets and the other things and went outside. In a corner of the veranda Sari sat leaning over a plate, picking through the grains of rice, humming all the while.

Lakhindar no longer thought of Sari's age. Nevertheless, after eight or ten years of marriage without children, her body was still in exceptionally fine shape. Her mouth was round with full, moist lips. Her complexion was dark, and she had an overall lustre like that of a shiny black chilli, her soft skin emanating a wondrous glow. Just to look at her would be enough to excite lust in a man and set his blood racing.

Lakhindar was the opposite of her. Once he had been broad and tall, but now he had become like a string of rubble, having wasted away considerably under the depredations of a variety of illnesses. He watched Sari with a look of easy indifference, putting down his nets and things and marvelling vaguely at how her childlessness and her abundant joy in song had preserved her so well.

Sari had by now finished her bath, and her hair, still wet, was spread out over her back. She was wearing a fresh, coloured sari laundered in washing soda. Sometimes, despite his indifference, she seemed to Lakhindar like a lady of class when she wore such fine clothes, although he had never bought her any expensive saris like the one she wore. There were also days when her body gave off a beautiful aroma, as though she had applied perfume to it.

Lakhindar could guess, generally, who gave her all these nice clothes and things. But when did he have the time to worry himself over that? He spent the whole day, twelve months of the year, in the wetlands just for the sake of survival.

'Is there any flattened rice?' Lakhindar asked.

Sari had looked around earlier at the sound of Lakhindar's footsteps. Looking at his face, she got up immediately. 'No, there isn't. Do you think we keep a never-ending stock of all these things?'

Gently, Lakhindar said, 'If there isn't any, it doesn't matter. Is there any leftover rice in the pot, then?'

Sari did not answer.

Lakhindar took that to mean 'yes'. 'Put some on a plate for me. I'll be back after I've washed my face.' And he left the veranda and went down into the yard.

Beyond the yard there was an open space, then a narrow canal full of water hyacinths, and over the canal was a bamboo bridge. On the other side of the bridge were scattered twenty or more poor, ramshackle houses like Lakhindar's. It was a village of extraordinarily poor people, none of whom owned even the smallest patch of paddy field. As in the past, they worked as seasonal labourers in the fields of others, and for the rest of the year they would have to eke out a living in whatever way they could.

Adjoining the village was a huge bamboo grove, some weedy underbrush, and a jungle of various unproductive trees, with here and there a few very tall palmyras and arecas.

'You were feverish and restless the whole night,' Sari called after him. 'So don't blame me if you eat rice and your temperature goes up again.'

Lakhindar said nothing. He wondered if the fever would come back if he had something to eat. He was now extremely weak and, in fact, unless he ate something, he would not have the strength to go after the birds near the canals and in the marshes. And if he did not catch any birds, how would the two of them survive?

Pushing aside the water hyacinths, Lakhindar washed his face in the canal, rinsed his mouth out, and went back. In the meantime, Sari had dished up some leftover rice and vegetables on a plate, kept a small jug of water beside it and put it on the veranda.

Maybe it was because of the fever that his appetite had increased, for Lakhindar quickly devoured the cold, hard rice. After he had again rinsed out his mouth, he put his bird-catching tackle together and said, 'Will you bring me my sweater?' Although the month of Magh had come to an end, the north wind still blew in gusts across the marshes and canals and the cold kept on rising up from the millions of holes in the earth. And in the mornings and the evenings, a thick fog blanketed the landscape.

Sari brought a moth-eaten woollen sweater from inside, put it down beside Lakhindar and went back to picking through the grains of rice. Lakhindar took up his tackle and went outside. Bhushan had arrived now. He too lived in the village, somewhere to the south on the other side of the bridge. Like Lakhindar, Bhushan spent his time these days hunting birds along the canals and in the marshes. He too was carrying some bird traps and nets.

Bhushan was around sixty. His greying hair stuck up, and there were tufts of whiskers on his cheeks. He had dull eyes, and the bones stuck out through his lanky, emaciated body. He wore a dirty, patched lungi and a loose cotton waistcoat. Over that he had a cotton shawl wrapped around himself. He was a weather-beaten and battle-scarred man like Lakhindar.

'I saw from some way off that you'd not gone out yet,' said Bhushan, 'so I came by. Are you going to the marshlands, then?'

'Yes.' Stooping slightly, Lakhindar came down from the veranda. 'Let's go,' he said.

Lakhindar had no answer to this question. From dawn to dusk he was rushing about, puffing and panting, in the fields and the marshes and by the canals, all for the sake of survival. And yet the birds and crabs and field tortoises that he caught, and whatever fallen grains he might glean, were never sufficient. There were so many other things needed in the house too, like oil and salt and spices and kerosene, all of which Sari had to get from the market a few miles away. Lakhindar suspected that it was there that Sari met Natabar. But one could not blame Natabar entirely, as Bhushan would. Lakhindar could see through Sari. He had never known a girl as scandalous as she. Who could say that she did not thrust herself at Natabar? And where did Lakhindar, chasing after birds the whole day, get the time to worry about such things? Anyway, who could prevent her waywardness?

Lakhindar said, 'I don't know how they met. And I'm not going to get myself worked up over it.'

Past the village limits an unmade road ran straight from north to south, on the other side of which was marshland. Now that it was the end of winter, it was completely bare wherever one looked, but just a few months back, before the harvest, the land had been covered with golden paddy.

Lakhindar and Bhushan crossed the road and went down into the field on the other side. Here most of the land would bear only one crop, the autumn rice. Of course, some sesame, pigeon-peas and mustard seed were sown here and there, but not enough to cover the vast emptiness of fallow fields.

The sun had now risen high above the horizon. There was virtually no one in the marshland; indeed, there were no more than two or three rustics to be seen anywhere in this vast emptiness. The sky was a brilliant blue and there was not a wisp of cloud or mist anywhere. There had been fog early in the morning, but that had lifted as the sun had risen higher. Very high up the white-breasted kites, their wings spread wide, floated on the breeze. Now and then they would swoop towards the horizon, then a mass of brilliant white breasts would sweep up overhead again. Below, bathed in the comforting sunshine of the end of winter, a golden iguana was wriggling lazily over the embankment and some field mice were scratching at the earth.

Since coming down into the field, Bhushan had forgotten about the business of Sari, and the anger and agitation of a little while ago had gone from his face. He walked on spiritedly, looking intensely all about him. Lakhindar too had his eyes cast over the marshland. Now, with winter coming to an end, small field tortoises came out seemingly from nowhere. A few of them might bring eight or ten rupees at the market.

At one time Lakhindar had been a very strong young man, with the energy of a wild buffalo and an indomitable courage in his heart. In those days, he could drive two bullocks on his own and plough eight or ten bighas of the Janas' or Maitis' land. But then about five years back he contracted some respiratory disease and suffered shortness of breath. His consequent weakness made it impossible for him to do any hard labouring work. Whereas the big landowners had once called on him for all their major labouring, after his illness no one would even look at him. Who would want someone who could not cultivate three kathas in a season? Lying about his health, Lakhindar would beg for work day after day at the doors of the Maitis and Janas, but no one had any interest in him. The man who once could plough the marshland so thoroughly each season had been completely forgotten by the big landowners.

But in work or out of it, he still had to survive. Constantly thinking of how to put something in his and Sari's stomachs, Lakhindar kept his eyes open in the marshlands, along the canals and in the boundless fields. There was still so much in the wide world that Jana or Maiti had not been able to possess: in the canals there were countless fish, crabs and tortoises, and in the jungles alongside of them there were sweet potatoes, beehives, wild bananas, yams, custard-apples and other fruits. Furthermore, all year – and especially in winter – a thousand varieties of birds would come. If he could catch four or five birds a day, that would somehow be enough for two stomachs. So the fields and canals and marshlands all around could, indeed, sustain Lakhindar and Sari.

Having caught his birds, he would go to a small town some three miles off where he would sell them to Mr Shashmal. Shashmal would not turn back anything – pigeons, blackbirds, parrots, kingfishers, come what may – and he would pay cash in return. It was not a credit business. Lakhindar had never concerned himself with how Shashmal sold so many different kinds of birds. He was satisfied just to get his money for what he had caught. The problem of filling two stomachs was the only thing in all the world he ever had the time to worry about.

In his dealings with him over a long time, Lakhindar had learned that Shashmal did not buy birds only from him, but that three or four others in the region also kept him supplied, and for all these birds he had a market in Calcutta at eight or ten times the price. In other words, he got eight to ten rupees for every one rupee he paid Lakhindar. That was something that had always bothered Lakhindar. For a long time he had thought that if he could go to Calcutta, then he would get a good price for himself. He had been there once or twice before; perhaps he would go again. But in such a vast city, how could he find someone who would pay him as well as Shashmal was paid? And so he had gone on through the years bringing the birds he caught to Mr Shashmal.

At first, he wandered around the canals and marshes looking for birds on his own, but then he found himself a partner in Bhushan. In no way did Lakhindar begrudge Bhushan's working the marshes and canals with him. Here in this vast realm of nature there was more than enough to feed twenty-five Bhushans. Like him, Bhushan also once had a body made of iron and could reap the landlord's fields as fast as the wind. But after a while his health broke down too, and from time to time he coughed up blood. A man in this condition was not worth a penny to the Janas and Maitis. Like Lakhindar, he too was rejected.

As they walked across the embankment they caught a field

tortoise. Along with the bird-catching equipment they carried a gunny sack, and they put the tortoise into it and went on their way. As they walked, each kept a hawk-like eye out, just in case they should get another one or two tortoises.

From time to time Lakhindar would look up and cast his eye over the sky, and Bhushan, seeing him do this, would do so too. Their purpose was to check on the movement of birds, but at that moment there was nothing in the sky except a flock of white-breasted kites. As they crossed a bare field and came to the canal, Bhushan said, 'It looks like today's not our day, Lakha. Nothing but one tortoise.'

Lakhindar stretched out his foot to the water. He did not have to see, but could tell by the smell on the breeze where a flock of wild geese had landed or where a group of parrots or wild doves might be sitting in the top of some tree. Preoccupied with looking about here and there, he said, simply, 'Yes.'

Bhushan went on, 'We've trudged through so many fields, my legs are ready to break. Let's have a rest now and a smoke,' he said, sitting down on the grass. From the knot in the waist of his dhoti he took out a small, round, rusty tin box, out of which he took a half-smoked bidi, saying, 'Take this. Have a smoke.' Lakhindar seemed not to have heard Bhushan. 'Hey!' Bhushan said, going over to Lakhindar and clicking his tongue, sounding like a wild parrot.

The marsh was about two miles long, and very wide. Most of the jungle thereabouts was quite sparse, with a few thickets, but to the south it was very dense with many different kinds of trees entwined by thick wild creepers. From the distance, Lakhindar could see a number of wild parrots sitting atop a luxuriant sissoo tree to the southeast of the marsh. Making a chirping sound, he hurried there, careful that his feet made no sound at all.

Lakhindar could imitate bird calls exceptionally well. It was something he had developed to an art form, and if one did not see him it was easy to believe that one was hearing a genuine dove, parrot or pigeon. Making bird calls was not a matter of pleasure for

Lakhindar, he did it purely to trick the bird into coming into his net. And yet only five years ago Lakhindar could not make a single bird call. So many different things he had had to learn for his livelihood!

Apart from the many wild parrots on the top of the sissoo tree, there were at that time of day no other birds near the canal, so Lakhindar simply had to catch at least three or four parrots, otherwise the two-and-a-half-mile walk across the marsh would have been in vain. Lakhindar moved close to the sissoo tree, making his chirping sound, and very circumspectly laid out his net a little way behind a bush. Then he went on making his call, varying the melody now and then.

Up in the tree the birds started to become restive at Lakhindar's call. From time to time they leaned forward as though trying to understand it. They fluttered their wings and moved further forward, a little at a time. Then, still more curiously, the parrots suddenly came flying down, and Lakhindar went on beckoning them as he warbled his song.

But just as the birds were about to hop into the net, Bhushan called out, 'Hey, Lakha! Where've you gone?' He had finished smoking his bidi and was coming from his rest on the other side of the canal.

Startled at the sound of his voice, the parrots flew off in all directions.

Lakhindar came out from behind his bush and sadly watched the birds flying away. All his plans had come to nothing. As the birds flew off, hidden now by the ample foliage, Lakhindar turned to Bhushan and said coldly, yet in no way accusingly, 'You've frightened the parrots away.'

Bhushan had had no idea. But seeing the net spread out and the birds flying away, he realized what he had done and was filled with remorse. 'I've caused you a great loss, Lakha,' he said. 'If only I'd seen the net a little earlier … '

Lakhindar did not answer, but went on folding up the net.

Bhushan spoke up again. 'If only four or five parrots had got into the net, that would have fetched a bit of money. What a bloody goat I am!'

Lakhindar knew that Bhushan's regret was genuine. He said, 'There's nothing we can do now. What's done is done. Today's just not our day.' He paused for a moment, then said, 'Come on, let's go into the jungle. We might find something there.'

There was no hope of finding any more birds that day, so the two of them went into the jungle. As the day started to decline and the sun's yellow became burnished, they came out with a collection of sweet potatoes, yams and a large ground potato after a lot of rummaging around in the undergrowth. This canal and jungle, as well as the field behind it, never turned them away empty-handed.

'Are you going home, then?' asked Bhushan.

'Yes.' Lakhindar slowly bowed his head.

They had left the canal behind them, crossed the winter fallow field, and were just coming up onto the dirt road that ran beside the village when they met up with Natabar once again. He was coming out of the village. Lakhindar had no trouble in working out where he had spent all his time since morning. Earlier that day, Natabar had had a few words to share with them, but now he said nothing, walking quickly by them with long strides up onto the dirt road and off to the west. The two men stood and watched him go.

Bhushan's eyes were blazing. Grinding his teeth, he said, 'That bastard son of a dog!'

Lakhindar did not respond. Calmly, he watched Natabar. When he had passed out of sight around the bend in the road, Lakhindar sighed and said, 'It's getting late. Let's go.'

They came down off the road into the village, and Bhushan repeated what he had said that morning. 'Mind your house, Lakha.'

Lakhindar did not answer.

Bhushan's house was close to the road, and he left Lakhindar after offering some more wise counsel and urgent advice about Sari and Natabar.

When he got home, Lakhindar saw Sari sitting on the veranda, a mirror in her hand and humming a tune, just as she had been that morning. It was a tune that could come only from one whose heart was light with joy. Lakhindar looked at his wife for a moment. Then he put down the wild vegetables on the veranda and took the bird-catching equipment inside.

Day after day, year after year, for so long Lakhindar's daily habits had been exactly the same. He would get up at daybreak, eat some leftover rice and hurry off to the fields and the marshes; whatever birds he caught he would take to sell to Shashmal, then return home at night. And so his days passed, set in this routine.

At the beginning of the month of Phalgun, Lakhindar returned home one evening to find that Sari was not there. He looked everywhere, but she was not to be found. Lakhindar became anxious, for he could not remember ever coming home at night and Sari not being there. Where could she have gone?

After his search he sat down on the veranda in the dark and thought for a while. Then he got up, went over the bridge and into the village to see if anyone had any news of her. After going to three or four houses, he found out that Sari had gone off with Natabar at midday.

The people of the village placed the blame for Sari's leaving squarely on Lakhindar. Why had he not been more cautious earlier? Why had the woman of his house been allowed to meet another man? Why did he continue to keep quiet even when he knew that Natabar was entering his house like a thief in the night? Why had he not given the bastard a good thrashing and driven him away? And so it went on.

Lakhindar's head was spinning with all their condemnation, and he went home and went to bed. He could not sleep the whole night. He tried to understand them all, but why should he have been angry at what Sari had wanted to do? If a woman has a mind to be wayward, who can stop her?

Then Lakhindar realized that his pillow was wet with tears.

He did not leave the house for two days after Sari had left. Bhushan would come and call for him, and then go away.

After two days Lakhindar again went out to the fields and the marshes with his bird-catching tackle. Lying at home for the sake of a heartless, wanton girl could do no good for his stomach. And, just as before, Bhushan was his companion.

With profound feeling in his voice, Bhushan said, 'The girl's made a real mess of you, Lakha.'

Lakhindar did not answer. He kept his hawk-like eye on the fields and the sky, his mind only on the birds in the air and the tortoises on the ground.

Bhushan said, 'How will you spend the rest of your life, then, Lakha?'

Without turning to Bhushan, Lakhindar said gently, 'We have the fields and the marshes and the sky, we have the birds and the tortoises and the fish. We have but one life. We must live it well.'

And then he raised his voice and called out, 'Hey! Ho, hey!' and, still calling, he ran along the embankment towards the marsh, raising his hand to the sky.

A flock of wild parrots was piercing the wind, flying in the same direction.

father and son
janmadata

The month of Agrahayan had just begun. By now the strong north wind was gusting everywhere like an unbridled mad horse and was as keen as the blade of a knife. This year the winter promised to be harsh.

It was midday and the sun was directly overhead, but there was neither warmth nor brilliance in its rays. Everywhere the timid sunshine held back from the dull and colourless day.

Let us look towards the ghat on the silted up river, some three miles from a small subdistrict town. Up above it was a terrace, on either side of which were seats permanently fixed for pilgrims who had come to bathe, although the cement bench on one side had collapsed a long time ago. There was still another bench, of course, with countless cracks in which the thriving families of a few generations of snakes dwelt in perfect peace. A total of eighteen steps led down from the terrace. All of them were broken, with the insides showing where the plaster had come away. The still water of the silted river came up to the foot of the bottom step.

Ninety years ago a certain Yajnanath Kundu had had the ghat built as a public service, perhaps to find favour with God, or simply to preserve his name. Indeed, in the middle of the terrace there was a white marble slab that indistinctly bore his name and the year that the ghat had been built. Now only half of it could be read, and it would not be long before people's feet had completely wiped Yajnanath from the face of the earth, his immortality having lasted not even a century.

On the terrace's one surviving bench sat Bishtupada, his chin resting on his knees, and in the cracks around him were a few dozen poisonous snakes, to which he bore no enmity. Bishtupada was about fifty. He had rough matted hair hanging down to his shoulders and tufts of whiskers all over his face. His skin was the colour of burnt copper and was dry and flaky. Big bones supported his tall and firm body, and his face was long and rough with numerous scars on his forehead and cheeks, as there were on his hands and thighs. He had heavy shadows under his eyes, and his jawbones seemed to push out through his skin. In all he was the embodiment of a reckless life; just a glimpse of him was enough to show that he was not a simple man. He sat staring ahead, an air of distraction about him.

For many years a sandbank had emerged right in the middle of the shallow, muddy river, and its sand shone in the dying Agrahayan sunlight. Three or four boats laden with hay and a flock of common cranes at one end of the sandbank was all that could be seen from one side of the river to the other. For some distance along the opposite bank, the chimneys of brick kilns puffing out their polluting smoke, rose up out of the indistinct line of trees and bushes.

About fifty yards to the right of Bishtupada was the region's old cremation ground. There was a huge banyan tree there, the roots of which had probably been buried deep in the ground since the dawn of history. Beneath it was Bhaga Dom's twisted and tumbledown hut with its tiled roof. It was now shut and the chain was on the door; goodness only knew where Bhaga had gone. Vultures were flying around the top of the banyan tree, and now and again their harsh, piercing cry would cut the air like a saw. This was the only sound to penetrate the profound, pervasive silence.

Neither Bhaga nor Bishtupada knew how many years the one had tended the cremation ground and the other had occupied Yajnanath Kundu's ghat. Bhaga's constant companions were a few hundred vultures, and Bishtupada's were dozens of snakes, creatures with whom both had had a long affinity.

Behind the ghat was an unsealed road which ran through vast stony fields towards the town. But here Bishtupada was the only representative of the human race amid the immense solitude of the still waters of the silted river, the sandbank, the cranes and the vultures and the snakes, the big cremation ground and the open fields. At that moment no one but he – and Bhaga – belonged in all of this.

He may not have shown it, but Bishtupada was extremely worried. For a long time his chest had felt as though someone were attacking his ribs with a crowbar. Although the air was pure on that desolate bank of the river, Bishtupada breathed with difficulty. There were two reasons for his distress and anxiety. One was that no corpse had been brought to the cremation ground for some days. It seemed so long ago that the noted traditional physician of the town, Aghor Chakravarty, had been cremated, even though it had actually been only three days, and since then not a pyre had been lit.

His and Bhaga's survival depended on the lighting of the funeral pyres. Bhaga was paid for burning corpses, and after the cremation the sons of the dead would come to the ghat and make offerings to the departed soul, and Bishtupada would be paid in cash for preparing the sacrifice. He would also get some rice; he was not really entitled to it, but he had a private arrangement with the priest. Anyone who wanted to make obeisance to their dead mother or father would come to the ghat. Then five or ten rupees would be collected, as well as rice, dal, fruit and vegetables. There was also something to be earned from the death anniversaries of forebears. However, all such post-funerary rituals had now become rare at the ghat.

Bishtupada had once done well out of it all, with three or four offerings a day and the occasional shraddha ceremony or anniversary, but for about six months the number of deaths in this region had dramatically decreased. Whereas three or four corpses were once being brought to the cremation ground in a day, now the pyres were not even being lit. This was the first time that for three days in a row not a body had been brought there.

But how could Bishtupada survive without people dying? Any increase in the longevity of others meant a decrease in his own. There were four stomachs dependent on his earnings – his own and those of Amodini and their two children. He had to work himself unstintingly to feed and clothe them, and now three days had passed without a corpse. For the last couple of days Bishtupada had been worried sick about all of this. And on top of it all, a little while back someone had brought the news that three days ago his own father had died.

At first, the report of his father's death had not sunk in. He did not even recognize Dhananjay, the man who had brought the news, though he was related to him in some way or other through his father. Bishtupada had only a vague recollection of this man who had come one hundred and fifty miles from a small town in Bardhaman district to tell him of his father's death, and he could not remember even thinking about his own father for the last fifteen or twenty years. Even if his father should at that moment emerge out of the earth and stand in front of him, it was doubtful that he would recognize him.

Old Dhananjay, sickly and short of breath, had had nothing at all to gain in covering the one hundred and fifty miles by train, bus, cycle rickshaw and on foot to seek Bishtupada at the ghat on this silted up river and give him the sad news. His only wish was that Bishtupada should get a share of his father's estate, and as he was leaving he advised Bishtupada that he should go home as soon as possible and have his say in determining the details of the matter of inheritance. Should he delay, everything would go into the stomachs of his brothers and there would be nothing for him to do but slap his forehead in remorse.

He appreciated Dhananjay's selfless altruism, but at first suspected that there might be some subtle stratagem concealed in it. Maybe he sought the discomfiture of Bishtupada's brothers. Bishtupada remembered that Dhananjay was an exceptionally wily fellow, but really he could not for a moment believe that this scheming uncle would have come all this way on some ulterior motive.

Bishtupada hardly reacted at all to being told of his father's death. In this world people are dying all the time and this death was just like theirs – one which had not the slightest meaning for him. He could not feel genuinely upset or perturbed by this information as it was now utterly irrelevant to him. He received Dhananjay's news with exactly the same indifference with which he would have received the news of the death of someone he had known a very long time ago.

Bishtupada had completely wiped away his past in coming to this place many years earlier, after which he had never looked back. He was totally preoccupied day and night worrying about providing for four stomachs.

Dhananjay had left a short time earlier, having delivered a great deal of moral advice and wise counsel. After that it was not the thought of his father's death that bothered Bishtupada but that of Aghor Chakravarty. The physician had died three days earlier, and today his sons ought to perform the fourth day's offering. The day was getting on, yet no one had come to the ghat. If the Chakravarty sons should perform the offering beside some pond near their home, then he would have no hope of getting ten or twelve rupees and a kilogram or so of rice. At present there was not a penny or a grain of rice in his house, so if he took nothing home from the ghat the oven would not be lit. Through all his anxiety, he continued to have great faith in the Chakravarty family priest, Nibaran Bhattacharya, who had been exceptionally kind to him ever since they had first met. Surely Nibaran would do everything to get the sons of the physician to come to the ghat at the river, provided there was nothing else in the way.

Under the weight of all these worries Bishtupada could not put his finger on the source of his distraction. The disinterest with which he had received the news of his father's death from Dhananjay was starting to be eclipsed by a slight feeling of inner discomfort. He had left his father twenty-five years ago, severing all relations, and he had but a dim memory of the man's face, so he could not imagine why he should feel at all uneasy about him. Yet, on the lonely bank of the river in the Agrahayan midday stillness, in the midst of a vast emptiness, Bishtupada found himself breathing with difficulty.

'Bishte! Hey, Bishte! Are you there?' A familiar voice suddenly came from some way off, and with it a bolt shot through Bishtupada's nerves and sinews. He swung around immediately and saw four cycle rickshaws that had just pulled up one behind the other on the road that ran beside the ghat.

Nibaran Bhattacharya got down from the leading rickshaw; then, one by one, the sons of Aghor Chakravarty along with two of their middle-aged relatives alighted from the rickshaws behind. Bishtupada recognized them all; like him they were all residents of the subdistrict town about three miles away, and in a small town everyone knew everyone else.

Bishtupada quickly ran up to the rickshaws.

Nibaran Bhattacharya was about seventy; because of his age his enervated body was bent and he looked like a hunchback. On the end of his nose, which was like a parrot's beak, was a pair of nickel-framed bifocal spectacles. His skin had once been bright and shiny, but was now shrivelled by the sun and crisscrossed with wrinkles. His cheeks were sunken and all his hair had turned grey. There was a flower in the thick braid at the back of his head. He wore a grubby cotton dhoti and, around his upper body, a long cotton shawl, his gleaming white sacred thread showing through its hole; on his feet were wooden sandals. Such was his dress all the year round. He was one of the last representatives of that quickly disappearing class of dedicated family priests.

Aghor Chakravarty's three sons ranged in age from forty to fifty, all of them worthy of their father's name. The eldest would have been much the same age as Bishtupada and taught at the college in the town. The middle son was a magistrate, and the youngest also had an important government job. They all bore the look of comfortable gentility and were dressed in the obligatory new white dhotis and cotton shawls, each with a blanket to sit on tucked into his waist.

Nibaran hurriedly told Bishtupada, 'Bring all the things down, Bishte, and quickly set out the elements of the food offering.'

In one of the rickshaws there were three or four big cloth bags crammed full of various things: top-grade Govindabhog rice, sesame seeds, bananas, honey, ghee, yoghurt, a brass can of pure milk, flowers, fruit, sacred grass, Ganges water and a packet of sweets.

Bishtupada strode down to the ghat carrying the bags with Nibaran beside him. Aghor Chakravarty's sons and the two relatives followed a little way behind.

'It's well past midday,' Bishtupada said. 'I was starting to think that you would probably not be coming. That maybe you'd do the ceremony somewhere over there.'

Keeping his voice down, Nibaran said, 'There'll be something in it for you, so how could I not come? We've come so late because they took so much time in all the preparations.'

Bishtupada said nothing.

Nibaran went on. 'Aghor the physician was a very wealthy man – do you know that?'

'I know.' Bishtupada inclined his head.

'His sons too have very good jobs. They make a lot of money. I bought for them two and a half kilograms of Govindabhog rice, two dozen bananas, and lots of ghee, honey, milk and yoghurt.' Nibaran winked and said, 'The offering ceremony doesn't require all this, but you understand why I bought so much, don't you?'

Bishtupada said nothing, but gave Nibaran a look of immense gratitude. Nibaran held no expectations of Bishtupada; the two of them led quite different lives, but the one was always ready with unsolicited help for the other. Without Nibaran's favours, Bishtupada and his family would probably die of hunger.

Nibaran said, 'I told them they would have to pay you twenty-five rupees.'

No one had ever given Bishtupada that much money. Doubtfully, he asked, 'Will they pay it?'

'Of course they will! They've got so much money. Would they want to be accused of stinting on their father's offering ceremony?' Whispering all the while, Nibaran went on, 'I explained to them that for the repose of their father's soul they would have to gratify everybody. Those sons are so big-hearted, they agreed straightaway. How could we survive without their generosity?'

It was taken for granted that as well as providing for Bishtupada, Nibaran would have negotiated a satisfactory fee for himself.

As they came down onto the ghat, Nibaran said, 'Hurry and get the altar ready. We don't want to delay any longer. There's still that three-mile haul back home.'

Spurred into action, Bishtupada put the heavy bags down on the terrace and said, 'I'll do it right now.' It seemed that his hands and feet were electrified. He kept a broom, some bits of sackcloth and an old plastic bucket permanently in one corner of the ghat. With extraordinary efficiency he swept the terrace clean, then filled the bucket with water from the river and brought up a big lump of mud in one hand. After washing the terrace, he wiped it sparkling clean with sackcloth. Then, with the lump of mud, he made a perfect little altar, eighteen inches long, eighteen inches wide, and six inches thick. Bishtupada took no more than fifteen minutes to do all this, so practised was he in the technique of preparing an altar that he could have done it with his eyes closed.

Aghor Chakravarty's three sons and the two middle-aged relatives were standing to one side. Once the altar had been prepared, Nibaran told the three sons to go and bathe, and they went on down the steps. Nibaran set out a place for them to sit, then took out from the bag the bundle of banana leaves, the lamp, rice, sesame seeds, flowers, the bunch of bananas, sweets, sacred grass, water container, and so on, and set them all in place. Then he said, 'Light the lamp, Bishte.'

Bishtupada poured some oil into the gleaming, five-sided lamp, twisted the cotton wick and lit it. Then, noticing the two brass jars that the sons of Aghor had brought, Nibaran told Bishtupada to fill them with water and then wash the banana leaves. Without a word, Bishtupada went down to the river with the water containers and his bucket and came back almost immediately to set about washing the bananas and their leaves, which he set to one side.

Nibaran was now making himself busy. Having folded his gamchha eight times and covered his head with it, he set in place the copper containers, twisted some of the sacred grass into rings, and arranged the flowers in bunches. Then he took up the bottle of Ganges water, opened it and poured some of the water into the palm of his hand, which he sprinkled over all the elements of the ritual, quietly mumbling the mantra, 'Make sacred that which is unholy ...'

The flame of the lamp was spluttering in the gusty north wind. Nibaran signalled to Bishtupada to place it up against the cement bench where it would be sheltered from the force of the breeze.

Having bathed, Aghor Chakravarty's sons came back. The eldest, Abhijit, was the executant of the offertory ritual and was obliged to perform his tasks in wet clothes. Nibaran said to him, 'Be seated, my son.'

Abhijit spread his blanket and sat on it facing south. The other two sons, Manojit and Surajit, may have put on dry clothes had they wished, but they chose to sit in wet clothes beside their brother. The two middle-aged relatives sat a little way apart from them.

As nothing remained for Bishtupada to do now, he went and sat in silence on a step below the terrace, his eyes fixed on Nibaran. He could not reckon the number of times over the years that he had had to prepare for offertories and other rituals at this ghat by the river. He had never been at all moved by any of them. Apart from the collection of a few rupees, some fruit and some rice, he had not the slightest interest in these rituals; he was merely a totally indifferent observer.

Nibaran poured out the entire two and a half kilograms of Govindabhog rice, over which he then dropped some of the honey, ghee, yoghurt, milk and sesame seeds. What was left remained in their containers. He peeled a dozen of the bananas and, putting them to one side, said to Abhijit, 'Mix it all thoroughly, my son, and roll it into balls.' He did not touch the remaining twelve bananas, which were left unpeeled.

After all the ingredients had been rolled into balls, Nibaran said, 'Wash your hands.'

Manojit poured water from a container onto his brother's hands.

Following Nibaran's instructions, Abhijit made holes with his fingers in the mud altar. Then he washed his hands again and took up in his fingers some of the sacred grass.

A short while ago when Bishtupada was somewhat mechanically preparing this offertory ceremony for Aghor Chakravarty, he had not given a thought for his own father's death, but now his former discomfort and dejection had returned.

Bishtupada would get all of the two and a half kilograms of sweet-smelling, sun-dried rice that Abhijit had rolled into balls. He would have to wash the ghee and bananas and sesame seeds and so on from the rice. He would be completely free from worry about four stomachs for at least three days. In the meantime maybe one or two corpses would be brought to the cremation ground. Surely they would! Humans were not yet immortal. Then after three days, someone or other would come to the ghat to perform an offertory or some other kind of ritual. Such was the way of the world.

Yet Bishtupada was not thinking about any of this as he sat on the step of the ghat, his eyes fixed on Abhijit. He had heard that Abhijit was very learned; he was no longer young, and much of his hair had turned grey. Yet despite knowing that death is inevitable and that parents are not immortal, this learned and accomplished man was so distressed with grief for his father that tears flowed from his eyes.

Nibaran Bhattacharya went on and on, chanting the mantras in his melodious voice:

To this food of the gods we bow, to this food of the gods we bow.
Here is the first rice offering to the soul of
Aghor Chakraborty Deva Sharmanah
Of the ancestral line of Shandilya.

In a deep and trembling voice Abhijit said with Nibaran:

To this food of the gods we bow, to this food of the gods we bow.
Here is the first rice offering to the soul of
Aghor Chakravarty Deva Sharmanah
Of the ancestral line of Shandilya.

The continual recitation of the mantras was all that could be heard between the vast fields on one side and the silted up river on the other, and the sound was carried on the breeze over the deserted cremation ground towards the horizon. The stillness of the Agrahayan afternoon gradually became heavy with grief.

As he went on watching Abhijit and his brothers, Bishtupada's chest felt as if it were shattering as a blurred picture of his father appeared from the dim depths of memory, as though on some imaginary cinema screen.

Twenty-five years earlier, Bishtupada had been a disgrace to his family in every respect. Such a wilful fellow had never been known. Even though he was the son of a good family, he indulged excessively in drink and bhang and always seemed to have his eyes set on some kind of mischief. There was no reckoning the trouble and scandals he had given rise to involving women, and so he was a constant cause of worry. But when Bishtupada announced that he was going to marry Amodini, a prostitute, his father threw him out of the house by the scruff of the neck, telling him that he was disinherited and that all relations between them would be cut off. Bishtupada was exceptionally obdurate: despite his father's threats he would not give Amodini up. He left Bardhaman with her, and they wandered from place to place, eventually settling in this subdistrict town and producing two children.

Amodini was a very fiery woman, quite capable of subduing such a turbulent man as Bishtupada, and she had tamed him to become a responsible family man. Apart from that, of course, his spirits had also started to ebb as he had got older.

Now, the faces of everyone at their home in Bardhaman twenty-five years ago came back to Bishtupada – his father, mother, brothers and sisters and other relatives. His father's face, especially, gradually loomed large before him as though it would cover the whole world. Indeed, it seemed that his time in Bardhaman had not been in this life but in some previous existence thousands of years before, and that he was watching scenes from it as one who remembers details of previous incarnations.

He went on listening to the indistinct recitation of the mantras.

> *You who are consigned to the flames of the fire, abandoned by your friends, bathe in this water, drink this milk, and be happy.*
>
> *You whose abode is the sky, left without a shelter, reduced to thin air, bathe in this water and be happy ...*

And while watching Abhijit and the others through misty eyes, Bishtupada was suddenly hit with the realization that his own father had died three days ago. As the eldest son, like Abhijit, he too would have been the executant in the post-funerary rituals. Given that he had been cut off, the next elder brother would be performing the offertory rites today.

Bishtupada's breathing grew laboured. He could not remember how many times he had even thought of his father in the twenty-five years before learning of his death. He could recall all that turmoil when he left home, severing all ties. However, as long as he watched Abhijit and heard Nibaran's mantras, the more the unlikelihood seemed true, that somewhere inside of him there was a kind of ineradicable root from which he had come.

Nibaran went on with his recitation of the mantras, and Abhijit echoed him.

> *Bathe in this water, drink this milk and be happy.*

After so many years of listening to them, Bishtupada knew all of these verses almost by heart. He could have performed any of the rituals without any difficulty at all.

The Agrahayan sun had passed its high point and was now leaning a little towards the western sky. The north wind had got stronger. The shrill cries of the vultures on the top of the old banyan tree in the distant cremation ground sounded their growing restlessness for corpses.

Abhijit was still sitting on his blanket, having now completed the offertory. Still standing, Nibaran said, 'Now bring the remaining offering on a banana leaf and come with me. We must make an offering to the crows.'

Bishtupada was still sitting as before on a step below the terrace, preoccupied with watching Abhijit as he followed Nibaran with the offering and stood under a Krishnachura tree on the other side of the terrace. Surajit and Manojit went with them. The two relatives remained seated on the terrace.

Following Nibaran's instructions, Abhijit set down the banana leaf with the offering and stood with his hands together, then recited a mantra with him.

> *This goes to the crows from all directions who live on the threshold of Yama, the God of Death, for the satisfaction of the soul of Aghor Chakravarty Dev Sharmanah of the ancestral line of Shandilya, to whom I bow ...*

After the recitation, Abhijit lifted up the offering and dedicated it to the crows:

> *I bow to the crow, his ancestors, the great souls that they represent.*

The dedication was finished, and Nibaran said, 'Come, let us stand away. Otherwise the crows will not take it up.' They walked a little way away, and three or four jet black birds swooped down and started to peck at the offering. Then Nibaran said, 'The crows now have their feast. Now you must consign to the river the food that is still on the terrace and bathe once more. Then your duty will be done. Come.'

They returned to the terrace. Abhijit took the food that had been rolled into balls, the flowers and the grass and all the rest on a banana leaf and went down the broken steps. His two brothers and Nibaran went with him.

As they came to the bottom step, Nibaran said, 'Put it all down together in the water, just here.' He indicated the place with his finger.

This too was an important part of the offertory procedure, and Abhijit laid the offerings very carefully in about six inches of water, although he did not know that there was a design in this. Should he put them out any further the rice balls would break up and blend with the water and the mud, and hardly any of it could be retrieved. But if laid down gently close to the bank in the still water of the silted up river, the lumps would not break up so easily. Later, when Bishtupada took them out, he would have well-washed rice. But this was a procedure known only to Bishtupada and Nibaran.

Having deposited the offerings and bathed for the second time, Abhijit and his brothers went back up.

Bishtupada was still sitting in exactly the same place.

Nibaran said to Abhijit's relatives, 'Will you pay Bishte his dues now? He will also have those leftover bananas, ghee, honey and milk.' He then turned to Bishtupada and said, 'Hey! How long are you going to sit there? Come over here.'

Bishtupada got up and went to him as though in a trance. One of Abhijit's relatives put twenty-five rupees in his hand and said, 'All right, then?'

Bishtupada had never got so much money for so little work, so he should have been overwhelmed by such a payment, but he could feel nothing other than an intense disquiet concerning his own father. Mechanically, he inclined his head.

Nibaran called Bishtupada over and said in a low voice, 'Hurry down to the river and get the rice out. Otherwise it will break up and spread about. And keep all that yoghurt and milk and the bananas,' he said, looking towards where the rites had been celebrated.

In a somewhat indistinct voice, Bishtupada said, 'All right.'

A little later, having gathered up the brass lamp, the various vessels and other things, Nibaran and the others went up to the unmade road on the other side of the ghat where the same four cycle rickshaws were waiting for them.

As he got into the rickshaw, Nibaran called out, 'We're off, then, Bishte!'

Bishtupada said nothing.

The rickshaws slowly went off into the distance across the empty, stony fields. Bishtupada was not aware of how much time had passed before he saw the sun sink further towards the west and felt that the warmth had gone out of the now dull sunlight. Far off over the vast open fields the cycle rickshaws were no longer to be seen.

At that moment there was no one other than Bishtupada at the ghat. The vultures in the cremation ground were no longer flapping their wings or crying out. The breeze had dropped and its whistling had ceased. On the sandbank in the river the cranes had stopped flying about and were sitting quietly under the cover of their wings.

Bishtupada was completely alone in a silent universe. For a long time he stood on the terrace as though in a dream, and then, almost staggering, he went down the broken steps to the river.

Near the bank in the still, clear water, the balls of rice remained intact. As he bent down and took them up, Bishtupada felt a pounding inside his chest and he burst into tears. He stood there awhile, dazed, with the offertory food in his hands. Then, unwittingly, he walked waist-deep into the water, held the balls of rice out in front of him, and mumbled the words:

> *To this food of the gods we bow, to this food of the gods we bow.*
>
> *This rice-offering is dedicated to the soul of Meghnad Deva Sharmanah of the ancestral line of Baradwaj ...*

Meghnad had been his father's name.

As he repeated the well-learnt mantras, he felt as though his eyes would burst with the hot tears flowing from them. After completing the recitation, he threw the food offering far out into the stream. Then he immersed himself a few times and, with tired legs, went back up the broken steps.

the supplicant
prarthi

Tauharlal was a famous leader. He was the Member of the Legislative Assembly – or the MLA – for the Piparganj region of north Bihar. The local people called him the 'emlay.'

In 1947, when the country became independent, he was just seven years old. He was only a toddler at the time of the August Movement in 1942, and he had been unaware of Rashid Ali Day and the Bombay Naval Mutiny. You will not find the name of Tauharlal on the list of those leaders of the Freedom Movement who, in aid of the country's independence, spent time in jail, gave themselves to the hangman or were sent into exile in the far-off Andaman Islands. Tauharlalji was a post-Independence patriot.

He had an inclination for politics, though in fact he was an extremely successful businessman. There was no timber merchant as big as Tauharlal within forty miles of Piparganj. In addition, he was the only dealer nearby in everything from vegetable oil, scooters and bicycles, baby food, kerosene, radios and sewing machines to detergent powder, bath soap and small pump sets. The merchandise sold by the small dealers in the vicinity was also bought from him. Apart from being a businessman, Tauharlalji was also a landed aristocrat, and the amount of land he owned, both in his own name and in aliases, would be hard to reckon.

Tauharlalji had very cleverly blended business and feudalism; consequently, he had mountains of money in the bank and in safes in his home.

But was there any honour in so much wealth, so much land, and so much business enterprise? Did he have any reputation in society? It was questions such as these that one day pushed Tauharlal into politics, for with political power he could bring the whole district under his thumb. As it is not very difficult for one who has money and the power of guns and lathis to acquire the votes of poor and illiterate people, for ten years Tauharlalji had remained the MLA for Piparganj district. Yet despite his immense wealth and great influence, he was a gentle and honest man – as long as his interests were not threatened and nobody annoyed him.

Tauharlal's huge, three-storey house stood inside a vast compound on one side of the town of Piparganj. Every Sunday morning, he held a public audience on the spacious veranda on the ground floor. Everyone in the district was free to come and go and voice their wants and complaints, their trials and hardships. In this way, Tauharlalji kept in touch with the people.

As on any other Sunday, the audience was in session. A huge mattress with a gleaming white cover was spread out on one side of the veranda, with many thick bolsters around it. Tauharlalji, wearing a finely woven punjabi and tight-fitting cotton pants, leaned back with four or five bolsters supporting his vast weight. He had no particular liking for sofas, chairs and tables, but felt comfortable sprawled out on the floor. In all respects, he observed the old feudal style.

He was surrounded by some of those close to him, a group of sycophants. The people of Piparganj spoke of them as a pack of boot-licking lapdogs.

On the other side of the veranda a huge, coarse cotton carpet was spread out for the group of poor and illiterate people who had come as petitioners. Sitting among them was Rajesh – Rajesh Jha – a bright, spirited young man of twenty-three or twenty-four. His eyes were riveted on Tauharlal.

A middle-aged, hunched man would write down the names of the petitioners and give them to Tauharlalji, beside whom he stood and at whose direction he called out the names in turn – Kamtalal, Chaudhury Dusad, Bajrangi, Mahadeo, Ramnagin, and so on.

As their names were called, the men would get up and, with hands pressed together, go straight to Tauharlalji, whom they would greet with 'Namaste, Master', after prostrating themselves and touching their heads against the veranda's marble floor. Then standing, still with hands pressed together, the litany of their needs or complaints would be heard.

One was in need of money for his daughter's marriage, and if the Master would be so gracious as to make some arrangement, the man would be his bondsman for the rest of his life. Another spoke of the need for a road in his village; someone else spoke strongly of a neighbour's having appropriated his wheat harvest and asked the Master to take action against him. And so it went on.

Tauharlalji gave assurance to all, raising his hand like a maharaja. He did not disappoint anyone. Observing his manner, it seemed as though he could fulfil the heart's desires of everyone in the region. Since he had become an MLA, everybody went to him as though to a wishing tree.

Sitting apart, Rajesh was tired of listening to these tales of woe. He was growing irritated with Tauharlalji's regal manner. This man, this post-'47 patriot, had not lifted even a finger for Independence. Of course, that did not mean much, for he was born in 1940 and in 1947 he was only seven, so how could he have fought against the British? Nevertheless, one big question remained: after Independence, what had he done for the people, what had he done for the country? He had never given a single paisa out of his own pocket.

In his youth, he had been an incorrigible womanizer and had got himself into trouble many times only to escape on the strength of his money. Later, of course, his womanizing lessened as his eyes turned to money-making, and after amassing immense wealth and becoming an MLA, he tried to cultivate an honourable image.

Rajesh privately hated this overnight patriot, who had made no sacrifice and had never lifted a finger for the common people. The only reason for his having to come to Tauharlalji as a supplicant was his father, Ramnath Jha, or else he would never have attended the MLA's public audience. It was only Ramnath's insistence that had sent him here; for Tauharlal, this was unexpected.

Ramnath was a greatly revered former freedom fighter who had spent nearly a quarter of his life in British jails. He had a backbone of steel and had never compromised with wrongdoing or taken the slightest advantage of anyone. This upright man had never bowed his head, even in the face of misery, oppression or hardship. He did not accept the copper plate which was awarded to long-suffering freedom fighters, and had even refused the pension to which he was entitled. Very politely and with palms pressed together, he had explained, 'Why should I get anything for having served my country? Please do not make me greedy. I have no wish at all to be one who receives a little and then wants to get more.'

The same man was now bedridden. He who had a spine that was straight and as hard as steel now had to stoop. The reason was Rajesh. The man who had never wanted anything for himself, had never held out his hand to anyone, had never for any reason lowered his dignity, had in the end sent a letter to Tauharlalji on behalf of his son in the hope of getting him a job.

A few years earlier, Rajesh had graduated with a BA pass degree. Although he had sent stacks of applications to various places, he had not even got an interview and employment was still just a dream. Of course, in his applications he had given his father's name simply as Ramnath Jha; he had made no mention at all of his having been a freedom fighter and a self-sacrificing patriot. Rajesh did not want to take any advantage of his father's name.

However, Ramnath understood that without lobbying Rajesh would not get a job: Rajesh needed an influential patron. Ramnath's days were coming to an end. What would happen to Rajesh? He was so worried about his son, that in the last stage of his life, he went against his own nature. Rajesh objected, of course, but Ramnath did not listen.

Tauharlal answered Ramnath's letter immediately. He expressed his profound respect for Ramnath, and entreated him to send Rajesh to him as soon as possible.

Rajesh was called after everyone else. As he went forward, Tauharlal welcomed him heartily, saying, 'Be seated, my son, be seated.'

Rajesh noticed that Tauharlal had not asked any other petitioners or visitors to be seated. He knew that his being treated differently and with such a warm welcome was on account of Ramnath. He sat silently on a corner of the mattress.

Having hurriedly ordered a servant to bring sweets, biscuits and some sherbet, Tauharlal now said, 'Have some, my son.'

Embarrassed, Rajesh said, 'No, no. There is no need for all of this. I ate before leaving home.'

'This is the first time you have come to my house. If you don't have just a little sweet, I will feel very bad. Please, eat.'

Had Rajesh again protested, he would have had to listen to more entreaties, and so he took a sweet and a glass of the sherbet.

Tauharlal said, 'I could have called you earlier, but I had to keep you waiting all this time. Do you know the reason?'

Rajesh turned to Tauharlal and did not answer.

Tauharlal went on without a break. 'The reason is that you are one of my own. I did not want to speak with you in front of all this hoi polloi. So I had to wait for them to go.'

Rajesh did not answer.

Tauharlal had been leaning back but now slowly sat up straight. A servant ran with another thick bolster which he arranged behind Tauharlal's back. Thus supported, Tauharlal leaned towards Rajesh and said, 'Ramnathji, your father, is the pride of us all. How much time he spent in jail for our country! In this entire land there are no more than three or four patriots who made such sacrifices. The whole of India is proud of him. But our pride is greater than that of others because he is a man of our district.' Having spoken so emphatically,

Tauharlal paused to catch his breath, and then went on, 'Ramnathji sent me a letter. It would have been proper to go and see him, but I didn't, for one special reason. I wanted you to come here. I have something very important to put to you.'

Rajesh was taken aback. Although he had seen Tauharlal from a distance in the street in Piparganj, he had never been introduced to him, nor had he required an introduction. Rajesh used to stay in his uncle's house while studying in Ranchi and, having come to Piparganj on holidays, he heard that Tauharlal had gone to his house once or twice, but he had never met him.

'What's the important matter you want to put to me?' he asked.

Tauharlal smiled mysteriously as he said, 'I'll tell you everything. But first I have some news.'

'What?'

'I have spoken with four or five big industrialists in Patna and Jamshedpur about the question of your employment. They would all like to have you in their companies. Within a month you will have a position. I will tell you the names of the companies. You can decide where you will work after discussing it all with Ramnathji.'

Even after hearing such great news, Rajesh did not show any emotion. He remained silent.

'Well, aren't you happy?' Tauharlal asked.

Rajesh was about to answer as a matter of courtesy when the thought came to him that a selfless, estimable patriot like Ramnath Jha had, for his sake, held out his hand to a dishonest, equivocating fellow like Tauharlal, and his antipathy towards the MLA returned.

Tauharlal did not wait for an answer. He said, 'The question of your employment is settled. Now let me come to that matter of importance.'

There was something in Tauharlal's speech that prompted Rajesh to be wary.

'The reason I am telling you this,' Tauharlal continued, 'is that you and your father are my own people. Had Ramnathji wanted he could have spoken to anyone else about your employment. So why did he favour me? Because he thinks of me as his own man.'

Rajesh did not like all this beating about the bush. Disinterestedly he said, 'What is it that you want to say?'

Tauharlal prepared himself by clearing his throat, then said, 'I'm sure you have heard that there will be an election in three or four months.'

'Yes.' Rajesh slowly nodded.

'The election battle will be very keen. I've heard that a Harijan candidate and a candidate from the minority community are standing for election. There are many votes here for Muslims and the scheduled castes, so the two candidates will have considerable influence. They could draw almost the entire Muslim and Harijan vote. So far I have always won, being able to depend on those votes. I'm sure you can understand my problem.'

Rajesh said nothing, but just looked at Tauharlal.

'Only your father can save me from this difficulty,' Tauharlal said.

Looking straight at Tauharlal, Rajesh frowned. 'How?' he asked.

'He is the most respected person in these parts. No matter whether one is Harijan or Hindu, Muslim, Christian or tribal, whatever Ramnathji says, the man will do it without hesitation. Ramnathji's public image and reputation are beyond compare. Apart from that, he is so much my own man, my own well-wisher.'

The whole business was now as clear as water to Rajesh. He said, 'You want my father to go into the Harijan and Muslim quarters and campaign for you – is that it?'

A smile lit up Tauharlal's face. He took Rajesh by the hand and said, 'That's right, my son. However, Ramnathji is not a well man. I would not want him to go about every day, but just one day, in the car with us, around various parts of Piparganj. Just one day. That will be sufficient.'

Tauharlal had worked it out wonderfully. How easily he would use Ramnath in his interests! Rajesh's spine stiffened and his jaw set as he watched this artful, scheming man. Slowly, he removed his hand and said, 'You would fix up a job for me and my father would win the election for you. This is the plan you have in mind, isn't it?'

Was there a sting in Rajesh's words? Tauharlalji was a little discomforted. Then, in a lighter vein, much like an affectionate mentor, he said, 'Naughty boy. You have it more or less exactly.'

'Surely you know that my father now has no connection with politics.'

'I know, of course. Certainly I know.'

'Earlier, a candidate had gone to get my father to speak at an election rally. Father sent him away.'

'You're talking about that Jaggilal Sahay?'

'Yes.'

'It was quite right for Ramnathji to send him packing. Jaggilal is a contemptible fellow. Like an animal – anti-social, depraved.'

'Be that as it may, it is not right to draw into your campaign people who are not in politics.'

With a tender smile, Tauharlal said, 'I tell you frankly – you and your father are my own, and I am yours.'

Rajesh held his gaze steadfast for some moments. Then he said, 'Let me tell you something. You have reckoned my employment at the cost of my father's working for your campaign. I won't submit to that at all. I don't need a position arranged by you. Now I am going.' As he spoke Rajesh got up. Without once looking back he strode off the veranda and straight out through the gate.

Ramnath had humbled himself enough for his son. Rajesh could not let him go down any further at this late stage of his life. He must maintain his honour.

an untimely flood

kartiker jhar, banya ebang chunao

Girdharlal Dube's great house in the town of Dharauni had been continually busy for some days. The reason was that in two months and eleven days the Legislative Assembly election would be held, and Dubeji was a candidate.

For the last fifteen years, Girdharlal had been the MLA for this region. While sleeping at home he had won three elections, for he was the biggest landholder within fifty or sixty miles of Dharauni. In his own name and in aliases, he held at least a thousand acres of land. He also had a private army of about fifty men.

About a mile and a half out of the town of Dharauni, the cultivated fields and low-lying stony ground stretched out towards the horizon, marked here and there with an age-old, forlorn and wretched village without electricity, a school or any educational facility. The villagers were untouchables, illiterate and utterly downtrodden. During earlier elections, Girdharlal had sent his armed thugs from village to village to repeatedly threaten villagers to stamp their marks on Dube-ji's election symbol, or else all their villages would be set on fire. And so it was accomplished. Like a flock of sheep, the villages had formed a long line to place a stamp beside Dube-ji's symbol, and Dube-ji had walked over rose petals to the Legislative Assembly in Patna.

But this time it would not be so simple. In the coming election, Dube-ji's opponent would be Ramdhani, a young, robust man of about twenty-five who belonged to the Koweris, a caste of untouchables. Ramdhani Koweri had given Dube some restless nights, and it now seemed to him that he would not win this election, as he had the previous ones, by sending out his armed goondas.

In his conversation and in his bearing, Ramdhani was not at all like the untouchables of these godforsaken villages of Bihar who, like timid animals, had traditionally kept their mouths shut. He was extremely spirited, fearless, irrepressible and dogged. In his younger days, he had come under the influence of the missionaries and gone to Ranchi. He returned a few years ago, educated and full of determination. Among these villages he was respected as the one and only literate man. The untouchables had a place in their hearts for him similar to the altar on which they raised the image of their god. There was a rumour that, at the coming election, Ramdhani would get all their votes.

Girdharlal had heard that, since his return from Ranchi, Ramdhani had been opening the eyes of the untouchables, who no longer seemed as cowed as they had been. On top of that were the various unsettling reports of untouchables and tribals having fought with landholders around Bhojpur, Motihari and Palamau, and of tanners and other untouchables having attacked Brahmin villages in some regions.

Dube-ji still relied heavily on lathis, guns and his private thugs, although his cool-headed, far-sighted supporters had advised him to have nothing more to do with weapons. This time he had to do what he had not done in the three previous elections: like a beggar he had gone three or four times to the untouchables' villages, soliciting votes – not without consequence, however. His village to village visits had led to tremendous excitement. Homage was paid to him by a host of people, from old men and women to five-year-olds, all touching their foreheads to the ground; nevertheless, Girdharlal was not free from worry. Who knew what intentions lay in the guts of these sons of swine?

One afternoon, a strategy for the election was being deliberated upon in Dube-ji's house.

In the ground floor sitting room, a sparkling white covered mattress had been spread out over the raised decking, around which large, old-style sofas were arranged. Girdharlal did not particularly like sofas, so he and his four special advisers were sitting on the covered decking and leaning back on thick bolsters. One of the four was a crooked lawyer, one was a big contractor, another was a retired headmaster, and the fourth was Dharauni's richest businessman. They formed Girdharlal's secret political cabinet, or his political cell. He would consult them on the polishing of his political image and on strategies for ensuring that he remained an MLA for the rest of his life.

The festival of Diwali had been celebrated a few days earlier. At this time the weather was usually wonderful, with a dry breeze blowing over Dharauni and not a trace of a cloud in the sparkling blue sky. Although the mornings and evenings would be a little cool, it was always very pleasant. However, this year it was different. For some days a strong wind had chased dark clouds across the sky. Today they had accumulated and looked like lumps of stone threatening to plummet down on Dharauni. The stormy wind gusted about like a mad horse, and the sky was suddenly rent by lightning. The menacing wind, the thunder and lightning all made it seem as though Dharauni was returning to some terrible, primeval chaos.

Looking through the window at the sky, Girdharlal said, 'Today is utterly wasted. We can't go out with all this thunder and lightning.' He looked terribly disappointed and worried.

The lawyer, Siyasharan, said, 'Who knows? With this weather, we may have to spend a few days inside twiddling our thumbs.'

In fact, they had planned that day to campaign in three villages but had not been able to go out on account of the bad weather.

Just as the headmaster, Ramnaresh, was about to say something, the sound of a jeep was heard, and a moment or two later Hansanath Tewari, the inspector from the Dharauni police station, came into the room. He was a big, rotund man of about fifty, weighing around one hundred and fifty pounds and carrying a great deal of fat.

He bowed his head, folded his hands and said most deferentially, 'Namaste, Dube-ji,' and proceeded to pay his respects to each of the other members of Girdharlal's special cell.

His loyalty to Girdharlal was in no way feigned or superficial, for it had been Girdharlal who had got him his position in the police force and, by virtue of his political influence, had seen to his promotion. Therefore, he was a frequent caller at this house, keeping Girdharlal informed about who was doing what, who was thinking what – indeed, everything that was going on in Dharauni. He got all these facts from informers.

'Sit down, Hansanath,' said Girdharlal. As the inspector sat diffidently at a corner of the floor covering, Girdharlal asked, 'What news? Is your work going well?'

'Yes, sir, with your blessings.'

'So what brings you out in this stormy weather?'

'Some very important information, Dube-ji.'

Whenever Hansanath brought any information, it was important. Dube-ji sat up. 'What information?'

Hansanath went on to say that a depression had suddenly come up across the Bay of Bengal causing much unseasonable cloud formation. At the same time, the snows of the Himalayas were starting to melt, as a result of which the Barakha river, two miles from Dharauni, was rising rapidly, and the villages and crops on both sides of the river would soon be flooded. Orders had come just today to Hansanath asking him to go to the villages on the banks of the Barakha and issue flood and storm warnings. The crops probably could not be saved, but to avoid loss of life villagers should be moved to safe places.

The contractor, Vishnukanta Singh, spoke up. 'Yes, yes, the storm was mentioned on the radio.' The former headmaster, Ramnaresh, and the lawyer, Siyasharan, said that they too had heard an announcement on the radio warning of turbulent weather. Girdharlal never had the time to listen to the radio; if he had, he would have had this news three days before. However, on hearing that there was the likelihood of a storm, with serious flooding of the Barakha river, an electrical reaction was triggered off in his mind as something suddenly occurred to him.

'Wasn't there a disastrous rising of the Barakha river ten years ago?' Girdharlal asked.

The others had forgotten about that flood. A ten-foot high force of water had flooded many of the untouchables' villages. Many people as well as cows, buffalo and goats had perished. But whoever remembered such insignificant news! Girdharlal's question drew back the curtains screening their feeble memories, and a picture of that fearful flood of ten years back emerged anew. Almost all together they said, 'Oh, yes, yes. There was.'

'Do you remember how many people died?'

Neither Ramnaresh nor Siyasharan could give the exact number of the dead. Only Vishnukanta ventured, 'About ten or fifteen people.'

'No,' Girdharlal corrected him. 'There were thirty. And cows, buffalo and goats?'

No one in the room could recall how many untouchables, cows, buffalo and goats had died in a flood ten years earlier. They slowly shook their heads, their faces reflecting shame at their weak memories. But on one point they were rather bewildered: why was Girdharlal suddenly so excited about how many untouchables and their livestock had died in that flood?

'You don't remember, then? All right, I'll tell you,' said Girdharlal. 'Two hundred cows, one hundred and twenty buffalo and two hundred and forty goats.' He turned to the inspector and said, 'There is a record of this in the sub-divisional officer's files. You can look it up if you wish.'

There was a brief silence, and then Girdharlal went on, 'You are probably wondering why I remember things from so long ago.'

They all looked eagerly at Girdharlal, for this was their own question.

'A politician has to remember many things,' explained Girdharlal. 'When something happened, who did or said what – if these could not be brought to mind at the right moment, then he would be lost. Without a strong memory you can't take a step in politics.'

Although they nodded their heads in agreement, they racked their brains over the political significance of the deaths of a few untouchables and a few animals ten years ago.

Girdharlal now turned to Inspector Hansanath and asked, 'After that flood, government relief came in, didn't it?'

'Yes, yes,' replied Hansanath. 'Charity kitchens were opened up in all the villages beside the Barakha river. The untouchables were given tents, money and some cows and goats.'

'Very good.' Looking at the inspector, Girdharlal's eyes sparkled as he said, 'If this time too Lord Shiva should by his grace deliver a flood, then there will certainly be government relief. The hardship of poor and helpless people must be alleviated.'

'Yes, yes. Of course.' Hansanath went on to explain that, while crops and houses might be destroyed in the storm and lives may be lost, government aid would indeed be forthcoming. This was the regular procedure.

Girdharlal interrupted him. 'I know,' he said as he settled back against a soft, plump bolster. Then, with some concern, he went on, 'If there is a flood this time, we will distribute the government relief. Government functionaries need not sweat over this task. We'll look after everything.'

There was a subtle hint in Girdharlal's words, which was grasped by the members of his own secret cabinet. The untouchables' villages on this side of the Barakha river fell within his constituency. If, after the flood, he could distribute the relief items there, the results might be very far-reaching. Girdharlal would eat sweets, and the government would pay.

Hansanath gulped and said, 'But ... '

'Do you want to say something?' Girdharlal asked.

'Yes, sir.'

'Speak up, then.'

'When the relief comes, it has to be distributed before the district magistrate and the sub-divisional officer. This is government regulation.'

Girdharlal remained calm. He had unlimited patience, for it was impossible to be a successful politician without this virtue. He said, 'How old are you?'

'I have gone fifty, sir,' Hansanath replied.

'And you still have no intelligence. I am an MLA, the representative of the people. The people will *want* to receive their relief from my hands. Understand?'

The inspector scratched his neck, saying nothing. A suspicion was brewing in his mind.

Girdharlal said, 'Don't you worry. I'll have a word with the DM and the SDO.'

After chatting a little more, the inspector got up and said, 'The sky is looking worse. Once I've warned the villagers by the Barakha, I'll have to hurry back to the station.'

The inspector was on his way out when Girdharlal said anxiously, 'No, no. You mustn't put yourself to any more trouble by going there. I'll do what has to be done.'

'All right, then. Namaste, Dube-ji.' Courteously and deferentially Hansanath took his leave. A few moments later the sound of the jeep was heard.

Inside, Girdharlal and the others were sitting close together. They were all of one mind in making the most of the bad weather that was coming by the grace of Lord Shiva.

Within an hour they had decided on their course of action. Then Girdharlal gave a self-satisfied smile and said, 'It is very important for a politician to keep his eyes and ears open at all times. From storm or drought or whatever, there is always profit to be made.'

Girdharlal's much desired disaster came to pass. For three days there was a storm and continual heavy rain. The Barakha river rose up twelve feet and the houses on both its banks, along with a great number of people and animals, were washed away. For mile after mile, crops were laid waste.

No one had gone there and given prior warning. If that had been done, at least a few human and animal lives might have been saved. But Girdharlal had not let the inspector go to the villages beside the Barakha that day, nor had he gone and given warning. Behind this there was a far-reaching scheme.

However, Girdharlal had had a word over the phone with the district magistrate and the sub-divisional officer about flood relief in the villages. Three days later, when the storm and flood had abated, a relief camp was set up for the villagers beside the Barakha river. Although the district magistrate formally opened the camp, the supervision and running around was done by Girdharlal and his men.

The villages were still a couple of feet under water as Girdharlal went barefoot from village to village, trudging through the mud washed up by the waters, taking whoever had survived to the relief camp. In all the villages, there was only sobbing, groaning and lamentation. Someone's brother had died, someone's father, someone's husband, someone's son, and people beat their breasts as they cried. Girdharlal gave a pat of consolation to each untouchable's back and head.

In the meantime, the district magistrate, the sub-divisional officer and all the other officials who had opened the relief camp had gone and were no longer to be seen on the banks of the Barakha. It was Girdharlal and his associates who carried out all the relief work.

It got about that it was Girdharlal who had saved the villagers by giving them food and water, shelter and medicine. It was also said that the great master was actually a god, for it was by his grace that they had been protected, and he was just like Lord Ram and Lord Krishna in his compassion. So it went on.

Ramdhani and his supporters made quite a noise over the business of the relief camp, alleging that Dube-ji had organized government relief in his own interests. But no one gave an ear to that.

Two months later, lines of untouchables from the villages beside the Barakha made their marks beside Girdharlal's symbol on the ballot paper in the Legislative Assembly elections. The untimely storm and flood had made Dube-ji an MLA for yet another five years.

the dumb show
mukabhineta

Today, as on other days, the ghat had fallen silent and still at midday when Keshtapada and his disciple, Natka, came to perform before the crowded and expectant gathering.

On this side of the vast river with its bend like the blade of a sickle was Nabiganj, on the other was Mukundapur. Some two thousand people would cross that river every day. Once there had been only two boatmen to take the people across and, as the stream was about one and a half miles wide, it would take a couple of hours to cross over. No one on either side had so much time on their hands, so two motor boats were bought to do the ferrying.

There was a wooden jetty reaching into the water at Nabiganj. Getting down from the boat one crossed the jetty to the high steps of staggered tree trunks. About thirty feet beyond were some shops with broken tin roofs. Some sold tea, biscuits and cheap packaged bread, some sold paan, bidis and cigarettes, and some sold rice, dal, oil and spices. In front of the shops at the ferry ghat ran an old cobblestone road, on the other side of which, facing the shops, were a few tall, luxuriant trees under which a number of cycle rickshaws were always to be found waiting in the shade.

A little way along the cobbled road to the north there were sawmills, rice husking mills, small lead cutting factories and countless warehouses. There was also a quiet colony with tiled roofs that was one of the world's most depraved red light districts. Beyond all of this for about a quarter of a kilometre was scrub, and just beyond that was the actual town, the rather formal-sounding Nabiganj district town, with its busy, crowded streets. After the partition of India, Nabiganj had experienced something of a population explosion.

On the bank of the river to the right of the jetty was the cremation ground. Flocks of vultures perched on the branches of a tall banyan tree there, under which was the tin and timber hut of the attendant, Bhaga Dom.

The sun had climbed directly overhead, and it was ebb tide on the river. The blazing sun of Jyaistha flashed off the clear, bluish water as though off glass. There was not a hint of a cloud, and a few hawks could be seen, wings outspread, floating against the blue so high up in the sky. The town of Mukundapur on the other side remained like a picture out of focus. There on the bank of the river were many brick kilns, their tall chimneys reaching high into the sky.

Apart from the sound of the river's current, it was so still that the world might have fallen asleep. It was midday, and at this time the river was closed for crossing for two hours. By mid-afternoon the launches would be running again.

As on other days, in the glimmering noon, Keshtapada and Natka were ready for the gathering assembled in the cool shade of the trees opposite the shops above the ferry ghat. The paan and tobacco shop on the other side of the road belonged to Keshtapada, and it was here that Natka worked at rolling bidis. Keshtapada was a restless man; sitting still was not in his nature. In the middle of the day, when there were no customers and it was boring, he would shut up shop for two hours and take Natka with him across the road. Then they would set about entertaining whoever was there at the ferry ghat.

Keshtapada was about thirty. He was tall and straight and looked like a palmyra tree that had been struck by lightning. He wore an ill-fitting pair of trousers of cheap, printed cloth, and a green-striped cotton waistcoat. Natka was exceptionally short and was balding. His small, flickering eyes suggested he was an artful devil. Like Keshtapada, he too was wearing trousers and a cotton waistcoat.

Everyday, Keshtapada would have his audience in fits with his imitation of the mannerisms and gait of certain persons in Nabiganj. There were no words in this show, just a humorous play of actions and facial expressions.

Keshtapada stood under the trees and looked around. Among the audience were shopkeepers and cycle rickshawallahs, a few labourers who had not been given work that day at the sawmill or the rice storehouse, and Bhaga Dom, who had come from the cremation ground, having at the time no corpses to dispose of. One shopkeeper who had not shut up shop and come was Nishi, who had the only tea shop on the other side of the road.

Nishi was about twenty-five, with gleaming skin, a strong and healthy body and a few pockmarks on her round face. She was pleasant to look at and to listen to. About three years ago, she had become a widow and, as she had not remarried, had set up the tea shop to make a living. She enjoyed the ribaldry and banter of her male customers, but too much of it or their attempts to grope at her would set her keen eyes ablaze. She always kept a sharp chopper at hand; she would suddenly flourish it along with a forceful stream of obscenity and abuse directed at them and fourteen generations of their ancestors. Except at midday, there was always a crowd in her tea shop, buzzing like a swarm of flies. Although she was particularly careful to avoid the touch of others, she would not move away from Keshtapada if he came in contact with her, nor would the chopper be raised. She would only frown and, looking at the man through narrowed eyes, say emphatically, 'Oh, hell.'

Nishi was never to be seen under the trees, and that day, too, she was sitting in her own shop, watching the other side of the road. In front of her shop, she had set up a couple of bamboo benches for her customers. Sitting at his ease on one of them, a glass of tea in his hand, Haren was watching Keshtapada. Short, stumpy and stupid-looking, he was a lowlife of the first order. Everyone in Nabiganj knew Haren and avoided him. However, he was never seen at the ferry ghat at midday. What purpose had brought him there today, and to Nishi's tea shop in particular?

As he looked at his audience, Keshtapada's glance rested on Haren, then moved on as he said, 'Today I'm going to do a take off on someone you all know well. I won't tell you his name yet. I'll see if you can get it.' Then he turned to Natka and said, 'Get up, partner.' 'Partner' was one of the several English words that Keshtapada had heard and kept in mind, and often inserted into his speech.

'All right, boss,' Natka said in Hindi, and stood up. (Because of television and the Bombay movies, Hindi had come like an unforeseen flood into Nabiganj, only a hundred and fifty kilometres from Calcutta. Natka spoke about two Hindi words in every ten.)

The show began. It was about a man who goes to a grog shop and drinks so much that he gets drunk and, in the dark of night, topples into a drain. His devoted wife, with worried face and lantern in hand, comes looking. At last she finds him, his body covered with the filth of the drain. Puffing and panting, she drags her revered lord home. The short Natka played the role of the husband and the lanky Keshtapada played the wife. Not a word was exchanged during the whole performance, Keshtapada and Natka creating the comedy through actions, gestures, looks and facial expressions.

Indeed, the whole thing was pure mime, although up until a few months ago this word was quite unknown to them. Amalesh Sanyal, having heard of their talents, had called them to his house and watched their performance. Amalesh was the most respected man in Nabiganj, a man with a wealth of learning who taught at a big college in Calcutta and had come home for the holidays. At first, Keshtapada had been reluctant to perform in front of him. Cowering in his diffidence, he had said, 'I can't. Such appalling vulgarity should not be shown in front of a gentleman like you!' But Amalesh would hear none of that, and so their silent entertainment was done in full.

Amalesh was astounded, saying, 'This is pure genius! Never in my life have I seen such mime.' So Keshtapada first heard the words 'mime' and 'genius'. He and Natka still did not know the meaning of 'genius', but they were able to guess that it was something good. Of course, Amalesh had made clear the meaning of 'mime'. He had also said that if he took them to Calcutta, they could do a grand 'show', and he would also arrange for their mime to be shown on television. Not only Keshtapada and Natka, but Nabiganj knew that Amalesh was not a man to indulge in baseless flattery and the villagers lived in anticipation of the day they would travel to Calcutta.

The sketch about the drunken husband and the devoted wife gradually became immensely popular, and Keshtapada and Natka's comic performances began to draw bigger and bigger belly laughs. The audience rolled in mirth and people said, 'Those buggers Keshta and Natka, what a couple of characters! Oh, Lord, I laughed so much I thought my stomach would burst.'

Haren was no longer sitting on the bench in front of Nishi's teashop, as he had fallen off it in an excess of laughter. He got up and said, as he sat down again, 'Those buggers have really got it down to a T! Oh, I think I'm going to die laughing!'

Nishi, however, was not so effusive or generous in her praise. She just clicked her tongue and, chuckling silently, said, 'Oh, God, just look at the pair of them!'

The sketch had reached the point where Natka, in the role of the husband, is lying covered in the filth of the drain, and Keshtapada, as his wife, lantern in hand, recognizes him, smacks her forehead, and bursts into tears. After wailing silently for a while, she takes the end of her imaginary sari and wipes the mess off her husband's body. As she drags him towards their house, she suddenly says to the audience, 'Can you tell whose wife is dragging her drunken husband home?'

The audience all cried out as one, 'Yes, we can!' The drunkard, indeed, was the proprietor of the sawmill, Kamakhya Kundu, who, almost every night, would live out this very episode with his devoted wife.

Once its characters had been recognized, there was not an iota of doubt about the success of the performance. Gratified, Keshtapada completed the remainder of the piece and sat down. For quite some time, the tranquil ferry ghat of Nabiganj had been rocked with raucous laughter.

When the laughter had subsided, Haren got up from the bench at Nishi's tea shop and walked across to the trees growing opposite. Condescendingly, he said to Keshtapada, 'That was a great act, brother! I never realized that you and that other bugger, Natka, had so much in you. Now I have something urgent to discuss.'

Haren's purpose was not clear. He had been an incorrigible criminal. There was no telling exactly how many cases of murder and robbery had been brought against him. Three or four times he had been dragged off to the police lock-up, but he was never kept there long. At the direction of an unknown person, all the charges were always dropped.

Of course, now Haren had become a gentleman. Bloodshed and thuggery were not his line of work. He was always in the company of political leaders, doing all sorts of work for them. He did not wield the knife or pistol himself; those who did jumped at his command. The people of Nabiganj, therefore, kept out of his way. Keshtapada was particularly worried, wondering what need Haren could have of him. He stood up and asked, apprehensively, 'What is it, Haren-babu?'

Haren laid a hand on Keshtapada's shoulder and drew him aside, saying, 'Not in front of everybody. Keep tomorrow evening free. I'll come and take you somewhere.'

'Where?'

'You'll see when you get there.'

'But … '

Whatever Haren might say in Nabiganj was, as a rule, automatically complied with. No one contradicted him. So Haren frowned and, with some displeasure, said, 'Well? But what?'

Keshtapada gulped and said, 'So many customers come to us in the evening. We make just a few paise a day. Please understand, we are very poor men … '

•

'Is that all?' Haren smiled and patted Keshtapada's shoulder affectionately. He said, 'You'll get more than you get from selling bidis! You come with me and you'll make more in one evening than you'd normally get in a month, you silly bugger! So be ready when I come tomorrow evening, and bring that Natka fellow, too. Oh – and no bastard needs to know anything about this.' Haren waited no longer, but hailed a rickshaw and went off.

All those gathered under the trees were waiting expectantly to find out why Haren had come. As soon as Keshtapada returned, they rushed to him with their questions, but Keshtapada only said, 'It's nothing important.'

Later that afternoon, when the ferries were running again and business was underway, Keshtapada put Natka in charge of the open shop and went to Nishi's. The tea shop was still largely empty. Sitting close to Nishi, Keshtapada said quietly, 'I need your advice, woman.'

Nishi had an idea of what advice Keshtapada had come for. When Haren had taken Keshtapada aside and whispered to him, she guessed that the man had some sinister design. After Haren had gone and everyone was clamouring around Keshtapada for information, Nishi had sat in silently in her shop. She showed no curiosity at all, for long before that she had put an invisible hook through Keshtapada's nose. Was the lanky fellow capable of keeping anything from her?

Looking at Keshtapada out of the corner of her eye, Nishi said, 'What's the rat up to?'

Keshtapada told her why Haren had come.

Nishi furrowed her brow. Clearly, she was very worried. She said, 'When the god of death beckons, you have to go. But be careful, and don't get involved in anything.'

'Sure,' said Keshtapada, slowly nodding his head. 'We must be careful.'

The next evening, when the shop was bustling with customers, Haren arrived in a jeep. Keshtapada and Natka had no alternative but to go with him. Nishi threw a look of warning at Keshtapada as they left.

Haren took them in the jeep to the other end of Nabiganj to the house of Bhabeshwar Chaudhuri. Before going inside, Keshtapada and Natka spent a few moments looking at the pillared three-storey home of a former era, set in the middle of twenty bighas of land. Before them lay a big garden of flowers, imitation mountains, fountains, a tennis court – so many wonderful things!

They followed Haren and saw things they had never even dreamt of. There was a huge reception hall where, about eight feet from the ceiling, two rows of ten identical chandeliers were hanging at uniform length. Another three times their size was in the middle; all gave off different coloured lights. Venetian blinds covered the stained-glass windows, and on either side of a vast oil painting on the wall was the head of a tiger and the antlered head of a deer. Velvet-covered sofas, too many to count, were arranged all around like thrones and all along one wall was a long, wide couch covered with sheets and strewn with cushions. An expensive red carpet was spread out on the floor; overhead were at least ten gleaming new fans.

Keshtapada and Natka's eyes bulged at the sight of it all.

Bhabeshwar Chaudhuri was the biggest landlord in the district and its richest man. Even though the old landlord system had been abolished, he still had so much wealth that simply by entering his house one could gain an idea of its vast extent. Keshtapada and others had heard that, after the recent growth in his landholdings, Bhabeshwarbabu and his associates had begun a business.

The reception hall was not empty, for lying on his side on the couch, watching them, was Bhabeshwar Chaudhuri himself. He was about sixty, with fair skin and the look of a man of luxury. His hair, hardly grey at all even at this age, was parted in the middle. He was wearing a finely woven dhoti and an old style, loose-fitting, silk jacket. In his dressing style, Bhabeshwar Chaudhuri upheld the values of a bygone time.

Keshtapada and Natka had seen Bhabeshwar before, but only from a distance. This was the first time they had come close to him.

As well as Bhabeshwar, many of the respectable citizens of Nabiganj were also there, sitting on the sofas. Among them were the principal of the Nabiganj Jaytara Women's College, Taraknath Raha, the chairman of the municipality, Haripada Tarafdar, and the eminent lawyer, Sahayram Putatunda. Keshtapada knew all of them.

Haren took Keshtapada and Natka before the couch and introduced them to Bhabeshwar. They both bowed deeply, offering a most deferential namaskar.

Bhabeshwar was touched. 'Sit down, sit down,' he said.

Keshtapada and Natka sat down on the carpet.

'Oh, my goodness, why there?' said Bhabeshwar. 'Sit up here.'

With folded hands, Keshtapada explained that it was not possible for them to sit on the same level as such a great man as Bhabeshwar.

Bhabeshwar did not press the point. He said, 'I have heard that you are very fine artistes. That you enact all sorts of amusing incidents.' His speech was tinged with the local accent.

Keshtapada and Natka were taken aback. They knew the word 'artiste', but they had not heard 'acting' before; however, they had no difficulty in realizing that Bhabeshwar was talking about their mime show. Lowering his head, Keshtapada said, 'Not really. At midday, to pass the time, we do a little ... '

He did not finish what he was saying, as he was interrupted by Bhabeshwar. 'None of this "not really"! I've heard a lot about you. Do you know why I have had Haren bring you here?'

'No, sir.'

'To see your acting.'

Keshtapada hung his head lower. Amalesh Sanyal had once cordially invited them to his house to see their show. Today, they had been called by Bhabeshwar Chaudhuri, and now they were suddenly in the middle of all these respectable people. Was what they did under the trees at midday a fit thing to show to these gentle folk? Hanging his head even lower and gesticulating with his hands, he kept on saying, 'No, no.'

However, like Amalesh, Bhabeshwar Chaudhuri was an extraordinarily persistent man and Keshtapada had no alternative but to submit. For how long can a poor man resist the whim of a great one? He said, 'What would you like to see?'

Bhabeshwar said, 'Do you know Byomkesh Majumdar?'

Keshtapada looked up. There were quite a few Byomkesh Majumdars in Nabiganj. The most noted of them was the proprietor of seven or eight rice husking mills, many lead cutting factories and a dozen or so big warehouses. Wanting to know whether or not Bhabeshwar was referring to him, Keshtapada asked, 'Which Byomkesh Majumdar? The one with the factories, all those warehouses?'

'Yes.' Slowly nodding his head, Bhabeshwar said, 'You know about this warehouse wallah. Have you actually seen him?'

'Many times.'

'What does he look like?'

'Nothing special. A little fat – you know. And his left leg is shorter than his right.'

Bhabeshwar held out his hands, palms upward, and raising his voice a little, said, 'You don't have to put it so nicely. Just say lame Byomkesh.' Then he suddenly dropped his voice to say, 'The fellow has a really bad name, don't you know? He has a poor reputation throughout the town.'

Keshtapada was going to respond, but before he could, Bhabeshwar went on, 'The lame one keeps a woman in a flat on the other side of the main bazaar. He goes to her secretly each night, all dressed up, and goes back home at daybreak. Did you know that?'

Many people in Nabiganj knew what Bhabeshwar had just revealed, yet Keshtapada was quite shocked. He just sat there, looking down at the carpet, holding his breath. That he should be listening to this kind of conversation from one such as Bhabeshwar Chaudhuri was something he could never have believed.

Bhabeshwar went on. 'So give us a funny sketch about Byomkesh going to his woman's house, limping and trying to keep his dhoti in place. Now you and Natka go with Haren and get changed.'

Keshtapada and Natka got up and went with Haren into a neighbouring room. When they came back fifteen minutes later,

Natka was wearing a silk sari and blouse, his eyes were made up, and his body gave off the smell of perfume. Keshtapada came out wearing a pleated dhoti, a brightly laundered, frilled punjabi, and expensive slippers. His hair was done ostentatiously. Byomkesh was always seen dressed in this fashion.

Using their own imagination, Keshtapada and Natka went on to enact the way in which Byomkesh – stooping, limping, and chin thrust forward like a thief – would go to his mistress, how the pair of them would indulge in playful bickering, and how she would react coquettishly to the gift of a golden ornament.

The effect was immediate. Bhabeshwar and the leading citizens of Nabiganj fell about laughing, even to the point of hiccupping, and they all said much the same thing, 'First class! But, oh! I nearly died laughing!'

Having recovered themselves somewhat, Bhabeshwar asked the college principal, the municipal chairman, and other special guests, 'Well, what do you think? Will it do?'

Taraknath, the principal, said, 'What do you mean, "will it do"? There can be no more powerful weapon to knock down our opponents. We must employ these mime artistes to wield the knife through laughter.'

Bhabeshwar agreed. 'That's right,' he said. 'I want to make a start with them.'

The chairman of the municipality, Haripada Tarafdar, said, 'You can do that, Mr Chaudhuri.'

Looking at Keshtapada, Bhabeshwar said, 'We're very happy with you. You've worked very hard today. Now have some rest. You can keep the costumes that you wore in your acting. Look after them, for you'll have to wear them again. Very soon I'll send Haren to tell you when to come.'

There was still no getting out of it! Keshtapada gulped and said, 'We have to come back?'

'Yes, yes! Why not? Many times. We have some very important work planned for you.'

Automatically, Keshtapada asked, 'What work?'

Bhabeshwar raised his eyebrows and smiled enigmatically. He said, 'Work in the national interest. Now take this.' And he took from his pocket two one-hundred rupee notes and held them out to Keshtapada.

Stunned, Keshtapada said, 'Who is this for?'

The eminent lawyer, Sahayram Putatunda, said, 'You have given us a great deal of pleasure. Won't you accept payment?'

Two crisp one-hundred rupee notes for a half-hour show! Keshtapada could not have imagined it in all his life and the next one as well!

Cordially, Bhabeshwar said, 'Take it, now, go on.' Overwhelmed, Keshtapada took the money. 'You can go now. Haren will take you back.'

It was very late when Haren got Keshtapada and Natka back to the ferry ghat. The motor launches had stopped, and all the shops were closed, except for Nishi's tea shop.

As soon as the launches stopped running at night, Nishi would not wait a moment longer at the ferry ghat, but would call a cycle rickshaw and go into the town, where she lived with her elderly mother. Apart from her mother, Nishi had no one else. Today, however, she sat waiting at the lonely ferry ghat for Keshtapada and Natka. That a primal thug like Haren had taken them away in a jeep was a reason for serious worry. How could she go back to town until they had returned and told her everything? Moreover, at night the two men would stay at the ferry ghat for, in fact, they had nowhere else to go. Keshtapada would spend the night in his shop, and Natka would sleep in Nishi's tea shop. Natka would also have to lock the shop.

Having got the full report from Keshtapada, Nishi's unease only increased. 'I smell a big rat,' she said. 'Who knows what these corpse-eaters are up to?'

Somewhat distracted, Keshtapada said, 'Yes, I feel the same way. But then it's good that we got these clothes and the two hundred rupees. We couldn't earn that much in two months.'

Heatedly, Nishi retorted, 'It'll bring you more misery than it's worth!' Still worried, she added, 'Let's wait a few days and see if Haren comes back or not. Things might change. But you still have to be very careful.' So saying, she looked up at the sky and became agitated. 'Oh, it's got so late. I'm going. Come with me a little way.'

The vicinity of the rice storehouses and the sawmills was deserted, but the red light locality was in full swing. With so many murderers, thieves, cheats and drunkards gathered there, it was a genuine outpost of hell. Nishi would never go out without her chopper concealed at her waist, for even though her courage was admirable, she was still a woman. It was not right that she should go alone past that disreputable neighbourhood, so Keshtapada and Natka would accompany her past the red light locality and onto the main road of Nabiganj, where she would go the rest of the way in a cycle rickshaw.

There had been no sign of Haren for a few days and their anxiety, especially Nishi's waned. They guessed that some whim had got into the head of a rich man to call on them to perform and now Bhabeshwar Chaudhuri would simply forget the whole thing.

But a week had scarcely passed, when they were faced with another catastrophe. At night, when the ferry traffic had ceased, the shops at the ferry ghat had closed, and Keshtapada and Natka had finished their dinner, the two men were enjoying a smoke before going to bed. A shiny red car pulled up in front of them and out got four of Nabiganj's notorious thugs – Jhante, Leto, Scarface Majid, and Palta.

Haren was an old-fashioned murderer, but Jhante and his mates were modern-day superstars. Keshtapada and Natka were stunned to see them, and their bidis fell from their lips.

However, Jhante and the boys had not come to make trouble. They were not carrying any knives or revolvers. Indeed, Jhante said with extreme courtesy, 'May I trouble you two eminent actors to come with us? We have brought a car for you. Please get in.'

As was the case with Haren, one could do nothing but obey.

Nevertheless, though terrified, Keshtapada asked, 'Where are you taking us?'

'Oh, sir, nowhere unpleasant,' said Jhante, hinting that they were going to make money, by rubbing the tip of his forefinger against his thumb. 'Come on, then, brother,' he said. 'Hurry up.'

'But we've been working really hard all day. We badly need some sleep. When can we be back?'

'The sooner we get there, the sooner we'll be back.'

They left the shop and got into the red car with Jhante.

Within a few minutes, they were in the middle of Nabiganj town outside a bright, brand-new, four-storey house that was not unfamiliar. The house belonged to the proprietor of rice storehouses and sawmills and the like, Byomkesh Majumdar. Their hearts almost stopped and then began pounding with frenetic force; in their alarm, they sweated so much that their clothes were sopping. Natka pressed his mouth close to Keshtapada's ear and, in a voice stricken with fear, said, 'We're finished, boss. The bastards have found out that we'd gone to Bhabeshwarbabu's house. Now they'll slit our throats.'

Not a word would come from Keshtapada's throat. Somehow he managed to force out, 'Yeah.'

However, it was with great cordiality that Jhante showed them into a spacious room, furnished with modern-looking lampshades, sofas and divans and even air-conditioners.

Sitting on a huge sofa was Byomkesh Majumdar, dangling both his long leg and his short one, and around him sat quite a few of the leading citizens of Nabiganj. The scene was almost the same as that seen at Bhabeshwar Chaudhuri's house some days before. Jhante formally introduced Keshtapada and Natka, and Byomkesh fawningly said, 'I have already heard about you. What a joy it is that Nabiganj has two such artistes. You do us proud. Now then, you have been brought here on urgent business. I am very pleased that you have taken the trouble to come, so late as it is. Can you guess why I have called you?'

'Oh, no.' Keshtapada slowly shook his head.

'Something hush-hush, top-secret. I've brought you here in the national interest.'

It was not clear if Byomkesh was aware that they had gone to Bhabeshwar Chaudhuri's house and performed a burlesque for him. Their heart-thumping had abated, but their bewilderment and nervousness had increased. Bhabeshwar, too, had wanted to employ them in the national interest. It was a funny thing that Byomkesh had exactly the same purpose. Almost stupefied, Keshtapada said, 'In the national interest?'

'Yes. You perform imitations of various people of Nabiganj at the ferry ghat, so I've heard.'

'But nothing of interest to a gentleman like you!'

'Oh, brother, no need to be so diffident! What you do is something good. It's called arty, er, art. Yes, that's it. Now tell me, you must know Bhabeshwar Chaudhuri?'

There was only a trace of the local accent in Bhabeshwar Chaudhuri's speech, for he spent many days each month in Calcutta. But Byomkesh Majumdar seldom left the town, and so his manner of speaking was heavily idiomatic.

Keshtapada's trepidation built up again. He said indistinctly, 'I do.'

Byomkesh said, 'Very few men as disgraceful as this scoundrel have been born in all the world. Do you know that Bhabeshwar bullies poor people with his thugs to evict them? That he then occupies their property and builds big blocks of flats and rakes in huge profits? And that he also runs smuggling rackets?'

Keshtapada did not know any of this. He just looked at Byomkesh stupidly.

Byomkesh went straight on. 'I have arranged some costumes for you. Go with Jhante and put them on, then come back.'

A little later Keshtapada came back from the neighbouring room dressed in a fine-spun dhoti and a loose-fitting silk jacket, while Natka came out dressed in the plain white cloth of a widow. Keshtapada's dress was an exact replica of Bhabeshwar Chaudhuri's.

Byomkesh then explained what Keshtapada and Natka had to do. In the middle of the night, accompanied by an armed gang, Bhabeshwar raids a widow's house. Having ejected the helpless woman from her home, he takes possession of it, razes it, and builds in its place a large block of flats. Keshtapada would mime the role of Bhabeshwar and Natka would play the widow.

Almost crying in his discomfort, Keshtapada pleaded, 'But sir, we've never seen Bhabeshwarbabu pull down somebody's house. So how can we mime it?'

Byomkesh smiled very tenderly, and said, 'Ah! But you're artistes. Put your minds to it, think about it, then it will all fall into place.'

Keshtapada knew that, once they had been brought here, it would not be easy for them to get away. He consulted with Natka, and the two of them gave a performance according to Byomkesh's instructions.

Byomkesh then inquired of the others in the room, 'Well? Will it do?'

They all spoke up as one, saying, 'What do you mean, "will it do"? It was brilliant! If we can show it three or four times, who can knock you down?'

Byomkesh took three one-hundred-rupee notes from his pocket and, offering them to Keshtapada, said, 'We have a real need for you both, Keshtapada. I'll send Jhante and the boys to bring you again later. But now it's very late, you must go and have your rest. But what you have done today must remain top secret.'

Bhabeshwar had given them two hundred, Byomkesh had given them three hundred. The fact that crisp notes seemed to be falling around them like bounty from the heavens did not particularly gladden Keshtapada and Natka, but rather it only made them more ill at ease. They could assume that there was great mutual enmity between Bhabeshwar and Byomkesh, each of whom had unlimited finances and an army of thugs. In between them, like reeds bending in the wind, lay their lives.

The next day Nishi was upset to learn of the Byomkesh affair. She said, 'This is very dangerous. You men must do one thing.'

'What?' asked Keshtapada.

'Get the advice of that college teacher, Amaleshbabu. He's a very good man. Do whatever he tells you.'

Indeed, they ought to have thought of Amalesh earlier. So Keshtapada immediately left the shops behind him and set off for Amalesh's house in Nabiganj. What he learned there made his heart sink: Amaleshbabu had left Nabiganj for Calcutta and would not be back for another fifteen days. In that time, they would have to try to put off Haren and Jhante on whatever pretext they could.

The next few days passed very quickly. Jhante and the boys, as well as Haren, came quite a few times to chat with Keshtapada and Natka, though both sides never came at the same time, and they praised the performance of Keshtapada and Natka. As long as their bosses valued the two actors so highly, they would be well looked after by the henchmen.

Keshtapada contrived to find out why they were being so well treated. A few months later the election would be held, and both Bhabeshwar and Byomkesh would be standing for a seat in the legislative assembly. Each had devised a strategy for the defeat of the other. There would be a cultural programme before the speeches at an election rally, and in that Keshtapada and Natka would perform their sketch, revealing to Bhabeshwar's voters what a low character Byomkesh was or to Byomkesh's voters what a low character Bhabeshwar was. It was up to the two actors to throw the mud in each side's character assassination of the other.

After fifteen days spent steeped in worry, Keshtapada at last had a meeting with Amalesh. After hearing the whole story, Amalesh's face hardened. He said, 'Those two are poor types. It's no good for the country if crooks like them get elected. You must keep away from them. I'll fix you up with some other work.'

Apprehensively, Keshtapada asked, 'How?'

'Narayan Sen will also be standing from here. He's a very honest and benevolent man.'

'I know. He does so much for people.'

'He has to win. I've taken a couple of months off to come back and work for him. In the coming week, Narayan will have his first election rally. I've found out that Bhabeshwar and Byomkesh still have not planned their rallies, so we'll get underway before they do. At our gathering, we'll put on a sketch in which you two will reveal their true characters to the people of Nabiganj.'

Keshtapada was jolted by this. 'But they've got so many thugs at their command!'

'There's nothing to fear,' said Amalesh. 'The country has not fallen into anarchy yet.'

'But they've paid us money ...'

'You didn't ask for it. If they want it back, then give it to them. We should all support men like Narayan.'

Keshtapada and Natka did their mime show revealing the low characters of Bhabeshwar and Byomkesh at Narayan's election rally. The audience was absolutely taken by it and did not want to stop clapping.

Hardly three days had passed when, suddenly, in the middle of the night, two of the shops at the ferry ghat were set on fire and reduced to ashes. Asleep inside the shops were Keshtapada and Natka. When the bodies of the two mime artistes were dragged from the ashes, they were no longer recognizable.